D0585423

A Corner of the Heart

Also by Jessica Stirling

The Spoiled Earth
The Hiring Fair
The Dark Pasture
The Deep Well at Noon
The Blue Evening Gone
The Gates of Midnight
Treasures on Earth
Creature Comforts
Hearts of Gold
The Good Provider
The Asking Price
The Wise Child
The Welcome Light
A Lantern for the Dark
Shadows on the Shore
The Penny Wedding
The Marrying Kind
The Workhouse Girl
The Island Wife
The Wind from the Hills
The Strawberry Season
Prized Possessions
Sisters Three
Wives at War
The Piper's Tune
Shamrock Green
The Captive Heart
One True Love
Blessings in Disguise
The Fields of Fortune
A Kiss and a Promise
The Paradise Waltz

As Caroline Crosby
The Haldanes

JESSICA STIRLING

A Corner of
the Heart

HODDER &
STOUGHTON

First published in Great Britain in 2010 by Hodder & Stoughton
An Hachette UK company

I

Copyright © Jessica Stirling 2010

The right of Jessica Stirling to be identified as the Author

**MORAY COUNCIL
LIBRARIES &
INFO.SERVICES**

20 31 21 68		
Askews		
F		

repro ... ny form
or by ... publisher,
nor ... r other
than ... dition

All c ... nblance

ISBN 978 0 340 99837 3

Typeset in Plantin Light by
Ellipsis Books Limited, Glasgow

Printed and bound in the UK by
CPI Mackays, Chatham ME5 8TD

Hodder & Stoughton policy is to use papers that are natural,
renewable and recyclable products and made from wood grown
in sustainable forests. The logging and manufacturing processes
are expected to conform to the environmental regulations
of the country of origin.

Hodder & Stoughton Ltd
338 Euston Road
London NW1 3BH

www.hodder.co.uk

PART ONE

Autumn 1934

I

It was all her father's fault. If he hadn't been so pushy she would never have met Vivian Proudfoot and wouldn't be speeding up the Commercial Road in the back of a taxicab on a rain-washed August evening a week before the bank holiday, leaving not just Shadwell but lovely, lively London behind.

She watched her father tip open the window in the partition and realised to her dismay that he was about to tell the cabby, a complete stranger, how he'd rescued her from the shackles of poverty. Not that she'd ever been poor, not poor the way she thought of it, not scratching in the gutter poor, not starving to death poor like her grandfather who'd worked the India Docks when the going rate was five pence an hour and you were lucky if you got eight hours continuous a week. To be fair, her dad had good reason to be proud. He'd raised her without any help and when the time came had scraped up the shekels to enrol her at Cowper's College of Commerce and keep her there even during the dock strike when her brother Ronnie's skimpy wage was all they'd had to live on.

'Our Susan,' her father said, 'was born with a head on her shoulders. All I ever done was encourage 'er to use it. Make 'er mother proud, she was still alive. Never been flighty, our

Susan, not like them young 'uns who get 'anded it on a silver platter. Right?'

'Right,' said the cabby obligingly.

'Ain't been no cake-walk, I can tell you, raising 'er on me own. But now she's hobnobbin' with toffs there'll be no lookin' back. Proves it can be done, don't it?'

'Right,' said the cabby, then, 'What can be done?'

'Silk purse, sow's ear: need I say more?'

Susan had heard the phrase so often that it no longer rankled.

Dad had insisted on hiring a cab for the trip across town to Paddington. No daughter of his, he said, was going to stumble out of the Underground all damp and draggled like a workhouse rat. She was leaving for green pastures at last and, by George, he was going to be there to see her off even if it meant sacrificing half a shift and forgoing his eight pence worth of steak and onion pie in Stratton's Dining Rooms to do it.

'What education's for, ain't it?' he rattled on. 'Diplomas, she's got five of 'em. An' she speaks proper. Four years that took; four years of Saturday afternoons with Miss Armitage at a half-crown a pop. Can fool anyone if you speaks proper. Saw that in a play, I did, when Susie weren't much more than a nipper.' He chuckled. 'Say somethin', sweetheart. Give the man a earful of King's English.'

Miss Armitage had been on the stage at one time and claimed to have acted with Mrs Patrick Campbell when they were girls. Susan didn't know whether to believe her or not. Miss Armitage didn't much care for Dad, though that didn't stop her taking his money and doing her best to plane away the worst excesses of Susan's cockney twang. Susan, in turn, had kept her end of the bargain and had practised her exercises assiduously at home in front of a mirror, though she'd hidden her new-found vocal mannerisms from everyone at school because she knew they'd only laugh. Later, however, when she'd gone out into the world as a registered stenographer her ability to 'speak proper' had landed her the agency's plum jobs.

She inched forward and in a soft, carrying whisper mischievously recited the first verse of a Christina Rossetti poem that had been one of Miss Armitage's favourites. '"Does the road wind uphill all the way? Yes, to the very end. Will the day's journey take the whole long day? From morn to night, my friend."'

'See,' her father said smugly. 'Told yer, didn't I?'

'Right,' said the cabby for the third time and, more irked than impressed, it seemed, reached behind him and snapped the little window shut.

'What's biting 'im?' her father said.

'It's been a long day and it's raining. I expect he's tired.'

'Yus, that must be it,' her father said and, not much mollified, rested his brow against the glass and watched the London landmarks rush past in the gloom.

Vivian Proudfoot waited by the station bookstall. She was a tall woman in the region of forty, unseasonably clad in a hacking jacket, tweed skirt and cable-knit sweater. She looked, Susan thought, more like a member of the Hoxton Ramblers' Club than a bestselling author. A briefcase rested against her calf and a bulging rucksack was strapped to her back, the weight of which tugged at her shoulders and made her bosom protrude alarmingly.

'Mr Hooper!' she trumpeted. 'I didn't expect to see you here.'

'Come up by taxi,' Matt Hooper said, 'to wave 'er ladyship off.'

'Don't you think a girl of twenty might be capable of waving herself off?' Miss Proudfoot said. 'Female emancipation's all the rage, you know.'

'Our Susie ain't never been away from 'ome before,' her father said. 'I don't want 'er to get into no trouble.'

'Susan will be fine,' the woman assured him. 'I'll take good care of her.'

Then, hoisting up the briefcase and adjusting the straps of her rucksack, she marched off towards the platform, leaving Susan to plant a hasty kiss on her father's cheek and follow on behind.

The summer sky still held hours of daylight but soot and rain had created an almost wintry murk through which signal lights and early lights in offices and shops blinked wanly as the train pulled out of the station.

Back home, to the east of Aldgate, the gutters ran like rivers and the river itself was the colour of rusty iron. You couldn't see the river from the terraced house in Pitt Street but on wet nights like this you could smell it. For three years Susan had temped for lawyers, bondsmen and stockbrokers in elegant rooms and panelled chambers but no matter how late she'd returned Dad would be sitting up with a pot of tea and a plate of toast, anxious to hear what she'd been up to. Tonight, with her brother Ronnie out drinking as usual, her dad would be all alone.

'You're not sulking, are you?' Vivian Proudfoot asked.

'Of course not.'

'Don't tell me you're scared?'

'Perhaps a little.'

'We'll pop along for afternoon tea soon; that'll perk you up.'

There were three men in the compartment busy reading newspapers and pretending they had no interest in the pretty young thing in the seat by the window.

Miss Proudfoot put a hand on Susan's knee.

'You're not afraid of me, are you?' she said. 'It's not as if we're strangers.'

'It's not you,' Susan said. 'I don't know what it is.'

'A crisis of confidence would be my guess.'

'Yes, I suppose you might call it that.'

Miss Proudfoot laughed. 'Come now, Susan, we're not lodging with the Astors. My brother and his brood aren't in the least intimidating.'

'Do they have servants?'

'Oh, yes, a few: a cook, a day maid or two and, I dare say, some lad from the village to do the boots; nothing for you to worry about. Now you've raised the subject, however, may I remind you that you are not – repeat not – a servant. You are my personal assistant. If anyone orders you to tote luggage or fetch tea you have my permission – nay, my instruction – to tell them to push off and if they come over all high-hat then refer them, whoever they are, to me.'

'Oh!'

'Don't look so stricken, girl. It won't come to that. There's an egalitarian streak in my brother that neither Harrow nor the Guards quite eliminated and if he does forget himself and become a trifle uppity his wife and daughters will soon put him in his place. Besides, my agent, Mercer Hughes, will be joining us. You've met him, haven't you?'

'No,' Susan said, 'actually, I haven't.'

'Then, my dear' – Miss Proudfoot patted her knee – 'you've

a treat in store. There's no one – repeat no one – quite like Mercer Hughes.'

By the time Matt Hooper reached Stratton's Dining Rooms, Georgie was already taking in the menu board. It was about the only thing Georgie was allowed to do unsupervised, for the poor lad was several pence short of a shilling and too clumsy to be trusted with saucepans, dishes or knives.

'Here, Georgie, let me give you a 'and with that,' Matt Hooper offered.

Taking an end of the board, he backed through the street door into the empty shop. The tables had been cleared but the green and white chequered cloths that Nora's auntie had sent over from Limerick had not been removed. Dishes clattered in the back kitchen where sinks, stoves and storerooms were situated and which served Nora Romano and her family as a living room when the business of the day was over. Matt leaned the blackboard against the base of the window so it wouldn't drip on the linoleum.

'Switch the slat, Georgie,' he said. 'I reckon you're closed for the night.'

Georgie Romano was over six feet tall, a head taller than Matt. He still had the baffled stare of an eight-year-old, though, and only his size and the stubble that fringed his jaw indicated that he wasn't some freakish child but a man in his twenties.

'Mammy, Mammy says . . .'

'Mammy says you're closed, Georgie.'

'She – she told you 'at?'

'She did.'

The obvious question was 'when' but nothing was ever obvious to Georgie. He clapped his hands and tackled the wooden slat that hung from a cord on the window. He took it in both fists as if he were about to crush it like a tin can and, tongue between teeth, twisted it from 'Open' to 'Closed'.

'Okay, Mr 'Ooper?' he asked anxiously.

'Spot-on, Georgie. Spot-on,' Matt said and, with a hand on the young man's shoulder, steered him through the shop into the kitchen.

Nora Romano's heart skipped a beat when she heard Matt barging about. She had her kids, her lodger and her cooking but Matt Hooper was the nearest thing she'd had to a man of her own since her husband, Leo, had emptied the cash drawer and scarpered with the tarty little piece from the Fawley Street fish bar.

Leo had always been an idle beggar whose 'line of work', as he called it, involved hanging about racetracks and drinking clubs and running errands for any of the shifty mob, Jews, Irish or Italians, who'd stand him a gin and grape juice and drop him a few bob now and then. When she'd first met him she'd asked him what kind of a name Leo was, fearing it might be Jewish, and he'd told her he'd been called Leonardo after the painter to distinguish him from a million other blokes named Romano who'd been born in the Eternal City.

The only decent thing Leo had ever done was help secure the lease of the dining rooms from old Harry Stratton. Even so, she'd been shaken by the manner of his departure. She'd even considered packing up and taking Georgie and her daughter, Breda, off to Limerick. Might have done it too if Matt Hooper hadn't told her how much he'd miss her steak and onions.

'Susie get away all right?'

'Right as rain,' Matt answered.

'Turn on the waterworks, did she?'

'Not 'er.'

'You?'

'Nah, not me neither,' Matt said. 'It ain't like she's goin'
off for good.'

He sat down, wiped his face with his cap, hung the cap
on the knob of the chair then disconsolately rested his chin
on his palm. He had broad shoulders, a determined sort of
chin, hair greying above the ears and blue-grey eyes that
didn't seem to have a laugh in them. He was handsome,
though. Even Breda thought so and Breda, at nineteen, was
notoriously picky.

'Anything good in the pot, Nora?'

'Mince,' Georgie chipped in. 'Mince on Friday, Mr 'Ooper.'

'Got enough for one more?'

'I reckon we can find you a plate,' said Nora.

Minced beef on toast was not the best meal on her menu
but she did her market shopping on Saturday and on Friday
night the family had to make do with leftovers. She placed
four thick slices of bread under the grill of the big gas stove
then stepped into the corridor at the rear of the kitchen and
called to Breda, who was putting on her face in the bedroom
upstairs.

'Can't believe Susie's gone,' Matt said. 'It's not for me to
stand in 'er way, though.'

'Stand in her way?' said Nora. 'What you talkin' about? It
was you what pushed her in the first place.'

'I only put a word in.'

'Some word!' said Nora. 'From what I hear you practically
had an arm lock on that Proudfoot woman.'

'It was all done through the typing agency.'

'It ain't being done through no typing agency now, though, is it?'

'That's true,' Matt Hooper admitted. 'But if things don't work out with Miss Proudfoot, the agency'll take Susie back. She's the best they got.'

'Not that you're biased, like.'

He had the decency to grin. 'Nah, not that I'm biased.'

Matt's wife, Freda, had died soon after giving birth to Susan and his mother had stubbornly refused to raise another baby. His father had slipped him a few bob to pay for a wet nurse and had offered sound advice. 'First thing you do is find some old woman to tend the kids while you're on shift. Second thing you do is register as a pacifist. Keep you out o' the war an', most like, on the dock. Be a long war, no matter what Asquith tells us. War or no war, the merchants of London won't starve. So tighten your belt, son, an' go an' do what has to be done for your kiddies.'

Matt had followed his father's advice to the letter. He'd sworn off tobacco, booze and women, every pleasure except an occasional night at the Adelphi when Leo Romano had finagled free tickets from one of his dubious acquaintances. But now, as he watched Breda Romano push away her empty plate and fish for the packet of ciggies she kept tucked in the leg of her drawers, a trace of the old appetites rose up in him again.

Breda tapped the pack, flipped out a cigarette, lit it, inhaled deeply and blew smoke though her nose. 'Whatcha gonna do now, Mr 'Ooper,' she said, 'now you got nobody to go 'ome to?'

'But I do have somebody to go 'ome to,' Matt answered.

'Who's 'at then?'

'Ronnie.'

'Ronnie!' The girl snorted. 'You ain't gonna see none o' Ronnie tonight.'

'Why's that?'

'He'll have himself a fancy piece. Ain't you got a fancy piece, Mr 'Ooper?'

'Nah,' Matt said. 'I ain't got a fancy piece.'

Breda wetted her lips and sat back. She had a chest on her, that much he had noticed, and she knew how to use those big Italian eyes. If he didn't know better he'd swear she was flirting with him.

''Ow about my ma,' Breda said. 'Ain't she fancy enough for yer?'

'*Breda!*' Nora snapped.

'I'm just 'aving 'im on,' Breda purred. 'Well, Mr 'Ooper, what is it? Ain't my ma fancy enough for you? Or ain't you man enough for 'er?'

Matt said, 'You want me to answer your question, Breda, it'll cost yer.'

'Cost me what?'

'One of them cigarettes.'

The girl smirked. 'Yeah, right!'

'Nah,' Matt said. 'I mean it.'

She shrugged, tapped the last cigarette from the packet, lit it and held it out across the table. When Matt reached for it she drew it away. He reached again and again she withdrew it, then, like the strike of a snake, he shot out a hand and caught her wrist. He drew her forward until her breasts were crushed against the table top.

Breda, round-eyed, opened her fingers and let him remove the cigarette.

Matt Hooper sat back and, tipping his chin towards the ceiling, savoured the cheap little smoke as if it were a fine cigar.

'Now,' he said thickly, 'what was your question again?'

There was something quaint about Hereford railway station, something not quite twentieth century. Lugging her suitcase, Susan followed her employer out on to the pavement to be greeted by a great canopy of sky, a broad well-lit high street and a taste of country air which, if not exactly wine, was a deal fresher than the stuff that seeped through the back streets of Shadwell. A mud-spattered, open-topped motorcar was parked outside the station. A man in a frayed army trench-coat, corduroy breeches and rubberised boots stood by it, grinning.

Dropping her briefcase, Vivian wrapped her arms around him.

'David, you scoundrel!' she cried. 'My God, you look like a scarecrow.'

'Been busy, old sausage. How you?'

'Me fine. Starved.'

'Gwen's waiting supper.'

'Glad to hear it.'

'Who's this?'

'My new assistant, Miss Hooper.'

He offered his hand. 'Proudfoot.'

The hand was dry and hard, the grip not quite crippling.

'Pleased ter – to meet you, sir,' said Susan politely.

Mr Proudfoot heaved Vivian's rucksack into the rear seat, followed it with Susan's suitcase, then, taking Susan's arm, helped her into the car. He slid into the driver's seat next to his sister.

'Now, remember, David, this is not Kop Hill,' Vivian told him, 'and you are not Raymond Mays. Don't go showing off.'

'Yes, my dear,' David Proudfoot said, slammed the car into gear and shot it forward into the high street while Susan cowered nervously among the luggage and, quite literally, held on to her hat.

In London you didn't have to think about where you were going. East was east and west meant the West End and if you got lost somewhere in between there was always a bus route to follow, a handy Underground station or some passer-by willing to steer you in the right direction. There were no such navigational aids in the country, Susan realised. Once they'd left the town behind, churches, humped stone bridges and timbered buildings leapt at her out of the darkness with, here and there, the glimpse of a barn or whitewashed cottage.

When Mr Proudfoot swung the car into a rutted lane the suitcase toppled into her lap, the rucksack pressed her against the door and it crossed her mind that if the door flew open she would be thrown out and no one – certainly not Mr Proudfoot – would be any the wiser.

The car flew past a listing signpost – *Hackles* – and a few yards further on a lawn, silvered by moonlight, the posts of a tennis court and – Susan blinked – a man seated on top of an umpire's chair. He rose, swaying. 'At last the goddess has come upon us,' he shouted at the pitch of his voice. 'About bloody time too.'

'Is that him?' Susan asked. 'Is that your agent?'

'Yes,' Vivian answered. 'That's Mercer playing the fool, as usual.'

The car nosed to a halt in front of a huge, two-storey, Tudor-style farmhouse and Susan sat back and let out her breath. Wherever she was and however she'd got here, she knew that at last she'd arrived.

2

He loped across the lawn, stepped over the knee-high hedge that bordered the tennis court and, in a gesture that struck Susan as very French, kissed Vivian first on one cheek and then the other. He glanced at Susan and obviously deciding that she wasn't worthy of attention, put an arm about Vivian's waist and escorted her along the pathway to the porch.

Four gnarled pillars supported a steep thatched roof that reminded Susan of a Rackham illustration in a book of fairy tales that she'd admired in the bookcase in Sir Alfred Pennington's chambers. Sir Alfred had noted her interest and, being a kindly old gent, had taken out the book and had shown it to her. He had turned the pages one by one, very gingerly, his hands so pale and spotted that they might have been drawn by the fairy-tale artist too.

'Theory is' – David Proudfoot came up behind her – 'that the whole tottering edifice started with the porch and just growed like little Topsy.' He paused. 'I don't suppose you know who little Topsy is, do you?'

Susan knew perfectly well who little Topsy was – she'd read *Uncle Tom's Cabin* in three different versions, courtesy of Shadwell public library – but she nursed a suspicion that ignorance was expected of her.

She shook her head. 'No, sir. I don't.'

'My daughter, Caro, was afraid of that porch when she

16

was little,' Mr Proudfoot said. 'Wouldn't set foot inside it even in broad daylight. Supposed to be haunted. Not the porch, the house. Ghost of some Civil War heroine is reputed to float about upstairs but I've never seen her. Not scared of ghosts, are you?'

'Never met one, sir,' said Susan. 'Don't suppose they'll do me no harm.'

'Sensible attitude,' David Proudfoot said. 'Viv will give you the grand tour tomorrow, I expect. The house is not entirely without historical merit. Hungry?'

'Yes, sir, I am rather.'

'Straight ahead,' David Proudfoot told her. 'Watch out for the step.'

He ushered her under the brow of thatch, through a doorway into a hall.

Black-painted beams and a sagging plaster ceiling loomed overhead. An electrical light bulb dangled from a twisted cord and a big lamp in a parchment shade flickered on a corner table. There were doors everywhere, black-painted like the beams. David Proudfoot nudged her with the suitcase.

'Kitchen's at the end of the passage,' he said. 'I'll take the luggage upstairs. Do you need to make use of the facilities?'

'The what?' Susan said.

'The lavatory.'

'No,' she said. 'Thank you all the same.'

She took off her hat, tidied her hair, then, throwing back her shoulders, pushed open the door and headed along a passageway. A moment later she found herself in a kitchen so vast that it might comfortably have accommodated three families from Shadwell with room to spare for lodgers and dogs.

'Ah, there you are!' said Vivian. 'Where's David?'

'Taking the luggage upstairs,' said Susan.

'Is he, indeed?' said Mercer Hughes. 'Isn't that your job?'

'Now, now, Mercer,' said Vivian. 'She isn't a skivvy, you know.'

A slim, very pretty woman with short fluffy fair hair was folding napkins. Beside her, holding a casserole dish wrapped in a towel, was a plump older woman. Two girls, clearly sisters, were seated at a long oak table set for supper. Mercer Hughes stood behind the elder of the girls, a stocky blonde not quite Susan's age.

'Where *do* you find them, Vivian?' he said. 'Selfridges' budget basement? Where are you from, my dear? You're a little too well scrubbed for Silvertown. Stepney, by any chance?'

Susan had encountered too many arrogant bullies while temping in the City to be cowed by a literary agent.

'Shadwell,' she said. 'You're out by only a few streets, sir. You seem to know the East End of London pretty well. Were you born there?'

Mercer Hughes laughed. 'I suppose I asked for that. Must say, Miss . . .'

'Hooper,' Vivian informed him. 'Susan Hooper.'

'Must say, Miss Hooper, you don't sound like a citizen of Shadwell.'

'Chelsea,' piped up the younger girl. 'She sounds like Chelsea.'

'She doesn't sound a bit like Chelsea,' said the blonde waspishly.

'Girls,' the woman spoke up, 'may I remind you it's not polite to discuss someone in the third person.' She glided round the table and held out her hand. 'I'm Gwen Proudfoot. These uncultured creatures are my daughters, Eleanor and

Caroline. Mrs Wentworth is our cook. You, I imagine, are Vivian's new secretary.'

'Oh, a typist!' Caro Proudfoot said. 'How exciting! Perhaps you'll teach me to type, Miss Hooper. I'd so much like to learn.'

'Susan won't have time to teach you anything,' Vivian informed her niece. 'She'll be far too busy. We're here to work.'

'Hammering out your next bestseller?' Eleanor asked.

'Absolutely,' Vivian answered.

'Another Bible story?' said Caro.

'*In Defence of Herod* was hardly a Bible story.' Mercer Hughes tapped the little girl lightly on the crown of her head. 'Haven't you read it?'

'Papa wouldn't let me,' Caro pouted.

'Papa wouldn't let you what?' David Proudfoot entered the kitchen. 'What slander is this you've cooked up against me now?'

'Aunt Vivian's book,' said Eleanor.

'Oh, that!' David said. 'No, well, you're far too young for political manifestos, Caroline.'

'I'm twelve,' Caro reminded him. 'You let Eleanor read it.'

'And how did Eleanor find it?' Vivian asked.

'Incredibly dull,' Eleanor answered.

'Oh, you fibber, Elly. You said you loved it,' Caro protested.

'To protect my tender feelings, no doubt,' said Vivian.

'Absolutely!' Eleanor Proudfoot declared and at that moment, Susan thought, not only looked but even sounded like a miniature version of her aunt.

Georgie had fallen asleep slumped across the table, his head cradled on his arms. Nora had stacked cups and plates on the draining board and had placed the greasy pots and pans in a neat row on newspapers on the floor.

All very orderly and methodical, Matt thought, her routine. It didn't occur to him to pick up a dish mop and help out. Eccentric he might be but not as eccentric as all that. Half the women in Pitt Street already thought he was a sissy because he wouldn't let his precious Susan play in the street and, like some fussy old hen, called her in to do her homework or eat her bite of supper off a plate. He'd even been spotted in the public washhouse rinsing blouses, knickers and vests, and whistling as if he were enjoying himself.

Nora was still trim and moved without the shuffle most women of her age developed when their arches fell. She was no doll like Breda, had never been a doll like Breda, not even when Leo had picked her out of the crowd. For a woman who spent the best part of eighteen hours a day slaving over a stove she was wearing pretty well, though.

'What you thinkin' about?' Nora said. 'You thinkin' about Susan?'

Matt realised with a start that he hadn't spared his daughter a passing thought for at least twenty minutes.

'She'll be all right,' he said gruffly.

'Sure an' I'm sure she will.'

There was still a trace of Irish in Nora's voice, a lilt that forty years consorting with cockneys hadn't smothered. When he'd been half seas over and maudlin with it, Leo had called her 'his fair colleen'. He'd called her a lot less flattering names when he'd been stone-cold sober and had often told Matt that she was no damned good for anything except cooking and thumping.

Nora sipped tea. It left a little milky bow on the hair of

her upper lip. She put out her tongue and, delicate as a cat, licked it off.

'This Proudfoot woman, not married, is she?'

'Not far as I know,' Matt answered.

'She the sort likes girls then?'

'Don't know what you mean,' said Matt, flushing.

'Sure an' you do.'

In fact, he didn't know what she meant, not exactly. He'd read articles in the *News of the World* about the queer things that went on in some clubs in Soho – women wearing monocles and top hats and dancing together – but he preferred to keep the door closed on all that sort of stuff.

'Look, Nora,' he said, 'you wanna know about Miss Proudfoot, I'll tell you about Miss Proudfoot. She wrote this book, see. Everybody read it – well, everybody with half a brain. When she come to talk at the Institute I toddled along to 'ear what she had to say. There was a mob protestin' outside, Jew boys an' Bolshies mostly. Sloane – you remember Sloane?'

'Can't say I do.'

'Pal of Leo's back in the old days. Anyhow, Sloane asked me to see Miss Proudfoot safe off the premises. Miss Proudfoot an' me gets talkin' while we're waitin' for her cab. She lets out she's on the scout for a new assistant.'

'And you just happen to have one handy.'

'Gave 'er Susan's name and the name of the agency but never thought nothing would come of it. Next thing Susan's working up in town where Miss Proudfoot has a office. Next thing after that, Miss Proudfoot asks to meet me, Sunday, in Regent's Park. We 'ave tea, very civil like. She tells me she wants Susie exclusive and she'll pay seventy shillings a week. Seventy shillings! Geeze, Nora, I never earned seventy shillings a week in me life. She asks my permission. I ask

Susan. Susan says yes. I say yes – and Bob's your uncle. I done the right thing by 'er, didn't I?' He paused, frowning. 'Didn't I, Nora?'

Oh yes, Nora thought, you done the right thing by her, but if you think she'll come trotting back to Shadwell the same girl as she went away you've another think coming, Matt Hooper.

'No man could've done better,' she assured him, then, irked by his self-righteousness, threw herself into her chores.

The living room was like something from *Country Life*, all squashy sofas and deep armchairs covered in flowery chintz. The fireplace, as broad as it was tall, was flanked by wicker baskets filled with logs. At the far end of the room was a piano and shelves crammed with books.

Mrs Wentworth brought in coffee. Mrs Proudfoot served it in tiny cups as delicate as eggshells while her husband busied himself pouring brandy.

'Here,' Vivian said, 'come, sit by me, Susan.'

Juggling her coffee cup, Susan lowered herself on to the sofa.

She'd already discovered that the girls were on holiday from a boarding school she'd never heard of, that Mr Proudfoot had a house in Mayfair where he stayed when business took him to London and that Mercer Hughes numbered several celebrities among his clients and wasn't above talking about them.

'I hope you don't spread gossip about me, Mercer,' said Vivian.

'What's there to spread? You're a hard-working author with an intellect H.G. himself might envy.'

'Who's H.G.?' said Caro.

The girl had planted herself on a cushion on the floor at Susan's feet. It was almost eleven o'clock but no one seemed to mind that the child was up so late.

'H.G. Wells. He wrote *The Invisible Man*,' said Eleanor.

'Oh, I loved that film,' said Caro.

'Nonsense,' Gwen Proudfoot put in. 'It gave you nightmares.'

'Do you know him, Aunt Viv?' Eleanor asked. 'Wells, I mean.'

'We've met once or twice.'

'You're far too modest,' Mercer Hughes said. 'Wells thinks highly of you.'

'Well,' Vivian said, 'I'm certainly not one of *his* disciples.'

'Yes,' Gwen Proudfoot said. 'One gathers that Mr Wells is vehemently against territorialism, though I've heard it said he's not opposed to Jews.'

'What makes you think I am?' Vivian asked.

'Your articles in *The Times*,' Gwen answered.

Vivian shrugged. 'Someone had to pay for my trip to Palestine. Thanks to Mercer's persuasive powers *The Times* agreed to foot the bill.'

'And got rather more than they bargained for,' said Gwen.

'The editor – Dawson – was by no means displeased by the controversy Viv's articles caused,' Mercer Hughes put in. 'In fact, he'd love to ship her over to Jerusalem right now to report on the Arab uprisings.'

'No, thank you,' Vivian said. 'I've no desire to be stoned by Arabs or shot at by Jews just to satisfy Dawson's need for increased circulation.'

'Who will you defend in your next book?' Gwen asked. 'Mussolini?'

'Il Duce needs no defence from me,' Vivian replied tartly.

Susan sipped coffee and kept her mouth shut. Her dad might be a crane operator on Shadwell Dock and her brother nothing but a butcher's assistant but when it came to politics they were probably better informed than anyone here. And if, by magic, she could whisk Danny Cahill, Nora Romano's dour Scottish lodger, into this chintzy living room then, by gum, the sparks would fly.

'Look at you, Susan,' Mrs Proudfoot said. 'Do you mind if I call you Susan?'

'Not at all.'

'Look at you; you can hardly keep your eyes open. We're used to sitting up half the night setting the world to rights but you must be exhausted.'

'Come along, ladies,' David said, 'up the wooden stairs to Bedfordshire.' He took the brandy glass from his sister and passed it to his wife, then, clasping Vivian's hand, heaved her out of the depths of the sofa.

'Breakfast at six, shall we say?'

'Six?' Vivian said. 'Don't be ridiculous. I'm a writer not a bloody milkmaid. You'll find me hovering over the coffee pot about nine if you're lucky. You, I take it, are sleeping in the cottage, Mercer?'

'Exiled from paradise as usual,' the agent said. 'Tomorrow we must have a little tête-à-tête, just thee and me, Vivian.'

'Business, I suppose?' said Vivian.

'Of course – business. What else would it be?'

'One lives in hope,' said Vivian. 'Are you down for the week?'

'Until Thursday.'

'Is Charles looking after the shop?'

'He is; the faithful Charles.'

'I don't know why he puts up with you.'

'Because I bring home the bacon. Don't I, my sweet?'

'That you do, that you do,' Vivian conceded and offered her cheek for a kiss.

3

The cow looked at Susan and Susan looked at the cow.

Caro said, 'Her name's Daisy. Not awfully original, I know, but Daddy bought her as a milker about four years ago and that's the only name she'll answer to. Quite pretty, isn't she? For a cow, I mean?'

'Quite pretty,' Susan agreed. 'Quite noisy too.'

'Oh, you heard her, did you?' Caro said.

'Hard not to.'

'She does kick up rather a fuss when her bag's full.'

'Her bag?'

'Where the milk comes from.'

'Oh!' Susan said. 'Who sees to the milking?'

'Mr Garrett or one of his girls.'

'Is Mr Garrett a farmer?'

'Not really,' said Caro. 'He's our manager. He does everything that has to be done – except for the apples. Mr Wentworth looks after the apples. Will you be here for the picking?'

'I really don't know,' said Susan. 'When is the picking?'

'Depends on the weather,' said Caro. 'Usually after we've gone back to school. You can stroke her nose if you like.'

'I think,' Susan said, 'I'll not bother, if it's all the same to you.'

The girl laughed. 'You don't like it here, do you?'

'I've only been here ten minutes,' Susan said. 'I don't know whether I like it or not. It's different where I live.'

Caro nodded. 'I know: the slums.'

'Who told you that? Was it Mr Hughes?'

'Mr Hughes? No, it wasn't Mercer. Why would you think that?'

'I – I don't know.'

The cow had wakened her at an ungodly hour. Wrapped in her raincoat in lieu of a dressing-gown, she'd tiptoed along the passageway to the bathroom. The bath was a great coffin-shaped object perched on dragon's claws and topped by a copper boiler that would fetch a fair bob or two, no questions asked, from any scrap merchant in Whitechapel. The cistern, hidden behind a panel, had groaned and retched after Susan had pulled the chain and was still retching and groaning when she'd scurried back to her room where Caro was lying in wait.

'It's a lovely morning. Would you like to go for a walk?'

Susan would have preferred tea and toast and a half-hour with the *Daily Express* but, for fear of giving offence, she'd said, 'Yes, of course.'

Little bundles of white cloud floated high overhead. The air smelled sweet, almost cloying. A bushy hedge flanked the pasture. Behind it were big trees, dense and green. There were sounds, strange sounds: clanking from behind the house and a faint faraway drone, like bees at a hive, and a dog barking and a rooster crowing, faint too and distant.

Caro steered her across the pasture into the wood.

The grass, wet with dew, swished against Susan's bare legs as she ducked beneath the monstrous boughs. Where the wood ended the land fell steeply in a chequerboard of fields, hedges and orchards. Riding on the distant horizon, like an inky scribble, was a line of hills.

'That's Wales,' Caro told her.

'What? All of it?'

'No, the mountains, just the mountains,' Caro said. 'Best view in England, Daddy says. Mercer has a painting of it from a hundred years ago and it looks just the same. Mercer says Daddy should move the farmhouse here, brick by brick, and then we could call it "Hackles Rising", but Daddy doesn't think that's funny. It wasn't always Hackles. On Daddy's old maps it's Hockles because that was the name of the family that owned the land.'

'How much land does your father own?'

'Oh, not much. Seventy acres, I think. This isn't our ground. Our ground stops at the hedge. Our orchard's on the other side of the house.'

'Is that where the cottage is?' said Susan. 'Where Mr Hughes sleeps?'

'Yes, closer to Gadney.'

'Gadney?'

'The village,' Caro said. 'Actually, it's closer to the priory, but that's just a ruin. Mercer says it should be taken down before it falls on top of him. Would you like to see the priory?'

'Not if it's going to fall on top of me.'

'That's just Mercer being silly. It's quite safe.'

'In that case I'd love to see the priory,' Susan said. 'But right now I think I'd better be getting back in case Miss Proudfoot has work for me to do.'

'Typing?'

'Typing, yes, and other things.'

'What other things?' Caro said.

'I'm not quite sure,' said Susan. 'Do we have a quiet place to work in?'

'The barn,' Caro said. 'Daddy's lending you the barn.'

'With or without the cow?' said Susan.

No vans or buses ventured along Thornton Street but by ten o'clock on Saturday morning through traffic, mostly pedestrian and mostly female, had all but obliterated Ronnie Hooper's view of Gertler's (Kosher) Butchers which lay directly opposite Herr Brauschmidt's High Class Pork & Beef where he, Ronnie, was employed.

It didn't bother Ronnie that Mr Gertler hired a *Shabbat goy* to ensure that his shop was kept open on Saturday and that gentiles were therefore free to purchase slices of Gertler's famous veal loaf and spiced beef sausage in spite of what God, or was it Moses, had set down as the thirty-nine principles of labour where there was written, Herr Brauschmidt ranted, not a word about unfair competition.

In the early years of the Great War Herr Brauschmidt's shop had been ransacked by anti-German mobs, while his three sons, English in all but name, had been running the gauntlet of the Kaiser's U-boats with the British fleet in the North Atlantic. Small wonder his boys had called Poppa crazy for staying put in Shadwell and, soon after the Armistice, had abandoned England and Poppa for a better life in America.

Unlike his employer, or his dad for that matter, Ronnie harboured no animosity towards the children of Israel. Indeed, on Saturdays he would hover outside the shop in the hope that Ruth Gertler would come strutting by on her way to the synagogue, swinging her hips and flashing her dark eyes. If Herr Brauschmidt caught him ogling the luscious young creature, though, Ronnie would be treated to a lecture on the perils of consorting with Jews, which completely ignored the fact that Ronnie had a reputation as a free-thinker who would consort with practically anyone provided anyone was female.

The fittings in Herr Brauschmidt's front shop were very up-to-date: tile, brushed steel and marble, glass counter guards and one small refrigerated unit that had cost an arm and a leg. The dead pigs, bald and headless, that hung outside the window were put there only to annoy Mr Gertler. When custom was slack, it was one of Ronnie's tasks to stand guard over these unappetising examples of the butcher's art and give them a whisk with a cloth to chase away the flies, which is precisely what he was doing when he spotted Danny Cahill with Georgie in tow weaving up the pavement through the crowd.

Georgie, as usual, was holding on to Danny's hand like a little kid and Danny, as usual, didn't give a toss.

'Haw, Ron,' Danny said. 'Has the princess come past yet?'

'Not yet.'

Danny Cahill had been resident in Shadwell for almost a dozen years but hadn't quite shed his guttural Glasgow accent.

He said, 'Your optimism never ceases tae amaze me.'

'She'll come round,' said Ronnie. 'Just give 'er time.'

'Admit it, man, she's out o' your league.'

'I'll admit nothing of the bleedin' kind,' said Ronnie. 'Hey, Georgie, you going for a ice cream?'

Georgie beamed. 'Breda gimme sixpence.'

'If he keeps his nose clean,' Danny said, 'he might get a toffee apple too.'

'Toffee apple, yum.' Georgie might have yanked Danny away there and then if Danny hadn't planted his feet like a boxer and held his ground.

'Missed you down the Crown last night,' Ronnie said.

'I was on second shift. Busy night for news an' all.'

'What happened to that geezer on trial at the Bailey; you hear?'

'Brief entered a special late plea.'

'What? Mitigation?'

'Self-defence,' said Danny. 'Claimed the wife threw a bottle at his client.'

'And he just hit 'er accidental like?'

'Aye, forty-nine times,' Danny said. 'Jury came in with a guilty verdict in less than an hour.'

'He'll swing, won't he?'

'He'll swing,' Danny confirmed. 'It was only worth half a para. Nobody gives a monkey's about domestics. Domestics don't sell newspapers. Chucked the copy at the night editor and shot the crow afore Bags could hand me some other item he's too lazy to gun up himself.'

Danny had worked for the newspaper since he'd arrived in London at the age of fifteen. By sheer persistence, he'd risen from messenger to subeditor in 'the whispering gallery', that enormous room through which news flowed from all corners of the globe.

'So what'd you do?' Ronnie asked.

'Grabbed a late pie an' a pint in Masefield's an' mooched off home. Bumped into your old man, by the way. He looked kinda down in the mouth.'

'He's missing his little pet,' said Ronnie.

'She went, did she?'

''Course she went,' Ronnie said. 'If she hadn't the old man would've thrown a fit. Nothing's gonna stop his golden girl, not if he can 'elp it.'

'Hereford?'

'Yeah.'

'With that fascist bitch?'

'Yeah.'

'I just hope your old man knows what he's let Susie in for.'

'Seventy bob a week and a *entrée* – is that the word?'

'Close enough,' said Danny.

'A *entrée* into high society.'

'They'll have her knickers off before she knows what's hit her,' Danny said. 'Those snotty bastards think young lassies like Susie are theirs for the askin'.'

'Okay, okay,' said Ronnie. 'No need to snap at me.'

'Sorry,' said Danny. 'I just hate to see your sister goin' the way o' all flesh.'

Two women, one young, stopped by the window. The elder of the two was wrapped in a shawl, a baby, barefoot, clinging to her breast. They glanced at Georgie and warily retreated three or four paces. The younger fished a purse from her skirt and, stooped over like a miser, stirred the coins with her forefinger, a sound that brought Herr Brauschmidt hastening to the door.

His apron was clean and his shirt so white it seemed dazzling in the sunlight. He was a big man, big-bellied, his cheeks ruddy with the exertions of the chopping block. He carried a thin, razor-sharp knife in one hand. The woman in the shawl pulled the baby closer to her chest as if she feared that the German was about to carve up her infant and feed him through the mincer.

'Got nice haslet for you today, ladies,' Herr Brauschmidt said affably. 'Nice bit of West of England brisket. Do hubby nice for Sunday dinner. Got nice cheap ox liver, go down a treat.'

''Ow cheap?' said the baby carrier.

'Ten pence the pound.'

The keeper of the purse scowled and shook her head.

'Bones?' Herr Brauschmidt suggested. 'Nice bones?'

Another shake of the head, another suspicious glance at Georgie and the women retreated, bound, it seemed, for Gertler's. With a pained expression Herr Brauschmidt watched them depart, then, wagging the knife, told Ronnie to stop cluttering up the pavement and get his arse inside.

Ronnie shrugged. 'Gotta go, Danny. See you later, uh?'

'Nah.' Danny hesitated. 'I've somethin' to do up west.'

'Skirt?'

'I should be so lucky. It's work – kinda.'

'I thought you was off Saturday?'

'I'm the eye that never sleeps,' said Danny. 'Remember?' Taking Georgie by the hand, he turned to leave.

'Hoy,' Ronnie called out. 'You mean that about our Susie?'

'What about your Susie?'

''Bout losing her knickers to a toff?'

'Nope,' Danny said, 'just kiddin',' and then, with Georgie straining at the leash, headed off towards Cable Street in search of an ice cream stall.

The little building was more like a library than a barn. There were no cows, no chickens, no feed sacks or bales of hay and the walls were lined with bookshelves packed with volumes old and new. A barrel stove and several oil-lamps indicated that the barn had no electrical supply but four vertical windows provided ample light. The desk and typewriter were almost new. The machine was flanked by a box of plain paper, three notepads and a pewter pot bristling with pencils. A hessian rug linked the desk to a sagging leather couch upon which Vivian was taking her ease.

'Do we have everything?' she asked.

'I'm not sure what everything is,' said Susan.

'Coffee, biscuits, cigarettes.'

'Yes, we have everything.'

'Well' – Vivian heaved herself to her feet – 'since I'm not here for the good of my health I suppose I'd better get on with it.'

From the mass of notes and clippings in Vivian's briefcase Susan had already extracted the slim cardboard folder that contained the outline of Vivian's proposed new book, *The Wheel of History*. Poised at the keyboard, she watched Vivian, a cigarette dangling from her lips, wander about the barn in search of inspiration.

'I don't know what Mercer expects from me,' the woman said. 'What if *Herod* was a fluke? I had things to say in *Herod*. I had a focus, a point of view that turned out to be more in tune with popular sentiment than I'd anticipated.' She peered, frowning, into the sunlight and sucked on her cigarette. 'What the devil am I doing here, Susan?'

'Working,' Susan suggested.

Vivian perched on an arm of the sofa. 'Did you happen to encounter Mercer on your morning perambulation? Did Caro take you to the cottage?'

'No.'

'He's probably still sleeping – or he's brought manuscripts to read. I tend to forget I'm not his only client.' Vivian sighed. 'I thought he'd show up for breakfast. I wonder if he's avoiding me?'

Susan cleared her throat. 'Perhaps we could start with the table of contents and begin filling in a few blanks.'

'You're right, Susan. What do we have so far?'

'Not a great deal.'

'I distinctly recall dictating heading notes to you before we left London. Didn't you type them up?'

'Of course I did.'

'Then read.' Vivian rolled on to the sofa and stretched out, forearm covering her eyes. 'Read, why don't you?'

Susan adopted her best Miss Armitage voice and rhymed off the headings. 'The Grand Sanhedrin; Freemasons, Jesuits and Jews; Priests, Mages and Men-Kings; The Folly of Moses Mendelssohn; The Role of the Inquisitor; The—'

Vivian groaned. 'That's enough.' She sat up. 'I have absolutely no idea where I'm going with this stuff. It's all so damned vague.'

'It is rather,' Susan agreed, then, after a moment, added, 'I know what sort of book my father would like you to write.'

'Do you?' said Vivian. 'What would that be?'

'A book of conspiracies,' Susan said. 'Secret plots to take over the world. I think that's why he liked *Herod* so much and went to hear you lecture.'

'I thought he was just trying to land you a job,' Vivian said.

'Oh, but he didn't know you were looking for a secretary.'

'I'm joking, child, just joking.' Vivian clicked her tongue against her teeth. 'However, I think you may be on to something.'

'My friend Danny Cahill says you can't go far wrong telling people what they're already disposed to believe,' Susan said.

'That's very sagacious of him. Is he a stevedore too?'

'Actually,' Susan said, 'he works in Fleet Street.'

Vivian brayed with laughter and was still laughing when, a second later, Mercer Hughes popped his head round the barn door.

'How goes it, Viv?' he asked.

'Smooth as silk, my dear,' Vivian told him. 'Now bugger off.'

Which, rather to Susan's surprise, he did.

4

When, in the winter of 1923, Danny stumbled into Stratton's Dining Rooms with nothing but seven shillings and a parcel of old clothes to his name the first thing he saw was Breda Romano perched on her brother Georgie's shoulders screaming like a banshee while Georgie, egged on by a room full of cabmen, lumbered about like a dancing bear, swinging the terrified kid round and round, her head bouncing off the light shade, her bare legs smeared with something that might be gravy or might be something a deal less savoury.

Despatched from St Finian's Orphanage in Glasgow with a rail ticket to London, three half-crowns and a torn penny map of the capital, Danny had clambered on to the wrong bus at Euston and had missed Fleet Street by a mile. He'd been too shy, or too proud, to ask the conductor for help but had twigged at length that warehouse walls and gigantic cranes weren't what you'd expect to find in the hub of a newspaper empire and had dropped off at the next stop which, as it happened, was fifty yards from Stratton's.

It was coming on dusk and it was raining. He'd eaten nothing all day but a bun and had no idea where he would lay his head that night. Though he was only fifteen years old, five feet five inches tall, skinny as a rake and alone in a strange city, bullying was bullying no matter how small you were or where you came from.

'Hey,' he shouted. 'Pit her doon.'

Eight pairs of eyes turned in his direction. Eight burly men with bull necks and forearms thicker than Danny's thighs set down their tea mugs and stared at the scrofulous little intruder.

Undaunted, Danny tucked the soggy brown paper parcel under one arm, stepped between the tables and, peering straight into Georgie's moon-shaped face, reached around the poor dummy, wrapped his free arm about the kid's waist and lowered her gently to the lino.

'Who the 'ell do you fink you are, sonnie?' one of the cabmen snarled.

'Danny Cahill. Who the hell're you?'

'Careful, Ernie, 'e's a Jock.'

'Aye, Ernie,' Danny said. 'Ah am a Jock. Wanna try me?'

The cabman laughed at the boy's bravado, which was just as well for Danny. When he asked where the girl's mammy was, the man pointed to the kitchen where Nora was frantically frying chops, too harassed to pay much attention to the commotion outside.

Eleven years had passed since that evening; eleven years in which Breda had blossomed from a weedy kid into what passed in Shadwell for a bombshell and Danny had become 'the lodger' and the envy of half the upstarts in Shadwell who assumed, quite wrongly, that one of the perks of his position in the household was to get a leg over the lovely Breda every time her mother's back was turned.

Danny had no interest in getting a leg over Breda. She would flirt with him from time to time just for practice and loved him as much as she loved any man but she knew that he knew that she was basically in love with herself.

Even so, when she crept into his room very late one night to tell him that she was in trouble, Danny had known precisely what the trouble would be and that he, and no one else, would be expected to get her out of it or, if the worst came to the worst, help her see it through.

Until she saw him bounding about the tennis court it hadn't occurred to Susan that Mercer Hughes was relatively young. His craggy features and hooded eyes reminded her of a picture she'd seen somewhere: a cowboy or explorer, a war hero, perhaps, peering stonily out from under the brim of his cap while the king pinned a medal on his chest.

In spite of Caro's urgings Susan refused to embarrass herself by taking up a racquet. She lounged in a deckchair on the path in front of the farmhouse with Vivian and Gwen Proudfoot, sipped a fruity concoction from a tall glass and watched the men pound the ball at each other while the sisters perched on the steps of the umpire's chair and squealed encouragement.

'They've been going at it for years,' Gwen said. 'Tennis, cricket, billiards, fishing, shooting, racing motorcars: whatever sport you care to name. How they keep a running score is beyond me.' She poked up an arm, caught a stray ball that zoomed over the hedge and tossed it back, all without spilling a drop of her drink. 'It will go on, I suppose, until one of them drops dead.'

'Don't you play?' Susan asked.

'With the girls now and then,' Gwen answered. 'It's too bloody playing with the boys. Besides, they don't much care for women getting in the way.'

Susan had worked all morning and for a couple of hours after lunch. In spite of her initial uncertainty, Vivian had soon found her voice and had reeled off screeds of prose at a rate that had Susan scrambling to keep up.

'Fifteen–forty.'

'What? Are you blind? That ball was well wide of the line.'

'Nothing of the sort. Look at the chalk.'

'Eleanor?'

'I saw it as out.'

'Traitor!'

Mercer Hughes was clad in cream-coloured flannels and a collarless shirt that clung to his chest and torso like a second skin. David, on the other hand, sported grass-stained breeches tied with string at mid-calf and a heavy woollen shirt. Both men wore pumps that had seen better days.

They sweated heavily in the hot August sun and squandered a great deal of energy in chasing balls that bobbed away into the cow pasture. When Mercer stepped over the little hedge to help himself from the jug of cordial Susan could smell his sweat, not stale and sour like the odour labourers gave off but clean and sharp and curiously masculine.

She watched him tip the jug and drink. His hair curled in damp ringlets across his brow. The shirt, plastered to his skin, shaped the long muscles of his back and shoulders like sculpture. He had long hands, long fingers and he drank the way she'd seen Spaniards do in photographs, the jug held high so that the cordial trickled into his mouth without touching his lips.

'We'll need a refill soon,' he said.

'No, we won't,' Gwen told him. 'We'll be having tea in ten minutes.'

'I'm four-three up in the set; I'm not stopping for tea.'

'Don't then,' Gwen Proudfoot said and stuck out her tongue like a child.

The agent looked down at Susan, wiped his mouth with the back of his hand and winked. 'What do you say, Shadwell? Tea or tennis?'

But Susan, having no answer to give, just smiled.

Old 'Bags' Bageshot, the crime reporter, might be the laziest man in Fleet Street but he did have his uses. His reputation rested on a string of sensational articles concerning 'The Vampire of Islington', who lured young girls into basements and allegedly drank their blood before he murdered them and dumped their bodies – five bodies in six years – in the Regent's Canal, and who, 'up to time of writing', as Bags put it, had not been caught.

There were those in Fleet Street who thought old Bags himself was the monster, for he lived in a house with a basement in Barnsbury Road but the fact that he was married with four children and in cahoots with half the detectives in the Metropolitan rather put the kibosh on that fanciful theory. The last victim had been found floating some seven years ago but every so often, on cold news days, Bags would resurrect the case, rehash the lurid details and scatter a few hints that he knew not only the fiend's identity but also where he was hiding: articles that the great British public lapped up, of course, and that gave the powers that be in New Scotland Yard a darned good laugh.

As a rule Mr Bageshot was grandfather to a clam when it came to imparting titbits of underworld gossip that might benefit his colleagues but he had a soft spot for the Glaswegian subeditor who corrected his factual errors and tightened his sprawling prose without a murmur of complaint and he was happy to do the lad a favour when the opportunity came his way.

The tip from Mr Bageshot backed by a couple of telephone calls led Danny to the outrigger of Soho that stretched from Wells Street off the Tottenham Court Road right up to Warren Street; not an area that Danny would have marked as a hotbed of criminal activity but one that Bags assured him housed upwards of a thousand crooks of various shades of grey.

Broad daylight late on Saturday afternoon: Oxford Street and the 'Tottie' as well as the byways of Soho were awash with folk. Danny walked briskly, hands in pockets, dodging this way and that like a winger with the ball at his feet. He knew London well – though not as well as Mr Bageshot – and loved the feeling that being loose in the city imparted: a feeling less of belonging than of possession, as if he, a shabby Scot, had usurped the natives' birthright.

The café clung to the edge of the 'real' Soho and wasn't a place you might drop into by chance. Four men and two women loitered on the pavement outside. The men wore natty hand-cut suits. The women were expensively coiffed and dressed but had the over-bright look of creatures that wouldn't be entirely comfortable until the sun went down.

Casually, almost lazily, they watched Danny approach.

The plate-glass window was painted dark green to half its height and, unlike Stratton's, carried no menu, chalked or printed, and no advertisements. The name American Lido was engraved low on the glass in a style too discreet to be anything other than ironic.

Danny stopped in front of the window and lit a cigarette. He lifted himself on the balls of his feet and pretended to peep over the band of green-painted glass.

The guy came up to him, not fast.

'What you after?' he said.

'Nothin',' Danny said. 'I just like the smell.'

'What smell?'

'Italian roast.' Danny paused. 'The coffee, I mean.'

'You sure that's what you mean?'

'What else?' Danny said. 'Unless you happen to be Vince.'

'What you want wiff Vince?'

'Bags sent me.'

'Who's Bags?'

'Aw, for God's sake!' Danny raised his eyes to heaven. 'You know who Bags is as well as I do.'

'You Danny?'

'Aye. Is he here?'

'He's inside,' Vince said.

He opened the door and ushered Danny into the coffee shop.

On the surface it was hardly what Danny would have thought of as a typical den of thieves. The room was long, stretching away into a shadowy interior where a young boy in an apron was wiping a marble-topped serving counter as he if were afraid of wearing it away.

There were no women in the room and fewer than a dozen men. Apart from the drone of a wireless system relaying sports results it was almost as hushed as a chapel. Two gents in Savile Row suits were playing cribbage at a table by the door and four others, a degree less well togged, were solemnly engaged in a round of solo whist, while at separate tables towards the rear a couple of ordinary-looking blokes were reading newspapers and drinking coffee from small white cups.

Before the card players could panic and scoop up the banknotes that lay among the cards Vince gave them the nod.

'Which one is he?' Danny whispered.

'Thought you knew 'im.'

'Never clapped eyes on him afore.'

'You 'ere to make trouble?'

'Not me,' said Danny. 'Mr Bageshot wouldn't stand for it.'

Vince looked down his nose and may, or may not, have smiled.

'That's 'im up there behind the *Pink*. You wan' a introduction?'

'Naw,' said Danny. 'That won't be necessary.'

The man was too absorbed in the *Sporting Pink* to notice Danny's approach.

He wasn't at all what Danny had expected. He wore a suit of fine chalk-striped material, a shirt with a high collar and four-inch cuffs fastened with rolled gold studs. On his wrist was a gold watch the size of a soup plate and on his fingers three or four rings. He was plump enough for his neck to swell over his collar and when he turned and glanced up his dewlap covered his tie. He looked smooth, though, smooth and sallow and very Italian.

'Mr Romano?' Danny said quietly. 'Leo Romano?'

No panic, no alarm: 'Who's asking?'

Danny pulled out a chair and sat down.

'I'm Nora's lodger, Danny Cahill.'

'Nora send you?'

'Nope.'

'How'd you find me?'

Danny tapped the side of his nose. 'Friends in low places.'

For a moment a glimmer of apprehension appeared in Leo Romano's brown eyes. He shook the newspaper and folded it carefully.

He said, 'Is it Georgie?'

'Georgie's just fine.'

'The other one then, the girl, Breda? She fine too?'

'No,' said Danny carefully. 'Breda isn't so fine.'

'She sick?'

'Not sick exactly, no.'

'Knocked up?' Leo said bluntly.

'Aye,' Danny replied. 'Knocked up.'

'You the daddy?'

'She doesn't know who the daddy is.'

'So what do you want from me, son?' Leo asked. 'Money?'

'No, Mr Romano,' Danny Cahill answered. 'Advice.'

At half past seven the gentlemen appeared in the dining room in white ties and tails as if the farmhouse were the Kit-Kat Club or the Café de Paris. Even Vivian had put herself out by struggling into a black rayon dress so tight that it showed every ridge and furrow of her Lastex girdle. Susan's best dress was calf-length and washable. The glances that Mercer Hughes shot in her direction added to her fear that she might be showing too much of something, though she couldn't imagine what. She had no chest to speak of and was so slim about the hips that Ronnie teased her by calling her 'sonnie'. Miss Armitage had told her that she had the perfect figure for a flapper but that flappers were 'very last year'. Being out of date in that department hadn't bothered old Mr Bottomly, Sir Alfred Pennington's clerk, who'd pawed her at every opportunity until she'd given him a resounding slap and had threatened to tell the judge if he didn't stop his nonsense.

The only admiring comment of any worth she'd ever received had come from Danny Cahill who, when she'd bumped into him at a Lyons Corner House off Leicester Square one lunchtime, had pursed his lips and uttered a soft 'wooo-hooo' that, even without embellishment, spoke volumes.

Candles in silver candlesticks cast light across the dining table. There was a great array of forks, knives and glasses to cope with. Mrs Wentworth had been joined by a very young girl, her granddaughter, who served and cleared each course and kept her eyes down and blushed furiously whenever anyone addressed her. The booze, as Ronnie would've put it, flowed like water; not cider tonight but wine. After one glass of a dry white stuff that tingled on her tongue, Susan covered her glass with her hand.

'Cautious, I see,' said Mercer Hughes. 'Are you afraid you'll lose control?'

'I'm not much of a drinker,' Susan said.

He was seated opposite her, leaning forward.

'What is it you drink down there?' he said.

'I don't know what you mean by "down there".'

'In Shadwell. What's your father's tipple, for example?'

'My father doesn't drink.'

'Now that's hard to believe.'

'True, though,' said Susan. 'He's teetotal.'

'Really! What about your mother?'

'My mother died when I was born. My dad – my father raised me.'

'No ladies to help out?' Mercer Hughes said. 'No transient aunts?'

'No,' Susan said. 'No transient aunts.'

'You do know what I mean by a transient aunt, don't you?'

'Girlfriends,' Susan said. 'My father's too concerned about paying the rent and finding my college fees to squander his wages on loose women.'

'One in the eye for you, Mercer,' Gwen Proudfoot said.

'Yes,' Mercer Hughes said. 'She's not just a pretty face, is she?'

'I didn't pick her for her pretty face,' Vivian said. 'Hidden depths she may have, Mercer, but I'd thank you not to try to uncover them.'

'Wouldn't dream of it, dear heart,' he said. 'Wouldn't even dream of it.'

After dinner the company repaired to the living room. Sheet music appeared from inside the piano stool. Eleanor and Caro, flanking their father, sang while Mercer Hughes danced, first with Vivian then with Gwen. He held his friend's wife very close, his hand slipping from her waist to her hip while she rested her brow against his cheek and whispered in his ear; an intimate flirtation that seemed to bother no one, least of all Gwen's husband.

Susan had never set foot inside a dance hall. Her father wouldn't even let her accompany Ronnie to church socials which, Ronnie said, were so carefully monitored the devil himself couldn't get into trouble there. Sometimes she resented her father's interference but more often than not she acknowledged that his rigid rules had rendered her 'different' from the girls who slaved in sweatshops and factories and whose only way out of the poverty trap was to marry a docker and have babies, not necessarily in that order.

'All right, Shadwell,' Mercer Hughes said. 'Your turn.'

'I – I can't. I mean, I've never . . .'

'What? Never?' He winked at Vivian. 'In which case it's high time you did.'

He offered his hand. Susan took it. He lifted her from the sofa. Gwen leaned by the French doors, watching. David struck a great trembling chord. Susan fitted her hand into Mercer's. The chord died away.

David said, 'All set?'

'All set,' said Mercer Hughes.

David hummed for a beat or two then broke into 'I'm Sailing on a Sunbeam' while his daughters, leaning on the piano, listened admiringly.

Susan had no notion if she was dancing a waltz, a foxtrot or a quickstep; nor did she care. She went where Mercer Hughes took her, the room and the people in it whirling past like figures seen from a merry-go-round.

'See how easy it is when you let yourself go,' Mercer Hughes said.

And Susan heard herself say, breathlessly, 'Yes, yes, I do.'

5

Susan assumed that Vivian and Mercer Hughes would treat religion with disdain; not so, it seemed. Vivian rolled down for breakfast already dressed for church and Mercer turned up a few minutes later in a navy blue suit that Susan thought added dash to his appearance, however out of place on a dusty country road. They walked the half-mile from Hackles to Gadney and entered the little church a few minutes before service was due to begin.

At school, where worship was mandatory, Susan had been obliged to join in daily prayers but being in a country church with its unvarnished wooden pews and wheezy harmonium was a novelty. The tousle-haired young vicar preached to a text from a letter by St Paul to the church at Corinth that seemed at first to have no relevance to a rural congregation but in the end delivered a telling message about the redemptive power of love.

After the service David lingered on the steps to chat with the vicar and two or three other men, who, Caro informed her, were apple growers too.

It was warm and still, the trees behind the church motionless.

Small boys in clean shirts and short trousers darted off to play among the stones in the churchyard. Women gathered by the gate to gossip. Susan guessed that they were the wives and daughters of farm labourers living in the tithed cottages that belonged to the squire or landowner. Mercer, Gwen and the girls wandered off to lean on the parapet of a stone bridge close to the churchyard gate, Vivian to chat to a pot-bellied gentleman in a panama hat and, Sunday or not, furtively smoke a cigarette cupped in the palm of her hand.

'Come and see this, Shadwell.'

Obediently, Susan joined the group on the bridge. Easing Eleanor from his arm, Mercer made room for Susan. She could smell the material of his suit, warm in the sun, and the lemony fragrance of the oil he used to slick down his unruly hair.

'What?' she said. 'What is it?'

'There, beneath you. Can you see it?' Mercer said.

The river ran brown and silver, dappled by sunlight and shadow. It straggled away in pools and shallows bordered by willows and meandered off into a meadow behind a row of small white cottages two or three hundred yards downstream.

It took Susan a moment to pick out the fish, motionless in the sluggish current: a long, sleek, olive shape with a prominent fin and a lean, thrusting jaw. She'd seen fish in glass bowls, of course, dainty flickering things, fish in ponds, fish dead on slabs or wrapped in newspaper but she had never seen one in nature and the sight gave her a strange thrill.

'Is it a trout?' she asked.

'God, no!' Mercer answered. 'Pike.'

'It's not doing very much, is it?' Caro said.

'Do not be deceived,' Mercer said. 'It's waiting for lunch.'

'What does it eat?' Susan asked.

'Anything it gets its teeth into,' Gwen answered, 'just like our own dear Mercer.'

'Now, now, Gwennie,' Mercer said, 'I'm sure you don't mean that.'

'Oh, but, indeed, I do,' said Gwen and swivelling abruptly on her heel went off in search of her husband.

One thing Matt Hooper hated more than any other was the hold religion had on the great unwashed, in whose unhygienic ranks, of course, he didn't include himself. He was forever quoting, or, rather, misquoting, the arch enemy, Karl Marx, and with tedious regularity would trot out the bit about 'the opiate of the people' while the bells of churches from as far afield as Limehouse pealed over Pitt Street. At least, he consoled himself, he didn't have to listen to Shadwell St Paul's calling the faithful to be duped, for the bells in the graceful steeple of the local church had been rendered speechless by wear, tear and acid dust.

While Nora, Breda and Georgie trudged off to mass at St Mary's, Matt lay in bed listening to his son's snores. Though he had no appetite for breakfast he was teased by cravings for a cigarette and, oddly, by a certain lumpy stirring in the region of his groin at the thought of Nora, or was it Breda, kneeling, open-mouthed, to receive the sacrament. Disturbed by this vision of female Romanos, he flung off the blankets, clambered over Ronnie and headed for the lavatory in the back yard in the hope that emptying his bladder might also clear his head.

It was a calm, cool morning with high flat clouds printed on a blue sky. Friday's rain had battered the petals from the rambler roses that clung, rather desperately, to the brick wall that separated the narrow yard from its neighbour. Matt scuttled out in nothing but a nightshirt and, sorted, paused on the way back to glare up at next door's cat, Toby, perched on top of the wall.

'What you lookin' at?' he said. 'You'll get no milk from me.'

Toby glared back and hissed reproachfully.

'Susie ain't 'ere, cat. Your soft touch ain't 'ere no more,' Matt said, then hurried back indoors.

By one o'clock the sun had climbed high over the rooftops to spear the kitchen with shafts of light. It wouldn't last, of course. By mid-afternoon the sun would dip behind the walls of the transit sheds that towered over Malabar Lane and Pitt Street's terraces would be smothered in shadow.

Matt had fried bacon and bread and, to add a little cheer to his solitary breakfast, had broken an egg into the dripping. Soothed by a mug of sweet tea, he rummaged under the cushion on the armchair and found an old copy of the *Star*. Still clad in his nightshirt, he immersed himself in an article on the white slave trade which, apparently, was the biggest employer of female labour this side of Rowat's pickle factory, though in his forty-four years in the East End he'd never seen a white slave or, indeed, a slave of any colour.

Caught up in his reading, he was startled when the knob of the kitchen door rattled and a female voice called out, 'Anybody 'ome?' and Breda tripped into the kitchen. Her pleated skirt was clenched tightly about her waist, her jacket thrown open to show off a lacy blue blouse. Her hat, a cloth thing with a flannel bow, was pushed back. Tiny beads of perspiration shone on her brow as if she'd been running which, this being Breda, Matt doubted was the case.

'You lookin' for Ronnie,' he said, 'he's still in his kip.'

'Not lookin' for Ronnie,' Breda said. 'Lookin' for you.'

'Me?' Matt said. 'What you want with me?'

He inched his chair close to the table and pushed his knees together.

'Could do with a cuppa, you got one 'andy,' Breda said. 'Ain't had nothin' this morning 'cause we was taking the wafer.'

'In the pot,' Matt said. 'You want toast?'

'Tea'll do,' Breda said.

'Help yourself.'

She found a cup on the draining board, rinsed it under the cold tap and filled it from the teapot. She seemed, Matt thought, quite at home, though to the best of his knowledge she'd never set foot in Pitt Street before.

She held the cup in both hands, sipped, and wrinkled her nose.

'Been in the pot a while. Sorry,' Matt said.

'Never mind. I like it strong,' Breda said. 'Got a message from me ma. She wants you round for supper.'

'On Sunday? I never come round Sunday.'

'Never been without Susie before, 'ave yer?'

'What you 'avin'?'

'Brauschmidt's best topside. Makes your mouth water just looking at it. You don't come, Ma'll be disappointed.' Breda paused. 'Me too.'

'I got nothin' to interest you, Breda.'

'Wouldn't be so sure of that,' the girl said.

She kicked out a chair, seated herself, stared at him across the width of the table then stretched out a leg and rubbed her ankle against his shin.

'I know what you need, Mr 'Ooper.'

'Do yer?'

'You need a ciggie. If I give you a ciggie, will you play the game with me?'

'What game's that, Breda?'

'Tease me.'

'I'm too old to go teasing young girls.'

'I ain't so young as all that – and you ain't so old.'

The lump had returned unbidden. He felt awkward, beyond awkward.

Breda laughed and rocked back. 'Got yah going there, didn't I?'

'Yus,' Matt said, not laughing. 'You did.'

She rubbed his shin again then took her leg away, fished out a fresh pack of Player's Weights, lit two from a match and without fuss passed one to him.

He relaxed his belly muscles, sat up a little and took in smoke.

Breda said, 'You comin'?'

'What?'

'Supper, you comin'?'

'I might.'

'Might?'

'Maybe I just need to be rubbed the right way.'

Breda frowned and blew smoke from the side of her mouth.

'Now you're the one doing the kidding,' she said.

'What if I'm not?'

'You got a cheek.'

'You started it, Breda,' he reminded her.

'Suppose I did.' She grinned. 'Can't 'elp it. See a good-looking bloke I just go all funny, like.'

'Even a good-looking bloke old enough to be your daddy?'

'Wish you was my daddy. If you was my daddy you'd do right by me same as you done right by Susie. My daddy never give me no start in life. Stuck, I am, waiting tables to a buncha animals can't keep their 'ands to themselves.

Deserve better, I do. Deserve a nice kind man to look after me.'

'You got time, Breda, lots of time.' Surrendering to paternal instinct, he reached for her hand. 'You'll see. Mr Right'll be waiting just around the corner.'

'What the 'ell's going on 'ere?' Ronnie growled.

He'd had sense enough to slip on a pair of old flannels before he'd tottered through from the bedroom but he was bare-chested, barefoot and his face so swollen that he looked as if he'd been through ten rounds with Max Schmeling.

'Thought I 'eard voices.' Ronnie scratched his chest. 'What you up to then? She been 'ere all night?'

''Course she hasn't been 'ere all night,' Matt retorted. 'She's been to mass.'

'Our Susie not gone ten minutes, Dad, and you're off chasing young birds. Does your ma know about this, Breda?'

'For Gawd's sake, Ronnie,' Breda said, 'it's got nothing to do with you.'

'You sure about that?'

'Swear on the Bible,' Breda said and crossed herself.

'Anyway,' Matt said, 'what 'appened to your fizz?'

'Division of opinion what got out of hand,' Ronnie said.

'He done you good, didn't 'e?' said Breda.

'Not as good as I done 'im,' Ronnie told her and, doing his best to swagger, reeled to the back door and headed for the lavatory.

Breda leapt to her feet and stuck on her hat.

'Gotta go,' she said, 'before Ronnie gets the wrong idea.'

'I think he's already got the wrong idea,' Matt said.

'See you tonight then, Mr 'Ooper?'

He looked up at her blonde hair and her lacy blue blouse filled to capacity with firm young flesh.

'Yus,' he said wistfully. 'See you tonight.'

Lunch was a rough and ready affair of cold meats, cheese and salad. Dinner, Gwen warned her guests, would be equally basic, for she had no intention of slaving in the kitchen on a lovely summer afternoon and Mrs Wentworth had Sunday off. David said he had something to do in the orchard and with Caro tagging along had gone off to do it while Eleanor, who was sulking for some reason, hid herself away in her room. Mercer and Gwen simply disappeared.

Vivian dragged a deckchair into the shade of the porch, declared that life was far too short to engage in intellectual cudgelling at the weekend, buried her nose in a Dornford Yates novel and within five minutes was fast asleep.

It was very, very quiet, almost uncannily so. Susan wondered if she should join David and Caro in the orchard or perhaps go in search of the mysterious priory. She was tempted to look for Mercer's cottage but a faint feeling of unease deterred her. She ambled along the path to the barn and slipped inside.

Hazy light stole through the windows, a grainy dust hung in the air. Not an ideal place to store books, Susan thought, but, unlike Sir Arthur Pennington, David Proudfoot didn't collect fine editions. Buchan, 'Sapper', the plays of Bernard Shaw, a broken run of Stanley Weyman, a colourful half shelf devoted to the novels of Jeffery Farnol: she ran a finger over the spines, then with a little shiver of surprise found herself confronted by a shelf of books on witchcraft, demonology, flagellation, black magic and fat histories of the Inquisition, titles that would surely never find their way into any public library.

She fished a volume from a bottom shelf and opened it

at a shocking engraving of a naked man tied to a stake. She hesitated, turned the page and found herself staring at a picture of a priest in flowing robes holding a baby above his head. On the next page was a scene of furious copulation between bearded men and sobbing, bare-breasted women.

Mercer Hughes came upon her as silently as a cat.

'Do you like that one?' he asked.

Susan started and swung round guiltily.

'No, 'course I don't like that one,' she said. 'I don't like any of them.'

'They're meant to engender disgust, of course, though some chaps find them quite stimulating.' He rested a hand on her shoulder. 'What you've stumbled upon, Shadwell, is a series of engravings collectively known as the *Analects of Magdeburg*; not the original, I might add. The original is virtually priceless. Only two complete copies are known to exist. The British Museum has one and the Vatican the other. This edition was printed for subscribers from the BM copy in the 1890s. I picked it up relatively cheaply just after the war to give to David.'

'Some gift!' Susan said. 'It's just filth.'

'Filth to some, art to others,' Mercer said. 'Until recently it was assumed that the engraver was Lucas Cranach or his son, famous painters in the court of the Elector of Saxony, but that's been disproved. It's also rumoured that the folio in the Vatican bears Martin Luther's signature, though personally I doubt it.'

'Why are you telling me all this?' Susan said.

'To educate you.'

'What makes you think I need educated?'

'You wouldn't be here if you weren't willing to learn.'

'It sounds to me as if you're trying to justify this sorry stuff.'

She caught a faint, puzzling whiff of perfume, not lemony like his hair tonic but light and flowery like the scent Gwen Proudfoot wore.

Mercer said, 'I don't have to justify anything to you, my dear Shadwell. Historians like Wells and philosophers like Russell will tell you otherwise but it's to the dark that we are drawn and in the darkness that we will find enlightenment.'

'In that case, I don't think I'm interested in being enlightened.'

'Why did you accept Vivian's offer of employment?'

'For seventy bob a week,' Susan said. 'Cor, I tell yer, Mr Mercer, ain't much a girl won't do for seventy bob. Vivian thinks I'm worth it.'

'Worth has nothing to do with wages,' Mercer said. 'Worth is something one puts upon oneself. That, I suspect, is a lesson you still have to learn.'

Susan seated herself on the edge of the desk, smoothed her skirt and crossed her ankles. 'Are you going to teach me?'

'Not I,' Mercer said. 'It isn't the same as learning to speak properly or take shorthand at a hundred and fifty words a minute. There are no handbooks to help you get what you want from life.'

'Folks round my way would think you lack for nothing, Mr Hughes.'

'How wrong they'd be, how very, very wrong.'

Susan said, 'My dad says your lot has better things to think about than where your next meal's coming from. My dad says it's your lot who keep the country from going to the dogs.'

'Do you agree with him?'

'Yes, I think mostly I do.'

'My, my!' he said. 'You do have a lot to learn.'

'About politics?'

'No,' Mercer said. 'About me.'

6

It took several days and much fretting for it to penetrate Nora's thick skull that Breda had become her rival. Sunday night supper hadn't been a success. She'd put on her best flowered dress and had spent an hour trying to do something with her hair only to be upstaged by Breda who had sallied down from her room looking like the proverbial million dollars and, without a blush, had kissed Susie's dad full on the mouth before she'd spooned out his meat and potatoes and, with another kiss, served him. All that kissing, all that flirting over cigarettes and bottled beer had seemed like an act at first, another of Breda's performances, though everything Breda did, from chopping liver to clearing tables, was a performance.

After she'd developed a bum and a bosom and the height to carry them, Breda had become the star turn in Stratton's Dining Rooms. Nora knew full well that she attracted custom that might otherwise have gone elsewhere: a host of ageing adolescents who goggled at her daughter as if they'd never seen a female before and hung around just for the privilege of watching her shimmy between the tables or bend over the counter to rake in the drawer for a fork.

Breda had never been short of boyfriends, of course: Syd, the cocky debt collector; Phil, who'd taken her up town and who, Breda had claimed, would have married her if he hadn't had a wife in Bethnal Green. Sixteen she was when Phil had ditched her but what he'd done before the ditching Nora didn't have the nerve to ask. After Phil came Nat, a nice lad, shy and courteous, who Nora thought would make an ideal son-in-law until the law caught up with him and a judge handed him a twelve-year stretch for a bit of armed robbery, of which offence, Breda had tearfully assured her mother, poor Nat was entirely innocent.

Last winter it had been Paddy, laugh-a-minute Paddy who was never sober enough to hold down a job and had eventually crept back to his mammy in Armagh with his tail between his legs. He'd been followed, briefly, by Chaz, a professional wrestler, built like a brick outhouse, who'd set off in March for a bout in Manchester and had never been seen again.

'Ain't no one, Ma, no one special.'

'Where you go when you go out then?'

'Down the Crown. Pictures sometimes – with Dora.'

'Dora? I thought she was carrying.'

'Not that Dora; the other one.'

Georgie was seated at the table trying to fit together the twenty-one pieces of a big wooden jigsaw that Danny had bought him. He worked patiently, tongue stuck out as if he intended to lick the pieces into submission. He had no interest in or connection with the conversation that took place over his head.

'You ever see him down there?' Nora asked.

'See who, where?'

'Mr Hooper, down the Crown?'

'Come on, Ma, you know Mr 'Ooper don't drink.'

'Drank enough Sunday, didn't he?'

'Two light ales is hardly drinking.'

'Why didn't Ronnie come with him?' Nora asked.

'Ronnie wasn't invited, was 'e?' Breda answered.

'Matt hasn't been in all week.'

'Maybe you scared 'im off.'

'Me scared him off? You, more like.'

To Nora's disappointment her daughter didn't rise to the bait.

'It's only three days,' Breda said. 'Expect he's busy. By the way, are we closing Monday? It's bank holiday.'

'Don't we usually close bank holiday?'

'Usually. I got plans, that's all.'

'Plans?' Nora frowned. 'What sort o' plans?'

'Thought I might go off for a sniff of the sea.'

'What sea?' said Nora.

'Southend,' Breda said casually. 'Maybe Margate.'

'Margate?'

'They got a new railway station at Margate.'

'You going with him?'

'Not going with no one, Ma,' Breda said.

'That's fine then.' Nora smirked. 'You can take Georgie with you.'

'I ain't looking after Georgie on me own.'

'Then we'll all go. Do us all good, a sniff o' the sea.'

'Ma!'

'It's him, isn't it? I saw how he looked at you. I saw what you was up to.'

'I don't know what you're talking about.'

'Mr Hooper – Matt: you got eyes for my Matt.'

'Your Matt? Since when did 'e become your Matt?'

'He's always been my Matt.'

'Not sure 'e knows that,' Breda said. 'Maybe you should tell 'im, case 'e's got other ideas.'

'Other ideas? Like you?'

'Me? For Gawd sake! What would I want with a old man like Mr 'Ooper?'

'He'd look after you. He'd take care of you.'

'Yer,' said Breda. 'I could do with being taken care of right now.'

'I knew it,' Nora cried. 'I know exactly what you're up to.'

'I bet you bleedin' don't,' said Breda.

They had 'done' the Lady Chapel and the crypt, sniffed the herb garden, walked past King Stephen's chair, been jostled in the cloisters by a motor-coach load of elderly tourists and had spent the best part of a half-hour in the famous chained library where Mercer, standing close to Susan, had delivered a lecture on Canute, Caxton and the *Nuremberg Chronicle*.

It was cool in the cathedral and Susan was happy to let Mercer lead. He seemed thoroughly familiar not only with the building's nooks and crannies but also with the histories of the bishops who lay entombed there. Vivian was less than enthralled, however. She claimed that she had been dragged round Hereford Cathedral so often she was surprised someone hadn't put up a monument to her and, leaving Mercer and Susan to it, had popped outside for a smoke.

For two days Vivian had rifled her brother's library in search of material on secret societies whose influence on the crowned heads of Europe, as well as its prelates, had shaped the pattern of history. On Wednesday morning, however, over a late breakfast, Mercer had suggested she take a break and proposed an afternoon trip into Hereford where David, chairman of a local growers' association, had business to conduct at Bulmer's sprawling cider factory.

'Now we come to it,' Mercer said. 'The cathedral's crowning glory, the pièce de résistance, a great treasure of the medieval world.' He parted the tourists who had gathered in the cathedral's south aisle and pushed Susan to the front. 'The Mappa Mundi, six centuries old; a gorgeous creation, is it not?'

The map was boxed in a wooden frame that opened out like a swing door. At first Susan couldn't quite take it in. She was conscious of Mercer pressed against her and the respect that the dodderers in the little crowd accorded him. His hands slid to her waist. He held her very steady, very still, his breath tickling the hair on the nape of her neck.

'It's the only intact wall map of the world to survive the Middle Ages,' he said. 'The supposition is that it was brought here as an altarpiece by Richard of Haldingham.' The little crowd hung on his every word as if he were more interesting than the map itself. 'If you look closely in the left-hand corner you'll see that Richard left an injunction for posterity: a request that we pray to the Lord to have mercy on his sinful soul and the soul of someone called Lafford, who apparently drew the map in the first place.'

'I can't quite make it out,' Susan admitted.

'Not surprising: it's in Norman French,' Mercer said. 'The Mappa is much more than a map, of course. It's really an encyclopaedia of knowledge and learning. The actual geography is haywire but just look at the figures. Adam and Eve, do you recognise them?'

Susan nodded.

'And these elderly gentlemen,' Mercer went on, 'are the cartographers of ancient Rome. Here are the mountains of Wales. There's the Nile flowing through Egypt. The unicorn, the centaur, the dragon; nothing was lost to the imagination. Naturally, Jesus and the heavenly host top it all, sitting up there in lofty indifference, thus proving that superstition ruled then just as it does now.'

Susan glanced round. He was standing very close to her, his thighs brushing her buttocks. 'Do you really think religious belief is nothing but superstition?'

'Of course I do,' Mercer said. 'Theism is strictly an excuse for waging wars.'

Behind Mercer's back someone tutted disapprovingly.

'Do you know what the Mappa reminds me of?' Susan said.

'No,' said Mercer indulgently. 'What does it remind you of?'

'One of those photographs in medical books: a germ or a cancer cell seen through a microscope.'

'Dear God, Shadwell,' Mercer said. 'What a perfect analogy for the world at large, especially with Jerusalem rotting at its heart.'

'How dare you, sir!' said a male voice from the crowd.

'You, I take it, are Jewish?' said Mercer.

'I am, sir, and proud of it.'

'In that case,' Mercer said, 'perhaps I'd better shove off,' and taking Susan by the hand he led her quickly away.

'Oh, she's smart all right,' Mercer said. 'Just to save face I even had to pretend I'd read *The Science of Life*. Where did you find this one, Viv?'

'I didn't find her,' Vivian said. 'She was laid at my feet, as it were.'

'Like Cleopatra.'

'Well, I wouldn't go that far,' said Vivian.

They were seated by the window in the Café Royal in St Peter Street where, by arrangement, David would pick them up for the journey home. Susan had gone to the ladies' room. Mercer and Vivian were alone, apart, that is, from a dozen or so day-trippers chattering over teacups and chocolate cake.

'She's quite the little jewel,' Mercer went on. 'Intuitive, articulate, well read. And that voice: she could probably just about pass muster at Henley. Tell me about the father.'

'Crane operator on the Shadwell Dock.'

'How on earth did he rear such a precocious child on a docker's wage?'

Vivian shrugged. 'By making every penny count, I suppose.'

'Siblings?'

'A brother: a butcher.'

'Literally or figuratively?'

'Literally,' Vivian said. 'Look here, Mercer, I'm rather keen on this girl. I'd like to hang on to her for a while, if you don't mind.'

'Really?' Mercer said. 'I've always had my suspicions about you.'

'Stop it,' Vivian said sternly. 'She's far too useful to scare away. I'd be obliged if you would exercise a degree of control over your lustful urges until I deliver publishable copy.'

'Is that an ultimatum?' Mercer said. 'The beauty or the book?'

'Take it that way if you wish.'

'What am I to do, my dear Vivian, if Miss Hooper falls in love with me? You know how irresistible I am. Am I to break the poor girl's heart by ignoring her?' He glanced out at the traffic in the street, at donkey-carts and pony-traps, motorcars and vans, at the façade of the quaint Old House across the square lit by a late afternoon sun. 'I think she may already be halfway to head over heels.'

'Don't flatter yourself,' Vivian said.

'When may I expect a first draft?'

'Are you changing the subject?'

'Merely being practical.'

'With a following wind and no disruptions – Easter.'

'Couldn't make it Christmas, could you?'

'Don't be ridiculous,' Vivian said. 'Why Christmas?'

'Because,' Mercer said, 'I may not be able to wait until spring.'

Danny wasn't surprised to find Breda in the kitchen when he arrived home from a late shift. The fact that she had to be up by six and ready to start serving at seven didn't seem to bother her. She was one of the lucky ones, Danny thought, who can tick along on five hours' shuteye a night and still be going strong at the end of the day. She wasn't going strong tonight, though; nor, come to think of it, was she one of the lucky ones. He removed his jacket and hung it on the back of a chair. He loosened his tie and unbuttoned his collar. He had rehearsed his story on the journey home on the night bus but he still needed a moment to collect his thoughts.

She served him a ham sandwich and a mug of Camp coffee then leaned against the draining board, doing her best to appear casual. Her washed-out kimono was half open. He could see her breasts rising and falling as she pumped herself up. He felt nothing for her sexually, not much anyway, just a thin trickle of pity for her predicament.

'For God's sake, Danny,' she blurted out. 'Tell me what you found out.'

No call for Breda to know he'd met her old man or that Leo was living on the fat of the land by running girls in the most lucrative club in Soho; a racket, Leo had confided, that was much less risky than tangling with the racecourse gangs who'd slit your throat as soon as look at you. Danny had thought it prudent not to enquire about the blonde from the Fawley Street fish bar who'd almost certainly been dumped years ago.

'Danny, please.'

He eyed the sandwich longingly but didn't dare take a bite.

'If you want it done safe an' near enough legal,' he said, 'it'll cost you a hundred quid, cash. I got an address in Harley Street.'

'Is 'e a proper doctor?'

'Physiotherapist.'

'For a hundred quid,' Breda said, 'I want a proper doctor.'

'He does for all the toffs, all the fashionable ladies.'

'It's only ten bob in Whitechapel.'

'I don't care if they're doin' it for free in Whitechapel,' Danny said. 'You aren't goin' tae one o' them backstreet butchers.'

Far too many stories about the fatal results of botched abortions had wafted across his desk over the years; arrests on manslaughter charges were so common that unless news was in very short supply they didn't even merit a paragraph. He'd taken a flyer on Leo Romano who, Bags had said, was one of the better known pimps on the west side and had connections with all sorts of useful people on the wrong side of the law.

'All very well for you . . .' Breda began.

'Listen, are you sure you're knocked up?'

'Positive. I ain't had a visit for two months.'

'Might be somethin' else,' Danny said.

'Like what?'

He shrugged. 'How do I know? Cancer?'

'Geeze! Thanks for that cheery thought.'

Danny said, 'You tell your ma you want Monday off?'

'Said I was going to Margate.'

'With me?'

'With no one. She wants us all to go.'

'Talk her out o' that if you can,' Danny said.

'I thought I'd do it Monday, be back all sorted Monday night.'

'It isn't that easy, Breda.'

'What do you know about it?' she said. 'You ain't a woman.'

'Naw,' Danny said, 'but if I was a woman I wouldn't be stupid enough to drop my knickers for some guy I'd only just met round the back o' the bloody Crown. You're not gonna tell me who put one in you, Breda, are you?'

'I don't know, I tell yer. Honest, I don't know who 'e was.' She let out a sigh that was close to a sob and sank down on a chair. 'Eat your sandwich.'

Danny bit into the bread and meat and chewed thoughtfully.

'You squeamish in the mornin'?' he asked.

Breda shook her head.

'Your – your things, they swollen?'

'Things? Oh, things.' She peered enquiring into her cleavage. 'They're okay so far. Is that a good sign?'

'Means you probably got a month to make up your mind.'

'Make up my mind about what?' Breda said.

'The kid,' Danny said. 'Isn't that what this is all about: the kid?'

'The kid? What kid? This is all about *me*.' She put an arm about his neck and nuzzled his cheek. 'You're not gonna let me down, Danny. I mean, you're not gonna abandon me, are yer?'

'No, Breda, I'm not gonna abandon you – not if you agree to do it my way?'

She gave up nuzzling and sat back. 'What way's that?'

'One step at a time, Breda,' Danny Cahill told her. 'One wee step at a time.'

Susan had no idea what the kiss meant, if it meant anything at all. All she knew was that it was different from the kisses he bestowed on Eleanor and Caro, on Vivian and Gwen. There was a brusqueness to his manner on Thursday morning, as if he were already preparing for the rush and bustle of the city. He came striding up from the cottage at half past seven dressed in his navy blue suit and sweating a little in the early morning sunshine.

Everyone, even Vivian, had risen to see him off. He would, he said, be in the office by lunchtime, leaving Charlie Ames, his partner, free to head off with *his* partner for ten days in Florence. He carried no luggage save a slim black leather attaché case and didn't enter the house. He planted the attaché case in David's motorcar and stood just outside the French doors, hands on hips, ostentatiously sucking in a last few mouthfuls of country air.

Gwen brought him coffee in a cup without a saucer and a single piece of toast on a plate. The women hovered around him while he ate, drank and glanced now and then at his wristlet watch as if every minute, every second had become precious and he was already on the clock.

Bank holidays, Susan had gathered, meant little to Mercer Hughes. All the publishing houses would be closed and half the capital's literati sunning themselves in Nice or Cannes or fishing for salmon in Scotland. He had promised to go 'upriver' with Anna Maples and her motley crew on Sunday and spend Monday with his wife, which, he said, through a mouthful of toast, was the least he could do for poor Rosalind.

David slid into the motorcar. 'Come along, old sport,' he called. 'Do your duty and kiss the girls, then we must be off.'

Gwen handed Mercer a napkin. He wiped butter from his lips and tossed the napkin on to the hedge. He skirted the half circle of grieving females and kissed each one in turn. Eleanor clung to him for a moment then ran off into the house. Caro, not to be outdone, attached herself to his thigh and told him how much she'd miss him. Vivian offered her cheek, Gwen her brow. Then he was looking down on Susan and, it seemed, had put all urgency aside. He placed a hand on her shoulder, holding her as if he feared that she might bolt. He lightly kissed her lips.

'See you around, Shadwell,' he whispered.

'Yes,' Susan said softly, 'see you around.'

Mercer vaulted over the passenger door and a moment later the motorcar zoomed off down the track by the tennis court.

Vivian lit a cigarette.

Gwen plucked the crumpled napkin from the hedge.

Susan watched dust settle over the hedgerows.

'A wife?' she said at length. 'Mercer has a wife?'

'Oh, yes,' Gwen said. 'Our Mercer has a wife. Did he forget to tell you?'

7

'I can see we're not going to get one jot of work done until you stop moping.'

'I am *not* moping.' Susan stripped the cover from the typewriter. 'I'm ready to do what you pay me for, Miss Proudfoot. I'm ready to work. Are you?'

'Now, now!' Vivian said. 'Don't come all high-hat with me, girl. You wouldn't be the first wide-eyed innocent to fall for Mercer Hughes.'

'I have not fallen for Mercer Hughes,' Susan said indignantly. 'And I am certainly not wide-eyed.'

'Are you aware that you go all posh when you're unsure of yourself? You sound like Paddy Campbell on one of her off days,' Vivian said. 'I don't suppose you know who Paddy Campbell is.'

'I do, too. Do you think I don't know nothing – anything? For your information my elocution teacher acted with Mrs Patrick Campbell. And while we're on the subject,' Susan said, 'I also know who Topsy is.'

'Topsy?'

'*Uncle Tom's Cabin* Topsy.'

'What's she got to do with it?' said Vivian.

'I'm not ignorant. I'm – I'm educated.'

'Yes, Susan, but education's a double-edged sword. It separates you from the girls you grew up with and alienates the sort of boys who might want to marry you. Education isn't enough to impress us, though. By "us" I mean the company in which you find yourself.'

'Landed gentry.'

'Landed gentry? If that's what you think we are then you'd better think again. We're not aristocracy or anything like it,' Vivian said. 'There isn't an Honourable among the lot of us. I may have taken lunch with Sir Oswald Mosley once – just once – and let me tell you if you think Mercer is charming he's a ragamuffin compared with Tom Mosley – but we aren't upper crust. We belong to a generation born with money but no family connections. My father made his pile by manufacturing chamber pots – repeat, chamber pots – in a factory in Stoke-on-Trent. Whatever we own we, or Daddy, worked for. Now if you'll just stop scowling at me for one minute I'll tell you about Mercer Hughes.'

Susan looked down at the typewriter keys. 'It's none of my business, really,' she said.

'I rather fear,' Vivian said, 'that it is your business, Susan.'

'Because he – he likes me, do you mean?'

'Oh, he doesn't like you. He wants you. You're young, slim and pretty and – what's the word? – unbroken. He'll flatter you, seduce you and toss you aside. The sad thing is that you won't hold it against him because he'll convince you that in a more equitable society you and he would live happily ever after – which is utter rot, of course.'

'Aren't you going to tell me about Mrs Hughes?'

'Rosalind? She's as mad as a hatter; genuinely, clinically nuts. She's presently shut away in what we politely refer to as a nursing home: a nursing home with barred windows and locked doors. Mercer knew she was unstable when he married her. Plenty of folk – though I'm not one of them – think Mercer drove her over the edge.'

'What's wrong with her?'

'God knows!' Vivian said. 'The psychiatrists have half a dozen different names for it. Paranoid schizophrenia seems to be the current favourite. They keep her doped to the eyeballs and more or less chain her to the wall when Mercer visits.'

'Why doesn't he divorce her?'

'It suits him to plead loyalty to Rosalind when one of his lady friends becomes too insistent.' Vivian paused. 'Truth of the matter is, he won't divorce Rosalind Carver because her father won't let him. He not only foots the bill for Rosalind's "treatment" but shells out whenever Mercer needs a few hundred quid to bail himself out of trouble.'

'I take it there are no children?'

'Was one once, but it died.'

'Boy or girl?'

'Boy,' said Vivian. 'Just a few weeks old when he passed away, poor child. No apparent cause, no reason, no one to blame. He simply fell asleep in his crib one afternoon and didn't wake up.'

'Perhaps that was the last straw,' Susan suggested.

'Probably,' Vivian agreed. 'Rosalind should never have become pregnant in the first place but her father insisted she deliver a grandchild and Mercer was nothing if not accommodating.'

'When did all this happen?'

'Four years ago, coming on five.'

'Before he became your agent?'

'Just before,' Vivian said. 'David had been at him for some time to take me in hand professionally – repeat, professionally.

74

'Trouble was I hadn't a clue what I wanted to write. Mercer came up with the notion of a book on Palestine, wangled a contract with Dawson of *The Times* and inspired me to write *Herod*. And now, you might say, I'm stuck with it.'

'Twenty-eight thousand copies in print is hardly being stuck with it,' Susan said, 'together with translations and the prospect of an American sale.'

'All right,' Vivian said. 'I don't need to be reminded that I'm earning a small fortune. Haven't I enough crosses to bear without you hounding me?'

'Talking of crosses,' said Susan, 'what's happened to the mail?'

'Mercer's dealing with it. He'll sift out the nasty stuff and bring the rest with him next time he comes up.'

'Oh,' Susan said. 'Is he coming back?'

'Of course he's coming back. Mercer may give the appearance of industry but, believe me, it's Charlie Ames who does the donkey work. Mercer will return to Hackles as soon as he possibly can – if only to see you again.'

'Me?'

'He's not going to pass over the chance of another conquest.'

'Have I no say in the matter?' Susan asked.

'Not much,' Vivian told her. 'You may surrender sooner or you may surrender later but I've no doubt you'll surrender eventually.'

'If you think that then you don't know me very well.'

'And you, my dear,' said Vivian, 'don't know Mercer Hughes.'

If Nora was puzzled by Danny's suggestion that Breda and he spend part of bank holiday Monday together she gave no hint of it. She was, in fact, relieved that her wayward daughter had abandoned the notion of going off to the seaside with some person or persons unknown. Danny Cahill was responsible and reliable. He'd make sure Breda had a good time without getting her drunk or taking advantage of her. She slipped Breda an extra half-crown to put in her purse and said she'd take Georgie across the river to the big bank holiday fair in Southwark Park to give him a bit of fun too. Then she kissed her daughter goodbye and watched approvingly from the pavement outside the shop as the pair headed off towards the Underground.

The surgery was in Malvern Place, a discreet cul-de-sac close to Harley Street. With shops and offices closed, great swathes of London were unnaturally quiet and the cul-de-sac, when they reached it, was deserted. In sunshine and warm shadow the houses looked immaculate: steps swept, brass plates gleaming, windows tactfully curtained, varnished doors implacable.

'This can't be the place,' Breda said.

'Why can't it?' said Danny.

'It'll cost too much.'

'I told you, I got the money.'

'Where did you get a hundred quid?'

Breda had spoken hardly a word since they'd left Shadwell. Only when they entered Malvern Place did she show signs of agitation.

'It isn't a hundred,' Danny said. 'It's twenty guineas, an' I got it.'

'This ain't right,' said Breda.

'I know it isn't right,' said Danny.

'What – what's he gonna do to me?'

'What he's not goin' tae do is stick a needle up you,' Danny said.

'You mean he ain't gonna take it away.'

'Not today he's not.'

'What you up to, Danny Cahill?'

'I'm just lookin' after you, like I always do.'

'Why are we 'ere if it ain't gonna happen?'

'All the doc does is induce a miscarriage.'

'Yer, then I won't 'ave to tell me ma.'

'Is that what worries you?' Danny said. 'Bein' caught out by your ma?'

'Another mouth to feed, me not working for a while, no room in the—'

'You still not goin' to tell me who the daddy is?'

'Don't know,' said Breda. 'Honest, I don't.'

'How about a short list?'

'It's not funny, Danny.'

'Bloody right it's not.'

'So,' Breda said, 'if the doc's not gonna do it today, why are we here?'

'To make sure you're expectin',' Danny said. 'Once we know for certain we can review your options.'

'Options? What bleedin' options?'

'Breda, you're a Roman Catholic.'

'What's that got to do with it?'

'If you get rid of a kid an' your ma ever finds out she'll go crazy. She might do the dance o' shame an' foam at the mouth at you bein' pregnant but she'll never forgive you if you kill the baby.'

'Kill the ... Oh, yeah, I see what you're up to, Danny Cahill. You're tryin' to make me say I'll keep it.'

'You don't have to keep it. You can give it away.'

'Give it away?'

'Put it up for adoption.'

'My baby!' Breda said. 'Not on your bleedin' life.'

'Fine,' Danny said. 'Now, if you don't mind, let's get you up those stairs an' have you properly examined. Maybe you're not pregnant at all.'

'Here,' Breda said, brightening, 'maybe I'm not.'

'Let's go an' find out, shall we?'

'Yer,' Breda said, 'let's go and find out.'

The boughs of the apple trees in David Proudfoot's orchard were laden with fruit which would soon be ripe for the picking. It was the same all over the country, David said, not just in Hereford but in Somerset and Devon too. Reports indicated a bumper crop and with it a glut of cider apples and a boom year for all. Bulmers had already taken on three hundred extra hands and with the construction of twenty-two huge concrete tanks had a storage capacity of close to five million gallons, more than enough to cope with all the apples in England.

The orchard was only a small part of the Proudfoot holdings. Harvesting was already under way in the wheat field by the river and the drone of a combine and a shimmering ochre dust hung in the air. David and his farm manager, Mr Garrett, had gone down to supervise the threshing and although Caro waved her father was too occupied to notice her.

'Shall we go and help?' Caro asked.

'I wouldn't know what to do,' Susan answered.

'Mr Garrett will find us something.'

Vivian had complained of a headache. Hot weather and early rising didn't agree with her, she said, and she'd be the better of a nap before lunch.

'We could go and look at the priory,' Susan suggested.

'Yes, I suppose we could,' said Caro. 'Follow me.'

The day had turned humid as if somewhere far across the rolling hills and valleys, in the mountains of Wales, perhaps, a thunderstorm was brewing. The air sizzled with clouds of insects but there was no birdsong.

They came upon the priory suddenly. It rose through the trees to a height of twenty or thirty feet, like a great stone cliff drenched in moss and ivy. There was little enough of it, just one tottering wall, cracked and crumbling, and a few blackened beams to indicate where the floors had been. At one time, Susan thought, there must have been gardens but there was no trace of them now. Tall weeds and rank grasses had taken over and even in the heat of noon the place had a clammy smell that reminded her of cat's pee.

'Is that it?' she said.

'Yes, that's it,' said Caro.

'Aren't there dungeons or something?'

'No, no dungeons. Even if there were Daddy would have had them blocked up. It's not safe, you see. Few people ever come here, just men with beards interested in local history, and not many of them.'

'I thought there was a cottage,' Susan said.

'There is: Mercer's lair – that's what Mummy calls it,' Caro said. 'Do you want to see it?'

'May as well, I suppose,' said Susan.

If the priory was disappointing the cottage was even more so. She'd expected something bijou and picturesque with roses round the door and a lovely little garden with a wicket gate. There was a lawn of sorts but it was thick with weeds and hadn't been mown in months. No fence, wall or hedge marked the territory. The cottage cowered in the shadow of three huge elms whose boughs drooped over its corrugated-iron roof.

There was no porch. The door hung half open on rusty hinges and from within came a muffled sound, like the panting of some woodland creature suffering in the heat. Caro clutched Susan's arm.

'What's that?' she whispered.

'How would I know?' Susan whispered back. 'Does Mercer have a dog?'

'No,' Caro said. 'It could be a badger or a fox, I suppose.'

'Whatever it is,' said Susan, 'we can't leave it here.'

'I'll fetch Daddy.'

'It's a person, I think,' Susan said. 'Someone's in there.'

'It must be a tramp or a gypsy. Daddy will soon sort them out.'

'What if they steal something?'

'There's nothing worth stealing,' Caro said.

'Stay here,' Susan told her. 'I'm going to take a look inside.'

She slipped around the half-open door into a cramped hallway. Boots and shoes were scattered on the wooden floor. Coats hung from pegs, a tennis racquet and a net of old balls too. She could see through the house to a kitchenette at the rear. To her right was a sitting room, door open, to her left another room the door of which was closed. Susan threw open the door and, with Caro at her heels, stepped into a bedroom furnished with a chair, a small dressing-table and a narrow cot.

Eleanor lay face down on the cot, weeping.

'*What – what are you doing here?*' she shrieked.

'We heard a noise,' said Caro.

'Well, yes, of course you heard a noise.' Eleanor leapt to her feet. 'I came to see if – if Mercer had left anything behind.'

'Like what?' said Caro.'

'A letter. I thought perhaps he'd left a letter.'

'Why would he leave a letter?' said Caro.

'He hadn't made his bed. I decided to – I was overcome by – I fell asleep,' Eleanor babbled. 'You won't tell Mummy, will you? Promise you won't tell Mummy.'

'Tell her what?' said Caro.

'That you found me here.'

Susan put a hand on Caro's shoulder and turned her to face the hall. 'Why don't we leave your sister to tidy up? Then we'll all go back for lunch.'

'Yes,' said Eleanor, sniffing. 'Lunch.'

Susan led Caro out of the cottage. The heat seemed to have become even more oppressive, the hum of insects louder.

'What's wrong?' Caro asked anxiously. 'Why is Eleanor so upset?'

'She fell asleep and we gave her a fright.'

'Is that all?' said Caro.

'Yes,' Susan said. 'I'm sure that's all.'

The manservant sloped off and left Danny alone in a wood-panelled waiting room. There were screens on frames with castors and a weird-looking machine in brushed steel with cables coming out of it and two half-moon dials on the front. The latest issues of *Tatler*, *Country Life* and *Punch* lay upon a table together with a crystal ashtray, a match stand and an onyx cigarette box filled with oval-shaped cigarettes. Danny wasn't tempted. He seated himself on a leather sofa and stared at the window which was shaded by fine net curtains. On the wall opposite hung a large, glossy painting of a sea battle, very detailed and dramatic. On the wall to his left were eight or ten diplomas in trim ebony frames. So far he hadn't clapped eyes on the doctor.

The manservant, a gaunt, grey-haired guy in a frock-coat, had swept Breda into the consulting room and, like a nightclub doorman, had stuck out a hand to keep Danny from following her. A fruity voice had called out, 'Ah, Miss Romano, my pleasure. Now if you'll be so good as to . . .' Then the door had closed. The manservant had hustled Danny across the hall and relieved him of twenty-one pounds; Danny wasn't daft enough to ask for a receipt.

The twenty-one quid had cleaned him out. He had about four quid left in his savings account. Sure he could have tapped Breda's old man for the dough – twenty quid was nothing to a West End pimp – but he had scruples about handling dirty money. Breda was his responsibility same as Georgie was his responsibility. God help them, he was the only bloke they had to lean on, apart from Breda's lovers, all of whom, including the daddy, had apparently done a bunk.

He sat forward on the creaking leather, fists clenched. He listened for sounds from the far side of the corridor. Heard sobbing, or thought he heard sobbing.

From far away in the half-empty city came the thump and bray of a marching band, very faint and fading then – nothing. The doc was sure taking his time; an unconscionable amount of time, as Bags would put it. He hoped that Breda and the doc weren't chatting about Leo. He'd used Leo's name to wangle an appointment and kept his fingers crossed that the doc wouldn't assume that Breda and her old man were chummy. Dragging Breda to see a posh doctor with diplomas on his wall had been the right thing to do, though. He could have taken her to any back-street midwife and had her condition diagnosed for five bob but if it went further, if Breda insisted . . .

The door opened.

The manservant said, 'Mr Romano.'

Danny didn't correct him.

'The doctor would like a word with you.'

He followed the manservant across the corridor into the doctor's office.

It was half the size of the waiting room but elegant, very elegant. The desk was antique, the lampshade had more coloured glass than a chapel window, the chairs were padded in leather and the wallpaper was flock. The one anomaly was a bed stretched out along the inside wall, the sort of bed you might find in a hospital, sheet and pillow stark in the light from the window. On the floor was a basin, a plain white enamel basin that Danny tried not to look at.

The manservant slithered away and closed the door behind him.

'Mr Romano?' the doctor said.

'Actually, naw. My name's Cahill.'

'I was under the impression you were Miss Romano's brother.'

'Uncle,' Danny said. 'Her uncle from Scotland.'

'I see.'

'I'm lookin' after her.'

'Yeah.' Breda nodded. 'He's looking after me.'

She sat bolt upright on one of the spindly chairs. She looked pale, Danny thought, paler than usual. Her eyes had the wide, unblinking stare that she put on when she was just about to start flirting but flirting was the last thing on Breda's mind right now.

'Well, Mr Cahill,' the doctor said, 'I've completed my examination and I'm happy to – I mean, Miss Romano is approximately ten weeks into a pregnancy.'

Danny said, 'Ten weeks?'

'Approximately.'

The doctor was a broad-chested man of about fifty. He was clad in a morning suit and a beautiful striped waistcoat. His features were meaty and, Danny thought, had the heavy, sensual look that some women found attractive. He certainly had plenty of hair, a great thick mop of snow-white hair that flopped across his brow and curled over his ears. He eyed Danny slyly, testing his reaction.

Danny said, 'How's her health – generally, I mean?'

The faintest of smiles tugged at the corner of the doctor's mouth. 'Oh, not good,' the doctor said. 'She's very frail.'

'Me?' said Breda. 'Frail?'

Danny licked his upper lip. 'Would carryin' a child tae term be too much for her constitution, do you think?'

'I honestly believe it would.'

Danny paused before he asked, 'Anythin' we can do about that?'

'It very much depends upon the circumstances,' the doctor informed him.

Breda opened her mouth but Danny, like a flash, reached out and gripped her thigh so tightly that all that came out was, 'Ow!'

Danny said, 'Miss Romano is her mother's sole means of support. To lose her services would bring great hardship tae – to the household.'

'May I enquire about the father?'

'Ain't got no father,' Breda said.

'The person who assisted in conception,' the doctor said.

'The what?' said Breda.

'The father' – Danny lowered his voice – 'is a married man; a peer o' the realm wi' a reputation to protect.'

'Is he aware of the girl's condition?'

'He is,' said Danny. 'He's also concerned about her health. If you think an intervention is advisable the gentleman says he's willin' to meet all costs.'

Nose resting on the vee of thumb and forefinger, the doctor covered his mouth with his hand. 'You must understand, Mr Cahill, we're treading on thin ice here. Termination of a pregnancy is, shall we say, frowned upon by the arbiters of law. However, there are certain loop – certain considerations that might permit me to put conscience before ethics, the health of my patient being one of them. I'm sure his lordship – whoever he may be – is aware of the delicate nature of the situation and the risks involved.'

'I'm sure he is,' Danny said. 'The fee quoted was a hundred quid – pounds.'

'Guineas.'

'Does that include your consultation fee?'

'No,' the doctor said.

'Ain't you gonna do it now?' Breda said.

Danny and the doctor ignored her.

Danny said, 'What you've given us is a presumptive diagnosis, right?'

The doctor's majestic eyebrows rose in surprise. 'Why, yes, it is.'

'How long do we have?'

'I *can* do it today, if you wish,' the doctor said.

'Can yer?' Breda said.

'Don't have the cash,' said Danny.

'In that case, I'm afraid . . .'

'How long,' Danny repeated, 'do we have?'

The doctor removed his hand from his face and sat back. 'You're no fool, are you, Mr Cahill?' he said. 'Very well, let me put it to you bluntly: conscience or not, I would not be prepared to terminate a pregnancy by dilation after the fifteenth week. Some practitioners will go as far as the eighteenth or even the twentieth week but I'm not one of them. After fifteen weeks the density of tissue and the size of the foetus add greatly to the risk – a risk I'm not willing to take on purely professional grounds. The rapid emptying of the uterus becomes—'

'Okay, okay,' Danny put in quickly. 'I think we've got the picture.'

'If Miss Romano's friend – this peer of the realm – is agreeable, I'll arrange to have the procedure done quickly. The recommended recovery period is, as a rule, three to four days.'

'Four days?' said Breda. 'Gerroff!'

'Thank you.' Danny got to his feet and offered his hand. 'Now we know where we stand, we'll take it from here.'

The doctor stood too. He was shorter than Danny had realised. He came around the desk and shook Danny's hand, then, taking Breda's arm, escorted her to the door.

'Now, Miss Romano, you mustn't worry. You're a healthy young woman—'

'I thought you said I was frail.'

'A relatively healthy young woman and if you put yourself in my hands all will be well, I assure you. Your problem will be resolved and in a week or so you'll be just as you were before.'

'Bleeding 'ell, is that the best you can do?' Breda said then, remembering her manners, thanked him and stepped into the corridor where the manservant was waiting to boot them out.

8

The girls had gone back to school, Caro willingly, Eleanor with much sulking and snivelling. By then, two weeks into September, the harvests had been gathered and the narrow roads that circled the farm were rutted by the wheels of the drays that lugged the loads to neighbouring barns. Most of David Proudfoot's acres were rented out and with Michaelmas not far off he was kept busy with accounts while waiting for the day, the perfect day, when Mr Wentworth would declare the apples ripe for picking and hands would be summoned from Gadney to shake down the fruit and box it for despatch to Bulmers' cider factory.

Susan was by no means oblivious to the seasonal activity or to rainstorms, russet sunsets and the huge custard-coloured moons that rose above the trees. She would have been more engaged with rural life, perhaps, if the big Tudor house had been a working farm, but Hackles' lofts lay empty and apart from Daisy, the amiable cow, no cattle or poultry were kept in the yard.

Whatever produce the Proudfoots required was purchased from local shops or markets and the only chore to which Gwen applied herself was supervising the laundry room where two young women boiled, steeped and scrubbed the Proudfoots' dirty linen and hung it out to dry.

Servants appeared and disappeared. A not so young woman

in an apron and mob cap ran a Ewbank over the carpets, dusted furniture, cleaned bathrooms and made beds. An exceedingly handsome young chap in stained overalls spent an afternoon mowing the tennis court and a boy, another Wentworth, turned up on his bicycle every day to deliver two newspapers, *The Times* and the *Telegraph*, which Gwen and Vivian devoured over lunch while David popped down to the pub in the village to share a plate of beef and a pint of bitter with friends.

Susan had no time to be bored.

Vivian spent six hours or seven hours a day in the barn working on her book. She had already borrowed heavily from a tubby English translation of a tract by an eighteenth-century philosopher, Giambattista Vico, *The New Science*, which was printed in blindingly tiny type embellished, to Vivian's delight, with marginal notes in pencil.

'David's been at this one all right,' she declared, holding the volume up to the light. 'I'm surprised he read it in translation; his Italian's excellent. Look here, he's even offering criticism. Always argumentative, my dear brother.' She thumbed the brown-edged pages carefully. 'What's this? The second cycle of history: the heroic age. Well, well, well! Old Mussolini gets an honourable mention, I see.'

'I hadn't realised Mussolini was as old as all that,' Susan put in.

'Not mentioned by Vico, you dolt: by David.'

'Is Hitler in there too?'

'If he isn't, he soon will be,' said Vivian.

On Sunday they drove to church in David's motorcar. On Monday David ferried Vivian to the bank in Hereford and on Monday evening Vivian paid Susan three weeks' wages in cash. On Tuesday Susan scribbled a postcard to her father to assure him that she was well. And on Wednesday evening, just as the sun went down, Mercer Hughes turned up crouched at the wheel of a raffish, long-bodied sports car that came roaring up to the front of the house through an early evening mist.

David was in the porch, unlacing his boots, Gwen in the kitchen, Vivian in the bath. Susan was in her bedroom, reading, when she heard the car.

She opened the window and peeped down at the men below.

'What the devil's this, Mercer?' David said.

'What does it look like?'

'Riley Nine.'

David stumped around the open-topped car while Mercer, still in the driving seat, grinned. 'I say, is this the Imp?'

'It is,' Mercer replied.

'New?'

'Straight from the factory.'

'Rented?'

'Purchased. She's mine, all mine.'

'Good God!' David said. 'Which bank did you rob?'

Mercer killed the engine and stepped from the car.

'No bank,' he said. 'Warner Brothers shelled out at last.'

'Oh, film people,' David said. 'On what?'

'Arlen's latest.'

'I didn't know you represented Arlen.'

'Rupert, not Michael.'

'He must be pleased,' said David.

'Who?'

'This Arlen chap: the author.'

'Oh,' Mercer said. 'He doesn't know yet.'

'Doesn't know?'

'Complications with the exchange rate. I'll tell him soon.'

'How soon?'

'Next week. Take him to lunch. Make a thing of it,' Mercer said. 'Never mind all that. Where is she?'

'Gwen? She's in the kitchen, I believe.'

'No, I meant—'

'I'm here, Mr Hughes.' Susan waved. 'See, I'm up here.'

Breda went dutifully to mass with her mother and Georgie on Sundays and now and then, to be on the safe side, sneaked into Friday night confession, an event that never failed to give the duty priest a thrill. She loved Christmas, put up with Lent and the Easter falderals and was always in the crowd when the boisterous procession to celebrate the feast of St Mary and St Michael came roiling down the Commercial Road. Once or twice, when she wasn't much more than a kid, she'd tried her hand at praying for a miracle to cure her poor dim brother but when that hadn't worked she'd shrugged off any credence in a god whose eye might be on the sparrow but certainly wasn't on her.

Nausea changed all that, nausea and tender breasts and crawling sensations 'down there' that may, or may not, have been imaginary. There was nothing imaginary about retching into the lavatory bowl every morning or gagging at the smell of braised liver or the sudden waves of panic as she shimmied between the tables, the awful feeling that all the men were staring not at her bottom but at her belly as if they were just waiting for her to pop.

'Sure an' I don't know what's wrong with you these days, Breda,' her mother said, shaking her head. 'You're going about like a half-shut knife.'

'Nothing, nothing. I'm fine, I'm fine.'

'You need a dose of the squills.'

'No, I do not need a dose of the squills.'

It could only be a matter of time until her mother twigged what was really wrong and dragged her off to see old Mrs Holloway, the midwife, and, suspicions confirmed, frog-marched her to Father Joseph who'd no doubt read the riot act and blather on about the wages of sin, after which there'd be no hope of quietly losing the kid short of tossing herself off Tower Bridge, which even in her desperate circumstances did seem a bit drastic.

She fished the rosary from the back of her drawer and the little silver-plated crucifix that her daddy had given her too many years ago to count.

Rosary in one hand, crucifix in the other, she took to kneeling on the stone floor of the back pantry to offer prayers for forgiveness, instantly followed by a demand that he, she or whatever blessed saint happened to be listening would sluice away the evidence of her stupidity. Not entirely convinced that she was a suitable candidate for divine intervention, however, she also set in motion certain measures to ensure that if heaven wasn't listening and Danny didn't come across she wouldn't be left entirely out on a limb.

'Breda, what do you think you're doing?'

'Doncha like it?'

'Didn't say that, did I?'

'Doncha wanna kiss me?'

'What if your mother sees us?'

'Time she found out.'

'Found out what?'

'How much you fancy me. You do, doncha – fancy me, I mean?'

'Well, you're a very attractive young lady, but . . .'

'No buts, Mr 'Ooper: you do or you don't.'

Matt slumped in a chair at one of the tables. He had the haggard look that a full shift on the dock laid on a man, though personally Breda didn't think shoving levers in a nice snug cab all day could be all that tiring. Tired or not, she could feel him rising to the occasion even through several layers of clothing.

She twined an arm about his neck and kissed him.

Matt Hooper sighed, puffed out his cheeks and shoved her away.

'Breda,' he said thickly, 'just what the 'ell's your game?'

'Game? Ain't no game, Mr 'Ooper. You're – you're my kinda guy.'

'Don't come the old soldier with me, Breda Romano. I'm no more your kind of guy than – than he is.'

'Who is?'

'Ronnie.'

She took a step back, hand to her bosom, as if mention of Ronnie's name had robbed her of breath. 'What's Ron been sayin'? Whatever 'e told you, it ain't true.'

''E ain't told me nothing,' Matt said. 'What should 'e have told me? You an' Ron got something going?'

'Ron?' Breda sneered. 'Your bleedin' Ron? Don't be so daft.'

'You could do worse.'

'Yeah, an' I could do a whole lot better,' Breda said. 'Ronnie ain't the type to look after a girl, not proper like.' She stuck out her chest. 'Not like you, Matt.'

Faint clouds of steam billowed through the half-open door of the kitchen, coupled with the sound of Georgie's raucous chanting. He was angry today, poor lamb; the big

moons of the autumn month often had that effect on
him.

Breda could hear her mother snapping at him to hush his
noise, for all the good it did. She thought of dumping herself
on Mr Hooper's lap again but, as if he'd read her mind, he
scrambled to his feet and, leaning on the table, addressed
her in a husky whisper.

'I reckon I know what's on your mind, Breda,' he said.
'You think 'cause my Susie's gone I got a urge to play fast
and loose. Well, maybe I do and maybe I don't. But I ain't
a big enough fool to suppose you want me for my sex appeal.
You're after a berth in my 'ouse, ain't yer? If that means
sharing my bed then you're willing to put up with that too.'

'Baloney,' Breda said. 'That's just baloney.'

'What's wrong with you, girl? I ain't rich. Why don't you
shake your hips at some toff with enough dough to set you
up nice in a place of your own?'

'I ain't that kinda girl, Mr 'Ooper,' said Breda loftily.

'You could've fooled me,' Matt said.

Georgie's chanting grew louder, augmented by the
hammering of a spoon on a pot lid.

'What's wrong with 'im?'

'He wants 'is supper,' Breda answered.

'He ain't the only one,' Matt said. 'Anyhow, you got it
wrong, Breda. My Susie'll be back 'ome in a week or two so
I got no room for another. Anyhow, last thing I need's a wife,
'specially a wife twenty-odd years younger than I am. Susie
wouldn't stand for it.'

'Susie can't never give you what I can,' Breda said.

'Like what? Like trouble?'

'Trouble,' Breda said. 'You don't know the meaning of the
word.'

'Maybe not,' Matt said, 'but it sounds like Nora has trouble enough back there in the kitchen without me adding to it.'

'Where you going?'

'Got a sudden fancy for fish and chips,' Matt Hooper told her, yanked open the street door and vanished into the night.

It didn't take Mercer long to make his move. Soon after supper he invited Susan to step outside and there in the shadow of the porch kissed her for the first time.

The night air had an autumnal nip to it but the house was stuffy and the French doors had been left open. David was tinkling idly on the piano. The notes drifted out across the tennis lawn and, Susan thought, went on and on, floating across the hedges like tiny leaves caught by the wind.

'Have you missed me, Shadwell?'

'Not much.'

'But a little?'

'Yes, a little.'

'Well, I've missed you. Try as I might, I haven't been able to stop thinking about you.' He laughed softly. 'Most infuriating, actually. There I am having lunch with a very important client and all that's on my mind is how quickly I can get back here to you.'

'I don't believe a word of it,' Susan said.

The Proudfoots remained in the living room, David at the piano, Vivian reading in an armchair. Seated on the sofa with wool and a darning egg in her lap, Gwen had barely glanced up from her needle when Mercer had led the girl outside. There were voices in the room now, though, muffled by the piano.

'Do you think they're talking about us?' Susan asked.

'No, they're talking of Michelangelo,' Mercer answered.

'Pardon?'

'Poem,' he said. 'Haven't you read it?'

'Not that one, no,' said Susan.

'I'll bring you a copy next time I come.'

'Are you leaving already?'

'In a couple of days.'

'Why did you bother to come at all?' Susan said.

'Fishing, are you, darling?' he said. 'I told you – to see you, of course.'

He drew her closer and placed one hand against her hip. She felt her dress and underskirt slither beneath his fingers. If he moved his hand a little to the left he'd be touching her intimately.

'Gwen told you, I suppose,' he said.

'Told me what?'

'About my wife.'

'Vivian did,' Susan said. 'How is she? Your wife, I mean?'

'Just the same. No worse, thank heaven.'

'Vivian told me some other things about you too.'

'Be surprised if she hadn't. Thing is,' Mercer said, 'Vivian believes she knows me inside out and she really doesn't know me at all.'

'She said you like girls.'

'That's true, that's fact.'

'She said you break their hearts.'

'Vivian is a crusty old maid.'

'Do you break their hearts?' Susan said.

'I think you ask too many questions, Susan.'

'And I think' – Susan pressed herself against him – 'that you just don't want to answer me. Why have you stopped calling me Shadwell all of a sudden?'

'I can't possibly let myself fall in love with someone called Shadwell.'

'But Susan's all right, is it?'

'Susan's just perfect.'

'I don't believe you're falling in love. I think you just want to – to kiss me.'

'So far you haven't objected.'

'That's because I rather like it.'

He kissed her again. His hand moved from her hip to her breast. She experienced a strange almost swooning sensation in the pit of her stomach and her legs felt weak. She closed her eyes, nose crushed against his nose and when he drew back she followed him greedily. It didn't matter if he loved her. He wanted her, this handsome, articulate, intelligent man wanted her and she knew even then that that was the most she could hope for from someone like Mercer Hughes.

'Patience, my dear,' he said. 'You must let me do what I do best.'

'And what's that?'

'Exercise my talent for persuasion.'

'Not,' Susan said, 'your talent for negotiation?'

'Oh, you are sharp, aren't you?' Mercer said. 'I can see it's not going to pay me to treat you too lightly.'

'I may just be an 'umble flower-seller, sir, but I ain't stupid.'

'A humble flower-seller?'

'Play,' Susan said. 'Haven't you read it?'

'It's *Pygmalion*, of course,' Mercer said.

'Didn't you expect me to read Bernard Shaw?'

'You're awfully prickly, aren't you?' Mercer said.

'I don't like being patronised.'

'I'm not patronising you, Susan. I'm attempting to make love to you.'

'Seduce me, you mean?'

He took his hands from her waist and stood upright against the doorpost. She could make out his face in the lamplight from the hallway, all angles and shadowy planes. When he spoke again the warmth had gone.

He said, 'You're not one of those callous little gold-diggers, are you?'

'I'm not a gold-digger,' Susan said, 'callous or otherwise.'

'But' – he paused – 'you are willing to negotiate.'

He had obviously expected her to be flattered by his kisses – which she was – to be carried away by promises that were far too premature to be sincere. She had only been kissed on the mouth once before when, last Christmas, Danny Cahill had given in to impulse and planted a smacker on her lips and, being Danny, had instantly apologised. She couldn't imagine Mercer Hughes ever being so impetuous, or ever apologising.

'Persuaded,' she heard herself say. 'I might be willing to be persuaded.'

'To do what?'

'Whatever you like.'

'Really?' he said. 'I don't think you mean that.'

'You didn't come all the way up to Hackles just to see me, did you?' Susan said. 'You're here to collect the outline of Vivian's new book.'

'Is it ready?'

'Vivian doesn't think so.'

'When can I have it?' he said.

'That's up to Vivian.'

'And the other thing?' he said. 'When can I have that?'

'Not yet, Mr Hughes,' said Susan. 'Not just yet.'

9

There were days that were rich in salient news and other days that weren't. With twenty-eight pages to fill and a schedule that demanded a hundred and twenty-four columns of news and features, dull days were a challenge to every hack in Fleet Street. Editors brought up in the austere tradition of, say, *The Times*, would accept that there was no big news today and that readers would just have to put up with it, but others, Danny's boss among them, were not above puffing some minor item to provide a sensational headline.

The editor-in-chief didn't exactly snatch up his bullhorn and bellow, 'Get me Bageshot.' Nevertheless, a messenger eventually arrived in Mr Bageshot's cubby to enquire if he had anything, anything at all – vampires excepted – that might give the vendors something to shout about. Bags, never a willing workhorse, reluctantly obliged and in a matter of a couple of hours had transformed a dull little report from a court stringer in Salford into a seven-hundred-word piece on 'devil doctors' that was really an article purporting to be news.

Only the nose of an experienced crime reporter pushed to provide splash copy could have sniffed out a lead buried in a two-line paragraph. Half an hour on the blower to the Salford stringer fleshed out the details of the unfortunate doctor's obsession with a young female whom he'd met at a dance hall in what Bags described as Manchester's lower depths. The fact that there had been no death and, as it happened, no sexual encounter, was skilfully blurred by a series of unallocated quotes from several female drug addicts and one on-the-record statement from no less a person than the king's publicity-hungry physician who, quite naturally, deplored the bad apples who had crept into the profession in the wake of the war.

By the time Bags's sheets reached Danny's desk the editor had already cleared a front panel and an inside page and the piece had become, 'Devil Doctor's Dance of Death'.

Danny flicked his pencil over the sheets, stroking out adjectives, inserting commas and replacing words that made no sense at all. He could, of course, edit in his sleep, a trick that some staff members mistook for dedication. Even so, he was in no mood to be interrupted and when a messenger tapped him on the shoulder he rounded on the boy with a snarl.

'*What?*'

'Geezer wants ter see yer.'

'What geezer?'

'Says 'e's a copper.'

'A copper?' Danny said. 'Is he in uniform?'

'Nope, no uniform.'

'Where is he?'

'Back lane.'

'Tell the gate man to let him in.'

'Won't come. Wants a word with you outside.'

'You sure he's a copper?'

'Ain't sure o' nuffink,' the boy said.

'Tell him five minutes.'

'Okay,' the boy said and trotted off.

Danny racked his brains to recall any offence that might bring a plainclothes copper to his place of work. He could think of nothing, nothing, that is, but his visit with Breda to the posh doctor in Malvern Place and the possibility that the posh doctor, like his Salford colleague, had finally fallen foul of the law.

The main attraction of the Crown of the Plantagenets wasn't its historical pedigree or the armorial shield nailed above the bar but the fact that it had a snuggery where ladies were made welcome and gentlemen might enjoy their company and, if so disposed, persuade some randy young thing to slip out into the alley at the back of the building to sample the wine of love.

Ronnie poked his head around the snug's frosted glass door and, finding no one there to whom he might offer his flagon, drifted back into the public bar where among the jellied eels and pickled eggs he'd left a slab of Gertler's famous veal loaf. He picked the slice from the plate, bit into it and, chewing, reached for his pint to wash it down. Then he did a fast double-take, for the drab little man leaning on the counter next to him seemed familiar – too bloody familiar.

'Dad?' he spluttered through a mouthful of pastry. 'What you doing 'ere?'

'What does it look like? I'm having a quiet pint. Do you mind?'

'I ain't never seen you take a drink before.'

'Then you ain't been looking 'ard enough,' Matt said.

'What's that – tap or bottle?'

'Tap.'

'You want another?'

'Wouldn't say no.'

Matt pushed the glass across the counter with his forefinger. Ronnie signed to the barman. Together father and son watched the glass fill.

Matt licked froth from the head with the tip of his tongue.

'Good stuff,' he said. 'Better'n it used to be.'

'Your 'ealth then,' Ronnie said.

'Bottoms up,' said Matt and sank the pint in one long swallow.

'You wanna watch it, Dad,' Ronnie said. 'I ain't gonna carry you 'ome.'

'I used to 'ave to do that,' Matt said. 'Carry your grandpa 'ome. She'd fly into a right old rage and kick 'im round the kitchen like 'e was a football.'

'Who? Grandma?'

Matt nodded. 'Wicked old bitch, she was.'

'Can't say I blame 'er,' Ronnie said. 'Since you was all starving.'

At Matt's request two more pints were drawn. He held the slippery glass securely in his left hand and leaned an elbow on the bar.

'Vowed none of mine would ever starve,' he said. 'And you never did, Ron, did yer? I mean, you never went 'ungry.'

'Not really,' Ronnie admitted grudgingly.

'Never went barefoot.'

'That's true.'

'Never got cuffed round the ear'ole.'

'You 'ere to talk about the good old days or what?'

'You see the postcard?'

'I saw it,' Ronnie said. 'She ain't givin' much away, is she?'

'Doesn't 'ave to. She says she's fine, she's fine.'

'Seventy shillings a week for sitting on my arse, I'd be fine too.'

'You never 'ad Susie's brains.'

'Never 'ad her chances neither.'

'You're not bitter, son, are yer?'

'Nah, not me.'

'When the time comes she'll see us both right.'

Ronnie said, 'What you mean – see us both right?'

'When she marries some toff with money, we'll want for nothing.'

'Have you set up our Susie to provide for us? Gawd sake, Dad, you're no better'n a ponce. 'Sides, she might not want to know us, she marries up.'

'Susan ain't like that,' Matt said.

'They're all like that.'

'Maybe the kind of girls you know, but not our Susie.'

'Kind of girls I know? What kind of girls is that?'

'Girls like Breda Romano,' Matt said. 'Tarts.'

Ronnie opened his mouth to defend young Miss Romano but somehow he couldn't find the gumption to present a case on her behalf.

His father sipped beer and stared blankly into space.

'She wants to marry me, you know,' Matt said at length.

'Nora? Yer, I know. She's been after you for years.'

'Don't mean Nora.'

'What? Breda?' Ronnie said. 'Breda wouldn't touch you with a forty-foot pole. Geeze, Dad, she's less than half your age; a good-looking kid but still a kid.'

'She's after somebody to take care of 'er – I mean, like a husband.'

'An' that's you?'

'Yus, that's me – or Breda thinks it is.'

Ronnie shook his head. 'You got the wrong end of the stick this time, Dad. Last thing Breda wants is to settle down, 'specially with an old guy like you. She don't wanna settle down at all, you ask me. She's—'

'Knocked up,' Matt said. 'She's knocked up.'

Ronnie said nothing for a moment, then, 'Did Nora tell you?'

'Nora doesn't know yet.'

'Who told you then? Breda?'

'Not Breda neither.'

'Then how can you—'

'What other reason could Breda 'ave for pitching herself at an old geezer like me?' Matt said. 'I may be green, son, but I ain't no cabbage. Take it from me, she's got one in the oven and don't know who the daddy is.'

'Don't tell me you're the daddy?'

'Hell, no!' Matt paused. 'How about you, Ronnie?'

'How about me, what?'

'Do you know who the daddy is?'

Ronnie sagged against the counter.

'She told you, didn't she?' he said. 'Breda bleedin' told you.'

'No, she didn't,' Matt said. 'But you just did.'

'Oh, bugger!' Ronnie groaned. 'Me an' my big mouth.'

The lane was crammed with vans waiting to collect the early morning editions. Half the drivers were down in Soper's pub topping up and the other half, including most of the paper boys, were clustered at the lane's end feeding their faces at a coffee stall. The metal shutters of the delivery bay had been rolled up and you could see right into the guts, if not the heart, of the building and smell the heady effluvia of oil, ink and paper that wafted warmly from within.

Danny emerged from the narrow staff entrance and glanced

left and right in search of anyone who might vaguely resemble a policeman in plain clothes. He had just stepped on to the broken cobbles to scan the lane when a hand closed on his upper arm and a soft voice said, 'Hey, Jock, got a minute?'

He was a big man, lean-featured, with a pinched fold of flesh – a scar – at the corner of his mouth. He wore a camel-hair overcoat and a silk scarf and the hat, pushed back from his brow, was a three-guinea fedora.

'You're no copper,' Danny said.

'Put the wind up your kilt, though, didn't I?' The man grinned. 'Leo wants a word wiff you. He's waiting round the corner.'

'Leo?'

'Mr Romano, you prefers it.'

'I'm supposed tae be working.'

'Five minutes,' the scar said, still softly. 'Ten tops.'

Danny nodded and let the scar guide him through the throng of down-at-heel paper boys. The motorcar, a black sedan with a bullet front, was parked behind the coffee stall, so close you could see the stall owner's fat backside reflected in the windscreen and hear sausages sizzling on the griddle. Another tall guy, younger, was leaning against the wing of the car, chatting to the stall owner's bottle-blonde daughter. In the front passenger seat, Leo Romano was sipping coffee from a mug.

The window was already rolled down. Leo stuck his face into the gap, peered up at Danny and winked. He winked not with one eye but with both, as if, Danny thought, he was sending semaphore signals.

Danny leaned into the open window.

'What?' he said.

'My medical friend's been waiting for a call,' Leo said.

'I think he'll have tae wait a while longer,' said Danny.

'Is it the dough?'

'Aye, it's the dough,' Danny said. ''Course it's the bloody dough.'

'I'll give you the dough,' said Leo.

'An' what's the vig on a hundred quid?'

Leo frowned. 'The vig?'

'Your extortionate rate o' interest.'

'You've seen too many films, son,' Leo said. 'Nobody round here calls it "the vig". Anyhow, I'm no shark. It wouldn't be a loan. It'd be a gift.'

'Some gift!' said Danny. 'You don't clap eyes on Breda for – what? – a dozen years then you pop up an' offer her a hundred quid for an abortion.'

'I didn't "pop up",' Leo reminded him. 'You came to me.'

'Aye, that's true,' Danny conceded. 'But only because I wanted the best attention for Breda.'

'Who paid the doctor's fee?'

'I did,' Danny said, adding hastily, 'but that doesn't make me the father.'

'You'd make my girl a good husband.'

'Whoa!' Danny said. 'I'm not gonna marry Breda just to ease your conscience, Mr Romano.'

Leo said, 'You don't want her to lose the kiddie, do you?'

'No, I don't,' Danny admitted.

'That's why you won't take my money.'

'It is.'

'Then marry her,' Leo said.

'Why should I?'

'Keep her mother happy,' Leo said. 'Keep me happy.'

'What about Breda? Who keeps her happy?'

'You do.' Leo placed the coffee mug carefully on the

ledge on the dash. 'Haven't you found out who the father is yet?'

'Breda still won't tell me. Says she doesn't know.'

Leo made a little popping sound. 'I'll come clean with you, Cahill. I don't want her to shed the kiddie. I seen the harm it can do. Whatever you think of me, Breda's still my flesh and blood. The kid will be my first grandchild.'

'You're breakin' my heart,' said Danny.

'Don't get cheeky, son. I lift my finger more than your heart gets broke.'

'That,' Danny said, 'I can well believe.'

'If you don't come through for her,' Leo said, 'will she do something stupid?'

'You mean, will she go back-street? She might.'

'She does,' Leo said, 'anything bad happens, I'll hold you to blame.'

'I'm only the bloody lodger,' Danny said. 'Breda's not my responsibility.'

'She is now,' Leo said. 'Capiche?'

'Capiche,' said Danny grimly.

IO

Planting, pruning, suckering, spraying: Mr Wentworth had nurtured David Proudfoot's orchard as well as if not better than he'd nurtured his own children and the crop of 1934 was heavy enough to delight the heart of any grower. Bittersweets in particular had ripened to perfection and Susan supposed that under Mr Wentworth's eagle eye they would be gathered as carefully as quail's eggs.

Picking began before Vivian and Susan came down for breakfast.

The kitchen table was covered with loaves of bread, butter tubs and great wedges of cheese to feed the hands at lunchtime. A tea urn, almost as big as the bathroom boiler, was already steaming away and David had wheeled out a crate of Bulmers' Woodpecker cider to carry down to the orchard for, he said, stripping apple trees was thirsty work even on a cool September day.

Susan had no idea how long it would take to pull down the crop. It was, she thought, rather like a question in an arithmetic test: if it takes ten men four hours to empty a van of its contents, how long will it take fifteen men to do the same job? She wondered if Mercer was already cavorting among the girls, dispensing his lordly charm or if he was closeted in the dank little cottage by the priory reading the outline of *The Wheel* that Vivian had reluctantly surrendered late last evening after Mercer and she had come in, somewhat flushed, from the porch.

The bundle of correspondence that Mercer had brought from London would keep Vivian occupied for a day or two, but then – what then? Would they stay on here in Hackles or return to London with Mercer? She knew little or nothing about Mercer Hughes and Ames, how the agency functioned or precisely what Mercer did in the firm's offices off Regent Street. How many people did he employ, for instance? How many girls?

Vivian scrambled eggs, made toast and, plate and coffee cup in hand, wandered into the living room out of harm's way.

Susan followed her.

'Are we going to work today?' she asked.

'Somehow I doubt it,' Vivian answered. 'Between cider and literature it's no contest. No doubt your presence will be required elsewhere.'

'To do what?'

'Pick apples, of course.'

At that moment the French doors flew open, Mercer put his head into the room and shouted, 'Come along, Susan. We need every body we can muster.'

He was dressed in an old pair of corduroy trousers, a flannel shirt and tennis shoes. He grabbed Susan by the hand and, before she could protest, dragged her out on to the path and closed the French doors with his heel.

'What about Vivian?' Susan got out.

'Vivian can cool her heels for a bit,' he said. 'She'll have me all to herself this evening. I'll take her out to dinner in Hereford: author and agent all alone with a bottle of wine and some serious business on the table.'

'The outline, I suppose?' Susan said.

'That, yes, but other things too.'

'What other things?'

'How soon she can deliver the finished product.'

'I take it you like it then?'

'Love it,' Mercer said a shade too quickly. 'Absolutely love it,' then, still holding her hand, led her through the yard and down to the apple orchard.

Ronnie could never quite fathom why Herr Brauschmidt insisted on travelling up to the Central Meat Market at Smithfield every Monday and Thursday and didn't follow Mr Gertler's example and order his meat from a reputable wholesaler.

What was good enough for Mr Gertler, however, was emphatically not good enough for Herr Brauschmidt who, since the dim and distant days before the war, had hired a pony and cart from the livery stable in Bosley Mews and trotted up to the market to pick his meat in person. This, Herr Brauschmidt implied without actually saying so, was what *real* butchers did and that he, being the genuine article – unlike that kosher upstart across the road – would continue to do until either he or the last pony in Bosley Mews dropped dead.

Herr Brauschmidt left for the market at an early hour, ungodly even by East End standards. Ronnie was charged with the task of opening the shop, mopping floors, washing counters and preparing the day's cuts. It was also left to Ronnie to take the 'float' from the safe under the sink in the rear of the shop and fill the drawers in the till with change, which, when he thought about it, was really very trusting of the old German even though the safe wasn't locked and would swing wide open if you kicked it hard enough.

By a quarter to nine, Ron had begun to shake off the dregs of his hangover. He was artistically arranging a display of loin chops on a window tray when, looking up, he saw Danny Cahill glowering at him through the glass. He motioned to his pal to come into the shop, which Danny promptly did.

'Where's the old guy?' Danny asked.

'Gone to the market. Won't be back for a couple of hours.'

'Good,' Danny said. 'I want a word with you.'

'With me?' said Ronnie, a note of panic in his voice. 'What've I done?'

'Breda's knocked up,' Danny said. 'Be obliged you wouldn't say anythin' tae her mother, though, since the matter's still delicate.'

'Delicate?' said Ron.

Danny frowned. 'You don't seem surprised.'

'It's natural you don't want Nora to find out.'

'I mean, surprised about Breda.'

Ronnie swallowed hard. 'Breda tell you who stuck it to 'er?'

'I thought she might've told you.'

'Me? Now why would she tell me?'

'She hangs out down the Crown, doesn't she?'

'Ain't seen 'er down there in weeks,' Ron said.

'What about that wrestler guy?' Danny said. 'He back in town?'

'Chaz? Nah. Hey, you think it might be 'im?'

'Or the Irish git?'

'Long gone,' said Ronnie. 'Anyhow, what's it got to do with you?'

'I have to find the guy,' Danny said.

'Why?'

'To persuade him to marry her.'

Although both he and his old man knew he was guilty, Ron had managed to avoid an out-and-out confession. He'd no idea if his father would side with Breda and her ma and force him to face up to his responsibilities or be sensible and just let it slide.

'What if 'e don't want to marry 'er?' Ron said.

'A shotgun up the arse'll change his mind,' Danny said.

'A shotgun?' said Ronnie shrilly. 'You wouldn't do that, would yer?'

'I wouldn't,' Danny said, 'but I know someone who will.'

'Who?'

'Her daddy.'

'You mean Leo Romano knows she's knocked up?'

'Aye, an' Breda's daddy keeps bad company.'

'Jesus!' Ronnie said. 'How bad?'

'Very bad,' said Danny.

It struck Susan as odd that fruit cultivated with such care was simply dumped in a great pile on the grass. She had expected something more leisurely, more traditional, more ritualistic, perhaps, but picking apples, it seemed, was just like the harvesting of any other crop. David and Mr Wentworth stood by the gate watching the fruit tumble from the baskets on to the pile from which, in due course, it would be transferred to carts to be transported to Bulmers' factory to be graded and weighed before pressing.

Susan was eager to perch on top of one of the stout wooden ladders up among the leaves but David would not allow it. He put her to gathering up the fruit that lay on the grass: plump, smooth, hard-shelled apples that rolled eagerly into the basket Mercer lugged round after her.

The other gatherers were friendly and called out to Mercer in a familiar manner. 'That's a ripe 'un you've got there, Mr Hughes. Be she your daughter?'

'No, she not be my daughter.' Mercer laughed. 'She's far too pretty to be any kin of mine.'

The women laughed with him but when he turned away whispered together and laughed again, slyly.

When cider was brought out they shared with Mercer and Susan, drinking in turn from the bottle, handing it round until the bottle was empty; three plump, dark-eyed women, a mother and her daughters, Susan guessed, red-cheeked, sun-sallow and flirtatious.

She felt awkward among the country women. She knew that in their eyes she was just some piece of city tat that Mr Hughes had fetched down from London. How many other pieces of city tat had he brought to Hackles? she wondered. She was tempted to explain herself, to assure them that she was different, but sense took hold and she kept her mouth shut and went swiftly back to picking up the fallen fruit.

'What's wrong, Shadwell? Why the sour face?'

'You're calling me Shadwell again.'

'All right, why the long face, Susan?'

'They're laughing at me.'

'No, they're not. Of course they're not. They're just jolly by nature.' Mercer rested a knee on the rim of the basket and made to pull her to him.

'Not here, please,' Susan said.

'Look,' he said, 'it's a beautiful morning. We're doing something half the dwellers in the great metropolis would love to be doing: we're picking apples in the heart of the

English countryside. If that doesn't strike you as romantic, Sha – Susan, then you're not the girl I took you for.'

'What sort of girl do you take me for?'

'You're behaving as if there's something between us,' Mercer said.

'Which,' Susan said, 'there's not.'

'I had rather hoped there might be.'

'They think I'm your mistress.'

'If they do – which I doubt – one can hardly blame them.'

'There!' Susan snapped. 'Even you think I'm cheap.'

He sighed and reached out once more. She would have none of it.

Mercer swung a leg over the basket and perched on the wicker rim. He spread his hands on his thighs and studied her with a tight little smile. 'One can hardly blame them for assuming that a man of my disposition – all right, my reputation – won't be able to resist someone as gorgeous as you.'

'You mean they're jealous?'

'Ah, now,' Mercer said, 'that's a loaded question.'

'What do you mean – a loaded question?'

'If,' he said, 'I agree that the ladies are jealous you'll accuse me of conceit. Susan, they're country girls. They've seen it all before. They know what's going on and they're not shocked. If anything, they're amused.'

'What is going on, Mercer? What—'

He put a finger to his lips. 'Hush. Not so loud.'

Tucking her dress into her lap, she knelt on the grass.

She wished that the women would go away, that all the teams that dotted the orchard would vanish so that she might be alone with him. She didn't want to play word games or have him soothe her with compliments. She wanted him to stretch her out on the grass and kiss her, to make love to her before she could protest, for what he chose to call romance was nothing of the sort.

She lowered her voice. 'Where do you take them, Mercer?'

'Take them?' he said, puzzled.

'Do you take them down to your cottage in the woods? I've seen your cottage in the woods and I don't think it's the sort of place I'd want to go.'

'I don't take them anywhere,' Mercer said.

'They come of their own free will, do they? In droves?'

'Oh!' he said. 'This is Eleanor. Eleanor's been talking out of turn again. Eleanor has it in her silly head that she's in love with me and that no other man – no other boy – will do. She's a spoiled child who's used to getting her own way. She doesn't have a brain in her head. It's all love, love and longing, though she has no idea what she's longing for.'

'And I do, I suppose?'

'No,' he said. 'You may be inexperienced, Susan, but you're no fool.'

'Well, that's nice to know.'

He pushed himself to his feet and before Susan could retreat, stood over her.

He said, 'Why does everyone assume I'm a heartless monster because I haven't been entirely faithful to a wife who, by the by, wasn't faithful to me and who, in all likelihood, will never see the light of day again? Why does everyone assume I'm incapable of love?'

She looked up at him towering above her and shook her head.

He said, 'I have what I came for, Susan. I've Vivian's proposal for her new book in my briefcase and tomorrow I'll head back to London to pitch it to her publisher for as much chink as I can screw out of the miserable old varmint.'

'Are you saying I won't see you again?'

'I'm saying that when we're back in London I *will* see you again; if you continue to work for Vivian it's unavoidable.' He reached out and brushed a wisp of grass from her hair. 'I already know what you mean to me, Susan, but, all evidence to the contrary, I'm a decent sort of chap. I want you to be sure, absolutely sure, that my feelings for you are honest and sincere. If you decide I'm as big a scoundrel as I'm supposed to be, or that you don't care for me at all, then it'll be business, strictly business, I promise you.'

'And if I don't do either of those things?'

'I'll count myself a very lucky man.'

He offered his hand and drew her to her feet.

For a moment they stood as close as lovers.

'Well, Miss Hooper,' he said, 'do we have a deal?'

'Yes, Mr Hughes,' Susan heard herself say. 'We have a deal.'

11

It was after nine o'clock when the back door creaked. Nora had cleared dishes and pots from the sinks, chopped vegetables and steeped lentils for tomorrow's soup and, in a half-hour or so, would bake a batch of the ginger biscuits that always sold so well. It was very peaceful in the kitchen. Breda had taken herself upstairs directly after supper and Nora had opened her copy of *Red Star Weekly*, which in spite of its title had nothing to do with left-wing politics and a lot to do with unrealistic love affairs that bridged the class divide.

She had drawn her chair close to the fire and with Georgie sprawled on the hearth rug at her feet like a great shaggy dog had begun to read aloud from the magazine. Though her son understood little of the fanciful story of love between a mill girl and a wealthy factory owner, he was soothed by his mother's Irish lilt and not well pleased when his sharp ears picked up the sound of a stranger creeping about in the corridor. He growled, rose and adopted a pugilistic pose but not being entirely without sense, shouted, 'Danny? You there, Danny?' before he charged out into the darkness to thump the intruder.

'Don't 'it me, Georgie.' Matt Hooper came into the kichen. 'I'm a friend.'

'Sorry, Mr 'Ooper. Thought you was a buggerer.'

'I ain't no burglar, son,' Matt said. 'I just dropped in to talk to yer ma.'

The bunch of flowers in his hand had been crushed by Georgie's affectionate hug and Matt tweaked the blooms before handing them over to Nora. He dug into his jacket pocket for a lumpy packet of peanut brittle.

'Sweets?' Georgie said. 'You got sweets?'

'Wait,' Matt said sternly. 'Gotter put yer teeth in first.'

Familiar with the rules of Mr Hooper's game, Georgie closed his eyes and opened his mouth. Matt placed a piece of brittle on the young man's tongue. Georgie's jaws clamped shut and, still with his eyes closed, he uttered a long, low moan of ecstasy as his molars crunched into the nuts.

'What you say to Mr Hooper, Georgie?'

'Thanks, Mr 'Ooper.'

Matt tossed Georgie the sweet packet. Georgie seated himself at the table to work his way noisily through the brittle while Matt turned his attention to Nora.

'What're the flowers for?' she asked suspiciously.

'A token of my esteem,' he answered.

'You find them on the dock or what?'

'Had 'em shipped in special from 'Olland.'

'Uh-huh!' Nora said. 'You know they aren't tulips.'

'Don't know what they are,' Matt said. 'Pretty flowers for a pretty lady.'

'Now I know you're at it,' Nora said.

She gave him a dig with her elbow by way of thanks and she went over to the sink to fill a vase. He looked uncommonly spruce tonight, she thought, chin smooth, hair combed. He'd even fitted a tie into the collar of his shirt, a stringy old tie, but a tie none the less.

'You ate?' she asked over her shoulder.

'Yus.'

'What you have?'

'Stew,' he said. 'Breda in?'

'Breda's always in these nights. Don't know what's wrong with the girl.'

'Where is she?'

'Upstairs,' Nora said.

She arranged the flowers in a vase that Leo had won for her at the Southwark fair back in the days when he'd still been trying to impress her. The vase was an ugly malformed thing but looked better with Matt's flowers in it. She planted it in the centre of the table and paused, hands on hips, to admire the display.

'Nice,' she said. 'Very nice,' then, giving in to impulse, stooped and kissed Matt on the cheek.

'What' – Matt cleared his throat – 'what's she doin' upstairs?'

'Blessed if I know,' Nora said. 'Why you askin'?'

'Need to talk to 'er.'

'What you got to say to her you can't say to me?'

Matt didn't hesitate. 'Gonna ask for her 'and in marriage.'

'*You what?*'

'You 'eard me, Nora. I'm gonna ask 'er to marry me.'

'You dirty old goat,' Nora shouted. 'You dirty old bastard.'

Georgie, blinking, looked up. 'Ma?' he said uncertainly. 'Mammy?'

Matt patted the young man's arm. 'It's okay, Georgie. It's okay.'

'Sure an' it's not okay,' Nora chanted. 'If you think I'm going to let any daughter o' mine marry a dirty old devil like you, Matt Hooper . . .'

'Calm down, Nora. Breda ain't interested in an old geezer like me. She might think she is, but she ain't. It's Ronnie she's after, my Ron. What's more, she's got 'im by the short hairs if she wants 'im. He's running scared right now and marrying your kid's his only way out. First, though, I gotta put the wind up Breda, force 'er hand and get everythin' out in the open. Best way I can do that's to propose.'

'Eh?' Nora said. 'You proposin' on your Ron's behalf.'

'Ronnie don't even know I'm 'ere.' Matt continued to pat Georgie's arm soothingly. To Nora, he said, 'Listen, you got to trust me. Will you do that, dear? Will you trust me?'

'Don't you "dear" me,' Nora said. 'I'm not your dear, nor never like to be.'

'Give 'er a shout,' Matt said. 'Fetch 'er down.'

Nora breathed like an old steam pump, chest rising and falling rapidly as if she couldn't force enough air into her lungs. Something was going on that she didn't understand but there were always things going on that she didn't understand. She wished Danny was here. She trusted Danny more than she trusted Matt Hooper.

'Go on,' Matt said. 'Do it, Nora.'

She stepped stiffly to the corridor. '*Breda?*' she shouted. '*Come down here.*'

After a long pause: 'Why?'

'*'Cause I say so, that's why.*'

Unlike some agents Mercer did not keep his client in suspense for long. He told her he was delighted with the outline and was sure that Martin Teague, her publisher, would jump at the chance to publish the book. Vivian's relief was palpable. She went around gaily kissing everyone, as if a publisher's agreement was the end and not the beginning of an arduous period of work.

Mercer and she were to dine in the County Hotel, no expense spared. From the depths of her rucksack Vivian unearthed an evening dress with a sleeveless bodice and a diamanté belt. From Gwen, after much twittering, she borrowed a suitable hat and a coat with a fat fur collar and sallied forth to the motorcar on Mercer's arm as if she were a blushing bride embarking on her honeymoon.

Down in the orchard lorries came and went. The women had all gone home. The labour of boxing and transporting the fruit was carried out by local men aided by a team from Bulmers. From the rear of the farmhouse the scene was dramatic: stripped trees lit by flares, the men mere shapes against a rising tide of ground mist, the lorries nosing cautiously down the slope to the field gate and growling up again. Tomorrow, David said, they would do it all again on Major Norton's spread north of Gadney, on and on throughout the rest of the month until there wasn't an apple left unpicked in the whole of Herefordshire or, for that matter, the whole of England.

Immediately after supper David hurried off to supervise loading and after Mrs Wentworth had gone home Gwen and Susan were left alone in the house.

Gwen carried coffee things into the living room. She poured and served, then, standing by the piano, cup in hand, looked out through the French doors into the bustling darkness.

Seated on the sofa, Susan sipped coffee. She was tired after a long day picking fallen fruit and there was something in the woman's manner that made her uncomfortable, though she couldn't quite put her finger on what it might be.

'You'll be going home soon, I expect,' Gwen Proudfoot said.

'Yes, I expect we will.'

'Will that make you happy?'

Susan said, 'I've not been unhappy here.'

'Mercer's seen to that, I suppose.'

'I – I don't know what you mean.'

'Of course you do,' Gwen said.

Leaving her cup on the piano lid she crossed to the sofa. She stood behind Susan, looked down on her for a moment then broke away and paced restlessly back and forth across the room.

'Have you been with a man yet?' she asked.

'I beg your pardon?'

'Have you been with a man,' Gwen said, 'in bed?'

'I don't think that's any of your business.'

'You haven't, have you?'

'No, in fact – no, I haven't.'

'He'll ruin you, you know,' Gwen said. 'He ruined me. Does that surprise you? He was my first, before David; while David was still in France.'

'Why are you telling me this?' Susan said.

'He was my first and there will never be another like him. Other men, you see, just don't match up. Mercer Hughes is like a drug, an addictive drug. He's not intentionally destructive but he'll ruin you without even trying.'

'I wish,' Susan said, 'you'd stop wandering around.'

'I'm sorry,' Gwen said. 'It's a habit I've fallen into lately.'

'When Mr Hughes visits?'

The woman laughed. 'My God, you are a shrewd little creature, aren't you?' She came to the sofa and seated herself by Susan's side. 'At this moment, Mercer is probably persuading Vivian that you're indispensable. She pays you well, I take it?'

'Yes, very well.'

'You are, of course, a legitimate expense; a point Mercer won't fail to bring to Vivian's attention.' She leaned back and rested her head on the cushion. 'What do you make of her book?'

The change of tack caught Susan off guard.

She hesitated. 'I – I think it's very interesting.'

'Will it be just another piece of contentious trash,' Gwen said, 'or will this one have political significance? I doubt, frankly, if Mercer gives a damn either way. It's all grist to Mercer's mill.' She turned her head and looked directly at Susan. 'Isn't history exciting, though? Isn't it glamorous?'

'I never thought of it that way.'

'Hasn't Mercer trotted out his line about how we are drawn to the darkness and in the darkness find enlightenment?' When Susan didn't answer Gwen went on, 'Nothing about Mercer is terribly original, you see. Most of the high-class women he encounters spot him as a fraud at once, but,' she sighed, 'it doesn't seem to matter. They believe they will be the one to – what? – cure him, redeem him, give him depth and bring out the best in him. You, however' – she reached out and stroked Susan's arm – 'you are a lovely little blank slate. He'll have lots of fun educating you once you're broken in.'

Susan drew her arm away. 'You don't like me, do you?'

'As far as I'm concerned you're just a sweet little mongrel, an oddity, a shabby little girl with clean underwear and a cultivated voice. Are you madly in love with him? Eleanor is. Eleanor would give herself to him at the drop of a hat, though she doesn't understand why she finds Mummy's friend so infuriatingly attractive. Are you after his money?'

'What? No, 'course I ain't – no, I am not after his money.'

'Just as well,' Gwen said. 'He hasn't any.'

'He has a new car.'

'Phooh! A new car is nothing to Mercer. Besides, it's probably leased or, more likely, borrowed from the husband of an adoring friend. If it wasn't for Charlie Ames the agency would have foundered years ago.'

'Doesn't Mercer have a family?'

'Family money, you mean? God, no. His father was an investor. He speculated in women as well as stock and when Mercer was twelve cut all ties with Mercer's mother and ran off with the wife of a Billingsgate porter.'

'I don't believe you.'

'It's true,' Gwen said. 'Well, perhaps not the part about the Billingsgate porter; she was a little better connected than that.'

'Where's his father now?'

'Dead,' Gwen said. 'He went bust in the 1929 crash, though, by all accounts, he was on his uppers long before that. Incidentally, he didn't throw himself from a tall building on Wall Street. He spent his last five cents on the Staten Island ferry and took a header into New York harbour. Left nothing behind but debts and, I dare say, a few broken hearts, Mercer's not among them.'

'That's dreadful.'

'Now you're feeling sorry for the poor fellow, aren't you? One thing you must never do, Susan, is give Mercer Hughes your pity. He'll feed on it, feed on it like a mosquito or one of those vampire bats you read about.'

'Why do you say these things? I thought you liked him.'

'I do,' Gwen said. 'I just can't stand him, that's all.' She plucked the coffee cup and saucer from Susan's hand and got to her feet. 'I assume he's already arranged to meet with you in London?'

'Not exactly, no.'

'He will; you know he will.'

Susan nodded. 'Yes.'

'And that it won't stop at a few discreet lunches or a dinner in some quiet little restaurant in a Soho back street.'

'I think,' said Susan carefully, 'that's rather up to me.'

'Oh, is that what you think?' Gwen Proudfoot said. 'Do you honestly imagine there's a point at which you can step back? Believe me, there's no such point. Once he has you, Mercer Hughes won't let you go. You'll never be quite free of him.'

'I know he can't marry me.'

'Won't, my dear, won't marry you. Even if he didn't have a wife conveniently locked away in the loony bin he wouldn't marry *you*. He pretends to be a man of the people but not your sort of people, not vulgar people. Once he's had you, he'll ditch you, though no doubt he'll convince you that a corner of his heart will always be reserved just for you. All I can say is that the corners of Mercer's heart must be the most crowded pieces of property in London.'

'Know what?' said Susan, getting to her feet. 'I think you're jealous.'

'Of you? Don't be ridiculous!'

'I think you're jealous 'cause Mercer loves me.'

'He doesn't love you. He'll never love you.'

'Wants me, then,' said Susan heatedly. 'Wants me and you can't have him.'

'God, but you're really no better than Eleanor.'

'No worse either,' Susan said. 'I'm young, Mrs Proudfoot. Isn't that what sticks in your throat? If Mercer likes me enough to . . .'

'Go on,' Gwen Proudfoot said. 'Say it. Say the word, Susan, even if you have no idea what it means. What do they call it in Shadwell? Do they call it making love? I'll bet they don't. Well, good luck to you, Susan Hooper. When you're lying under our mutual friend and he's pounding you with that thing of his I don't suppose it'll matter who you are or where you come from. We're all the same to men like Mercer Hughes, just – just—'

'If you don't mind,' Susan interrupted, 'I think I'd like to go to bed now.'

'By all means,' Gwen said. 'I do hope I haven't embarrassed you?'

'Of course you have,' Susan said. 'Wasn't that your intention?'

'Now, I suppose, you're going upstairs to cry into your pillow.'

'No, Mrs Proudfoot,' Susan said, 'I'm going upstairs to sleep,' and dropping the woman a mock curtsey, turned on her heel and fled.

Two days later Vivian and she left Hackles and returned to London by train. Three weeks after that Susan stood, slightly bemused, by her father's side in the East Arbour Street registry office and watched her brother Ronnie tie the knot with a tear-stained Breda Romano. And five weeks after that, on a cold Thursday afternoon in early November, she gave herself up to Mercer Hughes in a room in the Connaught Hotel.

PART TWO

Winter 1936

12

Mercer said it was guilt that drove her to kowtow to her father and present herself week after week at the family mansion in Pitt Street when, in fact, the Sunday afternoon trail from Kensington to Shadwell had simply become a habit. What lay behind it, Susan knew, wasn't her father's longing to see her but, rather, a desire to excuse what she'd become. When he glanced across the teacups and caught her bouncing her nephew Billy on her lap, what she saw in his eyes wasn't pride but disappointment, as if all his sacrifices, all his scrimping and saving had produced not a lady but a stranger.

In spring and summer, if the weather was fair, the gang would head for the park: Breda, Ronnie and Billy, Nora, Georgie and Dad. If he'd nothing better to do Danny Cahill would tag along too and, hand in hand with Georgie, chat to Susan while little Billy waddled and toddled and rolled about in the dirt.

Whatever the season her father's greeting was always the same.

'How's the boyfriend?'

'He's very well, thank you.'

'An' how's the new flat?'

'Fine, it's fine.'

The fact that he'd never met Mercer or set foot in her flat in Rothwell Gardens didn't seem to matter.

'Working 'ard?'

'Very hard.'

'New book on the stalks?'

'Yes, Dad, new book on the stalks.'

'Good, good,' he'd say, then, formalities over, throw open the kitchen door and cry, 'Look who's 'ere, Billy,' and depending on his mood, her nephew would pitch himself against her knees or, more often than not, scowl and paddle away on all fours to hide behind his mother or his gran.

On that rainy Sunday afternoon in September there was no escape from the crowded terrace house, no possibility of avoiding interminable accounts of Billy's precocious appetite for Gran's pork scratchings and how often he'd used his potty. On the surface they were reaching out, making room for her in the family circle. In reality all they required was an audience to applaud the little prince's pranks and foibles. Didn't it occur to them that she had a life too, a life so remote from anything they'd ever known that they couldn't begin to imagine it?

Seated at a table laden with ham sandwiches, pickle jars and rock cakes she'd watch her father fuss over the feeding of Billy's stubborn little face and wonder if resentment was at the root of her annoyance, if, perhaps, she was jealous of the boy who had become the apple of her father's eye.

Dutifully she drank Co-op tea, nibbled a sandwich, dismantled a rock cake, and smiled at Billy when he deigned to give her his attention. She even let him climb on her lap, smear her cashmere jumper with his sticky fingers and worry the big decorative buttons on her cardigan until he had them hanging by a thread while Breda and Ronnie watched slyly, waiting for her to snap.

Last night, Susan thought, I shared a dinner table with

Martin Teague, Anna Maples and Rupert Arlen. We argued heatedly about the war in Spain, Hitler's advance into the Rhineland and Mosley's decision to march his Blackshirts through the East End of London. After we got back to my flat my friend Mercer Hughes stripped off my clothes and kissed me in intimate places until I begged him to bring me off which he did, again and again. Of course, they'd never heard of Martin Teague or Anna Maples, had never read a line of Rupert Arlen's sugary prose and would no doubt be disgusted by what her lover had done to her which, in Breda's book in particular, wasn't love but perversity.

'Isn't Danny coming today?' Susan asked: no one answered. 'Breda, is Danny coming today?'

'Dunno. There's a goo' boy. Does 'e want 'is dum-dum den?'

The rubber teat was apparently not high on Billy's list of requirements. He pressed himself into Nora's legs and buried his nose in the folds of her skirt. She stroked his cap of dark hair and said, 'Sure an' he'll be finding himself in trouble, that boy, he's not careful.'

'What boy?' said Breda.

'Danny,' Nora said. 'He's in with a bad crowd.'

'What do you mean by a bad crowd?' Susan asked.

Nora lowered her voice. 'Jews.'

'Danny ain't in with the Jews.' Ronnie spoke from behind a veil of cigarette smoke. 'Danny ain't in with anybody, not even the commies.'

'All tarred with the same brush, you ask me,' her father said.

Billy made a rude sound with his lips and peeped up at his gran for approval.

'Oh, what's that I hear?' said Nora. 'Was that me?'

Billy's face vanished into her lap again. The game, once started, would go on and on until Billy grew bored with it. Georgie, not to be outdone, wiped crumbs from his mouth with his wrist and, blowing hard into his forearm, outdid his tiny rival in volume and vulgarity.

Susan said, 'I take it, Ronnie, you weren't at the protest in Finsbury Park?'

'Not me, kiddo.'

'Was Danny?'

'I doubt it. In spite of what Nora thinks, Danny's no militant.'

'They got our 'ouses, they got our jobs,' her father said. 'They won't be happy till they drag us into a war just 'cause Herr 'Itler won't let them ruin Germany the way they're ruining us.'

Susan had been privileged to hear some of the sharpest minds in England discussing international issues. Mercer was circumspect in expressing his opinions but Vivian's politics were there for all to see. She'd turned down *The Times*'s offer of a ticket to Madrid to report on the war in favour of a trip to the Berlin Olympics with her publisher, Martin Teague.

'You must be pleased, Dad,' Susan said, 'now Tom Mosley's set up a branch of the British Union of Fascists in Shoreditch.'

'In a bleedin' stable, so I hear,' Ronnie said.

'No,' Susan corrected him, 'the stable's in Bethnal Green.'

'Didn't know none of that,' her father said. 'You got your facts right, girl?'

''Course she's got 'er facts right,' Ronnie said. 'You still kept in touch, Dad, you'd know she's got 'er facts right.'

'Anyhow,' her father said, 'I thought Mosley's name was Oswald.'

'His friends call 'im Tom,' Ronnie said. 'You his friend, Susie?'

'No,' Susan said evenly. 'I don't travel in those circles.'

'What circles do you travel in?' Ronnie said.

At last, she thought, someone's asked me a straight question. She had no straight answer to give, though, none that would satisfy Ronnie.

She said, 'What else has Danny been up to?'

'You ducked my question, sis,' Ronnie said. 'Got something to hide?'

'I'll bet she's got something to 'ide,' said Breda.

'I have absolutely nothing to hide,' Susan said. 'I spend most of my time at the typewriter or on the telephone. When Miss Proudfoot goes off on one of her trips I deal with her correspondence and keep her diary of appointments. She's much in demand, you know. This summer she gave talks in Manchester, Leeds, Birmingham and Hull – and she's been to Germany.'

'Germany?' her father said. 'She meet Herr 'Itler?'

'No, but she did have tea with Dr Goebbels.'

'I'd like to meet Herr 'Itler. There's a chap got 'is head screwed on,' her father said. 'Germany for the Germans; way it should be 'ere.'

'Yeah, Germany for the Germans,' Ronnie said, 'and anywhere else Adolf can get his paws on. Before you know it there'll be jackboots marching down the Commercial Road.'

'He's got a right, ain't 'e?' her father said. 'It's a free country.'

'Jackboots, Dad, not Blackshirts,' Ronnie said patiently.

'Well, whoever they are, I'll be out there to cheer them on.'

'And you, Ronnie,' Susan said, 'will you be out there to cheer them on?'

'Not me,' said Ronnie. 'I'll be manning the barricades.'

'His nibs 'ere wants to go off to fight in Spain,' Breda sneered.

'Go like a shot.' Ronnie shrugged. 'She won't let me.'

'All very well for Danny Cahill,' Breda said. 'He's footloose an' fancy free.'

Susan sat up. 'Is Danny going to Spain?'

'He's talked about it,' Ronnie said.

'Commie bastard,' her father said under his breath.

Tired of blowing on his wrist, Georgie leapt suddenly to his feet and stamped around the kitchen, chanting, '*Heil, heil, heil, heil.*'

'For God's sake, Nora,' her father said. 'Shut 'im up, can't yer?'

'Where did he learn that?' Susan shouted above the din.

'Danny took 'im to the flicks,' Ronnie said. 'Saw it in the newsreel.'

'Don't care where he saw it,' her father said. 'Shut 'im up.'

Then Billy launched himself from his grandmother's knee, poked a tiny fist in the air and yelled, '*Eel, eel, eel, eel,*' until his grandfather swooped and scooped him up after which he kicked and screamed in such a fit of temper that it seemed as if he might choke.

'He's just tired,' said Nora.

'Soon be his bedtime,' said Breda.

'I think I must be going,' said Susan.

'Zat him?'

'Aye, that's him,' Danny said.

He watched the man fumble behind the florid handkerchief that sprouted from his top pocket and fish out a spectacle case. He opened the case, stuck the glasses on his nose and peered again at the photograph.

'Bonnie wee lad,' said Danny.

'Yeah, he's all that,' Leo Romano agreed.

He gazed in silence at the black and white snapshot but did not, Danny noticed, offer it to the red-haired girl who sat with them at the café table.

'When was this took?' Leo asked.

'April. You can see the daffodils.'

'Why'd you wait so long to bring it?'

'Had to finish the spool,' said Danny.

'Oh, you got more of Billy, have you?'

'Sure.' Danny tipped the remaining prints from the envelope and shuffled them on the table top like playing cards. 'Help yourself.'

The snack bar in Covent Garden was a brightly lit barn of a place with a long serving counter and racks of Bakelite trays. The coffee was puny and the pastries stale. Even so the joint was heaving with the usual collection of godless waifs to whom Sunday was only a day to be got through as painlessly as possible.

Leo seemed out of place here, the red-haired girl even more so.

She was young, about Breda's age. If you looked at her one way, you'd take her for a tart; if you looked at her another she seemed almost classy. Leo hadn't seen fit to introduce her and Danny had no idea whether she was Leo's girlfriend or one of his nightclub whores.

He watched Leo pick out another snap and hold it close to his nose.

'He talkin' yet?' Leo asked.

'Chatters away like a wee monkey.'

'Fast on his feet?'

'Like lightning.'

'Who's this?'

'That's Ronnie. That's his dad.'

'Not much to look at, is he?'

'Better in the flesh,' said Danny. 'He's okay.'

'This one? The filly?'

'That's Ron's sister,' Danny said.

'She got a name?'

'Susan.'

'Hitched?'

'Naw, not yet.'

He watched Leo stroke the snapshot against his upper lip and then, with a faint smile, pass it to the red-haired girl.

'What you think of her?' Leo asked.

The girl glanced at the photograph. 'Nice.' She pronounced it, 'Noyce.'

'She in work?' Leo said.

'Author's assistant.'

'What the 'ell's that?' the girl said.

'Glorified secretary,' said Leo.

'Bit more,' said Danny. 'If you don't mind, I think I'll keep that one. The rest are all yours.'

'Whose camera?'

'Mine – a Brownie.'

'I get you a better one,' Leo said. 'Leica maybe.'

'The Brownie's okay. It does the job,' said Danny.

'You'll keep the snaps coming, won't you?'

'Sure. If that's what you want?'

It was on the tip of Danny's tongue to ask why if Leo was so all-fired keen to watch his grandson grow he didn't go down to Shadwell and see the kid for himself.

Leo gathered the prints and put them into the envelope. He left the snapshot of Susan on the table and tucked the envelope into his inside pocket.

'At least lemme pay you for these,' he said.

'Nope. My treat.'

'You don't wanna take nothing from me, do you, son?'

'I'm not strapped, Mr Romano, thanks all the same.'

'How about a little gift? You wouldn't refuse a little gift, would you? I mean, you wouldn't wanna hurt nobody's feelings.'

'What sorta gift?' said Danny warily.

Leo jerked his head at the red-haired girl who, pushing back her chair, hitched the hemline of her skirt a little higher and crossed her legs. She wore black silk stockings that clung to her calf and thigh and the view, Danny had to admit, was appetising.

'Name's Rita,' Leo said. 'She's got a flat just round the corner.'

'Has she now?' said Danny.

'Yeah,' Rita said. 'Do you a nice bit o' supper, you like.'

Danny cleared his throat. 'Might take you up on that, Rita – but not today.'

'How come?' Rita said. 'I'm kosher.'

'Don't doubt it,' Danny said, 'but I'm goin' tae meet my girlfriend.'

Rita gave him the sort of eye that Breda had never quite perfected. Danny picked up the snapshot of Susan and holding it between finger and thumb gave it a little wave as if to dry it off.

'Oh, that's her?' said Leo. 'That's the girlfriend?'

'Aye, that's her,' said Danny.

'I guess she's not the sorta girl you wanna keep waiting?'

'Definitely not,' Danny said. 'So if you'll excuse me . . .' He gave Rita a little bow. 'Sorry about the supper.'

She unfurled her legs and swung them back under the table.

'Always there, you change your mind,' she said.

'He's not gonna change his mind, are you, son?'

'I doubt it,' Danny said, and shook Leo's hand.

'Call me, you need anything,' Leo said.

'I'll do that,' Danny promised, then, slipping Susan's photo into his pocket, threaded his way between the tables and hurried out into the rain.

13

Susan loved her little flat, especially when she had it all to herself. The building was relatively new and, Mercer said, very twentieth century, by which he meant more concrete than brick. It stood on the corner of Rothwell Gardens and Fenmore Street, a short walk from the King's Road. The second-floor window looked down on railings, trees and a patch of grass. Mercer had found the place and had offered to meet the rent. Susan wouldn't hear of it. Occasional presents, theatre seats and dinners in expensive restaurants were all very well but she wanted nothing from him that might seriously compromise her independence.

Mercer was a considerate lover. He rarely spent the night, however. He would lie with her in his arms until she was almost asleep then kiss her softly, wish her sweet dreams and slip off to his rooms in one of those enormous bride's cake buildings south of Kensington High Street where he lived with his mother and her companion; a place, Susan gathered, that Mercer regarded as more prison than sanctuary.

In May Mercer had sailed to New York to negotiate the sale of Anna Maples's novel, *Catharsis*, which a Broadway producer hoped to turn into a play, and to finalise US publication rights on Vivian's *Wheel*.

Vivian was already at work on her third book, *The Melting*

Pot, for which Martin Teague had promised a staggering advance of three hundred and fifty pounds. Encouraged by rising royalties, Vivian had exchanged her flat in Marylebone for a mews house in Salt Street, twenty minutes' walk from Rothwell Gardens. Susan accompanied her employer to lunches, launches and lectures but did not go out of town, for her task was to man the fort and, as Vivian put it, keep the wolves at bay.

Safe home at last, Susan switched on the light, lit the heater under the boiler and drew a bath to wash away the Shadwell smells. In nightdress, dressing-gown and slippers, she brewed a decent pot of Earl Grey and settled in an armchair in front of the gas fire to listen to the wireless and browse over a proof copy of Anna Maples's latest novel, *A Garland for Jocasta*, which Mercer had asked her to read.

Halfway through a programme of light classical music the doorbell rang; a modern electrical doorbell that shot sound through the flat like a tracer bullet.

Susan scrambled to her feet and hurried to open the door.

'Danny!' she exclaimed. 'My God! Danny! What are you doing here?'

At one time back in the 1890s Rodker's had occupied splendid premises on Pall Mall but the infamous clerihew scandal had so damaged its reputation that shortly before the century drew to a close it had moved across Piccadilly to club-cluttered Dover Street and had left its bohemian roots behind.

It catered now mainly to travellers from Ireland and Scotland who would put up for a night or two while passing through the capital and to local bachelors too lazy to cook for themselves. Its kitchen, if not famous, was certainly respected and its cellars were the equal of any in Westminster. Its dining room, tucked well back from the street, was noted for its gigantic bow window which looked down on a city garden so stuffed with exotic plants that one almost expected Mowgli to crawl out from among the leaves.

David had motored up from Hackles to join Mercer for an early bite. His motorcar, hood raised against the rain, was parked outside in Dover Street which, this being a solemn London Sunday, was relatively free of traffic. Mercer had hoofed it from heaven knows where protected only by a large umbrella, for the Riley, so he claimed, was in dry dock with a carburettor problem.

Car talk and apple talk occupied the gentlemen through soup, pâté and whitebait and they were well into the veal before the subject turned to women.

'She's coming up, you know. There's no stopping her now.'

'Who's coming up?' said Mercer.

'Gwen, of course. I'm here to open up the Mayfair house.'

'That'll rather cramp your style, won't it?'

'Oh, she's not coming to keep an eye on me. She's coming to keep an eye on you,' David said. 'She's peeved because you've been ignoring her.'

'I haven't been ignoring her,' Mercer said. 'Good Lord, man, I came down in April. What more does she want?'

'She wants you planted in that damned cottage, that's what she wants.'

Mercer sighed, fiddled with his fork and said nothing.

David ate a mouthful of veal. 'Eleanor's coming too.'

'Eleanor? What about school?'

'Thing of the past. She's eighteen now, you know.'

'My, my, how time does fly,' said Mercer. 'What's on the cards? Switzerland, France, the grand tour?'

'Since she isn't debutante material,' David said, 'she's taken it into her head she wants to be a famous writer, like her Aunt Vivian.'

'God!' said Mercer. 'Has she written anything, anything at all?'

'Not a line, as far as I know,' said David. 'She expects you to wave your magic wand.'

'My wand is fresh out of magic.'

'I'm not surprised.'

'Now what's that supposed to mean?'

David smiled. 'How is Rosalind, by the way?'

'Much the same.'

'And young Miss 'Oopah?'

Mercer hesitated. 'Blooming.'

'Blooming, not clinging?'

'No, David, she isn't the clinging sort.'

'Why haven't you got rid of her?'

'Not sure I want to.'

'Don't tell me you're hooked?' David said.

'Not – no, not hooked.'

'Were you with her this afternoon?'

'She goes to visit her family on Sundays.'

'And you do what – or should I say who?'

'I trailed out to visit Rosalind, if you must know.'

'Liar!' David said. 'If I were a betting man I'd put a quid on a rendezvous with Anna Maples.'

'Anna's a client; no more, no less.'

'Does little Miss 'Oopah know Anna was with you in New York?'

Mercer looked up. 'How the devil did you find out?'

David stroked his nose. 'I have my methods.'

'Does Gwen know?'

'Don't be daft. Of course Gwen doesn't know,' David said. 'You're not quite the man of mystery you believe yourself to be, old son. One of these days you're going to trip and fall and I'm not going to be there to catch you. Doesn't Anna Maples have a husband?'

'Neville doesn't give a damn what Anna gets up to,' Mercer said. 'He has his own pursuits to keep him occupied.'

'You mean boys?'

Mercer nodded.

David pushed his plate aside. A waiter removed it and, without being asked, filled his wine glass.

'Standards are falling even here, I see,' David said.

'It's Sunday; what do you expect on Sunday? When's Gwen arriving?'

'End of the week.'

'I'll take her to lunch. Take you all to lunch. Viv too.'

'Safety in numbers?' David said. 'I assume little Miss 'Oopah won't be included in the party?'

'Her name,' Mercer said, 'is Susan.'

'She's not a tenant in one of my buildings, is she?'

'No,' Mercer said. 'I know better than that.'

'None the less, if ever you decide to raise your sights and let Miss – let Susan slip from your grasp . . .'

'I've no intention of letting Susan slip anywhere.'

'If things change, if you do . . .'

'No, David, no.'

'Why not? She's already *in situ*, as it were, which would be very convenient for all concerned should you decide to move on to pastures new.'

'Vivian and I have a tacit understanding that I won't do

anything to upset Susan – no, don't laugh – who is, I gather, worth her weight in gold. She's smart, very smart, and now she's acquired a little bit of polish . . .'

'Between the sheets, you mean?'

'Oh, for God's sake! There's no talking to you, is there?' Mercer snapped.

'I fear,' David said, 'that the sylph from Shadwell has wormed her way into your heart.'

'Perhaps she has.'

'But not enough to smother your inclination to take what else is offered?'

'Be that as it may,' Mercer said, 'Susan Hooper's not for the likes of you.'

'Hands off, in other words?'

'Yes, hands off,' said Mercer.

There were eggs in the larder, half a loaf, a fresh pat of butter and a slab of fruit cake rich enough to fill the empty corners. She poached the eggs on the gas stove, made toast on the grill, sliced the fruit cake into four crumbly pieces and served supper on the little table that pulled out from the wall.

'How did you find me?' she asked.

'You gave me your address,' Danny answered.

'Did I? When?'

'Night before you moved out.'

'And you remembered it?'

'Sure, I remembered it,' said Danny. 'Why wouldn't I remember it?'

Susan poured tea. 'I really should change into something more respectable.'

'You look respectable enough tae me,' said Danny.

'I suppose you're used to it.'

'Used to what?'

'Seeing Breda in her nightie.'

'Not any more,' he said. 'Anyhow, it was never that much of a thrill. At least you don't have paper curlers stickin' out your ears.'

Susan laughed. There was something delightfully domestic about sharing an off-the-cuff supper with her old friend from Shadwell and, following Danny's lead, she attacked her poached eggs as if she hadn't eaten in days.

'Listen,' Danny said, 'I'm not intrudin', am I?'

'No, you're not intruding,' Susan said.

'Your friend . . .'

'Mercer? Not, as a rule, on Sunday.'

'I figured that might be the way o' it,' Danny said.

'Why are you here, Danny? Is it to say goodbye?'

'Why, where am I goin'?'

'Ronnie mentioned something about Spain. Is it true? Are you signing on to fight for the Spanish?'

'Hardly,' Danny said, 'since the Spanish are fightin' each other.'

'You know what I mean – joining the republicans.'

'I'm not jumpin' on the Spanish bandwagon just yet.'

'Vivian thinks Franco will bring stability to the country.'

'Your boss is a bigger fascist than Franco and Mussolini put together.'

'Is that why you're here, Danny? To convert me?'

He grinned. 'Naw, Susie. I reckon you're past redemption.'

He had never been much to look at and age hadn't improved him. He was small in stature, round-shouldered, coarse-featured, nobody's idea of a matinée idol, but there was warmth in his watchful grey eyes and when he grinned he looked almost impish.

Susan said, 'Nora thinks you're running with a bad lot.'

'I'm not runnin' with any lot. I don't approve o' bricks an' knuckledusters any more than I approve o' police batons.' He mopped up egg yolk with a finger of toast. 'Which brings me tae the reason I'm here. Next Sunday, Susan, steer clear o' the East End. There's gonna be bloodshed an' I wouldn't want you caught up in it. I take it you know what's in the wind?'

Susan nodded. 'The Blackshirts intend to assemble at the Royal Mint and march to Bethnal Green. They've been active in the East End for months.'

'Aye, but this isn't a propaganda exercise: it's confrontation,' Danny said. 'Every anti-fascist organisation in the country will be out in force. Marxists from the north o' England and half-mad Scots from Clydeside, plus every London hooligan fit to hurl a rock or lift a club.'

'Will you be there?'

'I won't be far away.'

'What about Ronnie?'

Danny frowned. 'He'll be there – somewhere.'

'What about my father?'

'I've persuaded him to go up to Stratton's tae look after Nora, Breda, Georgie and the kiddie.' He gripped her hand. 'Promise me you'll steer clear.'

'Very well, Danny.' She licked her forefinger and fashioned the sign. 'Cross me 'eart, I'll steer clear of Shadwell next Sunday. There! How's that?'

'You're not takin' me seriously, are you?'

'I've always taken you seriously, Mr Cahill.'

'This time,' Danny said, 'make sure you do.'

If Mercer had arrived five minutes later Danny would have cleared the building. As it was, Susan had barely stepped back from the door when a key rattled in the lock and Mercer barged in.

'Who the devil was that?'

'Who?' Susan said innocently.

'That fellow on the landing. He was here, wasn't he? He was here with you?' Mercer tossed his coat and hat on a chair and peered at the egg-smeared plates on the table. 'Damn it! He *was* here.' He rounded on her. 'A nice little supper for two. How cosy! What else did he get from you, Susan?'

'It was only Danny – Danny Cahill, my brother's friend.'

'What did he want?'

'Nothing, he – he just dropped by.'

Mercer caught the belt of her dressing-gown and pulled her to him.

'Don't tell me he hasn't been at you?'

'At me?' Susan said.

'At you,' he said. 'Down there.'

'Mercer, you're hurting me.'

'He's a damned commie, isn't he?' He wrenched the dressing-gown over her shoulders. 'Well, I'm not sharing you with any damned commie.'

He locked his leg behind her knees, hustled her into the bedroom and threw her down on the bed. She felt neither fear nor anger. Since they'd kissed in the twilight in the porch at Hackles she'd known she was his to do as he liked with. He caught her by the ankles and dragged her across the bed. She waited for his first furious thrust. She could even feel the length of him sliding against her thigh.

Then he pulled back. 'Can't do it,' he said. 'I can't take you like this.'

She sat up. 'There is no one else, Mercer.'

'Just me?' he said, frowning.

'Just you, darling,' Susan assured him and brought him down into her before conscience got the better of him again.

14

It was only when Ronnie saw newsreel cameras being hoisted at the corner where Royal Mint Street narrowed into Cable Street that he knew he was in the right spot. Ruth Gertler had told him that anti-fascist protesters were gathering from all over London and had rhymed off assembly points from the St Pancras Arches to the Prince of Wales pub in the Harrow Road. How Ruth kept track was beyond him. How anybody kept track was a mystery, for ten thousand protesters had poured into the East End that morning to keep the Nazis out.

Perched on the pediment of an ornamental lamppost, he wrapped an arm round Ruth's waist, pressed her against the pole and shouted, 'You okay, kiddo?'

'Never been better,' she answered.

Her gorgeous mass of thick dark hair was contained by a red bandana. She wore a white roll-neck sweater and a black woollen skirt fastened by a broad leather belt with a buckle the size of a fist; a useful weapon, she said, should she need one. On top she wore a short black overcoat, like a donkey jacket, thrown open to show off her breasts. When he dug his fingers into the material she swung gaily away from him as if the lamppost were a maypole.

Armies of protesters were swarming down from Aldgate, coppers on horseback trying to hold them back. Near the bottom of Mansell Street ranks of Blackshirts, sleek as seals in their uniforms, were protected by a cordon of policemen. The coppers had already begun to herd protesters into Dock Street and even into Thornton Street where Herr Brauschmidt and Mr Gertler had boarded up their shops and when last seen were standing shoulder to shoulder, one armed with a cricket bat and the other with a vicious-looking meat hook.

Ron's excitement quickened as a torrent of protesters poured out of Leman Street and swirled about the base of the lamppost.

Ruth yelled, 'What's happening, Myrtle, what's happening?'

Her friend, Myrtle, looked up. 'They got Gardiner's Corner blocked. Mosley can't get through. He's coming down this way instead.'

'Stuffed,' Ronnie shouted. 'They stuffed the bastard on Commercial Road.'

'Told you, didn't I?' Ruth Gertler said. 'You ready for the heavy stuff?'

'Ready and eager,' Ron told her. 'Let it rip.'

In spite of her promise to Danny, Susan was waiting under the 'John Bull' bridge in Fenmore Street when David Proudfoot's open-topped car arrived. The car was too narrow to accommodate six people comfortably. Vivian was perched on Mercer's knee up front, Gwen, Eleanor and she squeezed into the back.

Eleanor had grown taller since Susan had seen her last, her sulky petulance replaced by an air of *hauteur*. If Eleanor had grown up, Gwen had grown older. Her pretty face was marred by worry lines that powder couldn't disguise.

The car swept round Trafalgar Square into the Strand and on Ludgate Hill ran into a column of mounted police moving at a fast trot, a gaggle of small boys skipping alongside shouting insults.

'I do hope we haven't missed it,' Vivian called out.

'Missed what?' said Eleanor.

'The march, of course,' Mercer said. 'Don't you want to be part of history?'

They were still a half-mile or so from the Mint when a cacophony of cornets, clarinets and drums threaded with the skirl of bagpipes rose ahead of them and a swirl of young men and boys blocked the way.

David promptly reversed and cruised the car to a halt in a side street.

'It's certainly not safe to drive into Mint Street,' he said.

'Then we'll just have to hoof it,' said Mercer.

'No,' Gwen said. 'Take me home. I mean it, David. I want to go home.'

David hesitated. 'Well, if you insist.'

'I do,' his wife said. 'I absolutely insist.'

'In that case' – Vivian slid from Mercer's knee – 'I reckon I'll leave you to it.'

'You're not going to walk, are you?' Eleanor said.

'Of course I am,' Vivian said. 'I wouldn't miss it for worlds.'

'I think,' Mercer said, 'I'll join you – if Gwen doesn't object.'

He wore a long military-style trench-coat and a wide-brimmed hat. No copper, horsed or otherwise, would dare raise a hand against him, Susan thought. His voice alone would be sufficient to guarantee safe passage: that not quite imperious, well-bred voice, with every vowel rounded and every consonant in place, so different from the voices of the boys she'd grown up with, the men and boys who were shouting themselves hoarse in the name of democracy.

'Any more for the Skylark?' Mercer said. 'Susan?'

She felt a twinge of guilt, the merest twinge.

'Yes,' she said. 'I'm game.'

'Well, blow it,' Eleanor said. 'I'm not being left behind.'

'Mercer,' Gwen said, 'be careful, please.'

'I will,' Mercer promised, then, fashioning a mock salute, brought his little squad of females to heel and led it off, as it were, to the slaughter.

Nora said, 'Sure an' I wish you'd come inside, Matt.'

'I should be up there,' Matt said. 'Should be doin' my bit for the cause.'

'You'll get no thanks from Mosley for getting your head broke,' Nora told him. ''Sides, you're too old.'

'I'm not too old to fight for what I believe in.'

'What do you believe in then?'

'England for the Englanders.'

Standing outside the shop with his arms folded and a bulldog expression on his biscuit, Nora thought he looked like something peeled from one of the posters that were plastered all over Shadwell, even if he wasn't wearing a leather apron and brandishing a sickle.

Several men and women were huddled in doorways further down the street; unlike Matt, they really were well past it. Nora had heard nothing but fighting talk from her customers for weeks. Nellie Millar, the day girl who'd taken over from Breda, had told her it was all the fault of the Jews. Nora wasn't convinced by anything that came out of Nellie's mouth, for the girl was too young to have any sense and belonged to a family of thirteen – not even Catholics – and walked every morning from Whitechapel because she needed the wage.

'England,' Matt said again, 'for the English – like Spain for the bleedin' Spaniards. Now there's a cause I'd fight for if I 'ad the time.'

'Well, thank God you haven't,' said Nora. 'Come inside.'

'Ain't enough Jews in London to stop Sir Oswald, he puts 'is mind to it. He comes past the end o' my street, least I can do is cheer 'im on.'

'It isn't your street,' Nora reminded him. 'It's my street.'

'Whoever's street it is, I'll be proud to show 'im me 'and.'

'Your hand?'

When Matt demonstrated the fascist salute an old bloke two doors down released a mouthful of the sort of language Nora hadn't heard since Leo had left.

'Sod you too!' Matt shouted.

But when the old bloke lurched from the doorway and limped towards them furiously waving his stick Matt thought better of it and, to Nora's relief, elbowed her back into the shop and hastily bolted the door.

Even indoors you could sense the tension, a vibration not quite strong enough to make the plates rattle but just loud enough to cause Billy to mumble in his sleep. He was really too big to nap in the wash basket on the table now and one bare foot stuck over the wicker rim and his little toes twitched, almost, Nora thought, as if he were marching in his dreams.

Seated in Nora's armchair, Breda was smoking a Woodbine and rubbing some kind of jelly into her bruised nipples, for Billy, though weaned, was still greedy for the breast. Matt glanced at his daughter-in-law then looked away as if he found the sight offensive. Breda didn't care what Matt thought. Breda didn't care about anything these days except her baby boy.

'Don't you wake 'im,' she said. 'I only just got 'im down.'

On tiptoe, holding his breath, Matt peeped into the basket. 'He looks 'ot.'

'He always looks 'ot when 'is belly's full.' Breda coated her left nipple with pale blue jelly. 'What's 'appening out there? Any sign of what's-'is-face?'

'Not yet,' said Matt. 'He'll be 'ere, though. He'll be 'ere.'

'Yeah, so will Christmas,' Breda said. 'Ronnie told me it was happening at 'alf past one? It's gone three now.'

'Been held up, I expect,' said Matt softly. 'He's a busy man.'

'Who – Ronnie?' said Breda.

'Mosley,' Matt said. 'Where is Ronnie, by the way?'

'Out with 'is trollop,' Breda informed him.

'What you talkin' about, girl?' Matt said.

'Talkin' about Gertler's daughter,' Breda said.

'Now, now, Breda,' Nora put in, 'Ron's only doing his duty.'

'Poking that cow in some back alley ain't duty,' Breda said.

She wiped her fingers and tucked in her blouse. She screwed the lid back on the jar of jelly, lifted her cigarette from the ashtray and inhaled.

Matt cleared his throat. 'What's all this about Gertler's daughter?'

'That's who 'e's with most nights,' said Breda.

'I thought he went to the pub,' said Matt.

'Party meetings – with 'er.'

'Which party?' said Matt.

'The League – the Young Communist League.'

'What the bleeding 'ell's Ron doing with the YCL?'

'It's Spain,' Breda sneered. 'He talks about nothing else. You've 'eard 'im.'

'Yus, but I thought – I mean, we all talks about Spain,' Matt said.

'That bitch can twist 'im how she likes.' Breda blew smoke. 'He ain't going to no Spain with no commies.'

'Are you telling me my son's a communist?' Matt said.

'Your son blows whichever way the wind takes 'im,' Breda said. 'All he cares about is what he's got between 'is legs.'

The sounds were heavy and distinct: a thud, a clatter, another thud.

'What's that?' Nora sat up. 'Oh, my God! What's that? They're coming. They're coming to get us. Holy Mary, Mother o' God!'

'Nobody's coming to get you,' Matt said. 'Where's Georgie?'

'Upstairs,' Breda told him.

Matt went into the corridor past the larders. He stood at the foot of the staircase and called out, 'Georgie, you up there?'

Receiving no answer, he clambered up to the first floor, peered into Georgie's room and finding it empty checked the other rooms off the landing.

Nora was waiting for him at the foot of the stairs.

'What is it, Matt?' she said. 'What's wrong?'

'It's Georgie,' Matt told her. 'He's scarpered.'

Indignation and apathy, Danny Cahill thought, made strange bedfellows. For months Mosley's minions had delivered soapbox oratory via corner meetings and loudspeaker vans without serious opposition. In the past few weeks, however, every warehouse wall, every bridge, shop front and hoarding had been decorated with slogans urging patriotic citizens to rise up and support the republicans in Spain and thus, by some warped logic, keep the fascists out of Whitechapel.

Unemployment, deprivation and injustice had nudged too many folk into the arms of the Blackshirts but an hour reading the ticker-tapes, half a day sifting through reports from foreign correspondents or a glimpse into the editor's morning meeting would give pause to all but the most hardened, for the news that Danny's boss allowed to trickle into print wasn't half, not a quarter of the whole sorry story of what was really happening in Europe.

He skirted the spots where fighting had broken out and quit Gardiner's Corner as soon as it became clear that Mosley's Bentley wouldn't get through.

He hurried into St Mark's Street, took the lane behind the court building into Chamber Street and, shinning over a padlocked gate, crossed a school playground and came out into Royal Mint Street not far from where the Blackshirts were lined up in parade order.

Union Jacks and fascist banners fluttered in the breeze. Only one band was playing now and the Blackshirts sang lustily, as tuneful and well ordered as a Welsh choir, except it wasn't 'Bread of Heaven' but the 'Horst Wessel Song' that poured from their throats. Behind the uniformed ranks hundreds of Mosley supporters waved flags and sang too. Further up the street a line of Black Marias and limousines indicated that bigwigs from the Home Office and Special Branch were engaged in a pow-wow. The establishment obviously controlled Royal Mint Street but off to his left, in Cable Street, trouble was brewing. Not one black-shirted soul would make a move, however, until their leader gave the order and their leader was presently stuck somewhere north of the Mint.

Danny paused to light a cigarette and glancing up from the match saw Susan far down the line. She was walking arm-in-arm with the tall guy he'd almost bumped into in Rothwell Gardens. Behind her a heavyweight female in tweeds and a stocky, toffee-nosed blonde jogged to keep up.

Danny pressed himself against the wall, heart racing. He'd known that Susan had moved away from Shadwell, but until that moment it hadn't dawned on him just how far her journey had taken her.

He watched the ranks part and swallow her up, then he set off to join the Jews, communists and gangsters who massed behind the barricades at the narrow mouth of Cable Street.

'The boy?' said Herr Brauschmidt. 'The boy who isn't right in the head?'

'Georgie,' Matt said. 'Nora Romano's lad. You seen 'im?'

Herr Brauschmidt deferred to his comrade, Mr Gertler.

Mr Gertler was a small man, sallow and sinewy, with a mop of curly grey hair that stuck out from under his hat as if hat and hair were joined at the seam. He wore an expensive alpaca overcoat and the shiny steel meat hook that hung from his hand looked more like a fashion accessory than a weapon.

He shook his head. 'He has not passed this way.'

'Perhaps he is with Ronnie,' Herr Brauschmidt suggested.

'Have you seen Ronnie then?' Matt said.

'He has gone to look after my daughter,' Mr Gertler said, quite unabashed.

'Oh!' Matt exclaimed. 'Which way did they go?'

Mr Gertler pointed towards the head of Thornton Street where, like debris locked in a canal, a crowd of young men slopped back and forth.

Matt had worked the quays all his life. He'd seen things that wouldn't bear repeating but for Susan's sake he'd steered clear of picket lines, union meetings and the raucous wars of words and fists that provided release for his peers. But at least, he thought, I knew what was what and where danger lay – which was more than could be said for Nora's big soft-headed son.

'If Georgie comes this way,' he said, 'keep him safe, please.'

'We will, Mr Hooper,' Mr Gertler promised. 'We will.'

15

Susan didn't feel out of place among the fascists. Martin Teague, his wife and sons stood proudly behind the uniforms and behind them five or six women Susan recognised from literary luncheons. They smiled and waved to Mercer who, nothing loth, smiled and waved back while Eleanor, no longer bored, belted out the last verse of the Blackshirts' anthem and when it was over cried, 'Yes, Yes, Yes,' so loudly that several handsome chaps in the ranks glanced round, grinning.

'Where is he? Where's Mosley?' Eleanor asked.

'He'll be here,' Vivian answered. 'Just give him time.'

Mercer was chatting to an elderly gentleman with a stiff little goatee beard, eye-glasses and a silver-topped cane. He laughed at something Mercer said, then vanished into the crowd just as suddenly as he'd appeared.

'Who's that?' Vivian asked. 'Sigmund Freud?'

'One of Martin Teague's authors,' Mercer told her. 'Retired professor. Name's Kulgin – with a K.'

'Is *that* Eric Kulgin?' Eleanor said. 'I've read his book.'

'Have you, indeed?' Vivian said. 'Not a romance, I take it?'

'Aunt Vivian! Really!' Eleanor said. 'It's a history of the Medicis.'

'Any good?'

'Splendid,' said Eleanor. 'Deliciously gory.'

'Kulgin's of the opinion they'll try to stop him,' Mercer said.

'Tom Mosley won't be stopped by hooligans,' said Vivian.

'No,' Mercer said, 'but he might respect an order from the government. If he keeps to his plan and moves his troops down Cable Street there'll be bloodshed.'

'I want to march,' Eleanor piped up. 'I want to fall in and be counted.'

'Be more than spit in your face if you do, my dear,' said Vivian.

At which point Sir Oswald Mosley's Bentley, surrounded by police, nosed into view and all conversation ceased.

The cordon, three deep, meant business. Stones had been hurled at the open-topped Bentley as it passed down Leman Street. Say what you like, Sir Oswald had guts. He wasn't one for ducking responsibility or reneging on promises. He sat high in the rear of the car and defied the herd with the sort of arrogance you have to be born with. It was Matt's first glimpse of the great man. He struggled through the crowd of protesters that had been shoved into Dock Street and was on the point of raising his fist in fascist salute when, fortunately, the crowd surged and the Bentley, flanked by two motorcycles, swept past, heading for the Mint.

In the midst of all the pushing, shoving and shouting Matt experienced a pang of disappointment. For a split second he and Sir Oswald Mosley had been eye to eye – well, almost. Somehow Matt had expected more: an acknowledgement, a sign of recognition. He was inclined to chase after the Bentley but he was pinned on all sides by the crowd, swaying with it, surging with it, thrust forward by it as the coppers clubbed and punched and wrestled with those gamecocks who were eager to take them on. A woman in a knitted cap kicked the back of Matt's legs. He stumbled and might have fallen if the bodies all around hadn't held him up. He could see nothing but heads, heads and faces and a step or two ahead of him coppers' helmets, truncheons rising and falling and a horse, huge and dappled, galloping across the junction to slam its rump into the fray.

Then on the far side of the street he spotted Georgie, unmistakably Georgie, heading towards the barricades. He was coatless and hatless with only the loud-patterned pullover that Nora had knitted to keep him warm. He marched with a lumbering swagger, big head rolling, right arm stuck high in the air as he shouted out his battle cry: '*Heil, heil, heil, heil.*'

'Good God!' Vivian said. 'Mosley's capitulating.'

'Prudence over pride,' said Mercer. 'I imagine he's been given a direct order by the Police Commissioner. Looks as if we're marshalling for a march back into the city. Trafalgar Square would be my guess. Are we up for it?'

Vivian said, 'I assume we'll have police protection as far as the square?'

'Part of the deal, probably,' Mercer said.

'Hardly a triumph, is it?' Susan said.

'Much as I'd enjoy a good punch-up,' Vivian said, 'I have to agree that Mosley's doing the right thing.'

Bandsmen, policemen and Blackshirts were reorganising. Tom Mosley, grim-faced, inspected the ranks. A loudspeaker van made an appearance and broadcast an unintelligible message backed, oddly, by the strains of a popular dance tune.

Anna Maples appeared from the crowd. 'A Pyrrhic victory, I believe.'

'You know everyone, don't you, Anna?' Mercer asked.

'Who is this young lady?'

'My niece, Eleanor,' said Vivian. 'Anna Maples, the author.'

'I've read all your novels,' Eleanor gushed.

'And did you enjoy them?'

'Very much. When's the new one due?'

'Christmas.'

Susan was tempted to blurt out that she'd read *A Garland for Jocasta* and that it was even more tedious than *Catharsis*; just another thinly veiled account of Anna's passionate affair with the dyspeptic sculptor, Francis Warlock, whose member, according to rumour, was even longer than Anna's metaphors.

'Are you with someone?' Mercer asked.

'I came with Eric but he's toddled off,' Anna answered.

'We'll be going on somewhere for a spot of supper after the march,' Mercer said. 'You're welcome to join us.'

'Are you sure you don't mind?'

'Why would I mind?' said Mercer.

'I say,' Eleanor piped up, 'what's going on down there?'

'Looks like a last-minute baton charge,' Susan told her.

'Oh, good,' said Eleanor. 'Go get them, boys. Go get them.'

Dusk was gathering downriver before Danny got Georgie safely home. The final police baton charge had been pointless, for the word was out that Mosley's army had retreated and the East End had been 'saved'.

The East End, the parts that Danny could see, didn't look saved. There was debris everywhere, broken glass, broken planks, broken windows and gangs of young kids throwing stones. Every corner and shop doorway was crowded with jubilant street-fighters bragging how they'd stuffed the fascists and written a new chapter in working-class history, and a jolly little mob, mostly Irish, was gathered outside Stratton's hammering on the door and begging Nora to let them in.

Leaning on Danny's shoulder, Georgie stared blankly at the crowd. Some cabmen recognised him and waved but for all the response they got they might as well have been talking to the wall.

Danny steered Georgie into the lanes that led to the back of the shop. He helped Georgie negotiate the strip of paved yard past the lavatories, coal bunkers and bins and, fishing a key from under a flowerpot, opened the back door and pushed the boy into the passageway. Georgie lumbered down the corridor, bumping from wall to wall. He seemed to have no idea where he was. Danny directed him into the kitchen.

'Oh, it's you, is it?' Breda said. 'About bleedin' time.'

Nora leapt to her feet. 'Sure an' he was with Danny all the time.'

And Georgie, knees buckling, slumped to the floor at her feet.

The café on the Whitechapel Road was packed with boys and girls and they weren't all Jewish. One or two older blokes from the Unemployed Workers' Union shared a booth with a couple of organisers from the Stepney branch of the Communist Party who, Ronnie gathered, were shelling out bail money to hasten the release of those warriors who'd wound up in the cells.

Every booth was occupied and some of the girls were seated on the counter sipping soda pop and giggling every time a feller brushed against their knees. Mario, the café owner, no supporter of Mosley, dashed up and down dishing out cups of scalding-hot coffee and plates of macaroons.

Myrtle's boyfriend, Jacob, had been up on the Mile End Road near the cinema when an errant posse of Blackshirts had strayed into the territory looking for Jews to beat up.

'And did they find any, Jacob?'

'Did they not?' Jacob cried. 'More Jews than they could handle.'

'What did you do?'

'Broke heads,' Jacob said. 'Broke many heads. We had a rope slung over a lamppost and, I tell you, if the coppers had not arrived we'd have strung those fascists up by the heels.'

Ronnie was playing kneesy with Ruth and only half listening.

'Is that true about the lynching?' he asked.

Ruth smiled and shook her head. 'I doubt it.'

'They're hanging 'em in Spain, you know.'

'This isn't Spain,' she said.

'You coming to Spain, Ronnie?' said one young man. 'Some of us are heading out at the end of the month.'

'He can't,' Ruth said. 'He has a wife and child to support.'

'We've all got to make sacrifices,' the young man said.

'Try telling that to my wife,' said Ronnie.

'What? Is she a fascist?'

'No, but my old man is,' said Ronnie.

'You work for the German, don't you?'

'Yep.'

'Then you got nothing to lose.'

'I don't think I follow,' said Ronnie.

Ruth was still exhilarated by the day's events, high as a kite on the violence that had erupted around them. He was excited too but not as excited as the girl – maybe because he wasn't a Jew.

Ruth said, 'He means you can quit Brauschmidt's without a qualm.'

'The German only worries about his profits,' the young man said.

'An' what do you worry about?' Ronnie asked.

'Survival,' the young man answered.

That wasn't what he'd heard preached at YCL meetings and it certainly wasn't the party line: Ron was brought up short by the pungent little word.

He said, 'What's your name, anyway?'

'Moshe,' the young man told him. 'Moshe Gertler.'

'My cousin,' Ruth said and continued to stroke his thigh even as he reached across the table to shake the young man's hand.

Georgie was out cold for two or three minutes. When he came round he seemed, Danny thought, a bit more connected. He knelt behind the boy, supporting his head, and ran his fingers over Georgie's scalp in search of blood.

'It's the excitement, I expect, just the excitement,' Nora said. 'Georgie, do you know where you are?'

'Kitchen.'

'That's right,' Danny said. 'Know who I am?'

''Anny.'

'Tell me again, Georgie.'

''A – 'anny.'

With the acute sense of crisis that small children possess, Billy quit howling and clung to his mother.

Breda said, 'He get conked, or what?'

'Dunno,' said Danny. 'He's not bleedin' anywhere I can see.'

'Thought you was taking care of 'im,' said Breda.

'I didn't even know he was out there,' said Danny.

'Wasn't you with him?' said Nora.

Danny shook his head. 'I found him hidin' in a doorway.'

'Conked,' Breda snorted. 'Betcha 'e got conked. For all the brains 'e's got it wouldn't hardly matter.'

The Irish had given up hammering on the shop door. You could still hear shouting, though, as little groups of street-fighters romped past the window.

Nora soaked a washcloth, wrung it out and placed it across her son's brow. Reaching up, Georgie drew a corner of the cloth into his mouth and sucked on it.

'Should I give him something to drink, Danny?' Nora said.

'Make him tea,' Danny said. 'I'll get him up to his bed.'

'Best place for 'im,' Breda said. 'Then you can walk us home on the off-chance my bleedin' hubby's crawled in looking for 'is supper. Didn't see 'im out there, did yer?'

'Naw,' Danny lied. 'Be a miracle if I had.'

In fact, he had seen Ronnie, Ronnie and the Gertler girl perched halfway up one of the ornamental lampposts at the junction. They hadn't seen him, though, for they were much too occupied with each other. He wasn't about to tell Breda that; nor was he about to tell Nora what had been going on behind the breast-high wall of saw-horses and broken boards where, by chance, he'd stumbled on Georgie, head in hands, seated on a doorstep under a tailor's sign.

'Can you get up, love?' Nora asked.

Georgie seemed perfectly at ease sucking the end of the washcloth.

'Georgie?' Danny said softly. 'Did somebody thump you?'

'Be a copper, most like.' Breda hoisted Billy higher in her arms and coming around the table peered down at her brother. ''Ere,' she said, 'I don't think I like the look of 'im.'

166

'Me neither,' Danny said. 'Maybe I should fetch a doctor?'

'What, what is it?' Nora said. 'What's wrong?'

Georgie's skin was clammy. Icy beads of perspiration formed on his upper lip. The washcloth slipped from the corner of his mouth. His eyes rolled and he let out a sigh, something between a gargle and a snore.

'Georgie?' Nora said. 'Wake up, love, wake up.'

Danny sought for the pulse on Georgie's neck.

Then, looking up, he said, 'Oh, God, Nora, I think he's dead.'

16

Poor Georgie had never received so much attention in life as he did in death. In accordance with section 21 of the Coroners Act of 1887 his body was removed from his mother's house to an underground room in the London Hospital where, with the coroner and a minion from the Home Office in close attendance, the teaching hospital's most experienced pathologist undertook an extensive post-mortem examination of the corpse.

Official concern that young Mr Romano had been the victim of a police assault during the Cable Street riots was increased by the fact that Daniel Cahill was not only a friend of the family but a newspaper man to boot. It came as a vast relief to all – though not, perhaps, immediate kin – when the pathologist reported that no mark, scar, bruise or other significant contusion had been found upon the body and the cause of death had been a rare form of limbic encephalitis which had led to swelling in the cerebral cortex which in turn had resulted in a small but fatal embolism within the brain: in other words, natural causes.

Citing the Amendment Act of 1926 and egged on by a low-echelon representative of the crown, the coroner had used his powers to order an immediate inquest without jury and the awkward little case and awkward not-so-little Georgie had been sewn up in the matter of a week.

At Danny's insistence the body was returned to Stratton's in a sealed coffin.

Blinds were drawn, candles lit, rosaries unearthed and, consoled by religion, Nora and Breda mourned the passing of son and brother while the men, Danny in particular, took care of arrangements.

Then, on a blustery Thursday evening in mid-October, Ronnie, Danny, Matt and one of Nellie Millar's unemployed brothers carried the coffin out into the street. They eased it into a motorised hearse and followed the vehicle on foot to St Mary and St Michael Catholic Church while the good folk of Shadwell respectfully removed their caps and bowed their heads.

A small crowd had gathered outside the church for the receiving; men and women who couldn't bring themselves to join in a Catholic service but who couldn't quite bring themselves to stay away. Danny squinted from under the heavy coffin while a prayer was said, then, with Nora and Breda leading, helped carry what remained of Georgie into the church where the smell of incense brought back unwelcome memories.

In all his years at St Finian's Danny had never been beaten or bullied. In the musty old building's dormitories and classrooms he'd felt at home, whatever home meant for a kid who'd been dumped on the doorstep of the priest's house with the birth cord still attached to his belly and no indication to whom he belonged. Jesus is your father and the Virgin is your mother, Father Flynn had told him, and you will live in their sight for ever. He'd swallowed that when he was young but later when he'd looked more critically at the tormented figure on the Cross, at the passive blue stare of the Madonna he'd had doubts, doubts that Father Flynn and an awful lot of praying had been unable to quell.

Duty done, big Steve Millar clumped off. Ronnie and Matt stumbled into a pew while Nora and Breda went off to make confession.

Danny tarried by the coffin.

Tomorrow he'd help carry Georgie from the church. Nora and Breda would weep as the hearse left for Tower Hamlets, would say goodbye at the pavement's edge and go home to Billy, Nellie Millar and tables laden with food and drink. Matt, Ronnie and he would follow the priest and altar boys to the cemetery to watch Georgie put into the ground to sleep or perhaps, Danny thought, to hang about the gates of paradise waiting for a friendly face to show up to tell him what to do next.

'Ah, Jesus, Georgie,' Danny murmured. 'Jesus, Jesus!'

Then he turned and, looking neither right nor left, headed for the door.

Susan took the matchbox and lit his cigarette. She watched him draw smoke, his thin shoulders rising under his cheap black overcoat, hands shaking.

At length, he said, 'I see they've gone.'

'Yes,' Susan said. 'They didn't hang about for long.'

'Can't say I blame them,' Danny said. 'He wasn't much, our Georgie.'

'You don't really think that, do you?'

'Naw,' he said, ''Course I don't.'

'I take it *was* a brain haemorrhage?'

'That's what the experts say.' Danny dropped the half-smoked cigarette to the pavement and ground it out with his heel. 'Who told you?'

'Not you, that's for sure,' said Susan.

'I didn't think you'd be interested.'

'Oh, Danny! What a horrid thing to say.'

He rubbed his hand over his face. 'Aye, I'm sorry.'

'Ronnie called me.'

'What, on the telephone? He hates telephones.'

'He thought it was my place to be here.'

'Well, you're here now,' Danny said. 'He'll be out in half an hour.'

'I didn't come to see Ron,' she told him. 'I came to see you.'

'Why?'

'To find out what time the mass is tomorrow.'

'You comin' to the mass?'

'Afterwards – to the shop.'

The wind blew a shoal of leaves in a great rustling spiral across the face of the church. It was dark now and cloud scudded over the rooftops. Behind her were the Shadwell streets in which she'd grown up, streets that seemed both familiar and curiously remote.

'Danny,' she said, 'are you all right?'

'Yeah,' he answered. 'I'm all right.'

He'd always been a loner, a fellow they'd looked up to without ever getting to know and he'd kept one foot in Shadwell and the other in Fleet Street, balancing his separate selves with a skill she could only envy.

'Mass is at nine,' he said.

'Ten? Ten thirty at the shop?'

'Round about,' he told her. 'Look, Susie, I've gotta go to work now.'

She looked at the church rearing into the cloudy sky. No sounds came from within; no singing, no responses, no whispers of prayer. It was as if everyone she'd ever known in the old days was lying dead inside.

'How are you going back to town?' she asked.

'Tube.'

'I'll walk with you,' Susan said.

'Suit yourself,' said Danny.

But when she took his arm he didn't draw away.

Breda declared herself disgusted at not being invited to ride to Tower Hamlets to see her brother buried. Of course, she knew funerals were a man's thing and women, by tradition, were too emotional to be allowed anywhere near an open grave. That didn't stop her grousing about it, though, and she clung, yapping, to her mother's arm as they walked back from the church to Stratton's Dining Rooms after the cars had prowled off.

Anger at life's injustices had been Breda's answer to grief since her brother had passed away on the kitchen floor with little Billy looking on. She'd laid about her unremittingly, accusing Danny of carelessness, her mother of neglect and her husband of being in cahoots with his old man to make her life a misery. She'd also had a go at doctors and police sergeants and might have stormed the anteroom in the court building where the inquest was held if Danny hadn't talked her out of it.

Billy was the only person to whom she showed consideration but even he suffered, not from her acid tongue but from the sort of treatment any energetic toddler would resent. Shuttled forth and back from Dad's house to Grandma's, left for hours in the charge of a skinny stranger, Nellie Millar, Billy made his displeasure known and every fit of pique, every red-faced outburst drove a splinter of anxiety deeper into Breda's heart.

'Do you think there's something wrong with 'im?'

'What do you mean, wrong with 'im? He's just a bad-tempered little tyke.'

'No, Ron. I mean *wrong* with 'im – like Georgie?'

'Oh, I get it. You think Billy might be soft in the 'ead.'

'Well, look at 'im.'

'He looks all right to me.'

'Lying on the floor screaming is all right, is it?'

'He's just fed up,' Ron told her, 'like everybody else round 'ere.'

'Is that – is that foam at the corners of 'is mouth?'

'It's milk, Breda. It's only bleedin' milk.'

The blinds of Stratton's Dining Rooms were still drawn and the chalk board that Georgie had lugged out every morning was still propped behind the door.

Breda followed her mother into the shop.

Tables were set with plates and cups. Sandwiches were arranged on two long trays on the counter together with one bottle of whisky and one of gin. Nellie had lit the gas rings and on a raw October forenoon the place seemed inappropriately welcoming. Breda hoped that someone would turn up, even if it was only the old gits from down the road, otherwise it would be just family.

'Wanna cuppa tea, Ma?'

Nora nodded, seated herself at one of the tables and took off her hat.

'Nellie? You there?' Breda called out.

Susan appeared from the kitchen with Billy in her arms. Sucking on his dum-dum, Billy was, for once, at peace.

'What've you done to 'im?' Breda said.

'I haven't done anything to him,' Susan said.

'Why's 'e so quiet?'

'We've been having a little chat, that's all.'

'Chat? He don't know 'ow to chat.'

'Yes, he does,' said Susan. 'Don't you, Billy?'

'Hmm, hmm,' Billy agreed.

'Give 'im 'ere,' said Breda.

Billy was reluctant to quit his Aunt Susie's fragrant bosom and squealed when his mother reclaimed him.

'What you doing 'ere any roads?' Breda asked.

'I came,' Susan answered, 'to pay my respects.'

'Took your bleedin' time about it, didn't yer?'

'Well, it might have been nice if someone had thought to tell me.'

'Doncha read the newspapers?'

'It wasn't in the newspapers,' Susan said.

'Was too.'

'What, the *Advertiser*? No, Breda, I don't read the *Advertiser*.'

'Not bleedin' posh enough for you, I expect.'

As if waking from a trance, Nora slapped her fist on the table. 'Stop it, stop it, the pair o' you. I'll have none o' your squabbling.'

'I'm sorry, Nora.' Susan slipped into a chair and took Nora's hand. 'I mean, I'm really and truly sorry about Georgie.'

'Sure an' I know you are, dear,' Nora said.

The sight of Ronnie's sister smarming over her ma made Breda's blood boil.

Susie Hooper, molly-coddled since the day she was born, might wear fancy clothes and speak proper but she was no better than a stuck-up bitch who got paid for doing what Ronnie did to her every night.

'Is there anything I can do, Nora?' Susan said. 'Anything at all?'

Yeah, Breda thought, you can piss off back to your fancy man – and hugged Billy tightly to her breast. Billy was the only thing she had over Susie Hooper and Billy was worth all the cashmere money could buy.

'Ain't you, son?' she said and, jogging him up and down, stalked off into the kitchen to give Nellie a piece of her mind.

Try as he might Ronnie couldn't stop thinking about Ruth Gertler. Ruth was everything Breda was not; well educated, politically active and sexually alluring, not to mention that her old man was the owner of the best butcher's shop in Shadwell. Unfortunately Ruth also had scruples and when he tried to shove a hand up her skirt told him in no uncertain terms that she wasn't that kind of girl.

Ruth was a leading light in a tight little pack of fast-talking young men and women who weren't interested in the king's affair with an American divorcee and whether or not Max Schmeling would beat Joe Louis in the boxing ring but could tell you why Italy had devalued the lira and martial law had been declared in Belgium. When it came to Spain, they knew everything there was to know, for several of them already had brothers fighting with the republicans and would read aloud from their letters at meetings in Mario's café.

Standing in Tower Hamlets cemetery Ron tried to pretend that his brother-in-law, Georgie, had been a brave young fighter and a brigade of battle-scarred anti-fascists would arrive to salute the horrible hole in the ground, and after the priest had gathered up his clobber and led the altar boys back to the motorcar, Ruth would be waiting to kiss him on each cheek: no Ruth, though, no military heroes, only Dad and he and big Steve Millar left to toss greasy London dirt on to Georgie's coffin, while Danny Cahill, the pride of Fleet Street, snivelled like a kid.

'A sad day, a sad day, but your brother's at rest now, safe

in the arms of Jesus, our Lord,' the priest told him. 'He'll be made welcome in heaven.'

Ron shook the priest's hand. 'I'm sure he will, Father. I'm sure he will.'

He stepped back, stepped away, and found himself staring into the face of a plump, sallow-skinned geezer in a tweed overcoat.

'You Ron?' the man asked.

'Yeah, I'm Ron.'

'I want a word with you, son,' Leo Romano said and, taking him by the arm, led him off down the path to the gate.

The Chrysler's windows were rivered with condensation. Millar, Matt Hooper and he were on the bench seat in back, Ron and Leo up front, Leo scrunched behind the wheel. In spite of his bulky overcoat, he looked quite small in the motorcar's cavernous interior. He'd put on his hat – a homburg – and everyone else had put on their hats too, even Steve Millar who could do no better than a grubby cloth cap by way of funeral headgear. They were all pretty agitated, Danny reckoned, all except Millar who probably didn't know who Leo Romano was.

'Here,' Leo said, holding up his hand. 'Take it.'

'What is it?' Ron said.

'What's it look like?'

'Looks like money,' Ron said. 'A lotta money.'

'Not so much,' said Leo. 'Take it.'

'What for?'

'Expenses.'

'I don't want your money,' Ron said sulkily.

'Give it 'ere then.' Matt leaned forward. 'I'll take it.'

'Yeah, you would too, you greedy old devil.' The roll of banknotes was hastily withdrawn. 'You were always out for what you could get.'

'Look who's talking,' Matt said.

Danny pushed Matt back in the seat and Steve Millar clamped a hand on the old man's knee to keep him still. Leo lobbed the roll of notes into Danny's lap.

'You I trust,' he said. 'You looked out for my boy?'

'I didn't look out for him well enough.'

'Who killed him?' Leo Romano said. 'Some friggin' copper?'

'Georgie was sick,' Matt blurted out. 'He was sicker'n any of us knew.'

'What was he doing on the street?'

'The band,' Ronnie said. 'He ran off to hear the band.'

Leo faced his son-in-law. 'Where were you?'

'Me? I – I was . . .'

'On the barricade,' Danny said. 'Where else would he be? We were all out throwing bricks at Mosley.'

'He shoulda been home with his wife and kid,' Leo said.

'Georgie was *your* kid,' Matt put in. 'Where the 'ell were *you* Sunday week, Romano? Out screwing some tart?'

Danny cocked an elbow to keep the men apart. 'What's wrong with you? We just buried Georgie an' here you are arguin' like weans. Show a bit o' respect, for God's sake.'

'He started it,' Matt sulked.

'Like hell, I did.'

'Look, Mr Romano,' Danny said, 'you can't blame us for what happened to Georgie. Take it from me, Georgie was blown long before I found him.'

'Blown?'

'Burst blood vessel in his brain.'

'Nobody hit him?'

'Naw, nobody hit him. What do you want me tae do with this cash?'

'Split it between Nora and Breda.'

'Why don't you give it to them yourself?' Danny said.

'He don't want nothing to do with them,' said Matt. 'He's ashamed.'

'Ashamed, am I?' Leo Romano snarled. 'We'll see who's ashamed,' and reaching for the ignition key switched on the Chrysler's engine.

Dockers and cabmen who might have popped in to pay their respects were at work and only six or seven elderly female neighbours turned up for the feed. Herr Brauschmidt had sent down a pound of sausage meat and six pig's trotters, though how Nora was supposed to serve trotters at a funeral feast Breda couldn't imagine. It was, she conceded, the thought that counted but some thoughts that should have counted rankled instead. When a whole veal loaf, wrapped in the *Jewish Chronicle*, was delivered from Gertler's, Breda dumped it straight into the dustbin for, in her jaundiced view, the loaf wasn't a generous gift from the butcher but the equivalent of two fingers – Ruth Gertler's two fingers – raised in ridicule.

The old women fell on the sandwiches like half-starved gulls. Susie Hooper glided among the tables, laughing with the women, teasing them, even refilling their teacups as if she were hosting a garden party. Brash little Billy, good as gold, tagged after his auntie to be petted, fussed over and fed bits of cake.

'What do you say, Billy?'

'Fanks very much.'

Thanks for what, Breda wondered, thanks for what?

She tipped whisky into her coffee cup, then, glancing up,

caught sight of a motorcar drawing up outside. 'They're here,' she said to no one in particular. 'They're back.'

The door opened. The old women stopped chattering.

Nellie Millar's brother entered the shop, cap pulled down on his brow. He held the door for a plump little bloke in a natty tweed overcoat.

Breda put down her coffee cup and stood up straight.

'Daddy,' she said. 'Oh, Daddy, I knew you'd come back one day,' and flung herself into his arms.

17

Vivian was still in her pyjamas and dressing-gown which, Susan told her, might be the way Noël Coward chose to work but was not becoming attire for a serious lady author to wear to set about her labours. *The Melting Pot* was not going well. Vivian's solution to creative sluggishness was not to slip off to a quiet seaside hotel, like Anna Maples, but to rise late, linger over breakfast and gossip with her assistant until the muse came upon her. She settled on the couch in the low-beamed, ground-floor room that served as an office. The gas fire purred, the desk lamp glowed, the coffee was strong and her second cigarette of the day tasted even better than the first.

'So' – she blew smoke – 'a splendid time was had by all?'

'Hardly,' Susan said. 'Frankly, it was all rather a mess.'

'Funerals often are. By the sound of it your friend Danny made an error of judgement in bringing Romano back with him. He's a communist, isn't he?'

'Danny? No, he says he's just a man of the people.'

'One seldom meets a Scot who admits to being anything else,' said Vivian. 'Moaning about poverty and persecution keeps them happy, I suppose. Breda's father, this Romano chap, tell me more about him.'

'He's rolling in money,' Susan said, 'which is part of the reason the reunion went off the rails. He tried to slip a hefty wedge to Nora.'

'A hefty wedge?'

'Cash.'

'Conscience money, of course,' said Vivian. 'The young man's sudden death probably engendered guilt in his absent father. What does Mr Romano do?'

'Manages a club in the West End, I think.'

'I take it you don't mean the Carlton?'

'A club where girls can be had.'

'Ah! A procurer,' said Vivian. 'I wonder if my brother knows him.'

'Surely David doesn't visit those places?'

'He owns several properties in the region of Soho.'

'Properties? I thought he was a farmer.'

'That's what you're supposed to think,' said Vivian. 'Personally I prefer not to pry too deeply into what David does. Tell me, were you involved in the fracas?'

'Not at first. The trouble really started when Mr Romano let slip that he and Danny Cahill were acquainted. Apparently, Danny hadn't told Breda he'd been meeting with her father. Breda was furious.'

'It's not quite Galsworthy, is it?'

'No, it's not,' Susan agreed. 'I'm rather glad I'm out of it.'

'Are you?' Vivian raised an eyebrow. 'Are you really out of it?'

'I've come to the conclusion they're not my kind of people.'

'What led you to that conclusion?'

'I don't like being called a harlot,' Susan said.

'Who called you a harlot?'

'Breda.' Susan paused. 'My father agreed. I'd no idea he hated me so much.'

'He doesn't hate you,' Vivian told her. 'He's upset because you refuse to conform to the image in which he created you.'

'You make him sound like God. He isn't God; far from it.'

'No, but he thinks he is. All men do,' said Vivian. 'Tell me, if you were married to Mercer Hughes what would your father think then?'

'He'd boast about me to every Tom, Dick and taxi driver from Silvertown to Bethnal Green. I'd be his pride and joy again. It's all moot in any case: Mercer can't marry me.'

'Mercer isn't the only fish in the sea.'

'Beg pardon?'

Stubbing out her cigarette, Vivian got to her feet. 'You heard me.'

'You told me once there's no one quite like Mercer Hughes; remember?'

'That doesn't mean he's the man for you.'

'Bit late to tell me that now,' said Susan.

'Is he still in love with you?'

'He says he is.'

'He's certainly shown no sign of wanting to be rid of you.' Vivian leaned on the desk, tucked her fist under her chin. 'If I were a man I'd snap you up myself.'

'Vivian!'

'Oh, be easy, be easy. Despite rumours to the contrary I do not – repeat not – belong to the top hat and monocle brigade,' Vivian said. 'I've never been quite sure whether it's better to have loved and lost or never to have loved at all. However, my dear, that isn't your problem.'

'What is my problem?'

'Not having loved enough,' said Vivian.

Susan shuffled papers on her desk. 'Are you ready to work yet?'

Vivian sighed. 'No help for it, I suppose. Where are we?'

'Freud, the Jew and the Myth of Cathexis.'
'Oh, God!' Vivian said. 'How dreary!'

Cooking, baking and washing up kept Nora from brooding. During business hours she could pretend Georgie was out in the shop chatting to the cabmen or behind her in the kitchen quietly occupied with his jigsaw puzzle. Evenings were not so easy. Nellie left at seven: Danny returned at midnight. For five hours she was alone in a house that had once seemed too small and now seemed too large.

She spun out her chores as long as possible before she climbed the narrow staircase to the first floor where Georgie's room lay dark and empty and there was nothing left to do but kneel by the side of her bed and weep until her throat hurt and her belly ached, and Danny came home and knocked on her door.

'All right, Nora?'

'All right,' she'd say, though she was far from all right.

For the best part of a fortnight she saw nothing of Breda, Billy, Ronnie or Matt. They were mad at her for accepting Leo's money. Fifty quid was fifty quid, though. It made up for earnings lost, paid for Georgie's funeral and left her a little nest egg, something she'd never had before.

'What's wrong with them, Danny? Why are they ignoring me? I'm not asking for anything.'

'With fifty quid in your pocket you don't have to,' Danny said. 'If it's any consolation, Nora, they're not very happy with me either. Sometimes I'm glad I never had a family.'

'You had the nuns?'

'Not quite the same thing.'

'Sure an' wasn't it the nuns gave you your name?'

'Wet nurse,' said Danny. 'Willing though the nuns were,

breast-feedin' a day-old infant was beyond them. The wet nurse gave me her name – Cahill. My forename too – Daniel. Said I was her wee lion cub. Nobody had the gall tae straighten out her muddled grasp o' the Bible story. She had milk on because she'd lost one o' her own. I think she thought I was the one she'd lost. She reckoned I was gonna be a priest. She'd be fair disappointed tae discover how I turned out.'

'Danny,' Nora said, 'you're not going to leave me, are you?'

'God, no! What gave you that idea?'

'They keep talkin' about Spain.'

'Well, they can keep talkin' far as I'm concerned,' Danny said. 'Mind you, I wouldn't put it past Ronnie to join the International Brigades.'

'To get away from Breda, you mean?'

'He'll kid himself he's doin' it to make the world safe for Billy.'

'He might get killed, though.'

'He might,' Danny admitted.

'Would Breda get a pension?'

'I doubt it.'

'She could always come back here.'

'That she could,' said Danny.

'Have her old room. I mean . . .'

'Georgie's room,' said Danny. 'Yeah, it's big enough.'

'I wouldn't mind that.'

'Naw, but Breda might.'

'She should've married you,' Nora said.

'Holy Orders here I come,' said Danny.

The wheelchair was an affectation, not a necessity. His mother could walk perfectly well when it suited her. He had a suspicion

– more than a suspicion, actually – that when he was out of town dear old Mater and the redoubtable Mrs Hartnell legged it up to the Ritz for afternoon tea or, more likely, promenaded along Kensington High Street, arm-in-arm, heading for the Bonne Femme coffee house where bookmakers' runners, heavily disguised, were known to hang out.

Mercer didn't need a deerstalker and magnifying glass to deduce that his mother had been squandering her money again. Galoshes streaked with mud, a ticket stub in a coat pocket, a hat tossed gaily on to a chair in the hallway usually indicated that a long shot had romped home at Goodwood or Kempton Park. But romping long shots were rarely the order of the day and he didn't have to dig deep for evidence of his mother's losing streaks.

Neither his mother nor her companion had turned up in the breakfast room. It was left to Annie, the day maid, to fetch his ham and eggs and offer him a grilled kidney if he wanted one. Three or four minutes later, she brought him the morning's mail neatly laid out on the silver salver that his father had won for pigeon shooting in the year before he, Mercer, had been born.

'Will that be all, sir?'

'Yes, thank you, Annie.' The girl sidled away.

He riffled through the mail, what there was of it, and soon found the long envelope with the name of the bank embossed on the back and his mother's name on the front. He had no compunction about ripping open the letter.

'Mother,' he shouted. 'Mother, a moment of your time, if you please.'

Her voice, a silvery little wisp of a voice, floated through the apartment.

'I'm not decent.'

'Decent or not,' Mercer called out, 'get your ar – yourself in here.'

He sat upright, scowling at the open door; waiting.

The breakfast room lay cheek by jowl with the drawing room. Both had an easterly aspect which, in theory, meant they received sunlight in the morning. In practice, the sun didn't reach the windows of the Hughes' apartment until well after noon, for the street was little more than a canyon of enormously tall, elegantly fronted buildings where the well-to-do lived, at considerable expense, piled one on top of the other. The wheelchair's rubber tyres squeaked on the parquet; a slow, laboured progress from the bedroom across the hall.

Yes, there she was: the loins that had borne him covered by a blanket, shoulders raised like those of a sparrow that hasn't quite learned to fly; her face, the gamine little face that had once launched if not a thousand ships at least a dozen punts and one or two canoes, tucked modestly into her chest – presumably so he couldn't see the deceit in her beady old eyes. She wasn't really old, of course; still on the sunny side of sixty and no more an invalid than he was.

Rhoda Hartnell towered over her, steering the chair. Her jet-black hair was pinned in a bun, the collar of her grey dress buttoned to the throat like a prison warder or a captain in the Salvation Army.

'What is it, darling?' his mother asked. 'Is it the kidneys?'

'No, it's not the kidneys,' Mercer answered. 'It's this.'

'Oh,' she said. 'The doctor's bill? I'm so, so sorry, Mercer. I've been in such pain of late and Dr Mackenzie's injections do bring me relief.'

'What's he injecting you with now, Mama: gold dust?'

Mrs Hartnell edged the chair close to the table, pinning him in. His mother's knees were inches from his and his height made her seem small and defenceless. He wondered what role she'd chosen to play today: Dora from *David Copperfield*, perhaps, or Nadia, the tubercular waif from Rupert Arlen's last novel but one?

'Such pain. Such pain.'

Alfred Hitchcock had laughed when he'd been offered Rupert's novel and said he would only direct a film version if he could bump off Nadia in the first reel.

'It's not Mackenzie's bill, Mother,' Mercer said. 'It's from the bank.'

She made it a question: 'A misunderstanding?'

'It's no misunderstanding. You're overdrawn by two hundred and forty-three pounds. What, in God's name, are you doing with your money?'

'It's the depression,' Mrs Hartnell explained. 'Interest rates are down.'

Mercer interrupted. 'What "sure thing" let you down this time, Mama?'

'It was only a little flutter,' his mother whispered.

'Two hundred and forty-three pounds is *not* a little flutter.'

'Finish your breakfast,' his mother told him.

'I've had enough. More than enough.' He pushed his plate to one side and waved the banker's letter. 'Look, I know you're bored. I know you miss the old days but I can't go on topping up your account at this rate. I'm not made of money.'

She injected a tremor into her voice; not quite a sob, not quite a whimper. As a boy he'd fallen for it every time, had done every damned thing except lick her silver slippers to appease her.

'All right,' he said. 'I'm sorry. Please don't cry.'

In the old days, so he'd been told, she'd haunted the best

casinos in Europe; Deauville had been her favourite. His father had been rich enough to indulge her but not long after he'd been born his father's libidinous nature had led him into the arms of other women and in due course he'd abandoned her, leaving Mercer, the one and only, to support her passion for the sport of kings. Her recent affliction, which David called 'selective arthritis', had become her excuse for profligacy. She had a comfortable monthly income from gilt-edged investments of her own; why the devil couldn't she live on it?

'I don't grudge you anything, Mama,' Mercer said. 'If you really must lay bets on rank outsiders, however, please, please limit yourself to a pound or two. That's all I ask. It isn't unreasonable, is it?'

Rhoda Hartnell sniffed; a sign of disapproval that Mercer knew well. Wasn't it enough that he kept her at a good address in Kensington, paid Hartnell's wages and the wages of a cook and a day maid? Did she require him to feed the families of every off-course bookie in west London too?

'I'll apply for an overdraft,' his mother said. 'You won't be bothered.'

'Damn it, of course I'll be bothered. Where do you think the money comes from? It doesn't grow on trees. Besides, your bank won't give you an overdraft.'

'I'm sure if you explain . . .'

'Explain what? That I'm already mortgaged to the hilt?'

'Are you?' Rhoda Hartnell said. 'Isn't Mercer Hughes and Ames one of the most successful agencies in London?'

'Well, it's not,' said Mercer. 'I mean, we're not going down the drain or anything but there's a limit to how much I can take out of the firm.'

'No limit on how much you spend on your lady friends, though.'

'That, Mama, is a calumny.'

'You're just like your father. He deserted me too.'

'I'm not bloody – I am not deserting you, Mother.'

'You deserted your poor wife; now it's my turn.'

'Would you care for an egg, Millicent?' Rhoda Hartnell put in.

'Yes, dear, I believe I could toy with a little something.'

'Boiled, scrambled or coddled?'

'Coddled.'

Mercer sighed. He should have dismissed the impertinent bitch years ago but she was his mother's sole companion and her presence in the apartment left him free to come and go as he pleased.

He consulted his wrist watch. 'I must be off. I really must.'

'What are you going to do, darling?' his mother asked.

He folded the banker's letter, put it in his inside pocket and got up. He kissed his mother on the cheek, turned on his heel and strode off into the hall where Annie waited with his overcoat and hat.

'Mercer,' his mother called out. 'What *are* you doing to do?'

Pay up, I suppose, he thought, and, saying nothing, stepped out on to the landing and made good his escape.

Ruth Gertler had never been a member of any of the clubs or institutions that had sprung up after the war to protect the morals of young Anglo-Jewish womanhood. She was a butcher's daughter for one thing, the oldest of five girls in a household that, thanks to Poppa, mingled respect for tradition with a deal of liberal thinking. But even her indulgent Poppa wouldn't stand for an affair with a *goy* who might be able to dissect a lamb carcase in twenty minutes but who also happened to be married. Until recently she'd been half promised to Jacob but somehow Myrtle had come between them and she no longer knew where she stood in that triangle.

She was well aware, however, that she'd never be Ronnie Hooper's wife or 'know him' physically – okay, have sex with him – but that didn't stop her wooing him for all she was worth, since if she couldn't have Ron for herself she'd have him for the cause and ship him off to Spain to fly her colours in the fight against Franco; to be, as it were, her champion.

If Susie had been at home she might have deduced what was going on but Ron hadn't clapped eyes on his sister since Georgie's funeral and doubted if she'd show up for Sunday tea any time soon. Meanwhile, Breda yapped on about every little thing. The only time she shut her gob was when he was on top of her and as soon as it was over she was at it again, nagging him for his inadequacies.

He was rushing home to feed his face, change clothes and get out to a 'Campaign for Spain' fund-raising drive when he bumped into Nora loitering at the corner of Thornton Street.

'Hello, Ma.' He pulled up. 'What you doing 'ere?'

'Got nothing to keep me home now, have I?'

'No,' he said, softening. 'Suppose not.'

'Walk me back to the shop, Ron, will you?'

He didn't have the heart to shake her off. He took her arm and led her down the street. 'How's Danny?'

'He's fine,' Nora answered. 'Danny's a good boy. He looks after me.'

'You ain't been down our way lately,' Ron said.

'Not welcome, am I?'

'I wouldn't say that, Nora. You're always welcome at our 'ouse.'

'Isn't your house, though, Ronnie, is it?'

'Well, I pay the rent – half the rent.'

'Sure an' that doesn't make it your house.'

'My house or not,' Ronnie said, 'you come Sunday, see Billy.'

'Not till Breda asks me, I won't.'

'All right then, I'll bring Billy up to see you.'

He tried to make out the time on the clock on the steeple but the light was poor and the face dim. There'd probably be something to eat at the fund-raiser. Afterwards he'd buy a fish tea but not in Fawley Street; he was too well known to risk taking Ruth to the fish bar.

'You gotta girl?' Nora blurted out.

'I got Breda, that's what you mean?'

'Jewish girl.'

He paused. 'Who told you that?'

'Nellie Millar.'

'She's got a big mouth, that kid.'

'Is it true?'

'No, it ain't true. I ain't cheating on Breda.' He bristled. 'Entitled to have friends, though, ain't I? What's wrong with having friends? What other porkies has Nellie Millar been telling you?'

'She says you're going off to Spain.'

'Does she?' Ron said. 'Shows what she knows.'

'They're all going to Spain, all the lads.'

'All what lads?' he asked.

'Them what cares.'

'Nora, you don't know what you're talkin' about.'

'How do you get to Spain?'

'Lots of ways,' Ron told her. 'First you go to Paris where they give you the right papers to see you over the border.'

'Costs money, I suppose, the right papers.'

'That's why we're raising funds.'

'Funds? Who's raising funds?' said Nora.

They were almost at Stratton's, the window unlit, blind drawn. If he hadn't had a date with Ruth he'd have gone in, let Nora make him supper and to hell with what Breda thought.

'Everybody's raising funds, Nora. Ain't you heard?'

'Funds for what?'

'Clothing, medicine, guns . . .'

'Guns?'

'It's a war, Nora. 'Course they need guns.'

'You could get killed.'

'Yeah.' He tried to laugh it off. 'But not stood here in Shadwell.'

She was nothing much to look at, his mother-in-law; a plain face, moon-shaped like Georgie's. What age was she? Fifty maybe? He couldn't imagine being fifty. Come to think of it, he couldn't imagine being thirty.

'You want to go off with your friends,' she said, 'I'll give you the fare.'

'Thanks,' Ronnie said, 'but no thanks.'

'Leo's paying for the stone.'

'What stone?' said Ronnie.

'The stone for Georgie.'

'I don't see what that's got to do with Spain.'

'How much do you need, Ronnie? Ten pounds, twenty?'

'For God's sake, Nora! I don't want your bleedin' money. I got Breda and Billy to look after.'

'If you don't go, Ronnie, you'll regret it all your life.' She drew two notes from her purse and held them up. 'Take them.'

'Can't take them, Nora.'

'Why not?'

''Cause I ain't going nowhere,' said Ronnie.

18

Bun-fights were common in Bloomsbury and Chelsea; much less so in Mayfair. An invitation to David Proudfoot's 'At Home' was, therefore, a prize worth having. As far as Vivian could make out there was no particular reason for the shindig because neither she nor any of David's other close friends was launching a book. Susan's invitation arrived a fortnight in advance of the party and took pride of place on her mantelshelf where Mercer could hardly fail to notice it when he dropped by.

'Ah hah!' he said. '*Et tu, Brute.*'

'Oh, come now,' Susan said. 'It's hardly a dagger to the heart.'

'And I'm no Caesar.' Mercer kissed her cheek. 'Am I?'

'Too much hair for Julius: Augustus I'm not so sure about.'

He hung his overcoat and hat in the alcove and pulled out a chair. 'Do you realise, young lady, that you're becoming quite the sophisticate?'

'Why? Because I know the name of more than one Roman emperor?'

'At least you didn't compare me to Caligula,' Mercer said. 'I suspect you've just read Gaines's new translation of *The Twelve Caesars*?'

'As a matter of fact I have.'

'More than I've done. Viv's copy, was it?'

'My copy,' Susan said. 'Bought spanking new from Hatch-ards.'

'You've more money than sense,' Mercer said. 'What possessed you to plunge into Suetonius?'

'Eric Kulgin's review in *The Times*.'

'I see.' Mercer pulled her on to his knee. 'I've often wondered who bought books on the strength of Kulgin's reviews. He and Gaines shared the same wife once upon a time, you know.'

'Shared a wife?' Susan said. 'Literally?'

'Yup. In fact the wife they shared wasn't married to either of them. She was married to a Prussian officer who treated her abominably. She deserted him in Cherbourg, of all places, fled to England, straight into the arms of Selwyn Gaines who, as it happened, was living in a tiny cottage near Maidenhead and splitting the cost with – guess who?'

'Eric Kulgin.'

'Cosy, what?' said Mercer. 'It was all a very long time ago, of course. The scandal cost Gaines his chance of a post at Cambridge and rendered Kulgin *persona non grata* until the war came along and washed away their sins.'

'What happened to the woman?'

'She took up with another man and went off to New York.'

Susan punched him lightly on the shoulder. 'You're making this up.'

'No need to make it up. Truth is stranger than fiction, especially when it concerns the English middle class.' He stroked her calf. 'Three to a bed, though. What do you think of that, Susan?'

She slipped from his knee and smoothed down her skirt.

'I think,' she said, 'if we're going out to dinner, we'd better go now.'

'Yes,' he said. 'Perhaps we better had.'

It struck Vivian as outrageous that a perfectly adequate lunch, with coffee, could be had for half a crown in the Café Royal but that two respectable women were not permitted to enter the dining room unless accompanied by a male. 'Do they take us for street-walkers?' she fumed. 'My mother must be turning in her grave.'

'I didn't know your mother was a suffragette,' Susan said.

'She didn't tie herself to railings or throw herself in front of a horse,' Vivian said, 'but she endured forty years of marriage to my father which is surely enough to establish her feminist credentials? In fact if she was with us right now she'd probably chain herself to the sweet trolley and be dragged, shrieking, through the Grill Room. What are we going to do? I'm famished.'

'We could pop over to the Lantern House,' Susan suggested.

'Oh, so you've been to the Lantern House, have you? I thought Mercer reserved that little hideaway for clients.'

'Once.' Susan held up a finger. 'I've been there once. If you're not up to it there's a Lyons Corner House in Leicester Square.'

'Now you are joking,' Vivian said.

Taking Susan's arm she ploughed through Regent Street traffic into the cobbled lane that dipped down to the restaurant. Mercer's office was perched above the Lantern House at the top of a narrow, rather smelly stair. Neither Susan nor, oddly, Vivian had ever been in Mercer's office, for he preferred to conduct business by letter and telephone or face to face across a dinner table.

'If Mercer's here,' Vivian said, 'he'll think we're spying on him.'

'Well, aren't we?' said Susan.

'Fair point,' Vivian said, chuckling, and pushed on.

The morning's work on *The Melting Pot* had ground to a halt. Lunch, it seemed, had been an afterthought, though Susan suspected that the outing was simply an excuse for avoiding work. Even at two in the afternoon the restaurant was busy. Unlike many traditional chop houses the Lantern House did not discourage women. Several tables were occupied exclusively by ladies of a certain age scoffing zabaglione or delicate fruit-flavoured sorbets.

Coats were removed and taken away. The head waiter, Mr Sydney, showed them to a table at the rear of the panelled dining room.

'Well,' said Vivian, settling down, 'this is all rather splendid.'

'If,' said Susan, 'you cast your eyes to the left, it'll seem even more splendid.'

'Good God!' Vivian put a hand to her mouth. 'Is that who I think it is?'

Embarrassed, Vivian buried her nose in the menu card but Susan continued to stare until Mercer, sensing her presence, detached himself from the pretty blonde girl who shared his table and came over.

'Well, well,' he said. 'What a pleasant surprise. Won't you join us?'

'Wouldn't dream of it,' said Vivian. 'Two's company.'

'Come now, Viv. It's not as if we're strangers. Look, she's saying hello.'

'So I see.' Vivian waggled her fingers in Eleanor's direction. 'May I ask, Mercer, what you're doing with my niece?'

'Showing her the ropes, of course.'

'What sort of ropes?' said Vivian.

'I thought you knew; she wants to be an author, like you.'

'And lunching *à deux* is an essential part of her training, is it?'

'Don't be so sour. There's nothing to it.'

'Does Gwen know there's nothing to it?'

'What sort of question's that?' Mercer drew himself closer to the table and looking down at Susan, said, 'Don't you see what she's doing? She's trying to make more of this than it really is. That's why she brought you here.'

'She didn't bring me here,' Susan said. 'It was my idea.'

'They wouldn't let us into the Café Royal,' Vivian added.

'But you knew I'd be here, didn't you?'

'We certainly didn't know you'd be here with Eleanor,' said Vivian. 'Isn't she coming over?'

'Perhaps she's shy,' said Susan.

'Eleanor? Shy? Nonsense!' Vivian said. 'Fetch her over, Mercer. She is my niece, after all.'

'Vivian,' Mercer said quietly, 'do not go off half cocked, please. She's only a young girl setting out on the voyage of life.'

'Oh, for God's sake!' Vivian exclaimed, then called across the dining room, 'Eleanor, do come and say hello to your dear old auntie. I'm not going to bite.'

For some unfathomable reason, there had been a heavy run on sausages of late. Herr Brauschmidt was grinding rusk and measuring his special seasoning while Ronnie fed lean pork and back fat into the bowl of the Peerless Combination. On guard against small boys and marauding dogs, Herr Brauschmidt bobbed up and down over the utensils and paid no heed to what Ronnie was saying.

'So,' Ronnie shouted, 'what do you think then? Think I should go?'

'Uh?' Herr Brauschmidt paused in his beating. 'Go to where?'

'Spain.'

The butcher's brows knitted fiercely. 'Who is going to Spain?'

'Me,' Ronnie said. 'Ain't you been listening?'

'It is not for you to fight in the Spanish war,' Herr Brauschmidt said. 'Here you are needed more.'

'You ain't heard a word I've said, 'ave you?' Ronnie said. 'I've been asking if you'd spring me for a month or two; maybe half a year.'

'Spring you? What is that?'

'Let me go.'

'Go to where?'

'I just told you – Spain,' Ronnie said. 'I can travel with a group from the YCL next week but I'd like to be sure when I get home again you'll give me my old job back.'

Herr Brauschmidt dropped the pestle into the bowl and switched off the Peerless. 'Have the Jews done this to you, Ronald?'

'The Jews haven't done nothing to me,' Ronnie answered. 'It's not just Jews I'd be travelling with, Mr Brauschmidt. Anyway, I thought you'd buried the hatchet with Mr Gertler?'

'Gertler is taking you from me, is that how the way of it is?'

'Mr Gertler has nothing to do with it,' Ronnie said, with a sigh. 'What have you got against him anyhow?'

'He steals my trade.'

'Some of your trade, yeah,' Ronnie conceded. 'Look, forget Mr Gertler. Forget I even mentioned his name. Thing is, Mr Brauschmidt, I don't wanna burn my boats; I mean, my bridges.'

'Boats, bridges? What piffle is this?'

Ronnie rested an elbow on the casing of the Peerless. 'I know you don't like Musso and aren't too keen on Adolf. Spain's the place to stop the fascists. I wanna do my bit, Mr Brauschmidt, before it's too late.'

'You have a wife, a child,' Herr Brauschmidt reminded him.

'Six months, maybe a year, that's all,' said Ronnie.

'I would need to take on another boy.'

'I appreciate that,' Ronnie said.

'What happens to that boy when you come back? It is an easy matter to be courageous when you are here in London. When the bullets are flying you will not be so brave then. Manhood! What a thing it is to be a man,' Herr Brauschmidt said without a trace of irony. 'It is not an order too tall for you, Ronald?'

'Maybe it is,' Ronnie said. 'Won't know till I try, will I?'

Warily, he eyed the big-bellied man who'd been his boss since the day he'd left school. He'd been yelled at and lectured by the ruddy-cheeked German bully and, in spite of it all, had been taught a useful trade. He watched Herr Brauschmidt step back from the machine and vanish into the rear of the shop.

A moment later he returned holding up a spotless white apron.

'What's that?' Ron asked.

'Your apron,' Herr Brauschmidt told him. 'Here for you

when you return,' then, folding the apron over his arm, reached out and switched on the machine.

Susan wasn't surprised when, around half past nine that evening, Mercer stormed into the flat. He threw his hat and coat to the floor and kicked out a chair. 'If you ever, *ever* do that to me again, Susan, we're finished. Do I make myself clear – finished.'

She remained in her armchair, a book in one hand, a cigarette in the other and tried to appear unruffled. 'Do what, Mercer? I did nothing out of the ordinary.'

'You were spying on me, weren't you?'

'That' – Susan drew on the cigarette – 'is merely your interpretation.' She put the book aside and stubbed out the cigarette. She was astonished at the ease with which the question slid off her tongue. 'Are you sleeping with her yet, Mercer?'

'She's a child, for heaven's sake,' Mercer said.

'Vivian doesn't think she's a child. She thinks you're heading for trouble.'

'Eleanor Proudfoot is the daughter of a very dear friend.'

'Do you mean David,' Susan asked, 'or Gwen?'

'I mean both, of course.'

'Eleanor's in love with you.'

'Of course she is. I'm not in love with her, though. I'm in love with you.'

'Are you?' Susan said.

'You know perfectly well I am.'

'I'm not so sure I do,' she said carefully. 'I'm not even sure it matters very much whether you are or aren't.'

'And I thought I was a cynic.'

'It's not cynicism,' Susan said. 'It's common sense. Why

else would you take up with a girl like me except for the fun of it? You don't have to pretend you love me. And I don't have to pretend I love you. I'm not one of your Bloomsbury ladies to whom "art" is just an excuse for sleeping with everyone and anyone. If you leave me for someone else I won't fall into a black depression. I won't expect pity for the simple reason that I don't deserve it.'

'What if I were to ask you to marry me?'

'You won't because you can't.'

'If I could; if, say, I set about divorcing my wife?'

'Now why would you do that?'

'To prove I love you.'

'You don't have to prove anything, Mercer. You have me right here and now.' She smiled. 'Make the most of it.'

'Susan,' he said, 'is there someone else?'

'Do you take me for a complete fool?' Susan said. 'I've a job that pays three times what I'd earn in a typing agency, a flat in a nice part of town – and I have a man, a very nice man who takes me out to dinner, buys theatre tickets and makes love to me. Why would I want to risk losing all that just for the sake of sleeping with someone else?'

'Am I a very nice man?'

'I don't know. Are you?'

At length, he said, 'No, Susan, I am not a nice man.'

'Didn't you love her even a little?' Susan said.

'Once upon a time I thought I did but it was over before I met Rosalind.'

'With Gwen, you mean?'

He nodded. 'Yes, Gwen.'

'Does David know?'

'Of course,' Mercer said. 'He doesn't care.'

'Do you?'

He spread his hands. 'Things change.'
'Mercer,' Susan said, 'are you in trouble?'
He looked at her for a long time before he answered.
'Yes.'

19

It was typical of David Proudfoot to call his party an 'At Home' with its overtones of sedate afternoon tea parties where well-mannered ladies discussed the servant problem. There was nothing sedate or well mannered about the guests who drifted into Proudfoot's town house in a polished granite building west of Grosvenor Square to encounter friends – or rivals – in the huge drawing room which, with the carpet taken up, had been converted into a ballroom complete with, of all things, a five-piece Negro band.

'Black men, David? Black men?'

'Oh, you're quite safe, Cecile, provided we keep them off the rum.'

'You're doing this to torment me, aren't you, darling?'

'Of course I am, Cecile. Of course I am.'

There were no children in frills and satin shorts going the rounds with trays of fish paste sandwiches; no elderly gentlemen in mouldy dinner jackets reminiscing about the good old days on the river; no chatelaines fresh up from the country still smelling of dogs and horse manure; no dim-witted young attachés with prominent Adam's apples chattering about their year in the Middle East, or vacuous dumplings, powdered and primped, to flirt with them: the guest list had been hand-picked from the sixteen levels of society.

'What the devil are you playing at, David? Who are these people?'

'Friends and friends of friends.'

'My God, half of them look like gangsters.'

'Half of them are, Oliver, half of them are.'

Patou and Vionnet, Chanel and Mainbocher; princesse fronts, peacock's tails and jewelled belts; the cream of international fashion rubbed shoulders with cotton blousons, French berets and stiff little off-the-pegs taken in and trimmed by somebody's nervous maid with a mouth full of needles and pins.

'I'm really at a loss to understand what I'm doing here, David.'

'You're here to have fun, Philippa.'

'I've nothing in common with most of these people.'

'Oh, but you do, my dear, you do.'

'And what, may I ask, might that be?'

'You have money to burn,' said David.

Game pies, seafood flans and other cold collations were laid out on long tables in the broad corridor that linked the cloakrooms to the entrance hall. Barmen and waiters in tight white bum-freezers served drink in crystal glasses and food on gold-rimmed plates. The guests, juggling delicacies, sought space in adjacent rooms or seated themselves on the magnificent curved staircase that soared up to the floor above where from a little rococo balcony Gwen Proudfoot, champagne glass in hand, aloofly surveyed the scene.

Susan assumed that the kitchens and servants' quarters were tucked out of sight below and that family rooms, four or five at least, lay somewhere upstairs; a far cry in size and scale from the farmhouse at Hackles. She was amazed at the grandeur of the apartments; even more amazed that a modest, muddy-booted apple grower like David Proudfoot not only owned such a fabulous town house but that he was eager to show it off.

Two broad-shouldered gentlemen in evening dress had checked their invitation cards before admitting them to the spacious hallway where David, Eleanor and Caro waited to greet them.

'Hi, kid,' Mercer said. 'Long time no see. You've grown.'

'Have I?' Caro glanced down at her chest. 'Yes, I suppose I have.'

'And you, my dear young thing,' Mercer said, 'have never looked lovelier.'

'Thank you, kind sir,' said Eleanor and bussed his cheek.

Sweeping back the jacket of her new silk satin evening suit, Vivian gave her brother a bear hug. 'Proudfoot Manor's had a lick of paint since last I saw it. Been selling off the family silver?'

'Better than that, much better,' David informed her.

'Really? Do tell.'

'Later,' he promised. 'You know where everything is, don't you? Powder room's third left – that way. Drinkies – just there.'

'Dear Susan' – Caro reached for her hand – 'I do like your dress.'

'Thank you. You've had your hair cut.'

'Styled by Poggio, I'll have you know,' said Caro.

'No more pigtails?'

'Absolutely not,' Caro said, then stepped forward to welcome three men who were not, emphatically not, from her set.

★

Old Bags Bageshot would have pegged him immediately but reporters hadn't been included on David's list of invitations. Those in the know recognised the fellow, of course, and with the obsequiousness of born scroungers shook his hand and reeled away declaring that he wasn't at all what they'd expected and to judge by the cut of his evening suit wasn't even wearing a gun.

Susan left Mercer and Vivian to socialise while she explored the amazing house. Gwen was no longer poised on the wrought-iron balcony. David and his daughters were still hovering by the doorway as she drifted into a passageway that cut across the ground floor. Here couples were engaged in intimate conversation and four stout men, nursing whisky glasses, were so deep in discussion that they spared her not a glance. She was drawn to a brightly lit alcove, on the wall of which hung a large painting in a gilded frame; a painting that even she could tell was worth a bob or two.

'Horses,' said a voice behind her, 'you like horses?'

She glanced round. 'Mr Romano, what are *you* doing 'ere – here?'

'Got a white tie and tails like everybody else, ha'n't I?' Leo Romano said affably. He nodded. 'Know what that is? That's a Stubbs; one of the few not in captivity. Set you back the best part of three grand if it came on the market.'

'I hadn't realised you were an expert on art.'

'Expert on what's worth nicking, more like. How's my boy?'

'Billy? I haven't seen him lately, I'm afraid.'

'Don't get down that way much, I expect.'

'Not often, no.'

'Can't say I blame you,' Leo said. 'How'd you learn to talk proper?'

'Elocution lessons,' Susan said. ''Arf-cran a pop.'

He laughed. He didn't appear out of place here. His suit was immaculately tailored and there was no hint of ostentation in any of the accessories. He looked younger than she remembered him, rather chic too.

He said, 'Who you come with?'

'My employer, Vivian Proudfoot.'

'Yeah, the sister. Read one of her books once.'

'And you, Mr Romano, are you here with your wife?'

'Being polite, are we? Nora's my wife.'

'Of course,' Susan said. 'I'm sorry.'

'Shouldn't never have married Nora. Hadn't been for Georgie never would have neither. Had my sights set high even in them days – pardon me, *those* days. We got that much in common, Miss Hooper.'

'What's that, Mr Romano?'

'Ambition.'

'I don't think I'm ambitious, just . . .' She hesitated.

'Must be a word for it,' Leo Romano said. 'Ask your boss.'

'I'm not sure she'd know,' Susan said. 'Are you here with your boss?'

'Reckoned we'd get around to him eventually,' Leo Romano said. 'You wanna meet him, I suppose.'

'Not particularly,' Susan said, 'since I don't even know who he is.'

'Your friend Danny could tell you.'

'I don't see much of Danny either.'

Leo rested his shoulder against the wall close to the heavy gilt frame. 'Danny not been giving you the flutter then?'

'The flutter?'

'He carries your picture next to his heart.'

'Nonsense!'

'Nice girl like you don't know the flutter when you see it then Cahill isn't the man I thought he was,' Leo said.

'I already have a friend; a special friend.'

'One of Proudfoot's crew?'

'He's an agent, a literary agent.'

'Hughes, you mean?' Leo said.

'Yes, do you know him?'

'I know him,' Leo said. 'Sure I know him.'

'Who is your boss, Mr Romano? Is he an entertainment manager too?'

'I guess you might say that,' Leo told her, then with a hand on her waist, steered her out of the alcove and back to join the throng at the buffet table.

'Oh,' Vivian said, through a mouthful of seafood flan, '*that's* Leo Romano, is it? He doesn't look awfully fearsome to me. He arrived with Harry King.'

'Who's Harry King?' said Susan.

'Owns clubs all over London.' Vivian slurped a mouthful of champagne and scooped another forkful of flan from her plate. 'He's no Jack Spot, no thug from the streets who's gone up in the world. Comes from quite good stock, I believe, though I wouldn't want to get on the wrong side of him.'

'What's he doing here?'

'Business, probably,' Vivian said.

'Business with David?'

'I told you, I do not pry into my brother's affairs,' Vivian said. 'Rather a coincidence, though, you being related to one of King's cronies.'

'I'm not related to Leo Romano – well, not directly,' Susan said. 'He claims to know Mercer, though.'

'I doubt if Mercer knows him.' Vivian chewed vigorously. 'It's all so very incestuous at that level.'

'What level?'

Vivian had no opportunity to reply. Caro bobbed up to claim Susan's attention and Vivian wandered off in search of seconds.

'Do you like our house?' Caro began.

'I do.'

'It is rather splendid, isn't it?' the girl said. 'Mummy's not so keen. I think she prefers the simple life.'

'How long have you lived here?'

'Not terribly long. Five years, I think. Yes, five years,' Caro said. 'Daddy sold some houses somewhere and made a lot of money and bought this place. It costs a fortune to keep up. Awfully handy for the theatre, though, and the cinema. I like the cinema. Do you like the cinema, Susan?'

'I do,' said Susan again. 'Doesn't Eleanor get bored here?'

'In London? Not her. She's not a country girl, like me.'

'What,' Susan said, 'does she do with herself all day long?'

'She has friends, lots of friends. She goes to meetings.'

'What sort of meetings?'

Caro put a finger to her lips. 'That's a surprise.'

'Your family seems to like surprises.'

'Oh, yes,' said Caro. 'We're full of them.'

'Where are you taking me?'

'I know you like books so I thought you might care to see the library.'

'Are you sure your father won't mind?'

'No, he won't mind. I know where he keeps the key.'

The road that ran the length of the sugar warehouse was quiet at that time of night. There was romance of a kind in the shabby neighbourhood: cobbles glistened with a river mist, haloes surrounded the gas lamps and you could taste the air, sweet and almost sickly, on your lips. They were walking home, boy and girl striding out briskly, he with an arm over her shoulders, she with an arm about his waist like children playing gee-gees or a couple practising for a three-legged race. Every now and then one would stop and draw the other into a shuttered doorway or against the iron gates that closed off the alleys. They would kiss once then move on, linked in perfect unison and talking all the while.

'It's simple, Ronnie,' Ruth told him. 'You'll travel with the boys from the Stepney branch and you won't have to think for yourself.'

'Is Jacob going?'

'Jacob and Moshe and three others. Myrtle's trying to get out there too with one of the nursing units.'

'It seems – I dunno – premature.'

'Better now than never,' the girl said. 'If the French decide to close the border it might become difficult to get into Spain at all.'

'I don't have a passport.'

'That's the beauty of it,' Ruth said. 'If you travel on a weekend return ticket to Paris you don't need a passport.'

'Does Jacob have a passport?'

'Nobody has a passport. Passports cost too much.'

'How much for the ticket?'

'I told you – twenty-eight shillings. My poppa will pay your fare if I ask him. If he won't then the party . . .'

She swung him round and pulled him into a doorway.

She wore the short black coat and a sweater and had flung the coat open. Somewhere back at the meeting hall she'd taken off her brassiere and had hidden it in the handbag that swung against her hip. He could feel the weight of her breast, nipple rising against the palm of his hand. Ruth was nothing like Breda, not her lips, not her breasts. He didn't know if that was because she was Jewish or because she'd never had a kid, or if it was just one of those things.

They broke and moved on.

'It's not the dough,' Ron said. 'I can scrape up the dough if I 'ave to.'

'But you don't want to leave your wife with nothing, do you?'

'She won't go short,' Ron said, 'not Breda.'

'Think of it, Ron,' the girl said, 'boat train to Paris, then on to Perpignan, then straight over the Pyrenees.'

'Marching?'

'In trucks. I'm sure they'll have trucks. God, how I envy you.'

They had come round the long curve by the sugar warehouse and saw the bright lights of the Shadwell thoroughfare ahead of them, a tram rattling past. No shelter here, no nook or alcove to hide in. She pulled him against her, leaned on the wall, thighs locking his hips, skirt bunched up.

'Will you do it, Ronnie? Will you do it for me?' she said.

'Not for the cause, Ruth?'

'No,' Ruth said. 'For me.'

The library wasn't locked. The door was panelled oak, painted green. The brass knob was bigger than Caro's fist. She giggled naughtily, turned the knob, pushed open the door and ushered Susan ahead of her.

The windows were draped with heavy velvet curtains, the room lit only by firelight, two standing lamps and reflections in the many glass-fronted bookcases. A studded leather sofa and a pair of Georgian armchairs flanked a coffee table set with silverware, cups and glasses. There were two strangers in the room. One was eating a sandwich and sipping beer from a plain pint glass. He wasn't dressed for dancing but wore the sort of jacket aviators wear, all pockets and flaps.

'Hello, ladies,' he said in a high voice. 'Are you the entertainment?'

The other man rose politely from the sofa. He was munching a sandwich but appeared to prefer tea to beer. He was small and barrel-chested, with a thick mop of greying hair and a big moustache and his shirt was open at the throat in a style favoured by gauche young poets.

'Easy, Clive, easy,' the moustache said. 'What we have here are daughters.'

'Oh, I'm frightfully sorry,' Caro said. 'I had no idea. I mean, does my father know you're here?'

Clive winked. 'He does, but I'll wager he doesn't know you're here.'

'Nor would he be too pleased about it,' the moustache said.

'Do – do you require anything?' Caro stammered. 'Champagne?'

'A little of your big sister's company wouldn't go wrong,' said Clive.

'She isn't . . .' Caro began; Susan nudged her.

'Did David send you?' the moustache asked.

'No,' Caro answered, 'we just happened to be in this part of the house.'

'Then,' Clive said, 'I suggest you cut along.'

'And keep your mouths shut,' said the moustache.

Susan drew Caro out into the passageway and carefully closed the door.

'Who on earth are they?' Caro whispered.

'I thought they might be one of your surprises,' Susan said.

'A complete surprise to me,' said Caro. 'Why are they lurking in the library and why are they dressed like that? What do you think we should do, Susan?'

'Cut along and keep our mouths shut,' said Susan wisely.

By eleven o'clock the party was in full swing. Susan was treated to the comical sight of Eric Kulgin dancing with Vivian, his bristling little goatee not much above the level of her bosom. Gwen had fluttered down from her eyrie and was locked in the arms of an effeminate-looking fellow somewhat her junior who, whatever his other failings, was as light on his feet as Fred Astaire.

Even Caro had snared a partner: a mop-haired young Welshman who cared so little for convention that he'd turned up in a fisherman's sweater and had been lucky not to be thrown down the steps by the doormen.

'Wanna dance?'

He was a large man, broad in the shoulder, trim at the waist. He wore a red cummerbund under his dinner jacket. His jet-black hair was slicked down with Brylcreem and he had a scar, a pinched fold of flesh at the corner of his mouth. He spoke softly, persuasively.

'I'm not sure I'm familiar with this tune,' Susan said.

He held out his hands, large hands with perfectly manicured nails. 'Sure you are. Everybody knows "I'm Hitchin' my Wagon to You".'

She moved into his arms and followed his steps as best she could as he guided her past the bandstand.

'Woo-hoo, Susan,' Caro called across the room; she was still dancing with the curly-haired Welshman. 'Who's your friend?'

'Who is my friend, by the way?' Susan said.

'You can call me Eddie.'

'I'm—'

'I know who you are.'

'Yes,' Susan said, 'I thought you might. Did Leo send you?'

'Leo? Who's Leo?'

'Come off it,' Susan said. 'I may look posh but—'

'You don't look posh,' Eddie said. 'You look good, but you don't look posh.'

'That's disappointing,' Susan said. 'Where is Leo? In the library?'

'You talk a lot, doncha?'

'I'm just making conversation.'

'Best not to do that,' Eddie said.

'Aren't you supposed to add "If you know what's good for you"?'

'Be an insult to your intelligence, wouldn't it?'

'Yes, I suppose it would,' Susan said. 'What do you want me to do?'

'Dance,' said Eddie. 'Just dance.'

20

With nine people crowded into the library there weren't enough chairs to go round. The gentlemen gallantly yielded the sofa to the ladies while Harry King occupied a Georgian armchair as if it were a throne. Mercer recognised the women, Philippa and Cecile, both wealthy widows, but none of the men. Positioned in front of the fireplace, David rocked on the balls of his feet like a lord of the manor and waited for everyone to settle.

At length, he stuck his hands in his pockets and said, 'Gentlemen and ladies, welcome. I've invited you here this evening because I know you have money at your disposal and an interest in making more. Discretion, however, is required for the simple reason that the proposal I will shortly put before you is not quite legal.' He paused. 'Does anyone have a problem with that? Cecile?'

'Not I,' the woman answered. 'I barely know the meaning of the word.'

'How legal is not quite?' one man asked. 'I'd like to know who I'm getting into bed with. After that near-run thing in Hammersmith—'

David cut him short. 'This isn't Hammersmith, Oliver. It has nothing to do with building regulations – or bribes.'

'What does it have to do with?'

'Aeroplanes,' said David. 'The buying and selling thereof.'

'I take it,' Philippa said, 'you're talking about Spain.'

'I am indeed talking about Spain.'

'Aren't the Germans supplying Franco's army?'

'They are,' David said. 'But who said anything about Franco?'

'Oh, come now, David,' Philippa said, 'surely you wouldn't stoop to selling arms to the damned republicans.'

'Do the republicans have any dough?' said Oliver.

'Yes,' David said. 'They have dough. What they don't have is an air force. The government ban on the export of arms has hit them hard. The big aviation companies have no option but to close down dealings with both sides. Not that it's made a blind bit of difference to the arms dealers. Walk into the Waldorf Hotel in the Aldwych and you'll trip over a dozen of them eager to buy anything with wings.'

'Including junk?' said Oliver.

'Including junk,' said David. 'Croydon's littered with serviceable planes the vendors daren't move. Locked hangars at de Havilland are also the order of the day. So, yes, Oliver, junk is a highly marketable commodity at present.'

'And junk,' said Harry King, 'you have?'

'I do,' David said, 'or, to be more precise, these gentlemen do.'

'And who precisely are these – ah, gentlemen?' said Philippa.

'Pilots,' said David. 'Pilots with enough experience not only to service planes but to make sure they get to Spain unscathed.'

'You.' Harry King pointed a finger at Clive. 'Is what he says true?'

'Yes, sir, it is.'

'After the planes get there how long will they last?' Cecile asked.

217

'Not long, ma'am.' Clive grinned. 'Forty, maybe fifty hours' flying time. We change sound engines for duds before we ship 'em out.'

'In a sense, therefore,' Cecile said, 'we're doing the communists no favours?'

'We're draining their coffers, ma'am, that's all.'

'What if the planes don't get there?' said Oliver. 'What if they crash?'

'We die, sir,' Clive told him cheerfully.

'And how much do you get paid for dying, young man?' said Philippa.

'One hundred and twenty pounds per trip,' Clive told her. 'Plus six per cent of the selling price. All up front, of course.'

'How many planes you got, son?' said Harry King.

'Four,' Clive said. 'They don't have export licences and aren't registered to the original owners so the Air Ministry can't trace them.'

'What about the Foreign Office?' Cecile said. 'My friend the Honourable Mrs Bruce has had the devil's own problems with the Foreign Office.'

'The planes are lost property, ma'am,' said Clive. 'Let's leave it at that.'

'What are the planes?' Cecile said. 'What type?'

'Four Dragons used as air ambulances,' Clive said. 'They can be converted into bombers by somebody who knows what they're doing.'

'Does anyone in Spain who isn't German know what they're doing?' Philippa's remark drew laughter. 'Now, tell me, young man, what are four old Dragon aeroplanes worth to the republicans?'

'Twenty thousand the packet.'

'What's it gonna cost us, round figures, to buy four planes ready to ship?' said Harry King.

'Five thousand all told.'

'By my rough calculation,' David said, 'an investment of one thousand pounds each will earn us a profit of close to four hundred per cent.'

'Is there a risk?' said Oliver.

'Of course,' David said. 'It's an arms deal. There's always a risk. If there wasn't a risk I'd be taking on the whole bill myself.'

'Where are the planes now?' Philippa asked.

David answered, 'Hidden in barns and outbuildings in the vicinity of a private airfield in Herefordshire.'

'Oh, smart,' said Cecile. 'Very smart.'

'Well, gentlemen and ladies,' David said. 'If any of you want to walk, now's the time to do it.' He glanced round the room: no one stirred. 'Shall I continue?'

'Oh, yeah,' said Harry King. 'Please do.'

Susan was surprised when Eleanor appeared in the ballroom in fascist uniform. The black blouse and mid-length grey skirt emphasised her blondeness and she was certainly the most striking of the six young women who marched beneath the standard of the BUF. The flag, on its long pole, was too cumbersome for an indoor event and narrowly missed decapitating the piano player as the little parade swept round the room before, all very crisp and military, the flag was draped across the front of the bandstand.

'Geeze!' Eddie growled. 'What couldn't I do to 'er.'

'Which one?' said Susan.

'The blondie with the big – the blue eyes.'

'I'll introduce you later.' Susan felt it was the least she

could do. 'Her name's Eleanor, by the way; Mr Proudfoot's daughter.'

'Too posh for the likes of me then.'

'I wouldn't be so sure,' said Susan.

The Honourable Mrs Gertrude Brookes, commander of the unit, stepped forward and raised a hand. Her voice was almost as plummy as Tom Mosley's and quite loud enough, Susan thought, to rattle windows in Park Lane.

'It will not have escaped your notice,' Mrs Brookes shouted, 'that fifteen thousand Labour supporters were recently foolish enough to assemble in pouring rain in Trafalgar Square and under the guise – the deceitful guise – of mourning the republican dead voiced their condemnation of the nationalist coup d'état in Spain.'

'Hear, hear,' someone, a woman, called out.

'Thank you, Nancy,' the Honourable Mrs Brookes said with a smile. 'I trust you'll endorse our cause financially as well as vocally.'

'I will, Gertrude, be sure I will.'

'If the *DailyWorker* is to be believed the sum of four hundred and eighty pounds was collected that dismal afternoon in Trafalgar Square. Four hundred and eighty pounds with, no doubt, many a "bent tanner" included. Now, my friends – David's friends – are we not better than fifteen thousand rain-soaked communists?'

'We are, Gertrude, of course we are.'

'Can we, bone dry, not do better than five hundred pounds?'

'We can, yes, we can.'

'My girls will shortly be coming round with collection plates so let's do the British Union proud and in the process thank David for opening his home to us. Cheques made out to cash are acceptable, though banknotes are preferred. Dig deep, my friends; help stem the rising tide of communism and keep the Red terror out of our homeland.'

'What's the money for exactly?' Eddie whispered.

'Arms for Spain,' Susan said. 'No reason why the Popular Front should have it all their own way. They're collecting for Franco.'

Fishing in the pocket of his monkey suit, Eddie brought out his wallet.

'How much you think? Tenner?' he asked.

'A tenner would be a generous contribution from a working man.'

He grinned. 'There you go with that lip again.'

Eleanor came towards them, half-heeled shoes clopping on the wooden floor, cheeks glowing with excitement, bosom heaving. She held the plate in both hands and shook it as if it were a collecting can. Four large-denomination banknotes already adorned the silverware and one cheque, face down.

'Susan?' She thrust the plate forward. 'Surely you won't let us down?'

'My purse – I mean . . .'

Like a card trick, a feat of legerdemain, Eddie opened his fist and displayed a posy of banknotes. 'From both of us,' he said. 'Her and me.'

'Oh, really!' Eleanor said. 'And who might you be?'

'Eddie, Miss Proudfoot,' Susan said. 'Eleanor to her friends.'

Eddie waved the posy of notes tantalisingly out of Eleanor's reach. She glanced at Susan, then, squeezing the rim of the plate against her chest, grabbed at the cash as if she were chasing a butterfly.

'Don't tease me, please,' Eleanor said through her teeth.

'I ain't teasing you, Miss Proudfoot. Gotta question, though?'

'What,' she said, 'is that?'

'How much you charge for a dance?'

'What?' Eleanor cocked her head and gave Mr Eddie the full, fatal flutter. 'How much do you have in your hand?'

'Twenty quid.'

'Double it,' said Eleanor, 'and I'm yours for the last waltz.'

Susan watched Eddie's fingers close into his palm then open to show not a posy but a fan of eight pale five pound notes.

'This do?' Eddie asked.

'Oh, yes, that will do nicely.' Eleanor plucked the notes from Eddie's fingertips and dropped them into the silver plate.

'See you later, Mr Eddie,' she said.

'Miss Proudfoot, I can hardly wait.'

She pushed him away so hard that the bedhead thumped against the wall and brought down a little shower of dust and plaster.

'Get your bleedin' paws off me, Ronnie,' Breda snapped. 'You think you're gonna 'ave your fun when I don't know where you been?'

Ronnie brushed plaster dust from his bare chest and reached out again.

'Breee-da, come on, gal, don't tell me you don't want it?'

Nostrils pinched, lips compressed, cheeks swollen with indignation, she looked, Ronnie thought, like one of those bullfrogs you saw in magazines who can puff themselves up until they explode. He was tempted to tell her he'd done nothing with Ruth Gertler because he was saving himself for her; not that it was true, not strictly true anyway. He let out a sigh and throwing himself back against the pillow stared up at the damaged ceiling.

'Look at that crack,' he said. 'I really gotta do something about that crack.'

She exploded at last: 'Bastard!'

She humped up like a whale under the blankets and thudded down on her flank. He cocked his knee and experimentally nudged her buttocks. She let out a muffled grunt, jerked her hips and plastered herself against the corner wall. He'd had her like that before, feet braced against the wall, body arched against him, rocking – but probably not tonight.

He put his mouth close to her ear. 'You know where I been, Breda,' he said softly. 'I been to a meeting. Geezer talking about Spain. Just back from Madrid, he was. You think we got things bad 'ere, you ain't heard the half of it. When it comes from the horse's mouth it sure brings it closer to home.'

Still muffled: 'She there?'

'Who's that?'

'Your Jewish tart?'

'I don't have a Jewish tart, Breda. I don't have any sort of tart.' He paused. 'If you mean Miss Gertler, yeah, Miss Gertler was at the meeting and, yeah, we exchanged a few words afterwards.'

'And what else, Ronnie? What else did you exchange?'

At least she was talking; that was a start. If he played his cards right he might yet persuade her to give him what he wanted, but then it struck him just how demeaning it was for a man to have to beg for it, especially from his wife.

'Nothing,' he said curtly, and rolled away.

He lay with arms raised, hands behind his head, staring at the ceiling and listening to the night sounds, the house sounds, the sound of his father snoring and the stealthy creak of bed springs as Breda adjusted position. He wasn't really thinking about Breda now. He was thinking about Ruth and how soft her belly had been when his hand had found it; thinking too about Paris and riding over the mountains in the back of a truck, a man among men.

Breda raised herself on an elbow. 'You finished?'

'Finished?'

'You was telling me about the meeting.'

'I didn't think you were interested.'

'Interested in what you done afterwards.'

'I told you, Breda, I done nothing.'

She shifted once more and groped beneath the sheets.

'No, Breda,' he said quietly. 'No.'

'I thought you was ready for it?'

He didn't need his wife's capitulation or her charity. He just wanted to be left alone to think about Ruth; Ruth and Spain.

'Listen,' he said, 'is that Billy crying?'

'Nah, Billy's sound asleep.'

Billy isn't the only one, Ronnie thought.

And sliding away from her, he turned on his side to sleep.

It was close to midnight, perhaps a little after, before Mercer appeared. Loping across the floor, he swept Susan into his arms. She'd had her fair share of dancing by then and had been quite relieved when Eleanor, defying convention, had prised Eddie away from her in the middle of a tango.

She'd slipped off to the buffet, downed two quick glasses of champagne and nibbled a soggy slice of seafood flan while watching her employer and Anna Maples arguing with Eric Kulgin, Gwen Proudfoot and another, younger man. She'd also glimpsed Caro being kissed by the Welshman in a nook under the balcony and had wondered what Mama would say if she saw how readily her schoolgirl daughter had taken to the art of osculation.

'You've improved,' Mercer said.

'It's all the practice I've had – no thanks to you.'

'Who's Eleanor dancing with?'

'My instructor,' Susan said. 'Name of Eddie.'

'She seems very keen on him.'

'She's just over-excited,' said Susan. 'Where have you been?'

'Having a quiet drink with David. I didn't mean to neglect you, Susie. It was – well, a little bit of business.'

'Don't tell me you've persuaded Harry King to write his memoirs?'

'What do you know about Harry King?'

'He's my brother's father-in-law's boss.'

'Of course he is. I'd forgotten the family connection,' Mercer said.

'Eddie was sent to keep me out of the way.'

'I don't believe that for one minute,' Mercer said.

'He did it rather well, actually. By the by, you missed the collection.'

'Collection? What collection?'

'Cash for the nationalists.'

'Is that why Eleanor's wearing her uniform?'

'Oh, you knew she'd joined the party, did you?'

'I believe Vivian mentioned it.'

He seemed awkward tonight, almost ungainly.

Susan said, 'I wonder what they wear underneath?'

'Beg pardon?'

'Beneath the blouse and skirt. Does the uniform stretch to lingerie?'

'How the devil would I know?'

'I just thought you might have heard from – from someone.'

'What is wrong with you?' Mercer said.

'Absolutely not a thing. What about you? Are you in more trouble?'

'On the contrary,' Mercer said. 'My troubles have melted away.'

'Is that why you're touching my bum?'

'Am I? Gosh, I'm sorry.'

'I don't think you're in the least sorry. If you were you'd stop doing it.'

'Do you want me to stop doing it?'

'Not if it gives you pleasure – though it might get us talked about.'

'I doubt it,' Mercer said. 'Look at whats-is-name – Eddie; look what he's up to behind Ellie's back. One more chorus of "Tea for Two" and we might actually find out what female fascists wear under their skirts.'

'Whatever was in that drink David gave you has certainly made you frisky.'

'Aren't I always frisky?'

'Frisky enough to take me home soon?'

'Is that an invitation?'

'More of a challenge,' Susan said.

'Strike while the iron's hot sort of thing?'

'Is the iron hot?'

'Yes,' said Mercer. 'Very. As soon as this dance is over we'll leave.'

'Have you no more business to attend to?'

'Nope, it's all squared away.'

'What about Vivian?' Susan said. 'How will she get home?'

'Vivian,' said Mercer, 'can take care of herself.'

★

It took Ronnie a week to make up his mind. Tomorrow morning, Friday, he'd kiss his wife and son goodbye. Tomorrow evening, straight from work, he'd tote his bag to Euston for the night journey across the Channel. Moshe had told him he wouldn't need much more than a change of socks and some extra warm clothes. And Jacob had assured him if he couldn't rake up the shekels for the fare the treasurer of the Stepney branch would make up the difference.

Friday night Ruth would be home breaking bread or whatever it was Jews did on the eve of their Sabbath but he still nurtured a faint hope that Ruth would show up at the station with the other sweethearts and shed a bucket of tears.

Thursday evening, Thornton Street was uncannily quiet. The sky was clear, a big crystal moon clawing its way over the rooftops, the same moon, he realised, that shone down on the plains of that far-off country where people were killing each other. He was tempted to nip into the Crown for a farewell pint but, knowing his luck, Danny would be there or some other geezer he didn't really want to talk to right now. Anyroads, it was only fair he spend his last night in England tucking his kid up in bed and being nice to Breda.

He reached Stratton's just as Nellie Millar was leaving.

'Hoy,' he said, 'she in?'

''Course she's in, stupid. Where else'd she be?'

'What about Danny?'

'Late shift.' Nellie Millar eyed him suspiciously. 'What you after, Ronnie?'

'Not after nothing,' he said. 'Here to see Nora. Now scarper.'

'Huh!' the girl said. 'Snotty.'

She turned on her heel and trotted off towards the junction. He waited until she was out of sight before he knocked on the glass.

'It's me, Nora. It's Ron.'

He was just making ready to knock again when the blind lifted and his mother-in-law peered out at him.

'Me,' he said, dabbing a finger to his chest. 'Open up.'

She fumbled with the bolt and admitted him.

The urns were silent, the tables set for breakfast and the only light came from the kitchen. Nora was still in her apron, hair straggly, cheeks flushed. She closed and locked the door, adjusted the blind and glanced round the empty room as if afraid that someone might hear.

'Sure an' you've come for the money, haven't you?'

And Ron, sucking in a deep breath, said, 'Yeah.'

PART THREE

Spring 1937

21

There was no love lost between Martin Teague and Mercer Hughes. They might see eye to eye on politics and feign rapport in public but in the publisher's cramped little office in an old building in High Holborn it was daggers drawn.

'Cathexis?' Teague puffed on his smelly pipe. 'I'm not paying three hundred and fifty pounds for cathexis. Dear God, Mercer, I'm not even certain I know what the word means.'

'Her readers will, I'm sure.'

Teague looked down his nose at the typescript on his desk. 'And Freud, so much about Freud.' He glanced up, brows knitted. 'This isn't what I expected from Vivian. What's come over her?'

'Nothing's come over her, Martin. The book is fine.'

'Fine for Routledge, perhaps, but not fine for me.'

'Are you turning it down?'

'I didn't say that.'

'I'm not renegotiating the terms of the contract if that's what you're driving at,' Mercer said. '*Herod* and *The Wheel of History* are doing very well for you.'

'They were,' Teague said, 'much of their time.'

'Their time?' Mercer said. 'For God's sake, Martin, *The Wheel*'s in its fourth printing. Have you put the new book out to any of your experts yet?'

'Who do you suggest?'

'Well – Kulgin, for one.'

'Kulgin has about as much commercial sense as a rabbit. I've read it and I don't like it. That's judgement enough.'

More sucking on the pipe, more acrid smoke: Mercer waited for the *coup de grâce*. He was sure Teague had something up his sleeve. He watched the publisher drum his thick fingers on Susan's immaculately typed script and a few grains of tobacco ash drift on to the title page.

'Dead,' Teague said. 'It's dead. If you ask me her heart wasn't in it.'

Unfortunately Teague was right. *The Melting Pot* lacked Vivian's usual excoriating style. When he'd hinted as much over dinner last week Vivian had climbed on her high horse and informed him that he was just too stupid to grasp the book's premise and that she'd no intention of watering it down to provide Martin Teague with another piece of cheapjack fascist propaganda.

Mercer put on his professional face, inscrutable as a mandarin, and prepared to yield an inch before Teague demanded a mile. 'Vivian isn't going to be too happy about this, Martin.'

'She was happy enough to sign the contract.'

'What do you want her to do?'

'Trim down the esoteric rubbish and make the book more pertinent to the times we live in,' Teague said. 'After all, I went to a great deal of trouble to take her to Berlin last summer. We had tea with Dr Goebbels, you know.'

'I know; you told me.'

'There's not a word about any of that.' He tapped the typescript again. 'History's all very well if it leads to the right conclusion. Vivian's book doesn't.'

'If you wish Vivian to undertake extensive rewrites she'll need your notes.'

Teague sat back and tapped the pipe stem against his teeth. 'Basically it needs a grandstand finish. If Vivian's willing to sacrifice the psychological mumbo-jumbo and bring the book to a more positive conclusion I think we might look on it favourably.' He smiled smugly. 'You see, I do know what "cathexis" means: it means the concentration of emotional and psychological energy on one particular person or idea.'

'Like fascism?' Mercer said. 'Like Hitler?'

'Exactly: like Hitler – a myth no more. What do you think?'

'Well,' Mercer said, 'I take your point but I'm not sure Vivian will.'

'Oh, you're used to stubborn authors. You know how to handle Vivian.'

'I'm not so sure I do,' said Mercer. 'By the by, when do we get paid?'

'As soon as the revised draft reaches my desk.'

'Not sooner?'

'No,' said Martin Teague, very firmly indeed. 'Not sooner.'

The March wind that blustered up Salt Street and rattled the windows of Miss Proudfoot's mews house had nothing on the storm that raged within. At first Susan had been puzzled by Mercer's insistence that he call at the house in mid-afternoon instead of taking Vivian to lunch. Now she saw the sense in it; Vivian's fury was uncontrollable and she would surely have wreaked havoc in any restaurant that Mercer might have taken her to.

In lieu of plates and cutlery Vivian hurled books and papers all about the room. She might even have snatched up the Hermes and smashed it against the wall if Susan hadn't hastily shoved the typewriter into a drawer while her employer rampaged through the ground-floor rooms, slamming doors in a manner that reminded Susan of her nephew, Billy. Vivian was a great deal older and a great deal bigger than Billy, however, and no one, certainly not Mercer, was about to get in her way.

'I've never seen her like this,' Susan said.

'No more have I,' said Mercer. 'I fear that cheeseplant's had it.'

'Do all your authors behave like this?'

'None of them takes criticism very well but mostly they just mumble and sulk,' Mercer said. 'Anna did throw a vase at a maid once after a bad review in *John O' London's Weekly*. Missed, fortunately. Where's Viv now?'

'In the toilet, I think.'

'Perhaps she's throwing up?'

'Nothing would surprise me,' Susan said. 'I'd no idea she had such a temper. Quite alarming, really.'

'Quite alarming given that *The Melting Pot* is a bit of a mess.'

Susan leaned back and peeped into the hallway before she spoke.

'I know,' she whispered. 'I told her it was unbalanced.'

'The book's not the only thing that's unbalanced,' Mercer said. 'Perhaps I should leave.'

'Don't you dare,' said Susan.

The door of the downstairs lavatory opened. Two minutes passed without a sound. Tension in the office grew. Then Vivian appeared in the doorway, sheet white, a brandy glass in one hand and a cigarette in the other. Her eyes were red. Her hair was damp. With shaking hand, she brought the cigarette to her lips and inhaled. She blew out a cloud of smoke and, throwing back her shoulders, said, 'I haven't really been rejected, Mercer, have I?'

'Of course not, dear heart. Teague isn't that much of a fool.'

A mouthful of brandy: 'What does he want me to do?'

'Revise a little, that's all. Less Freud, more' – Mercer paused – 'more Hitler.'

'The Teutonic messiah sort of thing?'

'That's it exactly.'

'I'm not a Nazi, you know.'

'I know you're not,' Mercer said. 'Unfortunately—'

'Teague is,' Vivian said. 'What precisely did he say?'

'Hitler – a myth no more.'

'He'll want that for his title, I suppose,' Vivian said. 'How long do I have?'

Mercer shrugged. 'As long as it takes.'

Vivian dropped on to the couch, spread her knees and, holding the glass low, swirled the brandy round as if it might reveal a glimpse of the future.

'Damn,' she said. 'Damn, damn, damn.'

'You do have a choice, you know,' Mercer said. 'You can tell Martin Teague to stuff his contract and let Dawson send you to Spain.'

'Risk my neck for *The Times*? I think not.' She looked up. 'No, I'll give Teague what he wants. I just hope his judgement's sound.' She swallowed the last of the brandy and got to her feet. 'It's my fault – about the book. I hedged my bets. I refused to commit myself. Can't do that now, can I? It's all or nothing.'

'Your fans will applaud you for it,' Mercer said.

'My fans,' Vivian said. 'Yes, my many, many fans.'

'It's not as if he's asking you to sell your soul,' Mercer said.

'Too late, Mercer,' Vivian said. 'Too late,' and headed for the sitting room to refill her glass.

Sans Ronnie, as her snotty sister-in-law might put it, life for Breda had certainly perked up. Of course, she'd shed more than a few angry tears that Saturday morning before Christmas when she'd wakened to discover Ronnie hadn't come home and that far from being holed up with Ruth Gertler was halfway to Spain with a bunch of commies.

Her mother had shown up at Pitt Street at half past six just as the old man was rushing out to work and had handed her a brown envelope that Ronnie had left at Stratton's on Friday night. Inside the envelope were three five pound notes, his wage packet, unopened, and a 'Goodbye, Breda' note scribbled on a greasy piece of wrapping paper. The old man had been livid, so livid Breda had thought he was going to croak. It had been all Nora and she could do to calm him down and pack him off to the dock. Then, with Billy perched on her knee, Nora had suggested that if she didn't fancy staying in Pitt Street with the old man she would be welcome to come back to Stratton's until Ronnie returned. No, Breda had said, she'd remain loyal to her missing hubby and stick it out where she was.

There'd been quite a kerfuffle later that night, though, when Matt had staggered in half seas over. He'd given Billy the heebie-jeebies by bear-hugging him. And he'd given Breda the heebie-jeebies when he'd tried to crawl into bed beside her. No saying what might have happened if Billy hadn't screamed the place down.

By the time Nora returned from church on Sunday Breda was back in Stratton's unpacking her kit and sniffing about Georgie's old room to make sure she had the nerve to sleep there.

All in all, when you added in Danny and Nellie Millar's brother, Steve, it wasn't a bad exchange for one lousy husband.

'Lookin' good, Breda.'

'Lookin' good yourself, Steve.'

For somebody officially on the dole Steve was in great nick. He spent two hours every morning in Syd's gym on the Whitechapel Road skipping rope and sparring with up-and-coming cruiserweights. He came by most nights to pick up Nellie who, for some reason, no longer seemed capable of finding her own way home. He'd just be there, seated at one of the tables, waiting to chat to Breda while Nellie finished up in the kichen. He'd lift Billy on to his knee, put his big brown fedora on Billy's head and pull it down, then, knocking on the crown, say, 'Anybody in there?'

'Me, me, me.'

'Who's that then?'

'Billy, it's Billy.'

The hat wasn't the only thing new about Steve. His suit and overcoat, even his shoes, were all brand new.

Breda said, 'You got work then?'

'Sure, I got work.'

'Where?'

'Up town.'

'Doing what?'

'Complaints department.'

'What, in the Post Office?'

Steve just smiled that smile of his and changed the subject.

Ma took Billy into her bed and crooned some old Irish song to him until they both fell asleep. Breda waited up to serve Danny his supper. Her first words were, 'Any word about our Ron?' as if the newsgatherers of the world were billeted in Spain just to trace her errant husband.

'Nope, not a word, Breda. Sorry.'

Corned beef hash, piping hot from the pot; Danny hadn't lost the orphanage habit of eating mushy food with a spoon. She watched him fondly.

'Steve was 'ere again,' she said. 'He was asking after you.'

'Nice of him,' Danny said.

'He's a nice guy.' Breda paused. 'Wonder what 'e does for dough?'

'Search me,' said Danny without looking up from his plate.

'Can't be honest, like, can it?'

'What did he tell you, Breda?'

'Complaints department my backside. Come on, what does 'e do?'

Danny licked the spoon. 'Steve works for your old man, for Leo. He's paid tae keep an eye on you. He's your guardian angel.'

'I don't need nobody to keep an eye on me, 'specially a bleedin' gangster.' Breda pulled her cardigan over her breasts. 'I thought he might fancy me.'

'He does.'

''Cause he gets paid for it, you mean?'

'What he gets paid for is standing behind a palm tree in the Orchestra Room of the Brooklyn Club to deal with any complaints customers might have about the price of the cocktails, or guys who get the wrong idea about the nice young ladies they happen to meet at the bar.'

'No razors then?'

'If you're Steve Millar's size you don't need razors.'

'My daddy pays him?'

'Your daddy helps run the Brooklyn Club.'

'You know a lot about my daddy, doncha?'

'More than might be good for me,' said Danny.

'My daddy won't do you no harm,' Breda said. 'I won't let 'im.'

'That's nice to know,' said Danny.

She adjusted the cardigan once more, smiling to herself.

'I'm a lucky girl, Danny, aren't I?'

'Why's that, sweetheart?'

'I got two guardian angels to look after me now.'

'Aye,' Danny said, 'at least until Ronnie comes home.'

He looked awful, absolutely awful; so awful, in fact, that Susan didn't recognise him. He was seated on the pavement across the road from the door of her building, knees drawn up, back to the railings. She glanced at him, marked him as a tramp and wondered if she should summon a policeman to have him moved on. When he stood up, she quickened her pace; three steps would see her safe within the building. He staggered, lurched towards her and raised both arms like Lear calling curses from the pendulous air.

'Sue, Susie, Susan,' he shouted, still waving his arms. 'Susie, Sue. It's me.'

'Dad?'

She waited, rooted, as he gathered the skirts of his tattered old raincoat and made some attempt at tightening his belt. He took off his cap, licked his palm, ran a hand over his hair and put the cap back on. In the light of the streetlamp, wavering in the wind, he looked so insignificant that she experienced a pang of guilt at her neglect of him and might have hugged him if he hadn't smelled so bad.

'You've been drinking, haven't you?' she said sternly.

'A pint, just a pint to keep me going.'

'What is it? What's wrong? Why are you here?'

'Ronnie,' he said. 'You heard about Ronnie?'

Oh, God, she thought, he's dead: Ronnie's dead. Something thumped below her breastbone, like a punch, and in the same instant she began, selfishly, to reorganise the week ahead as if she were filling in Vivian's diary.

'Oh, Dad,' she said, and hugged him. 'I'm sorry, so sorry.'

'You heard then? Danny tell you?'

She pulled back. 'Tell me what?'

'How Ron went off and left me with never a bleedin' word.'

'You mean Ronnie's not dead?'

'Might be dead for all we know. Three months, three bleedin' months and never a bleedin' word. You heard?'

Ten days before Christmas, she'd received a postcard from Danny asking her to meet him for lunch at a Lyons Corner House near Leicester Square. She hadn't forgotten what Mr Romano had said about Danny's romantic inclinations and had turned up out of curiosity more than anything else.

Everyone had been jumping up and down about the king's abdication and half of London, it seemed, had packed into the Corner House. The racket was so deafening that Danny had been forced to lean across the table and bawl in her ear just to make himself heard; nothing intimate, nothing romantic, just news about Ronnie's enlistment and Breda's return to the bosom of what was left of her family, news to which Susan had responded with not much more than a shrug.

She hadn't seen or heard from Danny since.

She said, 'No, Dad, I haven't had a letter from Ron, if that's what you mean. Why would he write to me when he writes to no one else?' She sighed. 'Look, now you're 'ere – here, you'd better come upstairs.'

He stepped back and, craning his neck, glowered at the building.

'He up there?'

Susan sighed again. 'No, he's not up there. Are you coming or not?'

'You got a toilet?'

'Of course I've got a toilet. Do you need to pee?'

'Yus,' he said. 'Lead on.'

It wasn't a butler in full livery who admitted him to the opulent hall of the Mayfair house but a harassed little maid who relieved him, rather grudgingly, of his overcoat and ushered him into a sitting room where Gwen, in a faded floral tea gown, was playing two-pack solitaire at a huge oval table.

'I'm sorry,' Mercer said. 'I was hoping I might catch David.'

'You make him sound like a contagious disease.' Gwen continued to lay out cards. 'He isn't at home. Seldom is these days. Would you care for a drink?'

'No, no thanks. Do you happen to know – I mean, is he at the club?'

Gwen flipped a card from the pack and placed it in sequence. 'He's gone down to Hackles for a few days.'

'Ah, yes,' Mercer said. 'Bedding down the apple trees, I suppose.'

Shows what you know about apple trees.' Gwen looked up at last. 'What's he up to, Mercer? Is it a woman?'

'No, no. Well – I mean, I really don't know.'

'I think you do.'

'Look, Gwennie, I'm not quite as matey with David as I once was.'

'Or quite as "matey" with me either.'

'I don't think it's another woman. I really do think it's business.'

'Are you in on it?'

'I'm not "in" on anything,' Mercer said.

She drew her chair back from the table. She looked a little too rural, he thought, to be comfortable in this polished room. She folded her arms under her breasts and cocked her head.

'Talk to me,' she said. 'Sit down and talk to me.'

'I can't, Gwen. Honestly. I just popped in for a quick word with David.'

'At least have a drink with me. One drink. One damned drink.'

He said, 'Where's Eleanor?'

'Oh, so it's Eleanor you're interested in, is it?'

'Don't be ridiculous. Is she upstairs?'

Gwen put a finger to her lips and closed her eyes. 'Tonight? Now let me see: yes, tonight's a "Four Steps for Peace" lecture in Fulham town hall – or is it her class on breeding for the future?'

'Pardon me?'

'Breeding's all the rage, didn't you know? How to be the perfect wife and open your legs for race and nation. And to think we used to do it just for fun.' She got up and minced towards him. 'Do you remember how much fun it was, darling? How we used to go at it without a thought for the breeding of heroes? How irresponsible we were before Tom Mosley showed us the error of our ways?' She looped an arm about his neck, leaned into him and cupped his crotch. 'Once upon a time you'd have had me on the carpet or over the table by now. What a dreadful opportunist you were. Now we have a whole damned house to ourselves and beds galore to choose from' – she gave him a little shove – 'and you don't want me, do you?'

'It isn't that, Gwen. It isn't that at all.'

'What is it then?'

'I have an appointment.'

'With her, I suppose?'

She was still within range, poised for another assault on his crotch.

He nodded. 'Yes, with Susan.'

'Can't she wait for it?'

'That wouldn't be fair, Gwen, would it?'

'She's not your wife, Mercer. She's only a common little slut from Shadwell and you owe her nothing, nothing at all.' Gwen rested her hips on the edge of the table. 'Does she know about Anna?'

'I don't know what you mean.'

'It's a simple question, darling: does Susan know you're pleasuring Anna Maples on the side?'

'I'm not doing anything with Anna Maples.'

'You were always a glib liar, Mercer. If you'd told me the moon was made of green cheese I'd have believed you.'

'I'm not lying, Gwen. Anna Maples means nothing to me.'

'Anna thinks differently. We've even compared notes. We agreed that you were the handsomest beast in the jungle.' She stroked his cheek. 'You're still awfully handsome but you're not much of a beast these days. I suppose I could persuade you to spend the night with me if I really, really tried.'

'It would do you no good, Gwen, no good at all.'

'I know it, darling. I've lost you, haven't I?' She returned to her seat at the table. 'It happens to the best of us. I just didn't think it would happen to me. Don't pout, Mercer, your secret's safe with me but I'd be wary of Anna Maples if I were you. She's not the sort to take rejection lightly.'

'Gwen, I—'

'No,' she said, 'don't say it. Don't say anything. Go, just go.'

Relieved, he headed for the door.

She made him wash his hands at the sink in the kitchenette while she warmed a tin of minced beef, poured it on to a plate and topped it off with a poached egg. He'd sobered up quite a bit by then. The flat impressed him – daunted him, perhaps – by its gentility. She cut a loaf into extra thick slices, put a mug of tea by his elbow and joined him at the table.

'Does you well, this Hughes geezer, don't 'e?' her father said.

'Mercer doesn't pay for my flat, Dad. I pay everything myself.'

'Even the rent?'

'Even the rent.'

'One of them mean buggers, is 'e?'

'No, he's not in the least mean. He's very generous, in fact.'

He paused over a forkful of mince. 'I thought you was kept?'

'Is that why you let Breda call me a harlot?'

'She didn't say that,' he blustered. ''Sides, it's got nothing to do with Breda.'

'I thought she was the salt of the earth.'

'She's a selfish cow!'

'You've changed your tune, haven't you?' Susan said.

He ducked the question. 'You heard what happened?'

'Danny told me.'

'Oh, you been seeing Danny then?'

'Once – soon after Ronnie went away.'

'You know Breda left me in the lurch?' her father said. 'Went back to live with 'er ma, the ungrateful cow!'

Susan wasn't sure what he wanted from her, whether loneliness, curiosity or desperation had brought him across London. To judge by the state of his clothes he'd come straight from the docks with a stop off in some pub or other. He had that distinctive dockside niff: a woody, tarry, cheesy smell that had been part of his aura for as long as she could remember.

'Took Billy,' he said.

'Don't you see Billy then?'

''Course I do. Can't keep me away from my own grandson, can she?'

'You spend your evenings at Stratton's with Nora and Breda, don't you?'

'It ain't the same.'

'The same as what?' Susan said.

'Having your own 'ome.'

'Dad, are you tight?'

'On two pints of bitter, nah.'

'Tight for money,' Susan said, 'without Ronnie's wage coming in?'

'I done all right when you was young. I'm doing all right now.'

'Just asking,' Susan said. 'No need to get huffy.'

He mopped up gravy with a pinch of bread and pushed his plate away.

'Wouldn't 'appen to have a spare ciggie, would you, Susie?'

She brought the box of Churchman's from the drawer in the fireside table. He peered at the gold foil, at the rows of plump white cigarettes and, frowning, glanced up.

'Sorry, Dad,' Susan said. 'Ain't got no Woodbine 'andy.'

He grunted and smiled. 'Reckon I can make do.'

He extracted a Churchman's from the box and let her light it for him. He blew out smoke, coughed and reached for the tea mug. Susan seated herself again and waited for him to rap his gavel, as it were, and bring the meeting to order.

'Jews,' he said, 'went off with Jews. Can't forgive 'im for that. I mean, if he'd joined for Franco I could see sense in it. But Jews and commies – nah, nah, it ain't right.'

'Ronnie never did share your views, Dad.'

'Breda thinks he was tickling Gertler's daughter and she got 'im to join up.'

'Well, Ronnie's no saint,' Susan said, 'but I doubt if he's stupid enough to dash off to war just to please some girl – even Ruth Gertler.'

'You don't know where 'e is then?'

'How could I?' Susan said. 'Danny's the chap for that sort of thing.'

'Danny's drawn a blank.'

'Ron must be somewhere,' she said. 'He can't just have vanished into thin air. Have you spoken to Ruth Gertler?'

'Not my place.'

'You want me to do it, I suppose?'

'Maybe go along with Danny,' her father suggested.

'Why can't Danny go on his own? I hardly know the girl.'

'She ain't a girl; she's a woman. Anyroads, better if you go with 'im.'

'For heaven's sake!' Susan said. 'She's not going to seduce our Danny.'

'Never know with 'er sort.'

'All right, all right. I'll see what I can do,' Susan promised.

He nodded then, trying to appear casual, looked around the room.

'I suppose you like it 'ere?' he said.

'Of course I like it here.'

'You ain't coming back then?'

'No, Dad, I'm not coming back to Shadwell.'

'What about me? I took care of you. Now you should take care of me.'

'Who do you think you are?' Susan said. 'Old Mother Riley? Surely you can look after yourself until Ronnie comes home.'

'There's another bloke on the scene. Nellie Millar's brother. Leo sent 'im down to look out for her.'

'What?' Susan said. 'Are you telling me Romano employs Nellie Millar's brother to look after Breda? Is what's-his-name – Steve, is he sleeping with her?'

Her father shrugged. 'He hangs around a lot.'

'What does Nora have to say about that?'

'Nora doesn't 'ave much to say about anything these days.'

Susan sat back. 'You're trying to draw me in, aren't you? You're trying to get me mixed up in things that are no concern of mine.'

'Ain't I a concern of yours?'

'Yes,' she admitted, 'but you're not a doddering old wreck just yet, so don't try to pretend you are. For your sake, strictly for your sake, I'll get in touch with Danny and see if, between us, we can find out where Ronnie's fighting. Are you sure he's even in Spain?'

'Told Mr Brauschmidt he was going. Told his boss but not me.'

'All right,' Susan said. 'I'll do that much for you. But the rest of it – Breda and Nora – they're your problem.'

A key rattled in the lock and Mercer breezed in.

He stopped in the doorway, frozen like a runner in a

newspaper photograph. 'Dad,' said Susan, as evenly as possible. 'This is my friend, Mercer Hughes.'

Mercer closed his mouth and extended his hand. 'Mr Hooper, it's a very great pleasure to meet you at last.'

'Likewise,' her dad said. 'Likewise, I'm sure.'

She said, 'Dad was just leaving.'

'Surely not?' said Mercer. 'Stay a while, Mr Hooper. Do stay and have more tea. It's high time we became acquainted, don't you think?'

'Late,' her dad mumbled. 'Work. Tube.'

Mercer said, 'I'm sure we'll be able to find you a taxi.'

'No, I gotta go.'

'Look here, I do hope I haven't chased you away.'

'Susan?' her father said beseechingly. 'Where's me cap?'

22

No matter what became of him Danny would never forget how she looked that March evening as she stepped out of the Underground. The hat, the scarlet overcoat, the scarf thrown across her shoulder, stylish as any Chelsea girl. She paused and glanced about her as if there might be more to the meeting than obligation.

'Sue?' He came out from the shelter of the tobacconist's kiosk. 'I'm here.'

'So you are.' She took his arm. 'Where are we going?'

'Mario's caff. Apparently that's where Miss Gertler hides out.'

'Don't the YCL have an office in Stepney?' Susan said.

'They do,' said Danny, 'but if you think we'll be made welcome by the Reds, think again. These guys have given themselves over to the vision of a world where you – me too, probably – are the natural enemies of the proletariat.'

'Now I see why you're not employed by the *Daily Worker*.'

He laughed. 'By the way, this wasn't my idea.'

'Nor mine,' Susan said. 'I don't see why my father dragged me into it.'

'Homeland an' family,' Danny said, 'are the limits of your old man's vision. If he were in Spain right now he'd be cheering for Franco.'

'At least Franco isn't murdering priests and raping nuns,' Susan said.

'I think that might be a problem for some of the guys out there.'

'The idealists?'

'An' the adventurers.'

'I wonder what Ronnie is?'

'Missing,' Danny said.

The girl had thick dark hair and dark eyes and more than a touch of what passed for class. As soon as Susan saw her seated in a booth at the rear of the café she knew that Ronnie had fled to Spain not to escape his humdrum job, his wife and child or his father's half-baked ranting but to avoid the hurt that a girl like Ruth Gertler could unwittingly inflict on a simple soul like her brother.

Danny ushered Susan into the booth.

'Thanks for agreeing to meet us,' he said. 'This is Ron's sister.'

'I know who she is,' Ruth said. 'My aunt, Lena – Lena Gertler.'

There were no handshakes. The woman by Ruth's side was about Nora's age. She wasn't smartly dressed like her niece and looked drawn and tired.

'You know why I got in touch with you, don't you?' Danny said.

'To tell me to lay off Ronnie,' Ruth replied.

Susan said, 'We don't know where Ron is; do you?'

Danny said, 'I've tried every source I can think of, from party offices to the Red Cross. I even got through a cable to a journalist guy from our newspaper who's bunkered in Madrid. Nothing.'

'Can you help?' Susan said. 'Please.'

'I have letters,' Lena Gertler said, 'from my son, Moshe.'

'Does he mention Ronnie?' Susan said. 'Are they together?'

'They were,' Ruth said, 'until Moshe was killed.'

'God!' Danny said. 'I'm sorry.' He paused. 'That's not enough, is it?'

'No, that is not enough,' Lena Gertler said.

'Where was he killed?' Danny said.

'Jarama.'

'When?'

'On the 13th day of February.'

'Are you sure he's dead?' Danny said. 'Mistakes do happen.'

The woman dipped into her coat pocket, brought out a grubby envelope and tossed it almost contemptuously, Susan thought, on to the table.

She said, 'Is this a mistake, Mr Cahill?'

Danny took the single sheet from the envelope and carefully unfolded it. It was hand-printed in blue ink and bore a cramped signature at the bottom. More than that Susan could not make out.

'Who's this guy, Benson?' Danny said.

'Political commissar for the unit,' Lena Gertler told him.

'Is he a hard-line communist appointed by the Comintern?' said Danny.

'What does it matter?' Lena Gertler said. 'My son was not a communist. He was born a Jew and you can be sure he died a Jew. He just hated fascists.'

Danny folded the letter and returned it to the woman.

'Your son, Mrs Gertler, what unit was he with?'

'The British Battalion.'

Ruth said, 'I've letters from my friend Jacob too.'

'I suppose,' Susan said, 'we couldn't have a look at Jacob's letters?'

'They are private,' Ruth said.

'They are love letters,' the aunt said. 'Why do you hide it, Ruth?'

'Because Jacob is Myrtle's boyfriend.'

'These people don't care,' Lena Gertler said. 'Finding their brother is more important than your silly squabble with Myrtle.'

'It isn't a silly squabble,' Ruth said.

'It will seem so if Jacob . . .' The woman didn't finish the sentence.

'You're right, Aunt Lena, quite right.'

'What can I tell you?' Lena Gertler spread her hands. 'In December, soon after they'd arrived, the boys were sent to fight near Madrid. The guns did not work properly. Many were killed before the nationalists withdrew. Those who survived were rested. Food was scarce. Rice, beans, only a little meat. Wine to drink. Moshe didn't like Spanish wine. In January the British Battalion was assembled and the boys from Stepney became part of the International Brigades. Five hundred men in the battalion when it left the camp in Madrigueras. Moshe was excited to be marching to fight the fascists with a proper army.'

'An' that was . . .' Danny said. 'I mean, no more letters?'

'No.'

'Ronnie was still with them,' Ruth said. 'Jacob told me in his last letter.'

'Did Jacob tell you what company he was assigned to?' Danny asked.

'Number two company: machine-gunners.'

'Mrs Gertler,' Danny said, 'may I ask you where your son's buried?'

'In a grave near the town where he died.'

Ruth put an arm about her aunt's shoulders and held her tightly.

For half a minute no one spoke, then Danny said, 'Thank you, Mrs Gertler.'

'What do you know of it, you and her?' Ruth Gertler said angrily. 'You will not be happy until you know Ronnie's dead too, and my Jacob with him.'

'Stop it, Ruth,' her aunt told her. 'They are on our side.'

'Are they?' Ruth Gertler said.

'Thank you,' Danny said again. 'You've helped us a great deal.'

'I am glad of that,' Lena Gertler said. 'To your brother I wish the best.'

'If you find Ronnie,' Ruth said. 'Tell him . . .'

'Tell him what?' said Susan.

But the beautiful Jewish girl just shook her head.

They walked to the Underground. Danny held her hand. She remembered how he'd taken Georgie's hand when they'd all gone to the park and how bored and condescending and far too sure of herself she'd been then.

She said, 'Are you going back to Fleet Street?'

'Not tonight.'

'Will you be able to trace Ronnie now, do you think?'

'Maybe,' Danny said.

She stopped him short of the entrance to the Underground.

'You just don't want to upset me, do you?' she said. 'Tell me the truth.'

'It's hard to keep up with news from the front. I know guys who may have some information now we've discovered what company Ron's with. That's the best I can do right now, Susan.'

'What will you tell Breda?'

'Nothing till I'm certain of my facts.' He shuffled

uncomfortably. 'I'm not sure how Breda'll take it. She's havin' fun right now an' – well, you know Breda.'

'I used to think you might marry Breda.'

'Never crossed my mind,' Danny said.

'Don't you have a girl tucked away somewhere?'

'If I had I wouldn't tell you.'

'Why not?'

'Wouldn't wanna make you jealous.'

'Me? Why would I be jealous?' Susan said. 'Don't you have someone, Danny, some girl whose snapshot you keep in your pocket?'

'Matter of fact, I do.'

'Really?' Susan reddened a little. 'May I – I mean, who?'

'Greta Garbo,' Danny said.

'Very funny.'

'You okay now, Susie?'

'Yes, I'm okay.'

'Good.' He kissed her cheek. 'See yuh,' he said softly.

'Yes, see yuh,' she said and, half wishing that she was going with him, watched him walk away.

Everyone knew that Charles Plimlott Ames was devoted to his barrister companion, Freddie, who had once been his fag at school. In spite of that little idiosyncrasy, Charlie was universally regarded as a pillar of rectitude in the world of letters and disapproved of the goings-on of authors who traded partners, male and female, like cigarette cards.

Opera and ballet were Charlie's 'thing' and while he might now and then extol the beauty of a tenor's voice he would never, ever stoop to invading the tenor's dressing room; nor would he flirt with the muscular young men who floated about backstage at Sadler's Wells no matter how provocatively they padded their leotards. Charlie was a gentleman, born and bred. And he hated gossip. Woe betide the junior who tried to interest him in the latest titbit of scandal from Shaftesbury Avenue or draw his attention to the rumour that so-and-so had been spotted tête-à-tête in Claridge's with someone else's wife.

When any of Mercer Hughes and Ames's clients strayed from the straight and narrow Charlie was more than happy to let Mercer deal with it. He was also shrewd enough to turn a blind eye to Mercer's misdeeds, for although he, C.P. Ames, was the senior partner it was Mercer who did the dirty work.

Socially Mercer and Charlie lived entirely separate lives and rarely broke bread together. Once or twice a week the pair would meet in Charlie's spartan office with its view down into Lantern House Lane. Mercer would report on works in progress and contracts under negotiation and Charlie, meticulous to a fault, would remind his impulsive young partner that the selling of books was one thing and the keeping of books quite another: a warning that Mercer ignored.

On that March morning, however, all the signs indicated that Charlie's patience had finally worn thin. 'Mercer,' Charlie Ames said in a rumbling down-to-earth baritone, 'have you been tampering with the accounts again?'

'Of course not.'

'Is it your mother? Is she in over her head?'

'She's always in over her head. What, Charlie, is the problem?'

'The foreign exchange ledger has certain omissions . . .'

'I can explain that.'

'Explain what?' said Charlie.

'The Broadway money.'

'The Broadway money?'

'Isn't that what you're concerned about?' Mercer said. 'Anna Maples's payment on the *Catharsis* option?'

'Actually,' Charlie Ames said, 'I meant Arlen's money from Viking.' He paused. 'Perhaps you'd better tell me about the *Catharsis* payment.'

'Stalled,' Mercer said. 'That's all – stalled.'

'Not come through, do you mean?'

'Well, it may have come through,' Mercer admitted, 'but it hasn't been entered on Anna's account just yet.'

'Why not?'

'The exchange rate isn't all that favourable.'

'The exchange rate – yes, quite!' Charlie said. 'Where is the Maples money?'

'I told you. I'm holding it.'

'And Rupert's advance from Viking?'

'I've got the picture,' said Mercer. 'You want everything tidied up and squared away before the internal audit next month.'

'Look, if you need to borrow a pound or two . . .'

'No, Charlie, no,' Mercer assured him. 'Everything's fine.'

'Everything except the royalty statements.'

'Oversight, Charles, that's all; mere oversight,' Mercer said. 'If the beggars don't get their foreign earnings this half year they'll get them next half year.'

'That isn't the point,' said Charlie. 'If our clients are due payment then payment must be made on time.'

'Of course, of course,' said Mercer. 'What do you want me to do?'

'Fix it,' said Charlie Ames. 'Now.'

If there was one thing Breda liked more than any other it

was a taste of glitz and glamour. She was disappointed that Steve didn't whisk her off to the huge new Paramount picture house in Tottenham Court Road to see *Born to Dance* but took her instead to a cowboy film in the local flea-pit. She wasn't about to argue with Steve, though; a first date was a first date and she was glad to be dolled up and out of the house. Besides, she was already moony over the big feller, her guardian angel, and more than a little in awe of him.

They went in halfway through the main feature, groped their way into seats at the rear of the stalls and settled down. Steve had said he had to be back up town by half past ten and she'd said if that was the case she hoped he was a fast worker. Steve had just smiled his smile and hadn't taken her up on it. He'd brought her a nice box of Parma Violets, though, which, as Breda was well aware, made the breath sweet and the lips kissable.

She kept half an eye on Steve, half an eye on Wild Bill Hickock riding to the rescue of Calamity Jane. She offered the box of Violets to Steve who picked three and put them all in his mouth at once. He was a sucker not a cruncher, Breda noted, and took that as a good sign.

The usherette's torch probed up and down the aisle as more folk arrived to fill the empty seats. The beam of the projector flickered overhead. Music swelled and faded and swelled again. Wild Bill kissed Calamity Jane quite passionately.

Steve slid a hand on to Breda's knee.

She stiffened, thinking: He fancies me, he really does. He fancies me.

She shifted her weight, leaning to kiss him but apparently Steve didn't feel like being kissed. Anyway he still had his hat on and choosing the right angle to his mouth would be tricky. He slid his hand up her leg until his fingers reached the top of her stocking. She was just coy enough to draw in her belly and when the curtains closed and the house lights came on snapped shut her thighs. Steve snatched his hand away and taking off his hat placed it, crown up, on his lap.

He glanced her – that smile again – and said, 'You like?'

'Like what?' said Breda. 'The picture?'

'Yeah, the picture.'

'It's okay.'

'The best bit's still to come,' he said.

'I hope,' Breda said, 'I'm not disappointed.'

'You won't be, kid,' he told her. 'You won't be.'

House lights dimmed. The screen filled with stark newsreel images accompanied by a blast of martial music. The young couple to Breda's right began necking, the girl panting as if she'd never been kissed before. The couple in front were necking too. Steve put a hand on Breda's breast and, twisting in his seat, stuck his other hand all the way up her skirt.

Breda's scream rang through the cinema like a pistol shot.

She pointed straight at the screen and yelled, 'Ronnie. That's my bleedin' Ronnie,' while big Steve Millar struggled to extricate his fist from her underwear.

The most dispiriting thing about Anna Maples wasn't that she had a large backside and no ankles to speak of but that she persisted in talking all through lovemaking.

More often than not she was content to guide Mercer's endeavours as if she were reading from an instruction manual but every now and then, distracted by a stray thought that had nothing to do with what was going on south of the Maginot Line, she'd clamp her hands on his hips and say, seriously, 'Do you really think McClelland's review of *Garland* was fair?' or 'Marjory tells me Francis has been seen in Rome with that Irish girl,' or, worst of all, 'Lucy Pettingall is having her womb scraped next Friday; did she tell you?'

'No,' Mercer answered through gritted teeth. 'She didn't tell me.'

'A woman of her age. It's quite ridiculous!'

'Anna . . .'

'What? Yes, by all means continue.'

Anna's demands upon his patience, let alone his stamina, were considerable whether they were cohabiting in a quaint little hotel in Whitstable, the mausoleum-like bedroom in the family house in Richmond or, as now, in Anna's flat in Marylebone. Mercer had no idea why she still wanted him when, by her lights, half the men in literary London, not to mention most of the Home Counties, were so in thrall to her talent that they were practically queuing at the door to ravish her.

After what seemed like hours Anna pursed her lips and with a note of surprise, said, 'Oh! Yes! *There* we are!' and a half-minute later pushed him away.

Shrivelling inside the French letter, he lay back. He had no inclination to kiss her: she didn't expect it anyway. She lay motionless beneath the sheet, arms by her sides, head square on the pillow, frowning.

'I want you to give her up.'

'Give who up?' Mercer said.

'The Hooper girl.'

'Ah!' Mercer said. 'By the way, where's Neville?'

'Ceylon.'

'Ceylon? What's he doing in Ceylon?'

'You have me, Mercer. You don't need her.'

'Martin's rather keen to have another book soon,' said Mercer.

'I do have one or two ideas. How keen is he?'

'Contract keen,' said Mercer.

'Sight unseen?'

'Once you have something on paper.'

'Whatever happened to my American money?'

'Clearing,' Mercer said, 'takes time.'

'I really don't understand what you see in her,' Anna went on. 'My Broadway option, is Martin sitting on it?'

'It doesn't go through Martin.'

'No, it goes through you,' Anna said. 'What have you done with it?'

'I haven't done anything with it.'

'Have you been fiddling the books again?'

'I resent that remark, Anna. I really and truly do.'

'Give her up.'

'No.'

'I want you to be mine.'

'I am yours, aren't I?' Mercer said.

'You're not keeping me.'

'You don't need kept, Anna. You have a perfectly good husband.'

'You don't love me, do you?'

He made an effort, cocked an elbow and toyed with a wisp of her frizzy hair. 'Of course I love you. Everyone loves you. You're the most desirable woman in London. I count myself lucky to have known – to know you.'

'I think I'd really like to have my Broadway money soon.'

'Anna . . .'

'Give her up, Mercer. Give – her – up.'

He sagged against her shoulder.

'This is Gwen's idea, isn't it?' he said. 'Don't you see?'

'See what?'

'She's jealous; Gwen's jealous.'

'I'm not surprised.'

'Gwen's not jealous of Susan Hooper. She's jealous of you.'

Anna sat up. 'Really?'

'Plain as the nose – as a pikestaff. She's using Susan Hooper to split us up,' said Mercer smoothly. 'Susan Hooper's no more than a plaything. You know how I am? We're not like ordinary people. We have appetites that must be satisfied, passions that supersede the bounds of bourgeois morality. We care not a fig for what folk think of us. We're bound at the hip, you and me.'

'You're using me. You use everyone. Why should I be any different?'

'Because' – he paused – 'you're Anna Maples.'

In the silence that followed he could hear the roar of buses charging the traffic lights at the corner of Baker Street.

'Well,' she said, at length, 'you may be right.'

He waited, breathless, hanging over her.

'Mercer?'

'What is it, darling?'

'I'm ready.'

'Ready for what?' he asked.

And Anna answered, 'More.'

23

By the week's end the word was all over Shadwell and everyone who had ever shared a pint with Ronnie Hooper had visited one cinema or another to confirm Breda's claim that the man standing on the back of a flatbed truck somewhere in Spain was indeed her husband. He was clad in bits of soldier's uniform and glowered out at the camera from a row of republican prisoners who'd been rounded up by the fascists in the wake of the Jamara debacle. The Movietone version had a sympathetic commentary but the voice that accompanied the Pathé footage was marked by a faintly jeering tone as if to suggest that the prisoners were foolish not only for surrendering but for fighting on the wrong side in the first place.

Matt trudged off to the local pit with Nora who as soon as Ronnie's face flashed on screen burst into tears and had to be led out. Mr Brauschmidt and his wife nodded sadly when Ronnie appeared and were so disturbed by the experience that neither of them slept a wink that night.

Defying convention, Ruth Gertler slipped alone into the Bijou in North Street in the middle of an afternoon showing of *The Devil is a Woman*. She cried when she saw Ronnie up there but was so relieved that Jacob wasn't with him that she stayed on to watch the big picture which, in spite of her guilt, she rather enjoyed.

Flanked by Steve and Vince, Leo Romano trotted down from the American Lido to one of the tiny newsreel cinemas off Shaftesbury Avenue and sat through the one-hour show twice just to be on the safe side.

'Poor bastard,' Leo said as the trio emerged, blinking, into Dean Street. 'No wonder Breda was upset.'

'She was that all right,' Steve Millar said. 'Yeah, very upset.'

Danny was the first person Breda told about her 'discovery' and confessed that as well as being relieved that Ron was alive, she was proud, yes, proud, to see her husband up there on the big screen sharing a bill with Gary Cooper.

The following morning Danny telephoned Susan at work.

Susan had just changed the ribbon on the Hermes and was washing ink from her hands in the bathroom when the telephone rang.

Vivian was up and about. Surrounded by books and newspaper clippings, she was busily applying herself to demonising Hitler with the same thoroughness with which she'd libelled the Jews.

When Susan entered the office Vivian had just returned the receiver to its cradle. 'That was your friend Cahill,' she said. 'It seems your brother's turned up in a newsreel. Mr Cahill wants you to meet him at the Astoria to make absolutely sure it is your brother. Go and put your titfer on. We're off to the flicks.'

'My God!' Susan said. 'Are you coming too?'

'Why not?' said Vivian. 'I think it's time I met your Mr Cahill, don't you?'

Mercer told no one of his plans: not Susan, not Anna, not Gwen and certainly not his mother. He left before dawn, driving an old Ford banger he'd hired from a garage behind

Victoria Station. He cursed the day he'd been forced to sell the Riley, for the Ford wouldn't top fifty without the gearbox going on strike. Even so, he cleared London long before the sun came up and reached Hereford shortly after ten.

There were signs of spring in the fields and hedgerows: fading snowdrops, crocuses, daffodils thrusting through the grass, leaf bud on many of the trees and horse ploughs and tractors tearing up the arable tracts that flanked the country roads. There was no sign of activity around Hackles, however, and no sign of David. If it hadn't been for smoke purling from the farmhouse chimney and an appetising aroma of frying bacon Mercer might have supposed the place deserted.

He parped the Ford's horn and, leaving the car on the patio, ducked through the porch and called out David's name. At the top of the stairs a woman's face appeared; a woman he'd never seen before.

From the kitchen a voice called out, 'Come in, come in, whoever you are.'

Mercer followed the summons. In the kitchen two young women, both plump, were over by the stove, one tossing eggs in a pan, the other drinking milk from a bowl cupped in both hands. They eyed Mercer boldly. David was seated on one side of the big table, the man with the moustache, whom Mercer had last seen in the library of the Mayfair town house, on the other.

'Well, well, if this isn't a pleasant surprise,' David Proudfoot said. 'Come to join the party, old son? Bit late for anything but seconds, I'm afraid.'

'Have eggs, you be wantin' them, Mr Hughes,' one of the women said.

'Eggs would be good, thank you. Perhaps a bit of bacon too.' He removed his coat and peeled off his driving gloves, looked round and, with no one jumping to help him, tossed them on an empty chair.

'That's it,' said David. 'Liberty Hall.'

Mercer pulled out a chair, seated himself and lit a cigarette.

'You've met Roger, haven't you?' David said.

'Yes,' Mercer said. 'Not formally, of course.'

The man with the moustache raised his tea mug in greeting.

'Nothing formal about us, is there, Roger?' David said.

'Not a scrap,' Roger agreed.

He wore a cotton shirt and a pair of oil-stained flannels tucked into what Mercer assumed were flying boots. A quilted leather jacket with a mangy fur collar was draped on the back of his chair.

'You're the pilot, aren't you?' Mercer said.

'Navigator.'

'Ah!' Mercer said. 'Safe back from Spain then?'

Roger exchanged a glance with David who rapped his tea mug on the table and called out, '*Garçon*, a top-up, if you please.'

The younger of the women brought an earthenware teapot to the table and refilled David's mug. 'Will there be anything else, Your Highness?'

He looked up, merry-eyed. 'Aren't you going to stir it for me, May?'

'Ha'n't you had enough stirring for one night – sir?'

'Actually,' David said, 'I've had just about enough stirring for a week. Once you've given my good friend Mr Hughes his breakfast may I suggest you collect your sisters and make yourselves scarce?'

'Will you be wanting us later?'

'Mercer, are you staying over the weekend?'

'No,' Mercer answered. 'I'm driving back this evening.'

'There's plenty to go round, you know,' said David.

'I don't doubt it,' Mercer said. 'But I have to get back to London.'

'To the lovely Susan, of course,' said David.

'To my lovely mother – who isn't very well.'

'She never is,' said David. 'What a mama's boy you are, Mercer. I hope my daughters are as considerate of me when I reach my dotage.'

'I'm sure Gwen will take good care of you,' Mercer said.

The woman, May, put a plate of bacon and eggs before him.

'Tea or coffee, Mr Hughes?'

'Tea will do him fine,' David said impatiently. 'Leave the pot and buzz off. There's a good girl.'

The women ambled off, swaying their broad hips insolently. Mercer had counted three women so far. Even allowing for David's sexual appetite that seemed like one too many.

He said, 'Is the pilot – Clive, isn't it? – is Clive here too?'

'He's stuck in Bilbao,' Roger told him.

'Is that where he delivered our planes?' said Mercer.

'Unfortunately,' David said, 'there's been a hitch.'

'What sort of a hitch?'

'We lost one of the Dragons to the nationalists on landing,' Roger said.

'Really! How did that happen?'

Roger shrugged. 'Fortunes of war.'

'If Clive's in Bilbao what are you doing here?'

'Waiting for him to find his way home,' Roger said.

Mercer put down his fork. 'And the other planes, what happened to them?'

'Two were safely delivered.'

'So there is some money due?'

'Actually,' David said, 'I've been meaning to talk to you about that.'

The newsreels were spliced with shots of bombed buildings, refugees, orphaned children, soldiers frantically feeding shells into field guns; a harrowing flow of images intercut with clips of the German ambassador greeting King George, cricket from Australia, a giant ocean liner leaving port, Adolf Hitler delivering a speech in Frankfurt, and the enlightening sight of a thousand young women in vests and shorts performing gymnastic exercises in a national stadium accompanied by jaunty music that set Susan's teeth on edge.

The tiny movie theatre was shaped like a tunnel, steeply raked from back to front; fifteen rows of creaky seats occupied by a handful of men sufficiently engaged with world events to cheer when members of the International Brigades gave a thumbs up to the camera and hiss when von Ribbentrop strutted on to the red carpet to deliver his infamous Nazi salute to the king.

After half an hour Susan was so bludgeoned by the images that when the republican prisoners from Jamara finally flashed on screen she felt no affinity with her absent brother, who seemed like just another victim of the war.

Vivian nudged her. 'Which one is he?'

'Back row in the middle.'

'No hat?'

'No hat.'

Danny put an arm about her shoulder.

'At least we know he's alive,' he muttered.

'Or was,' said Susan.

It seemed a little odd to be ordering a half-crown lunch,

complete with finger bowls, under a Venetian chandelier in the middle of the Café Royal's enormous gilded dining room.

'Perhaps,' said Vivian, unfolding her napkin, 'they're hoping it'll fall on us.' She looked around. 'It's not so grand as all that, is it? I hope you don't mind me dragging you in here, Mr Cahill, but I have a score to settle.'

'Settle away,' said Danny. 'If it was good enough for Oscar Wilde, it's good enough for me.'

'Ah, but look what happened to poor Oscar,' Vivian said.

'He should've heeded Bernard Shaw's advice,' said Danny. 'I don't think he was much of a one for takin' advice, though.'

'Are you?' said Vivian.

'Depends who's givin' it,' said Danny.

Vivian smiled over the silverware. 'By the way, lunch is on me. It's the least I can do for playing gooseberry.'

'You're not playing gooseberry,' Susan said quickly. 'We're not . . .'

'Not what?' said Vivian.

'Nothing, nothing,' Susan said.

'Are you blushing, Susan?' Vivian said. 'I don't think I've ever seen you blush before. Mr Cahill, your opinion, please.'

'I've been in worse dumps, if that's what you mean, Miss Proudfoot?'

'I think you may call me Vivian – and it's not your opinion of the décor I'm after but a little insight into what you think of the situation in Spain.'

'Politically?'

'Yes, politically.'

'You didn't enjoy what you saw on the screen today, did you?' Danny said.

'I certainly didn't enjoy seeing Susan's brother – your chum – in chains,' Vivian said. 'I reluctantly have to admit that a picture *is* worth a thousand words. Where have they taken him?'

'At a guess,' said Danny, 'the prison camp at San Martin de la Vega.'

'I hear Franco's prone to having prisoners shot,' said Vivian.

'Aye,' Danny said, 'but if Ron keeps his nose clean they might put him up for a prisoner swop. Franco needs the support o' the British government to shore up the non-intervention treaty.'

'If,' Vivian said, 'I were to accept a *Times* commission to go to Madrid, would I be in danger of meeting a sticky end?'

'If you're in the front line, sure,' said Danny.

'Are you thinking of it, Vivian?' Susan asked.

'I am, to be honest, heartily sick of Hitler.'

'You'd be writing in support o' the nationalists, though, wouldn't you?'

'Yes, Danny, I would.'

'Would you take Susan with you?'

'No,' said Vivian.

'Why not?' Susan said. 'I'm no coward.'

Vivian paused. 'Mercer wouldn't stand for it.'

'Mercer has nothing to do with it,' Susan said. 'Mercer doesn't own me.'

'Does he not?' said Vivian. 'Really?'

'I thought we came here to eat,' said Susan testily.

'We did. Of course, we did,' Vivian said. 'Danny, see if you can catch a waiter's eye, please, and we'll save the war talk for later.'

'By all means,' Danny said and, as if to the manor born, raised an arm high in the air and loudly snapped his fingers.

After breakfast they ferried him out in Roger's truck to a

grassy field so remote it might have been on the steppes of Russia. Throwing open the door of a dilapidated barn, David declared, 'Here be Dragons,' which proved David knew as much about cartography as he, Mercer, did about aeroplanes.

He'd never flown and never would. He hated the idea of soaring above the clouds with nothing but a few bits of metal to support him. If he had been inclined to take to the skies, however, it certainly wouldn't be in the aeroplane concealed in the barn. Bird droppings peppered the wings, the propeller was set at a funny angle, the tyres were flat and rust, a lot of rust, lined the edges of the cockpit; a sneaking suspicion that his old chum David was playing him for a chump crept over him.

'I thought you were repairing it,' he said.

'Oh, it's been serviced,' David said. 'It's virtually ready to go.'

'Needs a lick of paint, that's all,' said Roger.

'When will it get this lick of paint?'

'Soon as Clive gets back,' said Roger.

'And when will Clive get back?'

'Soon as he can.'

'So,' Mercer said, as evenly as possible, 'it's one lost, two delivered and this thing ready for take-off.'

'What's wrong, old son? You sound a trifle miffed?'

'I thought we were selling aircraft not – not rust-buckets.'

'Told you; the republicans will take what they can get.'

'Were they happy with the two they've got so far?'

'No complaints,' said Roger.

'In which case, where's the cash?' Mercer said.

'We think Clive has it,' said Roger.

'You *think* Clive has it,' Mercer said. 'I was under the impression the chap in the Waldorf was paying up front.'

'No, no,' David said. 'The agent just makes the offer. You can't expect him to cut about London with thousands of pounds in cash in his pocket.'

'So no one's actually received a penny yet?'

'Not yet, no,' David told him.

'How does Harry King feel about that?'

'Harry King knows the game too well to be grouchy about a little delay.'

'The game? What game's that, David?' Mercer said.

'Planes aren't the only things Harry King deals in,' said Roger. 'He's got fingers in lots of other pies.'

'Talking of pies,' David said, 'I could do justice to a spot of lunch. The Trout okay with you, Roger?'

'Fine by me.'

'Mercer, have you seen enough?'

'More than enough,' said Mercer.

Soon after he passed through Gloucester heavy rain swept in and dusk settled swiftly into night. Neither headlamps nor wipers were working properly, which only served to increase Mercer's frustration.

It had been a wasted day; totally wasted. He'd left Hackles not only empty-handed but without proof that he'd receive a dividend any time soon. David had tried to explain things over lunch in a tiny thatch-roofed pub but a helping of squab pie and a single pint of bitter had rendered him too drowsy to make much sense of it. The fellow with the moustache, Roger, had backed David by nodding and 'yah-ing' in a manner so casual that it was almost insulting, as if, Mercer thought, he regards me as a fool for expecting to be paid at all.

What it boiled down to, and the fact he had to face, was

that Proudfoot might be pulling a fast one and that far from settling his financial problems the shady deal had only increased them.

He was, in other words, broke.

He'd been broke before, of course. His mother's mania for gambling large sums on small horses had seen to that. But he couldn't, in conscience, lay all the blame on her. He'd become too dependent on his father-in-law to bail him out of trouble in the past. Carver had no doubt heard that he'd taken a mistress and while the miserable old puritan might ignore rumours of an occasional fling he was still Rosalind's father and entitled to look after her interests.

There had been times of late when he wished that the quacks would come up with a cure for Rosalind's illness, some magic new treatment to restore her sanity and leave her as she'd been when they'd first met. She'd been sliding when he'd finally taken her to the altar, though, and had giggled all through the ceremony while his mother and Rhoda Hartnell had made a book on just how long the marriage would last before the blushing bride went completely gaga.

When he visited Rosalind now in the so-called nursing home, which was really no better than a luxurious prison house, he saw only the wreckage of a life destroyed by a condition that the experts couldn't identify let alone cure. The sad thing was that in repose she still looked fresh and young. But when the demon took hold she would age before his eyes, spew out words that would make a sailor blush and, if she wasn't restrained, spit and claw and – he shuddered to think of it – yank up her skirts, show him her belly and tell him that she wanted him to give her babies.

Perhaps if their baby had lived, if he'd had a son to care for, everything might have been different. The horror of that afternoon when he'd arrived home to find Rosalind walking up and down in the drawing room with little Jonny wrapped in a shawl while the doctors, two of them, and a police sergeant tried to persuade her to give up the baby. He'd loved nothing in his life so much as he'd loved his child and after Jonny's death everything had gone even more swiftly to hell.

Rain drummed on the roof and dashed the windscreen faster than the wiper blades could strip it away. Standing water hissed beneath the tyres. He craned over the wheel, peering into the darkness, struggling to concentrate.

The van came upon him suddenly.

Big, bulbous headlamps swung in an arc across his field of vision. He had a fleeting glimpse of the van driver's face, mouth agape, and the side panel of the van – *Farmington's Famous Jams* – lurching broadside across the roadway; then trees, a grassy bank and a field drain vomiting water.

The van roared past, tail lights winking and the angry wail of the horn ringing in Mercer's ears. The back end of the Ford rose up like flotsam on a tidal wave. Tilted on two wheels, the car thudded from the bank and with Mercer frantically fisting the wheel and pumping the brake, slithered at last to a halt.

There was no sound save the mutter of the engine and a series of small sighs from the springs as if the Ford were as relieved as he was to be upright and all in one piece. Motionless, he listened to the gush of the field drain and the flurry of wind in the trees for a moment or two and then drove shakily on towards London.

London had not escaped the rain. The King's Road was deserted save for a few late-night buses and an odd taxicab. Mercer parked the car close to the door of Susan's building.

It was well after eleven. Curled up under the eiderdown, Susan would surely be asleep.

The close call on the Gloucester road had been the final straw in a long, exhausting day. He felt old now, old, bone-weary and devoid of desire. Tomorrow he'd be himself again, striding out to do battle with publishers, but right now all he wanted was to lie in Susan's arms and be comforted.

He ducked into the building, climbed the stairs and let himself into the flat.

There were no lights in the room and the gas fire was dead. He opened the bedroom door with his forearm.

'Susan,' he whispered. 'Susan, it's me.' He waited for her to stir, to sigh, to lift her head from the pillow. 'Susan?'

He switched on the ceiling light.

The bed was empty.

He hurried into the bathroom which was empty too.

'For God's sake, Susan?' he said, as if she were teasing him. 'Where are you? Where the hell are you?'

He lit the gas fire, sank into the armchair and, in spite of himself, dozed off.

When he wakened it was half past two.

And Susan had not come home.

24

The changes Vivian had made to the original draft of *The Melting Pot* were numerous and Susan had been kept hard at it typing them up. Now, it seemed, Vivian had found her voice again. With an annotated copy of Dugdale's abridged translation of *Mein Kampf* in one hand and a cigarette in the other, she paraded up and down the office in Salt Street, dictating new material at so fast a lick that Susan could barely keep up.

They'd been at it for almost an hour before Mercer arrived. He rapped urgently on the horseshoe-shaped knocker and when Vivian, grousing, admitted him, shouted, 'Is she here?'

'Of course, she's here. Where else would she be?'

Mercer marched into the office and confronted Susan at her desk.

'Where the devil were you last night?' he said. 'You didn't come home.'

'Did too,' said Susan.

'When, when did you come home?'

'Three,' she said, 'or a bit after.'

'Three o'clock in the morning?' Mercer leaned on the desk. 'Who were you with, Susan? Whose bed were you warming instead of mine?'

Vivian tapped him on the shoulder. 'Hoy!' she said. 'That's

enough out of you, Mr Hughes. If there's any shouting to be done in this house, I'll do it.'

Mercer whirled. 'So you're in on it, are you? Who is it? I know it isn't your brother. It must be that commie, that Cahill fellow.'

'Danny Cahill is not a commie,' Susan snapped. 'But, yes, if you must know I was with Danny last night.'

'You deceitful bitch!'

'What about you, Mercer?' Vivian said. 'Who were you with?'

'I wasn't with anyone. I was out of town all day.'

Susan, red-faced, said, 'Why didn't you wait for me?'

'I've more to do than sit up half the night waiting for a little—'

'Careful,' said Vivian.

'Waiting for you to come home.'

'Home?' said Susan. 'Is that what you call it? You've a bleeding nerve, Mercer. You gallivant here, there and everywhere without a word to anyone and expect me to be waiting for you with my tongue hanging out like a . . .'

'Good little wife,' Vivian suggested.

'Yes, wife,' said Susan.

'But you are my wife, Susan. In all but name you are my wife.'

'Oh, no, I am not. You're not keeping me.'

'Because you won't let me.'

'Precisely,' Susan said.

'Far be it from me to interrupt a lovers' tiff,' Vivian said, 'but I've a book to finish.'

'The book, the book,' said Mercer, 'that's all you ever think about. Doesn't it matter to you that my life's going down the drain? Well, Vivian, I'm not leaving until she tells me where she was last night.'

'She was with me,' Vivian said, 'in the newsroom of Danny Cahill's newspaper poring over press photographs from Spain. It was a decidedly sobering experience, believe me.'

'Research?' said Mercer. 'In the middle of the night?'

'Sometimes it pays to have clout,' said Vivian.

'Danny's idea,' Susan said. 'The newsroom's quiet at that hour. The night editor was very accommodating when Vivian explained what we were looking for.'

'What were you looking for?' Mercer said.

'Information about my brother,' Susan said.

'Did you find any?'

'We did,' said Susan. 'He's in Talavera, a concentration camp the fascists opened up in the grounds of an old pottery factory. We were shown agency photographs newly arrived from Madrid, some so awful they'll never appear in print.'

'Unless the *Daily Mail* decides to use them for pro-Franco propaganda, of course,' Vivian put in. 'We found one – just one – of Susan's brother.'

'He's had his hair shaved off,' Susan said, 'all his lovely hair.'

'And you think your life's going down the drain, Mercer?' Vivian shook her head. 'You don't know the half of it.'

'Well,' Mercer said, 'your brother shouldn't be in Spain. It's not his fight.'

Vivian put a hand on Susan's shoulder. 'In a democracy – and we still live in a democracy last time I looked – a man's entitled to choose which side to fight for. Nobody's going to march you – or me for that matter – off to a concentration camp because we speak out for Tom Mosley. Oh, yes, my friend, you'll sue for peace at all costs provided peace costs you nothing. How long do you suppose that'll wash with Adolf Hitler on the rampage?'

'Don't tell me you're changing horses?' Mercer said.

'What?' Vivian said. 'And alienate my publisher, let alone my vast army of fans? Do you think I'm completely bonkers? No, Mercer, I'm not changing horses. All I'm saying is that as a freeborn citizen of this sceptered isle I'm entitled to change horses any time I want to. And so is Susan.'

'Now what's that supposed to mean?' said Mercer.

'Take it how you will,' Vivian told him. 'I'd be obliged if you'd fume elsewhere, however. I have a deadline to meet.'

'There's no deadline,' Mercer said. 'Is there?'

'You're my agent; you should know,' Vivian said. 'Even if there isn't a deadline I want this book off my hands as soon as possible. So shoo, scram and leave me to get on with it.'

'Yes,' Mercer said. 'Yes, of course.' He hesitated. 'We'll have dinner tonight, Susan. Talk things over.'

'No.'

'Will I come to the flat?'

'No.'

'Oh, God, you're not going to sulk, are you?'

'I'm busy, Mercer. I've things to do; important things.'

'More important than me?'

'Oh, boy!' said Vivian, throwing up her hands.

'For once, Mercer,' Susan said, 'you're not the centre of the universe.'

'Ah!' Mercer said. 'I see. Going out on the tiles with Cahill again, I suppose.'

'Hardly,' Susan said. 'I'm going home to Shadwell to see my father.'

'Really! And why is that?'

'Because he needs me,' Susan said.

'For what?' said Mercer.

'His son's in a stinking prison camp, Mercer,' Vivian said. 'Why do you think he needs her?' She took his arm and edged him towards the door. 'Now, please, just toddle along before you make things worse.'

'I'm not sure they can get any worse,' Mercer said.

'Oh, they can. Believe me, they can,' said Vivian.

Tightening her grip, she drew him out into hall, opened the front door and almost, but not quite, hurled him out into the street.

'Vivian?'

'Goodbye, Mercer,' she said and closed the door in his face.

The sky over the Thames was stretched thin as gauze and laced with pretty little clouds that caught the sun's rays around the edges. Even the smoke from factory chimneys was daubed with subtle colours and the brickwork around the dock gates had the rich, dense texture of a painting by Monet or Sisley or, she thought, that chap, Pissarro, whose name Ronnie had made fun of when she'd happened to mention it after her first visit to the Tate.

Such odd little thoughts milled in her head as she lingered at the corner across from the gates. The last time – indeed, the only time – she'd ever waited here, Ronnie had been holding her hand. She could still recall her father's look of alarm when he'd caught sight of them and how he'd covered his face with his hands when Ronnie had told him that Granddad had died of a stroke that afternoon.

He came up through the Garnet Street gate with a bunch of five or six men, hands in his pockets, cap pulled down.

The others were young and boisterous and when they caught sight of her they shouted and cavorted, showing off, and might have sloped across the road to accost her if she hadn't raised an arm, waved her scarf and called out, 'Dad.'

'Hey, 'Ooper, she yours?'

The same startled expression that she remembered from all those years ago crossed his face and he broke into a trot. She held up both hands, palms showing.

'It's all right, Dad,' she said. 'It's really all right.'

He clutched her sleeve, panting. 'Billy, is it Billy?'

'No, it's Ronnie. We've tracked down Ronnie.'

Her father let out breath in a roaring sigh.

'Geeze!' he said at length. 'Is that all?'

There was something going on between the big man and her sister-in-law. How far the affair – if it was an affair – had progressed Susan couldn't be certain but she had no doubt that Breda was smitten with Nellie Millar's brother and certainly wasn't pleased at having their cosy little twosome in the shadowy café interrupted.

When her father-in-law opened the door of the dining rooms, Breda sprang to her feet. 'You're bleedin' early, ain't yah?' Then, seeing Susan, 'An' what's she doing 'ere? Come to cause more trouble, 'ave yer?'

Steve Millar rose and offered his hand.

'Miss 'Ooper,' he said. 'Pleased to meetcha again.'

The hand was strangely soft, like squeezing a felt hat.

Her father said, 'She's got news about our Ronnie.'

'Has she?' said Breda, without enthusiasm. 'How come?'

'Newspaper,' her father said.

'Yeah, well, I can read as well as she can.'

'Danny's newspaper.'

'Where is Danny?' Susan said.

'Gone to work,' said Breda. 'He never said nothing to me about Ronnie.'

'No, we decided—' Susan began.

'You decided, did yer?' Breda said. 'Who are you to decide anything?'

This was not how Danny and she had planned it. Courtesy, tact and kinship were wasted on her sister-in-law, it seemed. Before she could devise an answer Billy came running from the kitchen and threw himself against her legs, chanting, 'Auntie Sue, Auntie Sue come to see me.'

Nellie Millar and Nora emerged from the kitchen.

'Sure an' this is a nice surprise,' said Nora.

'She's got news,' her father said.

'She says,' Breda added.

Breda was still half hidden behind Steve Millar and clung to his arm as if he were her rock, her anchor now.

'We'd best be going,' said Nellie Millar.

'No,' said Breda. 'You stay. Steve, you stay.'

'Family business,' her father said. 'Got nothing to do with 'im.'

Where, Susan wondered, was the big-hearted, all-encompassing loyalty that united families in time of trouble? No sign of it here.

'Come inside, have some supper,' Nora said.

'No,' said Susan firmly. 'I can't stay long.'

Once she stepped into the kitchen she'd be trapped for the rest of the evening. Gently, she detached her nephew's fists from her skirt.

'Ronnie's a prisoner of—' she began.

'Yeah, we know that,' Breda interrupted.

'He's in a camp in Talavera with—'

'Tents?' said Breda. 'That's okay then.'

'It's a concentration camp,' said Susie. 'I doubt if they have tents.'

'They'll shoot 'im,' her father stated. 'Sure as eggs, they'll shoot 'im.'

'Oh, God! Oh, God!' Nora sank down on one of the chairs. 'What've I done? What have I done?'

'You?' her father said. 'Ain't your fault Ron went off to Spain.'

Billy clung to his grandmother's knees, bewildered by her tears.

'They won't dare shoot 'im,' Breda said. 'Not my Ronnie.'

Steve put an arm about her waist and gave her a reassuring hug.

''Course they won't,' he said; then to Susan, 'What else you find out?'

'Not much,' Susan said. 'The news is reasonably up to date, though. Four or five days old, that's all. You'd be amazed at how much stuff pours into a newspaper office that never gets published.'

'Like what?' said Breda.

'Should never have done it.' Nora stroked Billy's hair. 'It's all my fault.'

'For God's sake, Nora, will you shut up,' Matt Hooper said.

'I gave him the money to go.'

'You did what?'

'Gave him some o' Leo's money for to pay the fare.'

'Oh, geeze!' her father said. 'What did you go an' do that for?'

'Ronnie wanted to go so bad,' Nora explained. 'Sure an'

I thought – I thought Breda would be better off without him.'

Breda shrieked, 'You cow, Ma! You interfering old cow!'

'Don't talk to your mother like that,' Steve Millar said. 'Ain't nice, Breda.'

'You keep your nose out of it,' Breda said. 'This is between me and 'er; nobody else.' She pounded a fist on his chest. 'How come *you* ain't out there fighting for – for freedom? Rather stay 'ome and poke an innocent widow, would yer?'

'You aren't a widow, Breda.' Susan resisted the temptation to add that she wasn't so innocent either. 'I didn't come here to make trouble. In fact, if you'll just calm down—'

'Calm down, calm down?' Breda cried. 'My own mother pays me hubby to go off to the war and you got the cheek to tell me to calm down. Only person in this wide world cares about me is Danny.' She thrust herself away from Steve and snatched up her son. Holding him high between her hands she shook him vigorously. 'Look at this poor little tyke, my poor orphan boy. See what you done to 'im, Ma? You took away 'is daddy.'

Billy, eyes rolling, was too stunned to wail. He swung between his mother's hands and meekly allowed himself to be shaken again.

'They'll trade 'im, won't they?' Steve Millar said.

Susan nodded. 'According to Danny—'

'Danny,' Breda yelled. 'Where's Danny? I want Danny.'

Anger welled up in Susan, a sudden rush of rage.

She stepped forward, pulled Billy from her sister-in-law's grasp and lowered the little boy to the floor behind her. Then she grabbed a fistful of Breda's hair and shouted, 'Keep your bleedin' paws off Danny, Breda. Danny Cahill's mine.'

★

Mercer picked her up in a taxi at half past nine. She had obviously put a great deal of effort into looking good, and it showed. The silk evening coat flew open as she came tripping down the steps from the front door of the Mayfair town house and he could see every curve of her body shaped by the white velour of the evening dress. He hopped out of the taxi, took her hand and kissed it before he helped her inside. He was pretty sure that Gwen was watching from the upstairs window but he wasn't cruel enough to look up and wave.

'Where to, guv?' the cabby asked.

'The Brooklyn Club. Do you know it?'

'Yer, I know it.'

Mercer settled back in the seat. Eleanor snuggled against him. She'd sprayed herself with a sensuous perfume, not one that Gwen would have chosen, and the effect was almost overpowering. In the flicker of the street lights her blonde curls shone like little gold ingots and until she opened her mouth you might have taken her for a sophisticated woman, not a girl of eighteen.

'I'm sorry about the short notice,' Mercer said. 'I'm so glad you didn't have anything better to do.'

'If I had,' Eleanor said, 'I'd have cancelled.' She snuggled closer. 'What happened to your regular girl? Has she ditched you?'

'Nightclubs aren't her thing.'

'It isn't over then?'

'No, Ellie, it isn't over.'

'Does she know about us?'

'Us?'

'I mean that you're taking me dancing.'

'Does it matter?' Mercer said.

'It would matter to me if I was your number one girl.'

'How' – Mercer hesitated – 'how did your mama take it?'

'Not well.'

'Didn't she try to stop you?'

'I do what I like these days. And what I like' – she blew into his ear – 'is you.'

'That's very – I mean, I'm flattered.'

'I'm the one who should be flattered,' Eleanor said. 'I know you've a string of girls at your beck and call. Aren't you going to kiss me?'

'Kissing usually comes later.'

She sat back and fixed him with her glittering blue gaze.

'Is there going to be a later?'

'You never know your luck,' said Mercer.

Nursing a glass of red wine and the inevitable cigarette, Vivian stretched out on the new American-style davenport that Heal's had delivered that afternoon. She blew out a thin stream of smoke and glanced fondly at her employee who had just polished off a mushroom omelette and seemed much calmer now.

'I must say,' Vivian said, 'it is very comfortable. Well worth the wait – the davenport, I mean. By rights, I suppose, you should be lying here and I should be perched on a hard chair with my knees together and my glasses on the end of my nose making notes.'

'Much as I appreciate your kindness, Vivian,' Susan said, 'I'm not sure I want to turn up as a case study in one of your books.'

'Fat chance of that,' Vivian said. 'Now, if you were Anna Maples's little helper she'd turn your comical encounter into a tragedy. You'd have to lob yourself off Waterloo Bridge on the final page, of course, that being Anna's idea of a happy ending.'

Susan managed a weak little smile. 'I don't know what came over me.'

'You spoke from the heart, that's all,' Vivian said.

'I mean why I came here. I just – I'd no one else to talk to. I'm sorry.'

'Don't apologise, my dear,' Vivian said. 'I rather like being your confidante. My nieces never had much time for me, even when they were young. Caro wasn't so bad, but Eleanor – well, that's water under the Waterloo Bridge now, I suppose.' She shifted her broad hips on the davenport and tipped cigarette ash into a tray balanced on her bosom. 'I honestly don't see why you're so upset.'

'I should never have lost my temper.'

'Wish I'd been there,' Vivian said. 'I haven't seen a good cat-fight since I left St Catherine's.'

'It wasn't really a cat-fight,' Susan said. 'I pulled her hair and she pulled mine but we didn't wrestle on the floor or anything. I suppose we might've done if Steve Millar hadn't separated us.'

'Steve Millar being Breda's lover?'

'I'm not sure. Possibly.'

'Are you angry with her for cheating on your brother?'

'Lord, no. I can't be judgemental when I'm – well, you know what I am.'

'But you're not married.'

'Mercer is.'

'Nominally,' Vivian said. 'Repeat – nominally.'

Susan leaned an elbow on the dining table and rested her chin on her palm.

'My brother's in one of Franco's hell-holes – you saw the photographs – and my father's convinced he'll be shot. In fact, I wouldn't be surprised if my father thinks he *should* be shot. Breda's behaving as if Ronnie were already dead and angling for another man to take care of her.'

'Steve Millar?'

'Perhaps.'

'Or your friend Mr Cahill?'

'Danny's too good for her.'

'I see,' said Vivian. 'Is Danny too good for you?'

'I can't answer that.'

'Put it another way,' said Vivian. 'Aren't you good enough for Danny?'

Susan sat up, frowning. 'Do you know, I never thought of it that way.'

'He is in love with you, you know.'

'How can you be so sure?'

'I may look like Grendel's mother but, believe me, I've had my moments,' Vivian said. 'I haven't forgotten what love light in a young man's eye can do for the heart rate. I take it Breda wasn't amused when you laid claim to Mr Cahill?'

'Anything but,' Susan admitted. 'I really put my foot in it, didn't I?'

'You did,' said Vivian. 'I imagine the first thing Breda will do when Danny turns up this evening is tell him what you said.'

'Or,' Susan said gloomily, 'take it as a declaration of war.'

'Throw herself at Danny, you mean?' Vivian said.

'She does have some formidable weapons at her disposal; not least the fact she's sharing a house with him again. Breda knows better than anyone that if she ever manages to drag Danny to the altar he'll never let her down.'

'Unlike, shall we say, the present incumbent?'

'Pardon me?'

'I mean your brother, of course, but it might equally apply to Mr Hughes.'

'Mercer doesn't take care of me,' Susan said. 'I won't let him.'

'I wonder why?' said Vivian. 'Could it be because you know that sooner or later he *will* let you down?'

'I didn't expect it to last this long, to be honest.'

'Nor did anyone else,' said Vivian. 'We are now approaching what may be the ultimate irony; that you are more of a cad than he is.' She frowned. 'What's the female equivalent of a cad? I must look it up next time I'm in the British Library.'

'Are you making fun of me, Vivian?'

'Wouldn't dream of it, my dear,' Vivian said. 'I may, however, be tempted to make fun of Mercer if ever you do decide to leave him in favour of a scruffy Scottish newspaper man with leanings to the left.'

'You don't like him, do you?'

'Mercer? Oh, no, I absolutely adore Mercer. Always have.'

'Actually, I meant Danny.'

'Ah,' said Vivian softly. 'Well, yes, I think if I spent enough time in Mr Cahill's company I might even fall for him myself.' She placed the wine glass and ashtray on the carpet and kicked her legs. 'Now, if you're feeling better, Susan, I suggest you cut along home just in case Mercer turns up with an armful of roses. You wouldn't want to miss a fine bit of grovelling, would you?'

'Mercer isn't much given to grovelling.'

'One of his more endearing traits.' Vivian kicked her legs

again. 'Before you depart, however, I wonder if you'd mind giving me a hand.'

'To do what?' Susan asked.

'To get out of this bloody sofa,' Vivian said.

25

The Brooklyn Club was a far cry from the Café de Paris. The staircase was too steep to be graceful and the gilded cherubim that topped the newel posts were chipped and peeling. The dance floor below was veiled in smoke, the table lamps in the dining alcoves dim. The only sources of strong light were a jagged neon sign that pointed the way to the Statue of Liberty Bar and the shell-shaped bandstand where an eight-piece orchestra was grinding out a quickstep.

There were twenty or thirty couples on the floor, more couples tucked away in the banquettes; men of a certain age in tuxedos and girls in evening gowns so revealing that Eleanor seemed overdressed by comparison.

It had been a mistake to bring Eleanor, Mercer realised, as he escorted her down the staircase. However grown up and modern she might imagine herself to be, in this company she was a lamb among wolves.

'Table, sir?' said a young man in a white jacket. 'You a party?'

'No,' Mercer said. 'Just two.'

'A couple,' Eleanor said, and hugged him.

The white jacket led them up the side of the dance floor past the line of banquettes. If Mercer had been in any doubt that eating and drinking wasn't all that went on in the red leather booths one swift sideways glance was enough to dispel the illusion. Eleanor, pop-eyed, tugged at his sleeve and whispered, 'Is she doing what I think she's doing?'

'Yes, I believe she is.'

The banquette was at the far end of the room close to a bare brick wall and a fire exit. The white jacket eased out the table.

'Is it always this busy?' Mercer asked.

'Most nights, yer,' the young man answered and, swinging from the hip, summoned a waiter in shirtsleeves and striped waistcoat to attend them.

The bill of fare was printed on a plain card; no prices listed. Mercer peered at it, invited an opinion and on the waiter's recommendation ordered whiting followed by ragout of beef.

'The lady?' the waiter said.

Eleanor waved airily. 'The same.'

The waiter wiggled a dark eyebrow. 'Champagne?'

'Of course,' said Eleanor. 'It has to be champagne, doesn't it, darling?'

He had thirty pounds in his wallet, fifteen of which he'd filched from the jewellery box in which his mother hid her gambling money. He nodded dolefully.

The waiter smiled and went away.

Eleanor popped up and down like a jack-in-the-box and might have kneeled on the leather bench and goggled at the couple in the next booth if Mercer hadn't pulled her back. She rested her bosom on the table and said, 'Is this where naughty men bring their girlfriends?'

'Yes,' he said. 'You'd never guess the country's in the middle of a slump.'

Eleanor didn't give a damn about the state of the country.

'If they don't bring a girl with them they can find one here, can't they? I mean, for money?'

'I expect that's true,' said Mercer.

'Haven't you been here before?'

'Certainly not,' said Mercer.

'It's all sex, isn't it?' She sounded like Caro discovering the year's first snowdrop. 'I mean, my God, I've read about these places in the newspapers but I thought it was all made up.'

'Well, it's not,' said Mercer. 'So be careful.'

'Tell me, darling,' she said, 'is this part of a writer's education?'

'I suppose you might say that.'

'Or are you just softening me up?'

'Softening you up?'

'You know – for sex.'

'Ah-hah!' said Mercer. 'Here comes the champagne.'

If he'd thought for one minute that Susan would still be at Nora's, he wouldn't have stopped off for a late night pie and a pint in Masefield's. But Susan, he was sure, would be long gone. It was after midnight before he let himself into the house via the back door. He paused and listened for sounds of distress – Billy whimpering, Nora weeping, Breda cursing – but the place was uncannily quiet. He took off his coat and hung it on the hook in the corridor before he padded into the kitchen.

She was standing by the stoves, arms folded, a cigarette in her fingers wafting smoke. She wore only a nightgown, a daffodil-yellow thing too revealing to be casual; no robe. She hadn't removed her make-up: her lips were bright red, her cheeks peachy pale, her eyebrows pencilled.

'Danny,' she said huskily. 'Thank God, you're 'ome.'

She tossed the cigarette into the fire, floated towards him and, to his surprise, held out her arms. 'Gimme a cuddle,' she said. 'I really need a cuddle tonight.'

He took her into his arms and patted her back. She pushed against him, sobbing dryly. The cheap cotton-silk material of the nightgown slithered under his fingertips. Without shoes she was quite small or, he thought, short; one thing Breda would never be was small.

She nuzzled against him, still more or less sobbing.

'She told you?' Danny got out. 'I mean, Susie told you?'

'Yeah. 'Orrible, ain't it? My Ronnie. My poor Ronnie, a prisoner.'

'Breda, you're chokin' me.'

'What? Yer, sorry. I'm just – just upset.'

''Course you are.'

Danny patted her again and managed to detach himself.

She stared into his eyes. 'I'm glad I got you, Danny. I really am.'

'I'm always here, Breda; you know that.'

She cocked her head and smiled wanly. 'You want supper? It's cold 'am?'

'Cold ham will be fine,' Danny said.

He seated himself at the table and watched her slide the supper plate from the bottom larder. She stood up, plate in hand, and glanced over her shoulder to make sure he was paying attention. She poured hot water into a tea mug, added a dash of coffee essence and, leaning over him, laid plate and mug on the table between his arms. Three slices of cold ham, four new potatoes lagged with salad cream and a pickled onion; Breda's idea of supper, not Nora's.

He picked up a fork and ate dutifully.

'How did your ma take it?' he asked.

'My ma's got a sin to answer for,' Breda said. 'Know this, she paid 'is bleedin' fare. I mean, can you believe it? She sent my Ron off to Spain 'cause she thought I'd be better off without 'im.'

'Nora tell you that?'

'Oh, she's sorry now,' said Breda. 'Crying 'er bleedin' eyes out now.'

'It's not as bad as she thinks it is,' Danny said. 'I'll talk to her tomorrow.'

'How about talking to me tonight?'

Seated across the table from him she reached for his hand. The strap of the nightgown slipped down over her shoulder. He gave her his left hand to hold and went on wielding the fork with his right.

'The old man, what did he have to say about it?'

Breda rubbed his knuckles with her forefinger. 'He don't care.'

'I think you're wrong there, Breda.'

'He's still mad 'cause Ronnie took up with that Jewish tart.'

'Well, for what it's worth,' said Danny, 'Ruth Gertler has another string to her bow. Ronnie's in for a surprise when he gets home.'

'Whatcha mean?'

'She's as good as engaged to some guy called Jacob.'

'Oh!' said Breda, then again, 'Oh!'

'You haven't lost Ron to Ruth Gertler, Breda; you've lost him, temporarily, to the fascists,' Danny said. 'The nationalists have hundreds of prisoners stacked in this camp at Talavera but the republicans have thousands of captured Italian conscripts too – an' Mussolini would kinda like to have them back. Sooner or later there'll be an exchange of prisoners. It's a fair bet Ronnie will be among them.'

'Oh!' said Breda once more. 'I thought he'd gone for good.'

'No such luck, eh?' Danny tempered his remark with a wink. 'No second chances, Breda, an' that includes me.'

She stopped stroking his knuckles and hoisted up the strap of the nightgown.

'You're a bastard, Danny Cahill.'

'Always was, always will be.'

'I dunno what she sees in you.'

'What who sees in me?'

'Bleedin' Susie Hooper.'

'Susie's not interested in me,' Danny said. 'She's got a guy.'

'I ain't the only one looking for second chances,' Breda said. 'I wonder what Susie would say if I told 'er what you done for me.'

'I didn't do anything for you, Breda.'

'If I hadn't been for you – no Billy.'

'Well, aye, but no Ronnie either,' Danny reminded her.

'In this life you gotta take the rough with the smooth,' Breda said.

'Very profound, sweetheart, very profound.'

She pushed herself up with both hands and looked down at him, shook her head and smiled. 'More 'am, Mr Cahill?'

'No, thank you, Mrs Hooper,' Danny said. 'I've had quite enough 'am for one night,' and ducked as she aimed a swipe at his head.

It had been Mercer's intention to find Leo Romano and, if possible, tease a few straight answers from the man. He'd brought Eleanor along as cover; not cover, actually, but protection. He had a holy horror of falling foul of gangsters and, in spite of David's assurances to the contrary, refused to believe that anyone who worked for Harry King didn't have a razor in one pocket and a knuckle-duster in the other.

Discreet enquiries made to one of the agency's less celebrated hacks, a writer of low-brow detective fiction, had elicited the information that King had carved out an empire in areas where the beetle-browed linchpins of London's underworld were too stupid to operate effectively. High-class knocking shops were only strands in a web of illegal activity that included blackmail, fraud and – Mercer had pricked up his ears – arms dealing.

In the hour before midnight, though, he was less concerned with Romano's thugs than appeasing Eleanor Proudfoot's insatiable appetite. Nourished by fish, meat and a gigantic ice-cream sundae and rendered playful by several glasses of inferior champagne, Eleanor insisted on throwing herself upon him with complete disregard for modesty. He was so busy fighting her off that if Leo Romano had ridden past on a white stallion he probably wouldn't have noticed.

She kissed his cheek, she kissed his mouth and, after she'd polished off the sundae, slipped off a shoe and massaged his thigh with her mischievous little toes; at which particular meeting of the women's branch of the BUF had she learned *that* manoeuvre, Mercer wondered.

'Dance,' he said, brusquely pushing back the table. 'Let's dance.'

Eleanor barely had time to fit on her shoe before he had her out on the floor which was now too crowded to give him much of a view of anything other than leggy blondes and brunettes being pawed by rosy-cheeked doyens of the establishment. Eleanor clung to him like a leech, belly locked against his, as he steered a course through the throng and set about scouting for Leo Romano.

The henchmen weren't hard to spot: a couple of big, hard-faced men in tuxedos and bow ties hanging about the mouth of the Statue of Liberty Bar; another standing off to the side of the bandstand and a fourth, a really big fellow, in a nook under the stairs discussing some issue with a skinny tear-stained girl in a torn dress.

There must be an office somewhere, Mercer told himself; a counting house, a back room, a private place where the girls deposit their takings and the books are cooked. He knew a little about the cooking of books but wasn't quite conceited enough to equate his tapping of authors' accounts with the sort of crooked dealing that went on behind the scenes in the Brooklyn.

Eleanor sang softly to herself. If it hadn't been for the occasional wriggle of her hips Mercer might have supposed she was falling asleep.

Then, chin resting on his breastbone, she looked up.

'Where shall we go,' she said, 'afterwards?'

'Uh?'

'Don't you have a place?' she said.

'No, I – I live with my mother.'

'I thought you lived with her?'

'Susan? She has a flat of her own.'

'Can't we go there?'

'Don't be bloody ridi . . . No, my dear, we can't go there.'

'It'll have to be a hotel then. I don't suppose one can do it properly in a taxi.'

It was on the tip of Mercer's tongue to tell her that her mother might be best able to answer that question when Eleanor stiffened.

'What?' he said. 'What's wrong?'

She pointed a trembling finger at a figure on the stairs.

'Oh, my God,' she said. 'It's Daddy.'

There was no disturbance, no commotion, barely a ripple of interest among the dancers as Eleanor was led off in one direction and Mercer in another. For a moment or two he thought they might be taking him out into the lane at the back of the club to beat him up and that David, hard on his heels, would do nothing to stop them. When they reached the banquette, though, the henchmen peeled away and he found himself seated in exactly the same position he'd been in before he'd hauled Eleanor off to dance. Plates and glasses had been removed but the girl's little silver evening bag was still on the table. David picked it up and put it in his pocket.

He wasn't wearing a tux, Mercer noticed, not even a suit and necktie. He had the look of a man who had thrown on whatever clothes had come to hand which, in David's case, happened to be a roll-necked sweater and a sports coat.

The white jacket appeared with two drinks on a tray and, saying not a word, unloaded them and went off again.

'What is that?' Mercer asked.

'Gimlet,' David answered.

'It's not drugged, is it?'

'Just drink it.'

Obediently Mercer sipped the cocktail which had too much lime in it for his taste. He pressed his tongue into his cheek to ease the sting.

He said, 'Where's Eleanor?'

'On her way home in a taxi with one of Leo's lads.'

'I thought you were still in Hackles?' Mercer said.

'Got back this afternoon,' David said. 'By the way, if you think my showing up here is wild coincidence, think again. Leo called me. Just because you didn't see him doesn't mean he didn't see you. What the devil do you think you're up to, bringing her to a place like this?' He swirled the mixture in his glass. 'Have you forgotten that she might be your daughter?'

The bully boys were still on call. Mercer could see them from the corner of his eye: a big fair-faced chap and the one who'd been Harry King's bodyguard at the Mayfair party. He was no longer afraid of them, or of David. He'd reached what Rupert Arlen would probably describe as 'a pretty pass' and with his back to the wall, quite literally, prepared himself for a scrap.

He said, 'Poor Eleanor. Given my seedy reputation, she simply can't understand why her allure has no effect on me. Oedipus, dear heart. Mourning becomes Electra, and all that.'

'Do not be flippant, Mercer; not about Eleanor.'

'What matter if I take her to bed? It's a fifty-fifty chance it won't be incest.'

'And that thrills you, does it?'

'Well, the odds aren't bad, are they?'

'We were drunk, remember. All of us, blind drunk.'

'I haven't forgotten, David. How could I? You, after your fashion, have been making me pay for it ever since. Does Gwen know what you get up to in Hackles when she's not there?'

'We have an understanding.'

'I know you do,' said Mercer. 'It isn't my fault she prefers to have me all to herself.' He sat back against the leather and took a long pull from the glass. 'Why are you doing this, David? Do you think if you put me in a tight enough spot I'll share Susan with you? She's not one of your apple-pickers, you know, or some bored farmer's wife.'

'She's common,' David said, 'and she's on the make.'

'There's a world of difference between being on the make and making your way in the world. Susan isn't about to sell herself to anyone; not me, not you, not anyone.' He put down his empty glass. 'Who's paying for these?'

'On the house.'

'In that case, I'll have another.'

He watched David signal to one of the henchmen who signalled to the waiter who, within seconds, delivered two more cocktails to the table.

'There is no money from Spain, is there? The aeroplane thing was a lie.'

'Come now,' David said. 'Do you think I'd lie to influential friends like Cecile and Philippa or to a man like Harry King?'

'King's dealing in arms, isn't he? The Dragons are only bait?'

'I knew you'd twig to it eventually,' David said.

'You used my money to grease the wheels? Quite clever, actually! Will I ever share in the profits or are you determined to ruin me?'

'Just giving you a helping hand, Mercer, that's all.'

'Some helping hand,' Mercer said. 'You're pushing me over the edge.'

'That,' David said, 'is my intention.'

'But why?'

'Eleanor has to be protected.'

'Rubbish! I'm not crass enough to lay a hand on Eleanor. It's Gwen, isn't it? Now I'm no longer willing to keep Gwen entertained you're closing the book on me. I mean, you're doing this for Gwen, right, and all because of Susan?'

'Oh, what a romantic you are, Mercer,' David said. 'I always suspected women would be your downfall but not, if you'll pardon the expression, love.'

'If' – Mercer paused – 'if I was prepared to give Susan up . . .'

'A little too late for that, I'm afraid.'

'Or share her with you?'

'Well,' David said, 'well, that might put a different complexion on things.'

'If I can talk Susan round,' Mercer said, 'would we be friends again?'

'Meaning, would I clear your debts?'

'Yes.'

'I take we're talking . . .'

'Three in a bed.' Mercer nodded. 'Just like the old days.'

'I thought you said she'd never wear it.'

'Oh, she might do it for me,' said Mercer.

'For you?'

'For love, let's say.'

'If she will, if she does . . .'

'My troubles are over?' Mercer said.

'Yes, your troubles are over,' David Proudfoot promised and shook his old chum by the hand.

That evening their lovemaking lasted for what seemed like hours; a much more satisfactory way of apologising than handing her a bouquet, Susan thought. Mercer had telephoned

her at Salt Street and had invited her to meet him in front
of Washington's statue at the Portrait Gallery at half past
seven.

'Are you going?' Vivian had asked.

'I see no reason not to.'

'Are you going to forgive him?'

'Yes, I expect I am.'

He was cautious rather than contrite; very polite. He had,
he said, booked a table in Simpson's but if she preferred
another restaurant he'd be only too pleased to go there
instead.

'The Lantern House, for instance?' Susan had said.

'Ah, no; perhaps, under the circumstances, not the Lantern
House.'

'Simpson's it is then,' Susan had said.

After dinner, they'd taken a taxi back to Rothwell Gardens
where he'd removed her clothes, pushed her on to the
eiderdown and made love to her.

She lay now, very relaxed, watching the lights from the
traffic in the Gardens flit silently across the ceiling. Mercer
stretched beside her, hands behind his head, a leg resting on
her thigh. He'd wait until she was almost asleep before he
slipped from the bed and with a kiss and an apology, dress
and depart for the apartment in Kensington within whose
walls his ailing mother lay in wait.

He rolled on to an elbow and looked down at her.

'Susan, I've a favour to ask of you, a very great favour?'

She raised her head an inch from the pillow.

'And what might that be?' she said.

Since the unmasking of the Vampire of Islington Mr Bageshot
had not been himself. He slumped at his desk day after day

brooding over the fact that his 'inside knowledge' of the monster's identity had been several thousand miles wide of the mark. The brute, like Whitechapel Jack before him, had decamped to America – Detroit to be precise – to carry on his filthy trade. He'd been caught in the act by a couple of Irish cops who'd saved the female from a fate worse than death – well, perhaps not worse than death – and had turned the perpetrator over to detectives who, being somewhat less scrupulous in their methods than their peers in Scotland Yard, had elicited a remarkably full confession from the – would you believe it? – house painter from London, England.

Old Bags had begged the managing editor to finance a trip to Detroit but the vampire was yesterday's news and too far away to merit more than a few page three items on what was going on across the Atlantic, for murder, even juicy murder, had taken second place to what was happening in Europe.

'There is, of course, a book in it,' said Danny Cahill slyly.

Mr Bageshot took his feet down from the desk.

'What d'you mean – a book?'

'A classic study of the case,' said Danny. 'Who else knows as much about it as you do?'

'You think so?'

'I know so,' said Danny. 'Have to wait for the result of the trial in the US, right enough, but you could have all the background stuff written up an' ready.' He paused. 'I've got a friend, a literary agent, who'd be keen to represent you.'

'Really?'

'Mind you, he's in a wee spot o' bother himself right now.'

Bags added another wrinkle to the cluster at the corner of his eye.

'What sort of bother?'

'Nothing serious,' said Danny. 'At least, I don't think it's serious. This guy's a friend of a good friend of mine an' he's being leaned on by Harry King. Somethin' to do with sellin' aeroplanes to Spain.'

To Danny's surprise old Bags let out a bark of laughter.

'Is that all?' he said. 'Okay, Cahill, out with it: what do you want to know about Harry King and the trade in illegal arms?'

'Oh!' said Danny. 'You're up on all this stuff, are you, Mr Bageshot?'

A glimmer in the tired old eyes, a crinkled smile at the edge of the bluish lips; Bags tilted his chair, leaned back and planted his feet on the desk again.

'Try me, son,' he said.

The University Boat Race took place on the Saturday before Easter. Anna invited Mercer to join her gang on Chiswick Bridge to watch the crews cross the finishing line, after which they would all motor out to Richmond for, as she put it, the party to end all parties. Neville, it seemed, was still in Ceylon and quite a crowd of arty types, male and female, would be making hay in the big blustery house overlooking the park. With rather less tact than usual, Mercer turned down the royal command and quite a little ding-dong ensued. Anna threw a bolster at him with such force that it wiped out a bedside lamp and an ormolu clock and the last time Mercer saw his celebrated client she was sprawled on the carpet drumming her heels in a spectacular fit of pique.

On Wednesday before Good Friday, David and Gwen left the Mayfair house and set off, with Eleanor grumbling in the back seat, to pick up Caro from school and spend the holiday in the dark heart of Herefordshire.

Meanwhile Charlie Ames and his bosom friend, the barrister, were motoring up to a quiet hotel in Cumbria where, braving wind and weather, they would pass a happy weekend tramping the hills and warbling love duets with only the spirits of the air and a few startled sheep to hear them.

On Friday evening, after the day's work was done, Nora sprang for a taxi to carry Breda, Billy, Matt and her up to the cemetery in Tower Hamlets where, true to his word, Leo had had a nice little stone erected to mark Georgie's last resting place. Flowers were put on the grave, tears were shed and, in the gloaming, Matt Hooper was sufficiently moved to offer Nora his shoulder to cry on. Later, back in Stratton's, he lay on top of the bed with her, chaste and fully clothed, and stroked her brow until she fell asleep and, for the first time in many years, he experienced a feeling that was perilously close to love.

If Breda had hoped that Steve Millar might invite her to do 'something special' over Easter, she was doomed to disappointment, for, it seemed, her guardian angel had lost a few feathers and, with Leo's permission, had fluttered off to cool his heels for a while.

On Saturday Mercer visited Rosalind who, pale and wraith-like, not only refused to acknowledge him but rocked in a corner of her little cell humming what may or may not have been a lullaby until Mercer could stand it no longer and caught the bus back to London where he spent a dreary evening playing gin rummy with his mother and Rhoda Hartnell.

Easter or not, in the mews house in Salt Street Vivian

and Susan were hard at work on the final chapter of *The Melting Pot* which, to Susan's surprise, had taken an unexpected turn. It was after nine o'clock before she got back to Rothwell Gardens and by half past ten she was in bed asleep, quite unaware that her life would soon be changed for ever.

26

Easter fell too early for the sun to have much warmth and the flowerbeds and leafy glades that gave Kensington Gardens their charm were still quite drab. It would be another month or so before the Serpentine attracted more than a handful of hardy bathers, though the banks were sprinkled with small boys and girls already armed with rods and nets in the optimistic hope that a minnow or two might be persuaded to exchange the murky depths for a short, happy life in a jam jar.

There were children everywhere, rolling eggs, playing rounders or skipping rope, since this was the twentieth century and the Lord's Day was no longer observed with Victorian propriety. Shell fragments and silver paper littered the pathways and more than an occasional small face was smeared with chocolate, for it seemed that some traditions were still respected by the young folk of London who, in spite of the chilly weather, were determined to make the most of the afternoon.

The Ring Tea House, a little north of the Serpentine, had once been a haunt of rank and fashion but on that March afternoon the customers who huddled at the outside tables in heavy overcoats and scarves looked more like Russian peasants than dandies.

Danny had already secured a table. He wore no overcoat

or hat and the breeze gusting along the walkway tousled his brown hair and tugged at the collar of his sports jacket. When Susan reached the table, he got to his feet.

'Glad you could make it,' he said. 'Whose idea was this, by the way?'

She seated herself on a cold iron chair. 'Mercer's.'

'Thought it'd be convenient, I suppose.'

'Well, it is – isn't it?'

He gave her a grin and a wink, determined, perhaps, not to let her see that he was just as nervous as she was.

'Aye,' he said. 'For polar bears.'

'Oh, come on. It's not that bad. You should've worn an overcoat.'

'Sold it,' he said, shivering ostentatiously, 'tae buy bread.'

'Stop it, just stop it,' she warned and, reaching, adjusted his collar and dusted his lapels.

Danny said, 'That him?'

She looked round and reached instinctively for Danny's hand as if the fellow in the long trench-coat and wide-brimmed hat were not her lover but a stranger. He loped towards them, long-legged, and the sun, poking through the clouds, laid a flittering little trail of light before him.

'Susan.' He kissed her cheek, then turning to Danny stuck out his hand. 'Mr Cahill, I presume. Heard so much about you.'

'Not all o' it bad, I hope,' said Danny.

'On the contrary,' Mercer said. 'I take it you know who I am?'

'Well, you're not Henry Morton Stanley,' Danny said.

Mercer frowned, then, picking up on the reference, laughed.

'Hughes,' he said. 'Mercer Hughes. Shall we sit?'

They squared off and eyed each other up. Mercer

exaggerated his breezy manner while Danny's Glaswegian accent became more pronounced. They argued politely about who would go into the Tea House to place an order until Susan, growing impatient, said she would do it and was gone before either man could protest. When she returned with the tray, Danny and Mercer were leaning across the table as if they were about to arm wrestle. It took her a moment to realise that an amnesty had been declared and they'd already buckled down to business.

Mercer said, 'By God, Mr Cahill, you've been a busy fellow. I take it your information is accurate? May I ask who the source is?'

'Crime reporter,' Danny said. 'He spoke to some guys in the Met.'

'Well, well, well,' Mercer said. 'It appears Mr Harry King hasn't been so clever after all. Why don't the authorities arrest him?'

'The evidence isn't strong enough,' Danny said. 'Sure, they could probably nail him for sending planes abroad without licences but all that'd get him would be a fifty quid fine. I mean, this is really small beer when you consider the swindles the government's up to. The aeroplanes are only the tip o' the iceberg. King's using the cash from the planes to pay for shipments of rifles and machine guns. He operates through a shady jewellery smuggler who's switched to selling arms cargoes, half o' which either don't exist or somehow never get delivered. If the republicans ever get their hands on him they'll probably hang the bugger.'

Mercer sipped tea and studied the two sheets of foolscap that Danny had given him. 'And this is – what?'

'Some names, some places an' dates,' said Danny. 'Best I could do.'

'Is that enough, Mercer?' Susan asked.

'Yes, plenty. I just need a few facts to convince my erstwhile friend that I know exactly what he's up to.'

'You're not gonna square up tae Harry King then?' said Danny.

'And wind up with my throat cut? No, I don't think so.'

'How did you get mixed up with this crowd in the first place?' said Danny.

'Greed,' Mercer said. 'Pure greed. I took my friend's word at face value.'

'Easy done,' said Danny.

Mercer studied the foolscap sheets for a few seconds, folded them and stuffed them into his inside pocket.

'I can't thank you enough,' he said. 'You've done me an enormous favour.'

'I did Susan the favour,' Danny said. 'Thank her.'

'Oh, I will,' Mercer said. 'Believe me, I will.'

Nora had spent many hours trying to explain to Georgie what the events of Holy Week signified but her son had been incapable of grasping the basic tenets of the Catholic faith. She experienced guilt as well as sorrow at having let Georgie down and, however unreasonably, blamed herself for not taking care of him properly. She walked home alone from St Mary and St Michael that Easter Day, as Breda had refused to accompany her.

She entered the house by the back door and took off her hat and overcoat in the corridor. She went into the kitchen, hoping that Billy, her little whirlwind, might help sweep away her gloom, but there was no sign of Billy; no sign of Breda either, only Matt Hooper over by the stoves stirring something in a big pot.

'What are you doin' in my kitchen?' she asked.

'Making your dinner,' Matt answered.

'You,' she said, 'cookin'?'

'I ain't entirely 'elpless, you know.'

She sniffed. 'What is it?'

'Rabbit stew. Me old ma used to make it when times was 'ard.'

'Where did you get a rabbit?' Nora asked.

'Brauschmidt's,' Matt told her. 'The secret's not to smother the flavour with seasoning, just onions, carrots an' a stalk o' celery. Be a hour yet, though, so sit yourself down, sweetheart, and 'ave a glass of stout.'

'Stout?' Nora almost shouted. 'What you playing at, Matt Hooper?'

'Thought you liked stout?'

'Sure an' I used to. Haven't had a touch since – oh, I don't know when.'

The shapely black bottle appeared as if by magic. She seated herself at the table while he screwed off the stopper, whipped a glass from the shelf and filled it. He passed it to her carefully and watched her sip from the thick foaming head that stopped just short of the rim.

'Does madam approve, like?'

'Yes,' Nora said. 'Madam does approve.'

'The Irish may not be good for much' – Matt poured a glass for himself – 'but, by gum, they sure know how to make stout.'

They drank in silence, appreciatively.

Then Nora said, 'Where's Breda?'

'Gone out.'

'With Steve Millar?'

'Nope,' said Matt. 'She took Billy up the park for to roll 'is eggs.'

Nora cocked her head. 'You shoved her out, didn't you?'

'What if I did?' said Matt.

'Why? What you up to?'

'Thought you deserved a bit of spoilin', that's all.' He paused. 'How was church? You been forgiven?'

'Forgiven for what?'

He put down the glass, leaned forward and touched her arm.

'Wasn't your fault, Nora. Ron would 'ave gone anyway.'

'I thought you blamed me.'

'Did at first,' Matt said. 'But I've been doing a lot of thinking lately.'

'Thinking about what?' said Nora suspiciously.

'How you can do things for the right reasons an' still 'ave them turn out wrong,' Matt said. 'Take our Susie, for instance, she didn't turn out right.'

'Right?' said Nora. 'What do you call right?'

'Livin' off a man, she is.'

'She isn't living off him,' Nora stated. 'You told me so yourself.'

'An' Ron going off to fight for the commies.'

'He's a grown man,' said Nora. 'He can fight for who he likes.'

'An' Breda not knowin' which way to turn.'

'They're young, Matt,' Nora said. 'Sure an' you've got to let them make their own mistakes – just like we did.'

'Worst mistake I ever made,' Matt said, 'was letting you go.'

'You didn't let me go. I was never yours in the first place.'

'I should've took care of you, Nora, after Leo ran off.'

'You was too busy taking care of Susie.'

'An' look where that got me.' He licked the milky stain from his upper lip. 'I should've chose you.'

'You making up to me, Matt Hooper?'

'Wonder what Leo would say if we set up together.'

'Set up together?' said Nora.

'Like man and wife.'

'Even if I wasn't still married to Leo, it'd be a sin.'

'Would it?' Matt said. 'Wouldn't you be forgiven for letting a old man take care of you while you takes care of 'im?'

'You don't want me,' Nora said. 'You just want a housekeeper.'

'I just want a place to lay me 'ead,' said Matt.

'And somebody to share your bed?'

'Been a long, long time since I shared a bed with anyone other than Ron.'

'You could've shared a bed with Breda, you'd played your cards right.'

'Nah,' he said, rather too wistfully. 'Never 'ave worked, that.'

'So it's me, is it?' Nora said. 'Bottom o' the hopper?'

'Well' – Matt spread his hands – 'I ain't nobody's catch, am I?'

Nora took another mouthful of stout and let it warm the cold lump of guilt in her stomach. If she'd had eight, ten kids she'd probably be all saggy and past it. But she hadn't had ten kids. She'd only had two, and one was gone. The only thing that brought her pleasure now was Billy and – she sat up straight in the kitchen chair – Billy was Matt Hooper's grandchild too and a bit of the future to share.

'What you got in mind?' she heard herself say.

'While we're waiting for the rabbit I thought we might go upstairs.'

'What sort o' arrangement, I mean?'

'Ronnie comes back, Breda, Billy and he can 'ave Pitt Street.'

'An' then you move in here,' said Nora, 'with me?'

'Yus.'

'What about Danny?'

'He can stay.'

'Oh, that's kind o' you,' said Nora. 'Got it all cut and dried, I see.'

'Just waiting the nod from you, dearest,' he said.

'Do you really want to go upstairs with me?'

'Yus,' he said. 'I really do.'

'Then turn down the gas,' said Nora.

The long weekend in Cumbria had filled Charlie Ames with *joie de vivre* and he arrived at the office in Lantern House Lane on Tuesday morning in the very best of spirits. Fresh air, exercise and good company had set him up for the spring rash of book launches, first nights and the usual complaining letters from authors whose statements of account had failed to come up to expectations.

Charlie was not one to be daunted by an occasional contretemps, though he preferred to deal with clients of the old school who would come to the office by appointment, say their piece, and depart without fuss. Others of more fiery temperament he might placate by standing them lunch in the Athenaeum where he could easily distract them – especially the provincials – by discoursing on the architecture or recounting tales of the Dickens–Thackeray feud or, if he were lucky, discreetly point out that the tall gentleman breaking a bread roll at the corner table was none other than the controversial poet, Tom Eliot.

Anna Maples, however, was not the sort of person to be distracted by anything when her dander was up, and her dander was most certainly up that forenoon. She was already seated in his office at a quarter past nine, looking, Charlie thought, even less well groomed than usual, her broad, square-jawed features sagging under the strain of what might be dissipation and might simply be ire. She was accompanied by a chap in a shiny lounge suit, a hang-dog sort of person with stooped shoulders and a pallid complexion who might, Charlie surmised, be a realist playwright from Huddersfield or some working-class genius from Salford whom she'd taken under the wing.

Charlie groaned inwardly, smiled outwardly.

'Anna, what a pleasure,' he said. 'Have you been offered coffee?'

'No coffee,' the woman stated.

Charlie flitted between the upright chairs and sought refuge behind his desk. He kept the smile fixed and placed his hands together, fingers delicately meshed.

'And this gentleman?' he said. 'I don't believe we've met.'

The man did not offer his hand.

'Grimes, sir,' he said. 'Sergeant Grimes.'

'Ah, a soldier?' said Charlie.

'No, sir – a policeman.'

'Fraud squad,' Anna Maples said. 'Where's Mercer?'

April had never been Mercer's favourite month; too many bills fell due in April and he was no longer young enough for his fancy to turn to thoughts of love.

He had half a dozen appointments lined up for the day, niggling little meetings organised around a mid-morning call on Martin Teague and a boring afternoon in a smelly screening room in Wardour Street where he'd be forced to sit through a couple of reels of *The Shadow of the Strangler*, a low-budget 'quickie' adapted from a low-budget novel by one of his hack authors. At some point, too, he'd have to confront Charlie and sue for a couple of days off to make yet another trip to Hackles.

Ridiculous, he thought, as he shoved a last piece of toast into his mouth and washed it down with coffee; utterly ridiculous that a man in my position should have to beg and borrow a few measly quid just to get through the week. He wiped his hands on a napkin, tossed it on to the breakfast table and headed for the hall.

The empty wheelchair was parked in front of the door. Behind it, arms folded, stood Mrs Hartnell. The day maid, Annie, lurked in the passageway, her little ears flapping.

'What,' Rhoda Hartnell said, 'have you been up to, Mr Hughes?'

'What I'm up to,' Mercer said, 'is scurrying off to earn a crust, so if you don't mind removing yourself and that contraption . . .'

'There's a thief in this house,' the woman said. 'It isn't Annie, it isn't Cook, and it certainly isn't me.'

'If you're referring to the fifteen pounds,' Mercer said, 'I only borrowed it. If Mother needs cash urgently let her draw from her own account. Where is my mother, by the way?'

'She's too upset to talk to you.'

'This is nonsense. Annie, my coat, please.'

Rhoda Hartnell stood her ground. 'Return the fifteen pounds and we'll say no more about it. Otherwise, we may have to summon the police.'

'The police?' Mercer said. 'Have you gone completely mad?'

'You took money without permission; that's theft.'

He brought out his wallet and peeped into the folds, though he knew exactly how much – how little – the wallet contained.

'I don't have fifteen pounds.'

'How much do you have?'

'Ten.'

She eased the wheelchair to one side and held out her hand. Far from humiliating him Rhoda Hartnell's gesture erased the last vestige of conscience. He waved the tenner in her face. She hesitated then took it.

'I'll pay you the balance this evening,' he said. 'Now, Annie, my coat, if you'd be so kind.' He slipped into his overcoat and with a facetious little flick of the wrist, threw up his hat and caught it. Then, with just seven shillings and sixpence to his name, he trotted downstairs to catch a bus into town.

Susan's shoulders ached and there was a knot the size of a fist at the nape of her neck but, gritting her teeth and rubbing her tired eyes, she continued to rattle the keys of the Hermes while Vivian, reeking of smoke, pencilled in the very last set of corrections to the very last chapter of *The Melting Pot* and clipped each page to a reading stand as soon as it was done.

Sunday afternoon seemed like an age ago. Susan had spent holiday Monday at the desk in the mews house in Salt Street and after snatching a few hours' sleep had been back at her post by eight on Tuesday morning.

It was now mid-afternoon. Apart from a short break to stuff down a sandwich she'd been seated at the Hermes, fingers flying, for what seemed like for ever. The only consolation to this obsessive burst of effort was that she had no time to think of anything or anyone; especially not Danny, especially not Mercer, especially not the sweet confusion of being in love with two men at once.

She blinked at the page Vivian clipped to the reading stand: not a page, half a page; twelve lines and then space, blank space.

'Is that it?' she said.

'That's it, my dear,' said Vivian just as the telephone rang.

Susan kneaded the knot at the nape of her neck, squeezed her eyes shut and opened them again. Five minutes, five careful minutes and it would be done: one copy for Teague, one copy for Mercer, and the third for the file.

She looked up to find Vivian waving the telephone receiver at her.

'It's for you, my dear,' Vivian said.

'Who is it?'

'Young Lochinvar,' said Vivian, and winked.

27

The breeze that had filled Mercer's sails early that fine spring morning had long since withered. Half an hour with Martin Teague, soft-soaping the little goat in the hope of persuading him to accelerate Vivian's payment on delivery had started the rot and by the time he'd dashed round three other publishing houses and endured an hour of murky footage in the screening room in Wardour Street he was almost fit to drop. He was certainly in no fit state to handle the weekend's mail that had accumulated in his office tray and barely had enough control over his temper to be civil to his venerable secretary, Miss Patterson.

'He wants you,' she said, giving him a strange look. 'He's been trying to find you all day.'

'Didn't you show him my diary?'

'He kept missing you, I think. I told him you'd be in before five.'

'Well, here I am,' said Mercer. 'I just hope this isn't going to take long.'

Charlie was dictating correspondence to his secretary, Janice, when Mercer entered his office but he wasted no time in dismissing the girl and, with one finger, pointed to a chair.

'Sit,' he said.

'Good weekend, Charlie?' Mercer said. 'How was Cum—'

'A year's hard labour,' Charlie Ames said.

'Beg pardon?'

'At least a year's hard labour breaking rocks in Wormwood Scrubs.'

'What,' Mercer said, 'are you talking about?'

'Criminal proceedings,' Charlie said. 'The question seems to be whether charges will be brought against the agency or against you individually.'

'Charges?'

'Fraud, I think, is favoured,' Charlie said. 'That will be a matter for the prosecution service. They may elect to go with embezzlement instead.'

The remnants of the pork pie he'd consumed in lieu of lunch rose in Mercer's gullet. He swallowed hard and slumped back in the chair, legs splayed.

'I've never been absolutely clear on the difference between fraud and embezzlement,' Charlie Ames went on. 'I assume it has to do with the sums involved and how the sums were extracted from the plaintiff.'

'The plaintiff?'

'Anna Maples.'

'Ah!' Mercer said. 'I see.'

'Do you?'

'Bluster, Charlie, it's all just bluster. She's mad at me because I won't—'

'I've no interest in your sordid affairs, Mercer,' Charlie interrupted. 'My sole concern is with the integrity of the agency. The Maples woman did not come alone. She brought the law with her: a police sergeant from the Fraud Office who, not unreasonably, requested sight of the books.'

'With or without a warrant?'

'No warrant,' Charlie said. 'I did not, however, consider it tactful to dig in my heels over protocol. I allowed him an hour in my office with the appropriate ledgers. Having discovered anomalies – anomalies I couldn't explain without implicating you – he says he'll return with a warrant to examine all our authors' accounts. I assume you know what that means?'

'Means we'll lose half our clients,' said Mercer.

'At least,' said Charlie. 'One whisper that Mercer Hughes and Ames is under investigation and we may as well shut up shop.'

'Can't you – I mean, can't we pay her off?'

'Perhaps,' Charlie said. 'But will that be enough? How many others have you diddled?'

'I haven't diddled anyone,' said Mercer. 'I mean, yes, sure, I've swung the odd payment here and there but that's hardly fraud, is it?'

'How many?'

'Three, just three: Arlen, Maples and Vivian Proudfoot. I swear that's all,' Mercer said. 'God, if she'd only held her water for another ten days none of this would have come to light.'

'I'm glad it did,' Charlie said. 'Truly, I'm glad it did. You've been plundering the authors' accounts for years, haven't you?'

'It's not as if I'm taking the bread out of the mouths of starving urchins. Every red cent is paid back – eventually.'

'How much is outstanding?'

'A few hundred.'

'How much, Mercer?'

'Eight hundred give or take.'

'Can you make it up?'

'Yes – in a week or ten days.'

'In a week or ten days,' Charlie said, 'the office will be

321

overrun with policemen and accountants and we'll be wiped out.'

'I'll see if I can talk some sense into Anna.'

'Seduce her, do you mean?'

'Well . . .' Mercer shrugged.

'You're no better than a gigolo, Mercer,' Charlie said. 'They say you're a charmer, a devil with the ladies, that half the women in London would love to be your paramour, to have – what is it? – a fling with handsome Mercer Hughes. Perhaps having no conscience is what makes you so attractive. But no one trusts you, not even, it seems, your lovers.'

'What are you going to do, Charlie?'

'Make good the deficiencies, of course.'

Mercer sighed. 'Thanks, Charlie. It won't happen again.'

'No, it certainly will not,' Charlie Ames said. 'In exchange for keeping you out of jail I'll require your resignation. I want you to resign from the agency and dissolve our partnership. Nothing less will appease Anna Maples.'

'And if I refuse?'

'I'd advise you to find a good lawyer.'

In spite of her brusque manner, Vivian had a kind heart and enough romance in her soul to pack her weary assistant off to meet young Mr Cahill on the steps of the National Gallery.

Danny leaned on the parapet overlooking Trafalgar Square. He seemed oblivious to the crowds that flowed beneath him, to the raucous sounds of traffic, and the little spots of rain that trailing cloud released into the late afternoon air.

'Wasn't sure you'd come,' he said.

'After what you did for me – for Mercer – how could I refuse?'

'Wasn't sure she'd let you away.'

'She sent me,' Susan said. 'She insisted.'

'Is that the only reason you're here?'

'Of course not,' Susan said. 'I'm curious.'

'Curious? About what?'

'Why you called – and why we're meeting here of all places.'

He chuckled. 'No flies on you, Susie, is there?'

'Why are we meeting here?'

''Cause I want you to remember it.'

'Remember what?' she said.

'The first time I kissed you.'

'You've kissed me before.'

'Aye, but not like this,' he said.

Taking her in his arms, he pressed his lips to hers.

From the street below a young man let out a whistle and two girls on the open deck of a bus cheered approvingly.

'Is that it?' Susan said. 'It's not awfully memorable, really.'

'How about this?'

He put his arms around her, drew her to him and kissed her again.

'Is that better?'

'Yes,' Susan said. 'That's better.'

'We need practice,' Danny said.

'I suppose we do.'

He released her and went back to leaning on the broad stone parapet between the pillars. 'If I didn't know it was hopeless,' he said, 'this would be a great opportunity for me tae ask you to marry me.'

'Why don't you ask me and then, you know, just let it slide for a while?'

'Aye,' he said. 'That's sensible.' He rested his shoulders on the parapet and peered up at the building. 'In fifty years,' he said, 'this place will still be here. Maybe we won't, then again maybe we will. Anyway, I hope you'll dot round the corner some afternoon an' look up at the gallery an' think, I remember a guy kissed me here once an' very nearly asked me to marry him.'

'Try it.'

'You sure?'

'Quite sure.'

'Susie Hooper, will you marry me?' Danny said. 'How's that?'

'Very direct,' said Susan. 'I'm sorry I can't give you an answer.'

'At least you didn't turn me down,' he said. 'You hungry?'

'Starved.'

'Wanna go for a bite to eat?'

'Love to,' Susan said. 'Where?'

'Somewhere cheap,' said Danny.

Breda hadn't a clue where her old man lived or who he lived with and in spite of much wheedling on her part Steve Millar refused to tell her. She'd been used to a society in which everyone knew everyone else and it didn't occur to her that Steve might not know where his boss put his feet up and that her daddy might simply vanish into thin air when the day's work was done.

She had one lead – the Brooklyn Club. She didn't even know where the Brooklyn Club was, though, or what went on there or at what hour of the day or night it opened its doors. She fancied it might be the sort of club you saw in the pictures with palm trees, bartenders rattling cocktail shakers, handsome men playing cards and elegant women in ball-gowns dancing to the strains of a forty-five-piece orchestra.

Steve wouldn't tell her and Danny claimed he didn't know but the cabmen were less cautious, for they naturally assumed that Breda was just inquisitive and that giving her a straight answer would do no harm.

'Leo's place? Nah, love, you don't wanna go there.'

'I don't wanna go there. I just wanna know where it is.'

'Up west.'

'Where up west?'

And they told her.

It was half past six, and raining, when, with little Billy strapped into his pushchair, she struggled off the bus and headed down the side street in search of gilded pillars and neon, and found nothing but a number on a door and a peeling painted sign that said, *The Brooklyn*.

She'd dressed Billy in a pale blue romper suit and combed his hair. She'd fed him toffees to keep him quiet on the bus ride, though, and had strapped him into the pushchair under a waterproof cover which had accumulated enough rainwater to give him a puddle to dabble in and, soaked and sticky, Billy was no longer a picture of childhood innocence.

Further up the street, which was hardly more than a lane, three men were noisily unloading a van and the stink of fish, beer and drains was almost overpowering. It dawned on Breda then that she'd made a mistake in bringing Billy to see his grandfather; that she'd made a dreadful mistake in coming here at all.

She pulled the chair back from the doorway and had just swung round to retreat when who came strolling round the corner but Steve Millar; big Steve with his hat shoved back and a leggy redhead clinging to his arm. They were laughing fit to burst and Breda, who had experience in such matters, knew at once what they'd been up to that afternoon.

Steve stopped in mid-stride, mouth open. The redhead glanced at him, frowning, then, following his gaze, let out a squeal of delight, trotted forward and swooped on the pushchair.

'Who we got 'ere, then?' she crooned. 'Ain't 'e a lovely boy?' Billy stared up at her, cocked his head and simpered like a little coquette. 'He's a charmer, 'e is,' the woman said and before either Breda or Steve could stop her began to unbuckle the straps that held Billy in check.

'Rita,' Steve said. 'Leave 'im alone. He's Mr Romano's kid.'

'His kid?' Rita looked up. 'Leo's got a kid?'

'I'm 'is kid,' said Breda. 'Billy's my kid.'

'Is 'e now?' Rita hoisted the little boy into her arms. 'Has Billy come to see 'is granddad den?' Holding Billy tightly, she advanced on the door and with a fist like a sledge-hammer rapped on it while Breda and Steve looked on helplessly.

'Milligan,' Rita shouted. 'Open up. We got visitors,' and when the door opened swept inside, carrying Leo's grandson with her.

There were no palm trees and, at that early hour, no orchestra. The interior door from the kitchen was wedged open and you could see cooks in aprons and shirtsleeves leaping about amid clouds of steam. An old bloke was listlessly sweeping the floor with a broom while waiters in white jackets nipped around setting tables in the alcoves. Two young women were seated on the edge of the bandstand swinging their legs and on the stand itself a chap with a saxophone played little riffs and snatches in a dreamy kind of way. You could see all this from her daddy's office. You could also see Billy, Rita and Steve playing hide-and-seek among the chairs and tables and hear Billy's shrieks of laughter ringing through the room which, Breda noticed, made the waiters smile.

Her father had shifted his chair from the side of a roll-top desk littered with bits and pieces of paper and had angled himself so that he could keep an eye on his grandson, which he did with such thoroughness that, Breda thought, she might not be there at all.

'So,' her daddy said, 'Matt Hooper got a leg over at last, did he? God knows, he's been trying long enough. Has he moved his dunnage in yet?'

'Nah, not yet,' said Breda. 'Only a matter of time, you ask me.'

'She happy?'

'What?'

'Your ma – she happy?'

It hadn't occurred to Breda to enquire whether or not her mother was happy. As far as she, Breda, was concerned the stuff that went on upstairs was just nasty. She didn't quite know why she was so offended by her mother's new lover who, after all, might have been her lover if he'd been twenty years younger and who, like it or lump it, was still her father-in-law and as much a fixture in Stratton's Dining Rooms as the tea urn.

'Hooper was never much of a one for the ladies,' her daddy said. 'Had his wife and his kids and that was enough for him. But, Catholic or not, he'd have married your ma if she'd been free – which she wasn't, since I'd got there first.'

'Doncha mind, then?' said Breda.

'Mind what?' her father said.

'Ma havin' – I mean, Matt 'Ooper takin' your place?'

'He ain't taking my place,' Leo Romano said. 'I gave up that place years back so I got no right to reclaim it now.' He nodded out into the club. 'Look at our Rita. You'd better be careful, Breda, or she'll have Billy off yah.'

Rita had trapped Billy between the tables and, scooping him up, swung him round and round, his little legs flying out in all directions while he screamed in delight at the rough handling.

Breda said, 'That woman – she Steve's girl?'

'Could be,' her father said. 'What a little terror he is. You'll have a handful there when he grows up.'

'Gotta handful now,' said Breda. 'You not gonna do anything about it then?'

'About what?'

'Ma.'

He stopped watching Billy's antics and inching the chair round, faced her.

He looked fat, she thought, in the half-buttoned shirt with the garters pinching his arms. Dark stubble shaded his jaw and showed up the heaviness of his chin. His hair was thinning and in a year or two he'd have one of those pates like monks have and be even more soft and buttery than he was now. She wondered what he did with the girls who came here, how he kept them in order. She wondered too if he'd have taken her on to work here if she hadn't been his daughter. Better here, perhaps, than round the back of the Crown with . . .

He said, 'What you expect me to do, Breda? Knock Matt's teeth out, show him the door, tell him he got no right to mess with my wife? My wife? Nora ain't my wife, except under law. No, darlin', I can't right all them wrongs for you.'

'What wrongs?' said Breda.

'Georgie going that way. Your husband running off. It's

worse for your ma; she has you to put up with. I reckon she deserves what she can get after what she's been through. And you . . .'

'Me?' Breda stiffened. 'What about me?'

'You grouse about an old guy sharing your ma's bed when you got a husband out there in Spain. I saw those newsreels, Breda; just looking at them gave me the shakes. You want something to worry about, worry about your husband.'

'Steve says—'

'Steve says what I tell him to say,' her father said. 'You thought I sent him along to take Ronnie's place, didn't you?'

'Well, kinda,' Breda admitted.

'Nobody can take Ronnie's place,' her father said. 'He's your husband.'

'He ran off and left me – just like you done.'

Her father let out a wry grunt. 'No, sweetheart, not like I done.'

'I don't need Steve to look out for me. I got Danny.'

'Sure you got Danny. There's one guy who'll never let you down. I reckon he might have married you if he hadn't practically raised you.'

'Anyhow, he fancies somebody else – Susie bleedin' Hooper.'

'I know he does.' Her father tipped back the chair and pushed himself to his feet. 'Listen, Breda, you have a husband and a fine little boy. What I got' – he shook his head – 'you don't want. Now, go home, give your old ma a hug, tell Matt Hooper I said hello and wait for your husband to come back. You need money?'

She sighed. 'No, Dad. I don't need money.'

'Better go then. I got work to do. Don't forget what I said, will you?'

'Nah, I won't forget.'

She followed him out into the club where Billy was perched on Steve Millar's shoulders, wearing Steve Millar's hat.

'Hey, Rita?' big Steve said. 'How'd you like a kid like this?'

'Give me a kid like that,' Rita said, 'an' I'll be yours for ever.'

Then, lifting Billy down, she kissed him and with manifest reluctance handed him back to Breda.

If there was one thing Anna Maples wasn't good at it was keeping her mouth shut. She was well aware that imitating a police officer was an indictable offence but she was so confident that C.P. Ames would sort things out discreetly that she couldn't resist bragging about her 'prank' to the guests at Eric Kulgin's dinner table.

To give him his due, Eric knew how to host a dinner party and was sufficiently savvy to hire a caterer from the French restaurant four doors down rather than tackle cooking in his miserable little kitchen. There were six people squeezed into the basement room which made for an intimate atmosphere and, with wine flowing like water, Anna's tale of revenge on the larcenous Mercer Hughes occasioned, as they say, much merriment.

'This actor fellow, where did you find him?'

'I found him,' Rupert Arlen said. 'It wasn't too difficult. Bar in Mayberry Street is littered with them – out-of-work actors, I mean.'

'Do we know this chap?'

'I doubt it,' Anna said. 'Provincial rep. Done a bit of wireless, he claims, but I'd never heard of him.'

'Nor had Charlie Ames apparently.'

'Grimes, Sergeant Grimes: isn't that wonderful?'

'Absolutely spot-on. Who dreamed up the name?'

'I did,' said Anna.

'How much did he charge for the performance, Anna?' Eric Kulgin asked.

'Ten guineas.'

'Bargain, I'd say. Hughes has had it coming for a very long time.'

'I expect,' said Anna over the rim of her glass, 'Mercer is scratching at the door of my apartment even as we speak. "Anna, Anna, forgive me, forgive me."'

'Like the chap in *Washington Square*?'

'Exactly.'

'Takes a strong woman to bring a fellow like Hughes to his knees,' Rupert Arlen said. 'Well done, Anna. Cheques all round come Monday morning, I imagine, and letters of apology from Charlie; guarded, of course, very guarded.'

'And a roasting for our dear Mercer.'

'No more than he deserves.'

'I wonder what he'll do.'

'Not much he can do. Charlie Ames won't let fraud go unpunished.'

'Charlie wouldn't sack him, would he?'

'Not sure he can,' said Eric Kulgin. 'Wouldn't want that, Anna, would you?'

'I'd be happy just to have him throw out his little tart,' said Anna.

'You don't suppose he loves her, do you?' Rupert Arlen said.

'Of course he doesn't love her. He loves me,' said Anna Maples, tilting up her chin. 'Me, and no one else.'

'But we all love you, Anna,' Eric Kulgin said.

'Absolutely.' Rupert Arlen raised his glass. 'To Anna.'

'Anna.'

'Anna.'

'And Sergeant Grimes,' said Eric which made everyone laugh once more.

28

In hindsight it seemed fitting that her affair with Mercer Hughes should end in the apple orchards of Herefordshire. It was all so very different from her first trip into the country over thirty months ago. Seated up front with Mercer, watching the small towns and villages rush past, Susan sensed that a chapter of her life might soon close and that, come what may, she would have to move on.

'I must say, this is a big improvement on that sporty job,' Vivian said from the rear seat. 'Whatever happened to the Riley?'

'Unreliable,' Mercer said, 'like most things these days. I'm glad the Rover is to your liking, Vivian; you're paying for the hire.'

'Am I?'

'I'll pay you back, of course.'

'That's very kind of you, Mercer,' Vivian said, 'though you still haven't explained what I'm doing here.'

'I told you, we're making a surprise visit to your dear brother.'

'But why?'

'I thought you'd prefer to get out of London rather than wait about for Martin Teague to summon you to face the firing squad.'

'So you've read it, have you?' Vivian said.

'*The Melting Pot?*' Mercer said. 'Yes, I've read enough of the revised version to know that you, my dear Viv, have burned your boats with Herr Teague.'

'You don't sound surprised,' said Vivian.

'Oh, I'm not,' Mercer said.

'Or disappointed,' said Vivian.

'Being a good little agent – evidence to the contrary – my copy of the typescript is even now on its way to Routledge, a firm much more in tune with your ideas and, I might add, your ideals.'

'I didn't know I had any ideals,' said Vivian. 'What will Teague do?'

'Rant and rave and call you a traitor,' Mercer said. 'He'll ask for his signing fee back and we'll probably have to concede him that much, though God knows he's made enough profit out of you these past three years. Tell me, my dear, what on earth came over you?'

'A little too much Hitler, I suppose,' said Vivian. 'By a process of degrees I realised that no matter how one looks at it, the Jews aren't to blame for all the ills in Europe. It's the hubris of national governments and the dictators, elected and otherwise, who concoct the conspiracies that will, I fear, bring us all to our knees. They don't call them conspiracies, of course; they call them alliances, but it comes to the same damned thing.'

'Try explaining that to your brother,' said Mercer over his shoulder.

'I don't have to explain anything to David,' Vivian said. 'He's just as corrupt as the next man. You can't expect him to be otherwise given the hogwash he's had poured into his ears since he came out of short clothes.'

'Kindred spirits, your brother and I,' Mercer reminded her.

'It was only a matter of time until he turned on you,' said Vivian. 'He has, hasn't he? Turned on you, I mean?'

'He's not the only one,' said Mercer.

Vivian leaned forward. 'I think the sight of my niece in fascist uniform delivering a Nazi salute was really the turning point. Who's next, I wonder? Caro? Will he give Caro up to Moloch too?'

'For king, country and the British Empire? Probably,' Mercer said. 'Tell me, Vivian, why do you never visit the Mayfair house? Do you prefer to preserve the illusion that your brother's a straightforward cider-maker, a yeoman devoted to his little patch of land and not some bloated plutocrat?'

'While you've been busy doing your little deals, Mercer, I've been out on the road, out in the jungle,' Vivian said. 'I've spoken in halls packed with men to whom Tom Mosley is a god and, yes, I've preached Mosley's gospel for all it's worth. I'm not oblivious to the voices outside, however, to protesters and dissenters, the so-called rabble. In spite of my personal convictions I've been struck by the fact that they can't be silenced and should not be silenced, which does not – repeat not – make me a communist or an anarchist or even a Labourite; just a little less conservative than I used to be.'

'God preserve us from the voice of reason,' Mercer said.

'The voice of reason,' Vivian said, 'to which no one ever listens.'

'Until it's too late' said Mercer. 'Susan, do you agree with her?'

Before she could answer, Vivian said, 'Susan agrees with her friend Cahill, I suspect. Can't say I blame her. He's a very sensible young man.'

'Ah, the honourable Danny; the friend with whom she doesn't sleep.'

'If she did,' said Vivian, 'would it matter to you, really matter to you?'

'Of course it would.' Mercer took a hand from the steering wheel and squeezed Susan's thigh. 'Susie's my little girl. She doesn't want anyone else. Do you, darling?'

'May I remind you,' Susan said, 'that if it wasn't for Danny Cahill we wouldn't be heading for Hackles in the first place?'

'True,' said Mercer, 'very true,' and returned both hands to the wheel.

Susan knew something of what had been going on and that Mercer had become involved in a shady scheme to sell arms to the republicans. She hadn't forgotten the party in David Proudfoot's town house or the strange assortment of characters he'd brought together; nor had she forgotten how little she'd seen of Mercer since that evening. What really stuck in her mind, however, was the meeting in Kensington Gardens on Easter Sunday, how well Danny had handled it and how elated Mercer had been with the information Danny had provided.

On arriving at Hackles they were greeted with hugs and kisses out on the terrace by the tennis court in the half-dark of the April twilight: Eleanor, Gwen and David, but no Caro; she had gone back to school.

David insisted on showing Susan upstairs to her room while Mercer, at Gwen's insistence, was consigned to the damp little cottage in the shadow of the priory. David put down her overnight case and switched on the bedside lamp. It was almost dark outside, just warm enough to bring out the first of the season's moths which thumped softly on the window glass and hung there, fluttering, in the lure of the light. David drew the bedspread from the bed and turned down the quilt and blankets.

'Keeping you apart in this day and age is rather silly,' he said. 'I mean, sharing a bed with your lover is hardly going to shock Eleanor.' He closed the bedroom door and showed no sign of leaving. 'God, but you are pretty,' he said softly. 'Mercer is a very lucky man.'

'Thank you,' Susan said.

'How long are you staying?'

'Just one night, I think.'

'A flying visit,' he said. 'Why did he bring Vivian?'

'Mercer thought she needed a breather.'

'Rather a nuisance, though, what?'

'I don't know what you mean,' Susan said.

'If you happen to feel lonely in the wee small hours,' he said, 'I doubt if anyone would mind if you slipped down to the cottage. Indeed, I'll accompany you.'

'No,' Susan said firmly. 'That won't be necessary.'

'If you do change your mind, I shan't be far away.'

'I won't change my mind.'

He said, 'In that case we'll have to divide to conquer, will we not?'

'Conquer what?' Susan said.

David Proudfoot didn't answer.

'Supper in half an hour,' he said, then went off and left her alone.

Eleanor, half asleep, lay on the couch with her head in Mercer's lap. David played a selection of tunes from West End shows on the piano. Vivian smoked and sipped brandy, Gwen knitted and Susan, seated cross-legged on the carpet at Mercer's feet, waited for the uneasy truce to end.

There was, she thought, an element of farce about it: four women and two men trapped in a rambling farmhouse with, off stage, a dank little cottage under the crumbling walls of a priory to which one couple would steal away at the second act curtain while the others stumbled about in comic confusion, bumping into each other in the darkness. Only it wasn't funny, wasn't farce, wasn't remotely light-hearted; the deceptions and betrayals were all too real.

Mercer said, 'Shall we play a game?'

'Must we?' Vivian said. 'Can't we just be at peace for once?'

Eleanor opened her eyes and sat up. 'Charades? I'm good at charades.'

'No,' Mercer said, 'a brand-new game.'

'What game would that be?' Gwen asked.

'It's called "Let's swop prisoners." Very popular in Europe, so I'm told.'

'Mercer, that isn't funny,' Vivian said.

'What are the rules, old sport?' said David.

'Oh, we make up the rules as we go along.'

'Doesn't sound like much fun to me,' said Eleanor. 'Do we need dice?'

'No, dearest,' said Mercer. 'It's not a game of chance.'

'I rather like the sound of this,' David said. 'How do we begin?'

Mercer placed a hand on Susan's shoulder. 'Let's imagine that what I have here is a prisoner of the class war; a healthy specimen, relatively undamaged. However, I find I'm no longer able to supply her with nourishment or guarantee her safety. I am therefore obliged to exchange her for someone from the other side.'

'This,' Vivian said, 'is not – repeat not – on.'

'Be still, old sausage,' David said.

'Tell you what, Viv,' said Mercer, 'why don't you pretend you're the Geneva Convention and sit back and ensure fair play?'

'Miss Geneva Convention,' Eleanor said. 'It rather suits you, Auntie Viv.'

'Now, David,' Mercer continued, 'who will you offer in exchange?'

'Is she a fighter?'

'Oh, yes, she'll pull her weight.'

'Is she on our side?'

'That remains to be seen.'

'Is she – what did General Mola call them – a Fifth Columnist?'

'Quite possibly,' Mercer said. 'That's a risk you have to take.'

'What are we talking here?' David said. 'One for one?'

'Take me,' said Eleanor. 'I'm not a Fifth Columnist.'

'No one's quite sure what you are, Eleanor,' said Mercer, 'but you're definitely not part of the exchange.'

'Oh, for God's sake!' Vivian exclaimed. 'This has gone far enough.'

'Of course,' Mercer said, 'with the agreement of both parties the prisoner might be set free; might be, as it were, repatriated.'

'If you weren't willing to make a trade, Mercer,' David said, 'why did you bring her with you in the first place?'

'New rules,' said Mercer. 'New game. What do you say to a little bit of arms dealing instead? Suppose you were to offer me a thousand pounds.'

'For Susan? I mean, for the prisoner?'

'No,' Mercer said. Plucking Danny Cahill's list from his pocket, he tossed it across the room. 'For this.'

Stooping, David picked up the papers from the carpet and scanned them.

He looked up. 'Where did you get this stuff?'

'I have, as the saying goes, my sources,' Mercer replied.

'What is it, Daddy?' said Eleanor. 'What's wrong?'

David ignored her. 'These numbers?'

'Dates,' Mercer said. 'Dates linked to forged bills of lading.'

'I don't believe you.'

'Well, that's your prerogative. I'm sure Harry King will believe me.'

'You wouldn't dare.'

'Actually,' Mercer said, 'I'm far too much of a coward to antagonise your friend Mr King. I'll leave it to you to break the bad news and let the great man draw his own conclusions about who might be selling him short.'

David wafted the typed pages in the air.

'You bastard!' he said. 'You absolute bastard!'

'Four clapped-out aeroplanes? How big an idiot do you take me for?' Mercer said. 'It's a pyramid, isn't it? I'm just one tiny insignificant stone in the heap. King's not interested in me. You, however . . .'

'All right, all right, what do you want?'

'Only what I'm entitled to – a cheque for one thousand pounds.'

'Daddy?' said Eleanor again.

'Be quiet, girl,' David told her. To Mercer he said, 'What does that buy me?'

'My silence,' Mercer said. 'You get to keep the list.'

'Why are you doing this to me now, here?'

'So that I have reliable witnesses,' Mercer said. 'Who better than a wife, a sister, a daughter and an innocent young woman from Shadwell?'

Eleanor leaned on Susan's shoulders. Gwen put her knitting to one side and sat back in the armchair, a little smile on the corner of her lips. Vivian craned forward in her chair, hands on her knees.

'They don't know anything about it,' David said. 'You didn't have to involve them in any of this. You're doing it to humble me.'

'I'm doing it,' Mercer said, 'because I don't trust you.'

'What *do* you want from me, Mercer?'

'I told you: one thousand pounds.'

'All right.' David got to his feet. 'We'll go out to the library, just you and me, and discuss it like gentlemen.'

'We're not going to resort to fisticuffs, are we?' Mercer said.

'Don't be a damned fool,' David said and, throwing open the French doors, ushered Mercer out into cool night air.

It was too soon for the apple trees to be showing blossom. Even so, there was a sweet and pleasing fragrance in the early morning air. The tennis lawn was white with dew, the sky to the east petal pink. There was no sign of the cow in the pasture, no sign of life at all save for a hawk circling above the trees that screened Hackles from what Caro had once described as Wales.

Susan had slept hardly at all and at first light had risen, washed, dressed and packed her overnight case. She carried the case downstairs and went outside to put it in the boot of the Rover.

Shaved, dressed and sipping coffee from a saucerless cup, Mercer stood by the hedge looking out over the tennis court.

'Want some?' he said. 'I've made a pot.'

Susan shook her head. 'When are we leaving?'

341

'As soon as Vivian's ready. We'll stop for a proper breakfast on the way.'

'It's all over then?'

'Yes, it's all over.'

'You were gone long enough last night,' Susan said.

'Well, you don't shake off an old friend in five minutes.'

'Did he give you what you asked for?'

Mercer patted his breast pocket. 'I have the cheque right here.'

'Would you really have shopped him to the authorities?'

'God, no!' Mercer said. 'He's far too slippery to fall foul of the law. I wouldn't have shopped him to Harry King either, but David doesn't know that. He's not afraid of much in this life but gangsters like King, they play by different rules. Did he make up to you, Susan?'

'He did a little.'

'He thought you were there for the taking,' Mercer said.

'I never have been.'

'Oh, I know that,' Mercer said. 'If I hadn't known that I'd never have fallen in love with you.' He put the coffee cup on the ground and came to her. He looked down at her from what seemed, again, like a very great height. 'I want you to remember that I loved you, Susan, that you weren't just a – how do they put it in these parts? – a roll in the hay.'

'Why are you talking in the past tense?' Susan said.

'I'm sailing for New York early next week and I'm not coming back,' he said. 'My mother will have to learn to live within her income. Charlie Ames will patch up my contracts. Vivian will find a new publisher and a new direction. My wife – well, her father already looks after her, poor woman, and in a month or two she'll have forgotten I ever existed.'

'In other words, you're running away?'

'Yes, I'm running away. I've one or two contacts in New York but if they don't work out then I'll jog down to California where there are lots of opportunities for a charming Englishman to make his mark.'

'You could take me with you, you know.'

'I love you too much to do that, Susan.'

'You're such a liar.'

'You see,' he said, 'even you don't believe me.' He put an arm about her and kissed her. 'My partner, Charlie Ames, says I've no conscience; I'm trying to prove him wrong. When I was young I used to dream that one day I'd meet a girl like you. And now I have. And now it's too late.' He let out a little snort of amusement. 'A docker's daughter with a polished accent who happens to be an independent spirit. Just my luck, eh? Just my bloody luck.'

'Have I no say in the matter?' Susan asked.

'None,' he answered. 'I'm doing you a tremendous favour, you know.'

'By ditching me along with all the other problems in your life.'

'You wouldn't like America.'

'How do you know?'

'Because your future is here.'

'Without you?' Susan said.

'Yes, without me.' He kissed her again. 'In any case, your friend Cahill's lurking in the wings, isn't he? Poor devil won't stand a chance if I'm still around, now will he?'

She didn't answer him at first.

'Come on, Susan, admit it,' Mercer said.

And strictly to appease his vanity, Susan answered, 'No.'

On the drive back to London he was just as he had always

been, relaxed and charming, chatting to Vivian as if nothing were going to change; nothing, that is, except her publisher and the shape of her career. When they stopped for breakfast in a tearoom on the far side of Hereford, he kept the conversation light and with a skill few men could emulate parried Vivian's questions about her brother and the sorry state in which he found himself.

'David?' Mercer said. 'No, he's not in any trouble. Never will be, not that old reprobate. It was all really just a bit of sport. We'll be right as rain in a month or two, you'll see. Back to beating tennis balls without a care in the world.'

Vivian was not convinced. 'Some sport, with a thousand quid at stake.'

'It's only money, dear heart, only money.'

'But you won, Mercer, didn't you?'

'Oh, yes,' he said. 'For once in my life, I won.'

On reaching the city he dropped Vivian off outside the mews house and drove Susan back to Rothwell Gardens. He was no longer chatty, no longer breezy. He drove quickly through the noon traffic. He circled the Gardens and drew up at the kerb outside the flats with the Rover facing towards Fenmore Street. There were no last-minute kisses, no promises to send for her or even keep in touch.

He sat quite still, hands resting on top of the steering wheel.

'Are you coming up?' Susan said.

'No,' he said. 'I've a lot to do and you must be tired.'

'Yes,' she said. 'I am rather.'

After a moment, Mercer said, 'I think you'd better get out now, Susan.'

'Is this it, Mercer?'

'Please,' he said, 'just get out.'

He didn't open the door for her or take her case from the boot, perhaps, she thought, because he couldn't bear to see her tears. She stood at the pavement's edge, looking down through the half-open window.

Mercer looked up and whispered, 'See you around, Shadwell.'

'Yes,' Susan said softly. 'See you around.'

Then, without another word, he drove away.

29

It galled Danny more than somewhat that he wasn't the one to break the news that political negotiations had finally secured the release of a number of prisoners and that Ronnie might be on his way home. Not surprisingly the *Daily Worker* had stolen a march on its competitors and was first to announce that a handful of unnamed British prisoners were heading for the Spanish frontier at Irun where they would be met by Communist Party representatives and escorted back to England.

They would not, of course, be welcomed as heroes, not officially at any rate, and if public sentiment hadn't been running high in their favour the brave boys from the International Brigades might have been branded traitors and arrested as soon as they stepped off the ship.

In terms of news it had been a packed spring season. The Germans had finally shown their hand by bombing the little market town of Guernica in the Basque Country, an act of calculated savagery that had no military purpose and that clear-eyed pundits saw as a rehearsal for what might soon be a future war. In May, too, while London draped itself in bunting ready to celebrate the coronation of King George VI, the giant airship *Hindenburg* exploded in a ball of fire over New Jersey; a ghastly spectacle that everyone who cared to shell out for a cinema ticket could go and see for themselves.

Only days later, amid all the pomp the nation could muster, a new king was crowned in Westminster Abbey and the shame of Edward's abdication in the name of true love was, in part, erased. And as if that wasn't enough excitement for one month Stanley Baldwin retired as Prime Minister and Neville Chamberlain took his place, though no one, at the time, cared too much about that.

In the midst of all this sensational stuff, the crossing of prisoners from Spain into France was lost to the front pages. It was all that Danny could do to keep track of their progress to Dover where, after being questioned by the CID and fingerprinted, they would be put on a train to transport them to London's Victoria Station late on a fine June evening.

'Breda,' Matt yelled, 'do you know what bleedin' time it is?'

'Don't shout or you'll waken Billy,' said Nora. 'I've just got him settled.'

'He should be comin' with us, Billy should,' Matt growled. 'It ain't right that the boy won't be there to welcome 'is dad 'ome.'

'Danny says there might be trouble from Mosleyites.'

'What does Danny know?'

'Anyhow, it's far too late for Billy to be up. He's only a baby.'

'Ron'll expect 'im to be there.'

'Will you kindly stop moaning,' Nora said. 'You're worse than a baby yourself, Matt Hooper. Sure an' I don't know why you're fussing so since you thought you'd never see Ronnie again.'

'Now that ain't true. I was always – always confident.'

'You're not going to start ranting, are you?'

'I might 'ave a few choice words to say, yer,' Matt admitted.

'Not tonight, Matt, please. I want smiles from you tonight,' she told him. 'Nothing but smiles. Are you bringing him back here?'

'I ain't taking 'im to Pitt Street. He'll want to be with 'is wife.'

'He won't want to see me, not after what I done to him,' said Nora.

''Course he'll want to see you. So you'll be waiting with arms wide open an' the kettle on when we fetch 'im back from the station. Hear me?' He paused then yelled. 'Breda, what the 'ell you doin' up there?'

'She's making herself gorgeous,' Nora said.

'In case that Jewish tart turns up, I suppose.'

'Ruth Gertler ain't no tart,' Nora said. 'She lost her cousin, remember.'

'Yer, so I 'eard. Long as she keeps 'er claws off our Ron.'

'Danny says—'

'Danny don't know 'is backside from 'is elbow these days.'

'He's in love, Matt, in case you hadn't noticed.'

'In love? Who's 'e in love with?'

'Your Susie.'

'My Susie!' Matt snorted. 'He's got no chance there even if 'er posh boyfriend 'as done a bunk. Breda?'

Breda stepped into the kitchen. 'What?'

'About bleedin' time,' Matt said, then, 'Here, gal, what you done to yourself?'

'Like it?' Breda said, twirling. 'Ma done all the stitchin'. Fixed me 'air up proper, too. Ruth Gertler ain't gonna top me in the looks department.'

'I'll bet she ain't,' Matt said.

'I thought you was in a hurry,' Nora put in.

'Well, we got a hour. I booked the taxi for nine.'

'Taxi?' said Breda. 'You think we're made of money?'

'Not every night a man's son gets 'ome from the war,' Matt said. 'Where's Danny? I thought he was coming.'

'He's goin' straight from Fleet Street,' Breda said.

'To pick up Susie an' Miss Proudfoot,' Nora added.

'Miss Proudfoot? What's she got to do with our Ronnie?'

'She's Susie's friend,' Nora said.

'Now's your chance,' Breda said. 'Give the old bird a bit of docker's charm, Pappy, an' you could find yourself married to the upper crust.'

'Don't go puttin' ideas into his head,' said Nora.

'See,' Matt said, 'I already got a ball an' chain.'

'Sure and don't you forget it,' Nora said. 'When Breda moves back to Pitt Street an' Danny leaves, I'm going to need a man about the house permanent.'

'Don't tell me Danny's leaving?' Matt said.

Breda and Nora exchanged a glance.

'Can't see past the end o' your nose, Matt Hooper, can you?' Nora said.

'Or the end of somethin' else,' said Breda.

The day had been oppressively hot. It wasn't until the mid-part of the evening that a cooling breeze stole into the mews house in Salt Street and Vivian and Susan found relief from the heat.

Precious little work had been done since Mercer's departure. In spite of C.P. Ames's gentle nudges Routledge had taken their own sweet time in coming up with a contract for *The Melting Pot*. It wasn't the book itself that had given the editorial board pause but Vivian's reputation as a fascist propagandist. Only her assurances that she was no longer affiliated to the British Union or willing to be Martin Teague's mouthpiece had finally swayed them into offering a modest advance; that and the promise of a foreword by no less a person than Herbert George Wells who, it seemed, was impressed with Vivian's change of stance as well as her vision.

Routledge's advance for a scholarly work like *The Melting Pot* was considerably down on Teague's offer. But, said Vivian, shrugging, one has to pay a price for respectability and with a small private income to fall back on she wasn't exactly on the breadline.

'Will you start another book soon?' Susan asked.

'Of course, though Dawson is still badgering me to go to Spain to cover the conflict for *The Times*. I'm not sure, though,' Vivian said, 'that the real conflict isn't much closer at hand. I think I'll stay put and keep my nose to the grindstone.'

'Will you still require an assistant?'

'Unless you have other plans.'

'Like what?'

'Sneaking off to America.'

'No, that's over.'

'Haven't you heard from him?' Vivian asked.

'I don't expect to. I doubt if anyone knows where Mercer is, apart from Mr Ames and I question if he'll let the cat out of the bag.'

'David's been fishing, too,' Vivian said, 'but to no avail. Eleanor's bereft, or pretends to be. Gwen, I gather, has taken up residence in Hackles and says she'll never set foot in the Mayfair house again. I really don't know what will become of my family and, to be perfectly honest, Susan, I don't much care. As for Mercer's clients – well, Rupert Arlen has found himself another agent and apparently Anna Maples threw such a fit after Mercer left that her husband had to be summoned back from somewhere or other with a view to having her sectioned.'

'Is that true?'

'Oh, I doubt it. It's a good story though,' Vivian said. '*Do* you have other plans, Susan? *Is* there a change in the wind?'

'I take it,' Susan said, 'you wouldn't employ a married woman?'

'I don't see why not,' said Vivian. 'At least until babies come along.'

'Oh, yes,' said Susan. 'Babies. I hadn't thought of that.'

'Has Danny asked you to marry him?'

'Yes, and he's patiently waiting for an answer.'

'Don't make him wait too long, Susan.'

'In case he changes his mind, you mean?'

'I think there might be a war coming and a war changes everyone's mind about all sorts of things,' Vivian said.

It was dusk now, the light in the windows almost gone. Vivian and she were seated at the dining table nibbling cheese and sipping wine. In a half-hour or so Danny would arrive with a taxicab to take them to Victoria Station in the hope that the Dover train would be on time and that Ronnie would be on it.

Vivian lit a cigarette. 'Do you miss him, Susan? Mercer, I mean.'

'Yes, of course,' Susan answered.

'Do you still love him?'

'I don't know. I really don't know. I'm not being coy. I was dazzled by him. I'd never met anyone like him before.'

'Few of us have,' said Vivian.

Susan paused before she spoke. 'He told me I'd be better off without him. Is that a lie, Vivian, or is it Mercer's version of the truth? I don't suppose I'll ever know for sure.'

'Which,' Vivian said, 'is probably just as well.'

'It's hardly fair on Danny, though, is it?'

'Young Mr Cahill is too much of a realist to hold it against you, Susan.'

'I don't think Danny's a realist,' Susan said. 'I think he's a romantic.'

At that moment the doorbell rang.

Susan wiped her lips with a napkin and brushed crumbs from her dress.

'He's early,' she said.

'He's eager, that's all,' said Vivian, and went to open the door.

Back in the days of Phil and Syd, when she was footloose and fancy free, Breda had thought nothing of travelling in taxis. First time she'd been seriously kissed had been in the back of a taxicab, but apart from a trip to Tower Hamlets cemetery at Easter, which hardly counted, she hadn't been in a cab for years. Now, all dolled up and quivering with nervous excitement, she felt as if she were a bride again, though, come to think of it, she hadn't ever felt like a bride before; the shabby ceremony in the East Arbour Street registry office had been more like facing a firing squad than a celebration of love everlasting.

Through the open partition the old man was telling the cabby how brave Ron had been and how the Lord Chamberlain had wrote to General Franco and demanded Ron's release in exchange for three hundred Eyeties – five hundred, if that's what it took – and how there was even talk of a special medal in the offing.

'Right,' said the cabby.

'Go, I told 'im. Go, I says, an' do your duty, son. An' he

looks me square in the eye an' says "I'll do it for you, Dad, an' for England."'

'England?' the cabby said. 'What's England got to do wiff it?'

'Ain't been no cake-walk, I can tell yer, keeping the 'ome fires burning when 'e was banged up in a Spanish jail.'

'What battalion was 'e with?' the cabby said.

'I – er – Breda, what'd Ron do over there?'

'Machine-gunner,' Breda said.

'Yer, right,' said the cabby and, to Breda's relief, closed the glass partition with a sceptical little snap.

Danny had warned her that in spite of scant press coverage the arrival of twenty-eight battle-scarred Britons newly released from Franco's prisons would not go unnoticed. Reporters would be on hand to show off or show up the bravery of the International Brigadiers and collect a few horror stories, if, that is, the Home Office allowed the lads an opportunity to speak out, which Danny rather doubted.

When the cab swung into Buckingham Palace Road, Susan experienced a wave of apprehension at the sight of so many people flowing through the station arches. Then it dawned on her that the soldiers' return was a sideshow and most folk were only interested in boarding the boat train for the Continent or securing a seat on the trains that trundled south through Clapham.

'Hmm,' said Vivian, as she stepped out of the taxi, 'at least they don't have a regiment of the Household Cavalry lined up to defend the railhead from communist invasion.'

'They'll have snipers hidden in the bookstalls, I expect,' said Danny.

Susan clung tightly to his hand. 'Do you know where we're going?'

'Platform eight, I think.'

There was quite a crowd in the vicinity of the platform. Chains had been slung between the barriers and half a dozen policemen were loitering in the region of the gate together with a stationmaster, a ticket collector and a couple of geezers in soft hats and belted raincoats who Danny identified as plainclothes detectives.

In the forecourt a group of young women in BUF uniform marched round in a circle waving placards that called for peace at all costs which, Susan knew, was the latest slogan of Mosley supporters who, it seemed, remained oblivious to irony. She noticed Eleanor among the marchers and, still too slight to fill her blouse, Caro tripping along behind her sister.

Eleanor had already spotted Vivian and chose to ignore her but Caro, gauche as always, called out, 'Auntie Viv, Auntie Viv,' and waved a paper flag until a stern-faced female commander barked at her to keep line, an order that Caro, with some rue, obeyed.

Vivian shook her head. 'Sickening, isn't it? Quite sickening.'

She might have gone on to say more if Susan's father hadn't arrived at that moment with Breda, flushed and breathless, in his wake.

'Danny,' Breda cried, 'is he 'ere?'

Danny shepherded her into position against the chains.

'Not yet, sweetheart, not yet.'

To the right of the gates reporters had gathered, together with officials from various left-wing groups. Ruth Gertler, her aunt and two or three other Jews formed a separate group close to the barrier. They were first to see the signal drop and the locomotive steam into the station.

'It's coming, it's coming,' Breda cried, jumping up and down.

The train squealed to a halt at the buffers.

The coppers had truncheons in their belts but didn't draw them even when the crowd of anxious relatives swayed against the chains. Danny put both hands on Breda's shoulders. Susan's father blinked and blinked, his lips curled in a hideous parody of a welcoming grin. The crowd swayed again and, through steam and drifting smoke, saw the carriage doors open and men jump out: ordinary men, ordinary travellers, one or two women among them, some toting suitcases, others not. Murmurs of doubt and disappointment grew as the civilian passengers yielded up their tickets and quickly left the concourse.

A guard climbed down from the van at the rear of the train. He glanced at the foreshortened line of carriages, half the doors hanging open. An elderly woman carrying a little black dog shuffled up to the gate where she fiddled and fussed with her handbag until she found her ticket and gave it up. A copper bent over her, whispered something in her ear and courteously led her away.

'Where are they?' a reporter shouted. 'We got deadlines, you know.'

The sounds of the station going about its business echoed beneath the vaulted roof; a sound like the sea, Susan thought, quite vague and distant.

She heard Breda say quizzically, 'Where's my Ronnie?'

'Wait,' Danny said softly. 'Just wait.'

The men in soft hats and raincoats slipped through the gate, followed by the stationmaster. They conferred for a moment and one of the hats nodded. The stationmaster signalled to the guard at the far end of the platform then briskly set off down the line of carriages, slamming doors with foot and fist as he went.

Far down the line, almost at the platform's end, a carriage door opened and a man appeared. He stood for a moment as if dazed and then, without looking round or behind, came swinging up to the gate, walking very, very fast.

He was tall and angular and wore the top part of a soldier's uniform, a cheese-cutter not a beret on his head. He looked at no one, no one at all, and stood stalk still while the detectives had a word with him. Released, he strode through the gate and swung left. One man, just one, stepped out of the crowd to greet him. No hugs, no back-slapping; they shook hands briefly, pushed through the gang of reporters and disappeared.

Two more soldiers appeared: a matched pair, short in stature, scruffy and scraggy and not quite sober; Jocks for sure. They dropped out of the end carriage, staggered, righted themselves and sticking out their chests marched, step in step, to the gate. They wore no caps and only the brown shreds of uniforms. They saluted the detectives smartly and on being ushered through the gate, raised their arms high in the air, fists clenched, and roared, '*Salud*, y' bastards,' before setting off, quite aimlessly, to find their way to Euston.

Men in groups of four and five spilled on to the platform. They laughed and shouted and looked back as well as forward, reluctant to let their comrades go.

Susan peered through the stragglers in search of her brother who, holding on to another young man, was last to emerge. It seemed as if they were also reluctant to say goodbye to whatever glory they had shared but when they reached the barrier Susan saw that the young man was limping badly.

One of the detectives reached out to help but Ronnie shoved him away.

He looked like her brother – and yet he did not. His face was white as suet, his cheeks hollow, big teeth protruding through the gaunt outlines of his face. He wore a ragged pullover over a khaki shirt and a pair of stained corduroys and one hand was wrapped in a grubby grey bandage. He pushed open the gate and helped his comrade hop through, for the boy, a dark-haired Jew, had one leg fastened up behind him with a strap, the foot, what might be left of it, swaddled, like Ronnie's hand, in a grubby grey bandage.

The reporters surged forward to catch what they could of sentiment and sorrow before the crowd dispersed.

Danny held Breda firmly by the waist.

'Wait,' he said again. 'Just wait.'

Ronnie steered his friend to the little group in the corner and handed him over to Ruth Gertler. She clung to her young man desperately, her eyes searching his face and then, in that awkward pose, they kissed, while Ronnie, stepping aside, spoke quietly with Ruth's Aunt Lena.

'Who the 'ell's she?' Susan's father said indignantly.

'Shut up, Matt,' Danny told him, and let Breda go.

She ran across the angle of the forecourt, stopped in front of her husband and looked up at him.

'Hey, kiddo,' Ronnie said. 'How's tricks?' and had just enough strength left not to stagger as Breda, with a joyous little yelp, threw herself into his arms.

30

Porters and stevedores, cabmen and carriers would soon be rolling out of bed to begin the labours of the day, for it was June and the sun had hardly set before it rose again. In just a few hours the markets would open, not the Baltic or the Royal Exchange but the produce markets where meat and fish, fruit and flowers were ferried in from fields and quays and from the ships, large and small, moored in the basins of the Thames.

They had strolled hand in hand up the Mall, happy to be alone at last and, not by chance, had found themselves in Trafalgar Square.

Late though it was, traffic still circled the square, buses growling past and taxicabs whizzing down to Charing Cross. But it was peaceful enough for a soft summer night and Susan was glad she'd lured Danny away from the maudlin family reunion. She'd call in at Stratton's tomorrow when the tears had mostly been shed and the shouting had faded and Ronnie, fed and rested, had had his broken fingers set and the rope burns on his wrists professionally dressed.

Vexed at seeing her nieces in uniform, Vivian had made polite excuses and had left for home. And Breda, after a token argument, had waved Danny, her guardian angel, goodbye and, clinging on to hubby, had sent the old man off to join the queue at the taxi rank.

Ronnie had kissed her and winked, as if they still shared secrets. But his secrets were too dark for her now and she might never learn where her breezy brother had gone or what he'd done and just how much of him had been left behind in Franco's prison camp.

'He won't tell you, you know,' Danny said.

'No, but he might tell you.'

'Aye, he might, but I doubt it.'

'Will he go back to Spain?' Susan asked.

'If he does an' he's captured, it's the firing squad for sure,' Danny said. 'Naw, he won't go back, not with that hand.'

'Will Brauschmidt take him on?'

'If Ron can hold a knife,' Danny said, 'I expect he will.'

'Once a butcher, always a . . . I shouldn't say that, should I?'

'Probably not,' said Danny.

She rested her head on his shoulder and was quiet for a while.

At length, she said, 'When are you on shift?'

'Eight.'

'Are we going to stay here all night?'

'I dunno: are we?'

'I've a perfectly good bed at my place.'

'No pyjamas,' Danny said.

'Do you really need pyjamas?'

'No toothbrush.'

'I have a spare: never used.'

'How about breakfast?'

'Eggs,' Susan said, 'any way you like them.'

'How about an answer first?' he said.

'Why do you think we're here?'

He looked up at Nelson on his column, at the guardian

lions, at the lit columns of the National Gallery. 'Fifty years,' he said. 'Fifty years at least, Susie Hooper, that's the deal. I play for keeps, sweetheart.'

'I know you do,' she said.

Then in the very heart of London with no one looking on she kissed him.

And said, 'Yes.'